Loving Patience

by

Jennifer Simpkins

The Patience Series, Book 2

This is a work of fiction. Names, characters, places, and incidents are either the product of the author's imagination or are used fictitiously, and any resemblance to actual persons living or dead, business establishments, events, or locales, is entirely coincidental.

Loving Patience

Cover Art by *Diana Carlile*

The Wild Rose Press, Inc.
PO Box 708
Adams Basin, NY 14410-0708
Visit us at www.thewildrosepress.com

Publishing History
First Edition, 2022
Trade Paperback ISBN 978-1-5092-4398-3
Digital ISBN 978-1-5092-4399-0

The Patience Series, Book 2
Published in the United States of America

Her breathing reached an even point as she fell deeper into slumber, sounding like a melody playing in his head. He strained to look over his shoulder at the bedside clock; it read ten nineteen. For almost an hour he had been watching her rest. It seemed like just minutes ago he looked down and noticed she'd fallen asleep on him. He could watch and hold her for the remainder of his life, and still, it wouldn't seem like forever to him. Watching her gave him time to take in her beauty and get to know the body he enjoyed pleasuring so much.

Dedication

For my loving husband

Chapter One

Liza Dyer didn't know that today her life would dramatically change, but it was looking like a day full of unwanted surprises.

The first being the coffeepot was bone dry when she woke earlier that morning. The one sure way to guarantee a disastrous day—have no coffee brewing in her beloved coffeepot. Was it too much to ask someone to make another pot for the person expecting her morning cup of hot joe? Liza guessed so, and she was still pissy about it, just not enough to make her forget the real reason she was shooting flames. No. Forgetting to make her drug of choice couldn't compare to the betrayal that had kicked her in the gut a few short hours ago.

She'd cried the first hour of leaving her hometown, Linden. Then she'd been on the road for a couple of hours longer than she should have, only because she stopped several times for coffee—which then had her stopping to pee every hour—and she really had no more tears to shed on the rat bastard.

Seriously, why was she bawling her eyes out anyway? Yeah, she and Greg had a relationship, but in all honesty, was it perfect? Did she love him? He obviously didn't love her. Now, with a little clarity, she realized that maybe she and Greg had moved to the next stage in their relationship by living together without putting much thought and emotion into it. She was crying for nothing. At thirty-five, she was a single woman destined to disappoint her mother because she wasn't ever going to marry and give the woman two-point-five grandchildren.

She was well past the point of feeling sorry for herself. Now she was in the *if he was around, I would beat him with my ballbuster* stage. She'd never been forced to use the ball bat before, but Greg would have been the perfect man to break it out on. No, he wasn't a serial killer sneaking through her window at night while she slept, but he was a man who made her feel weak and vulnerable, and for that reason alone, he deserved to be whacked over the head a few good times with her Louisville Slugger.

There was where she wanted to be for the next few hours: Ollie's, the first and most likely the only bar in Patience, Tennessee. As soon as she saw the neon lights promoting brands of beer in the front windows, she pulled into the gravel lot and instantly had mixed feelings about the place. She yanked open the scarred wooden door and stepped into an overly amplified room booming with twangy country music.

Now that she was seated at the bar, she decided it wasn't that bad of a place to hang out for the couple of hours it would take her to forget about her extremely bad day.

A petite, spunky woman with black hair highlighted pink stood in front of her, wiping down the bar. "I don't mean to be blunt, but you look like you've had one hell of a day. What can I getcha?"

"You have no idea," Liza said with a heavy sigh. She hung her oversized bag on the back of her stool. "Do you serve wine here?" She was desperately hoping she didn't have to settle for a beer, but if she had to, so be it. If she could make it through one, the next ones probably would go down without her even tasting them.

"Yep. Ollie started carrying a variety of wines when we started to get more women customers. He felt it important to accommodate everyone," the bartender said.

"I think I need a few glasses of red if you don't mind."

"Coming up…"

"Liza. Liza Dyer."

"It's nice to meet you, Liza. I'm Minny. I'll be back in a sec so you can start having a better night, and maybe, if you want, you can tell me about it."

****

Tex wasn't ready to leave the bar, the place he found himself more nights than he should. He shot a few games of pool with some guys, blowing off steam after a long day, and lost twenty dollars in the process. Oh well, he was doing okay for himself. Laughing with the guys and putting off the inevitable night spent on his mom's couch was fun.

While he was playing his second game of pool, an expensive perfume scented the stuffy bar. Every man at the table stopped what they were doing, ogled the woman who was overly dressed for a place like Ollie's, and then had to wipe their drool with the backs of their hands. He was one of those men who couldn't take his gaze off the beautiful woman who looked out of place for the local hangout. He should blame her for him losing twenty bucks. He didn't know if he was succeeding in hiding from the guys the fact he couldn't keep his gaze off the brunette for more than a few minutes at a time.

Minny served her several glasses of wine, so he guessed the woman probably needed it. Minny was a good bartender. She cut people off when they needed to be, talked to the sloppy drunks who just wanted to slur their words around, and took care of the regulars. If Minny was keeping the drinks coming, the brunette probably was having one awful day.

That was the only thing keeping him away for the moment. He understood bad days, and the woman deserved to sit and drink alone if she wanted.

Plus, Minny and the woman moved from the bar to a table in the back, looking to be having an intense conversation, and Tex didn't want to interrupt girl time. He was learning women needed girl time—whatever the hell that was. He didn't know what was being said but sensed his lovely distraction was feeling better on her second…her third glass of wine.

At one point, she stood and twirled, and Tex thought he would lose it right then. He had never seen a woman wear a sweater as a dress, but she did with some type of plaid tights and boots that reached right above her knee. She was so out of his league, and he damn well knew it. He had to readjust himself to make room for the hard-on he was getting just by seeing her do a simple dance, stumbling just a tiny bit.

A woman like that knew what she wanted, and she didn't take no for an answer. She had a rocking body and wasn't afraid to show it off. Her snug dress showed off her toned figure and hugged every part of her slim yet curvy physique. The dress was an instant turn-on for him and probably every other male in the joint. For some reason, it bothered him other men were most likely looking at her as some piece of ass. Why, he wasn't sure, because he had done the same thing with plenty of women.

The women he went for lately were willing to go all in, no strings attached. It worked for him, but lately he questioned the way he looked at women. Did he want to continue down that road of just sleeping with women and never trying for the other stuff? A relationship. He was going to have to be content because, in the end, he would just become a disappointment, and it wouldn't be fair to the woman.

Minny looked as if she were going back to work, but not before bringing the babe another glass of wine. Man, how many was that? It had to be like…four. No way could she drive. He decided to keep an eye on her, and if she needed, he would get her wherever she was going.

He would like her stripped naked in his bed, but that was unlikely. For one thing, he was pretty sure she was drunk, and sleeping with intoxicated women was a nonstarter for him—a standard all men should have. The other was she didn't look like a woman interested in anything but the bottom of her glass.

She didn't seem to notice all the men staring her way or the women giving her the dirty eye. She was classy, sexy, and wasn't going around flaunting herself in tight skirts and low-cut shirts that showed too much cleavage. That fact made her even more attractive and desirable. But even with her face tilted downward, he could tell when she smiled and laughed a few times with Minny that she had a contagious smile. He wondered what it would be like to taste those full lips.

As he continued watching her, glued to her every move, he noticed the way she tugged at her dress, the way she sipped her drink without seeming to taste it. She was a mystery to him, and he was determined to figure her out. Who was she? What was she doing in Patience? And what had her drowning herself in a bottle of wine? A woman like that was too beautiful to have such sad eyes. God—those eyes, the way she had them done up made them look big and bold and seductive.

Just when he was ready to make his move and volunteer a ride to wherever she was staying for the night—Jefferson, a ballsy young kid, strutted up to her table, looking his fill and showing no hesitation. Tex could tell the boy was on his way to being drunk, if not already there. He clenched his fists. Jefferson was only interested in one thing, and it wasn't just a ride to her hotel room. He'd seen the young guy drink a few beers, so maybe he was feeling brave, thinking he could handle a woman like the brunette. He'd probably just turned twenty-one and most likely had never touched a woman in his life. The boy didn't stand a chance, but it still didn't settle well with Tex. He held back even though his first instinct was to send the guy back to his group of friends laughing and cheering on the little punk. Jefferson's flirting was probably some dare. Who was brave enough to talk to the classic beauty sitting alone, showing no interest in anything except drinking her wine?

Tex sat, turned to face the bar, and polished off the rest of his beer. It was cold and smooth, and he was feeling more relaxed. He couldn't help glancing over his shoulder at the table, Jefferson talking to the woman, and damn it, he was actually making her laugh.

"You want another, Tex?" Minny had approached without him noticing.

"No. Three's my limit if I want to drive home, but

thanks." He turned back to check on the woman and Jefferson.

"Her name is Liza, and she's in no mood to be messed with tonight," Minny volunteered.

"I noticed her come in. It was kinda hard not to."

"She said she's here to visit a friend. She's had a pretty rough day, so please don't try anything with her. She's had a lot to drink, mostly my fault, but she looked like she needed it. I'm trying to keep an eye out for her. Make sure nothing happens to her."

"Well, it looks like Jefferson has the same idea." Both Minny and Tex looked at Jefferson and Liza. Jefferson was catching Liza before she stumbled to the peanut-covered floor. Her dress rose, revealing awesome-shaped legs. They would feel good wrapped around his body, rocking into him. *Shit*. Now he was for sure hurting. Where did that come from? He was no fucking better than the kid.

Jefferson twirled her around, and Tex admired her womanly figure. When the punk suddenly brought her close, her smile faded. She seemed uncomfortable.

"Tex, she's a strong woman. Don't go over there acting like a superhero. Believe me—she wouldn't appreciate it tonight. She can handle Jefferson," Minny assured him.

Minny knew more about Liza than he did, but he had the sneaking suspicion something was about to go down.

"I just don't like to see a man take advantage of an intoxicated woman," he proclaimed.

Minny laughed. "What's gotten into you? Usually, you're the guy that would be putting the moves on the woman and not letting a young guy like Jefferson get in your way."

He thought about it, and she was right. He didn't know what had gotten into him, but he'd changed over the last couple of months. Yeah, he'd taken a woman or two to bed but not like he used to. He and his best friend, Bradley, would sit at the bar and brag about all the hot babes they banged. They were always out to have a good time.

However, Tex had been spending less time with Bradley and more time working at his landscaping business and the coffee shop and bookstore he was helping remodel. He hung out mostly by himself, and he was becoming less interested in the one-night stands.

"I don't know. Maybe I'm just finally growing up."

"Well, I can tell by the way you're gripping your beer bottle you are itching to go over there and save Liza, but just chill for a minute. If things get too out of—"

Minny didn't get the chance to finish before Liza shouted for Jefferson to let her go or she was going to knee him in the nuts.

Tex turned completely around on his barstool, and before he knew it, he was on his feet. He smiled at the woman he'd never met and was proud. Seeing a tough woman stand up for herself and not wait for someone to rescue her was refreshing. Most everyone in the bar stopped doing their various bar activities, including the band playing some ballad, and turned their attention to the action.

Jefferson was obviously drunk. Tex knew the boy. He wasn't the type to approach a woman who was at least eight or ten years older than him. Being drunk was probably why the kid didn't let Liza go when she threatened to bring him to his knees.

Jefferson tugged a little tighter and started to sway

back and forth.

Liza slurred her words a bit, but she was clear. "Let me go, you jackass."

"Minny, I think it's time I step in." Minny said something, but Tex had already moved away from the bar. When the argument started to heat, all he could think of was getting to Liza and getting her out of there. Where he wanted to take her, he wasn't sure.

****

Liza was enjoying her time alone. Her wine was pleasant, even though she was past the point of tasting it. She wasn't completely plastered yet, but if Minny kept being generous with the drinks, she would be, sooner than later. She was feeling good, though.

She knew what was going on around her, but she could only hear her own inner voice. That voice was louder than any bad country ballad excessively amplified. It reminded her that she was a thirty-five-year-old woman with wonderful parents, a sister and nephew she loved, and good friends. Nevertheless, no matter how great those things were and how grateful she was to have those relationships, she still longed to be wanted. The real Liza—the person she was only with herself—had no other choice but to want a connection with a man.

She just wanted the simple things—a good man who liked to hold her after sex, who didn't want to rush off in the morning, a person to watch a movie with on a Saturday night, and it would be nice if he loved and wanted only her. Was that so much to ask for? She didn't think so, and she wasn't the settling kind. She would rather be alone than be something she wasn't. So if she couldn't have what she thought she deserved, then screw it. She would just be Liza. Fuck all the jackass men she was lucky never to meet.

"Was your father king for a day? He must have been to make a princess like you."

She took a minute to process what the young cowboy just said. Not because she didn't understand his words, even though he was way drunker than she was, but because she couldn't believe any man would think a cheesy line like that would work.

She had to give him credit for having the worst pickup line ever. "Excuse me? Who are you?" she asked, arms crossed and hopefully sporting a smug expression.

"Just the man of your dreams," the not-so-smooth talker proudly proclaimed. He sounded as if he were reading off a teleprompter.

She tried to be badass, but he was kind of cute in a teenage-boy kind of way. She let out a laugh. "You're sweet."

"I will be anybody you want, baby. Can I buy you another drink?"

"Okay, first, lose the awful pickup lines, because if you ever plan to actually pick up a woman, you are going to have to come up with something a little more original and a little less corny. Secondly, I'll pass on the drink." She stood, apparently a little too quickly because she staggered a bit and fell into Casanova Cowboy. He caught her and must've taken that as some kind of sign, because he didn't let her go.

"Whoa there, while you're already in my arms, why don't we dance?" he said with a lopsided grin.

He awkwardly twirled her around, and he didn't try to hide running his gaze up and down her body. Liza sensed he was harmless. She was probably the first woman he'd ever had so close, but she didn't appreciate him being all in her space.

She tried pulling out of his hold, but her attempts went unnoticed. The boy whose name she didn't know was seriously starting to piss her off.

"All right, cowboy, time to pack it up. The dance is over."

He waggled his eyebrows. "Baby, I can go all night."

Okay, now he'd passed the point of pissing her off. What her friends liked to call her *Liza mode* was kicking in all kinds of high gears.

"I said the dance is over, so you can remove your hands from my ass."

"I'm not through with you yet."

"If you don't let me go this second, you won't be getting any woman in the near future, because my knee is going to do major damage to your balls," she warned.

He was still not listening. Did he not understand she wasn't interested? After tugging her a little tighter, he started to sway side to side to the music that had just suddenly stopped. The once-loud bar was now quiet. God, she was making a scene. Why couldn't the cowboy stay at his table and save his lame pickup lines for a girl his age? He had a better chance of hooking up with a girl who actually found him charming. She'd thought he was sweet the first few minutes, but now he was being an asshat.

"All right, this is the last time I will warn you. Get your scrawny hands off me! I'm not having a good day, I have a lot of built-up anger, and I have no problem taking it out on you."

She was close to finally reaching him, but a lean

hunk appeared out of nowhere and pulled the boy back several steps by his shirt collar. The hottie called the boy Jefferson. She was pumped with adrenaline, and it took all she had to not push this new man out of the way and tell him to mind his own damn business. She would have done that, but she liked looking at his backside.

His snug, washed-out jeans shaped to his fine ass. She was sure she stood there with a funny-looking grin on her face while the hunky man sent Jefferson back to his table of buddies, but she was drunk enough not to care.

Before she made a bigger fool of herself for the night, she reached down, grabbed her glass of wine, and drained it. Her purse had fallen off the back of her chair and now sat on a pile of peanut shells. She put what she thought would cover her drinks and a large tip for Minny on her table. After throwing her hobo bag over her shoulder, she made her way through the bar. A lot of people stared. It might have been the only action they'd seen in a while. She just wished she wasn't the one to provide it. What was Anna going to think if she ever found out?

Minny walked right in front of her and stopped. "Liza, I think you've had a lot to drink tonight. Why don't you stick around for another hour? Then I can sneak out of here early and take you home."

"Don't worry, Minny. I'm f-fine."

"I'll take her, Minny," a strong, male voice commented from behind her.

Liza turned around, making sure she didn't fall in the process. All the wine she'd drunk was going straight to her head. *Oh my.* Her stomach surprisingly fluttered, and where was that coming from? It was the major hottie again. His chestnut hair cut short, a couple of days' stubble covering a strong jaw, and a solid, long-sleeve shirt clinging to broad shoulders and a well-formed chest left her heart beating a little faster. She knew by her own hometown that small southern towns grew some of the best-looking men…but wow.

"You're hot." *Oh shit.* "No, I mean it's hot. Hot in here." She fanned herself. Clearly, her consumption of alcohol was messing with her ability to think and speak at the same time.

He cracked a full-on grin but thankfully didn't comment. He probably heard women say such things to him on a daily basis.

"I hope Jefferson didn't bother you too much. He's too young to handle his alcohol. I'm sure he won't feel as much pain as if your knee had made contact with his balls, but believe me, he will feel like crap in the morning."

She adjusted her purse on her shoulder, very aware of the incredible, sexy man in front of her. Except for Minny, who had moved to her side, Liza shoved all other commotions going on in the background out of her mind.

"Did everyone hear me?" This was not going to be one of her finer moments. She just knew it.

"Sorry to say, but yeah. Don't worry. Jefferson had it coming. Even though you've probably scared him shitless to ever approach another woman, especially a woman as beautiful as you."

"Well, I hate to be the one to teach him a lesson, but he needs to learn to drink less and come up with some better material to pick up women. What he has now just isn't working."

"Sadly, I don't see women in his future for a while.

He's going to feel like an idiot when he wakes up tomorrow, remembers you, and realizes what a jackass he made of himself."

This stranger was pure male, and her heat factor was raising the roof. She was going to have a stroke if she didn't get into the cool October air.

"I have to say you have a slightly better way with a woman than Jefferson over there."

Jefferson was staring a hole in the table while his buddies slapped him on the back.

"Just slightly?"

Ignoring the question, Liza turned to Minny. "Thanks for the offer, Minny, but I'll be fine. I just need to get some fresh air." She outstretched her hand to the mystery man. "Thanks for your help…"

"Tex. You're more than welcome, Liza."

How did he already know her name? Maybe Minny had told him.

"Take this." Minny held out a bottle of water. "You look hot."

Liza accepted the water, then left Minny and Tex.

Her legs only slightly wobbled as she moved toward the exit. She pulled the door open, and finally, she breathed in the air filled with the distinctive smell of tobacco firing in a barn and felt slightly better. She stood in place and gave herself a few more minutes to settle before she left the night air and got in her SUV. Where was she going? When she'd left Linden earlier that day, her only plan had been to make it to Patience.

Her next order of business was to settle her nerves before calling Anna. She'd accomplished both of those things and more, if she added killing a young man's hope of ever finding a woman and having a hunk with the

14

perfect mixture of blue-green eyes charm her.

She lifted her arm to the beaming lamp pole. The watch on her wrist showed the time was after ten. Her best friend, the reason for being in Patience, was probably still awake because of her love for the night and ongoing insomnia, but Liza didn't want to phone her just yet. She didn't want to call and say, "Hey, Anna, I'm in Patience. I'm drunk because of my cheating boyfriend, and sorry to interrupt your alone time with your fiancé, but I need you to come pick me up at a bar and let me sleep on your couch for the night."

Anna wouldn't judge her or show her anything but support, but Liza wasn't used to being vulnerable in front of other people—Anna included. Liza was the strong friend who let everything roll right off her back and took on everyone else's problems. She'd learned early that she was a fixer.

Music streamed through the opening door of the bar, and she turned back. Tex.

"You really shouldn't drive," he called out.

"Why's that?"

"I think you had about four or five glasses of wine, and it wasn't Jefferson grabbing you—you fell into him. Not that he was right to not let you go, but it was you who stumbled into his arms." He crossed his arms over his broad chest and leaned one work boot back against the concrete building.

"And h-how would you know that?" Damn him for being right.

"I've been watching you for most of the night," he admitted.

Why did that excite her more than annoy her? He didn't need to know she felt a tad bit sexy with the knowledge that he was drawn to her for some reason.

Again, she couldn't help but question him. "And why were you doing that?"

"Your beauty distracted me from my pool game. I couldn't take my eyes off that sweater thing that I guess is a dress and the way it clings to every curve. If you didn't notice, you had every man in the place staring at you."

"You flirting with me?" He was really good at it, and she was just drunk enough to enjoy it. Jefferson needed to take lessons before he went prowling around again.

"Maybe I am. How's it working?" He moved away from the wall and walked toward her.

Unlike with Jefferson, she didn't mind this gorgeous male in her space. A strand of hair blew in her face, and when she brought her hand up to put the tendrils behind her ear, Tex stopped her. He moved his hand gently and placed the fallen hair back in place. She stared up at his face and lost all train of thought. What did he just ask her? Oh, right…flirting.

"I guess you're doing okay. I have to be going. I need to find a hotel or something in the area."

"Even though you said my flirting abilities were just okay, I will let it slide because you're new to town. How about I take you to the Town's Inn? It's just a few minutes down the road. It's right before you hit Main Street."

A hotel sounded good for the night. It would give her time to recoup and get herself back to normal. "I think I can make it to the hotel if it's just right down the road." Just as she finished voicing her claim that she was fit to drive, her mouth started to water. *Oh no. I won't do it…the worst possible thing.* She threw up right on Tex's boot. So now that was like the sixth time she'd made a fool of herself in one day. She was seriously going for breaking the world record for how many times she could make an ass out of herself in twenty-four hours. What more could happen?

He took a bandana he must have pulled out of his pocket and wiped her mouth. It should have made her feel like a small child, but it didn't. It was sweet and something no other person had done for her in a long time. She kept her eyes locked on his and swore something sexual was between them. This was crazy. *Seriously, Liza, how many seconds have you known this man? Will you ever learn your lesson?*

She couldn't even see her ex wiping her mouth after she threw up on his slick, shined-up shoes. No, Greg would have taken a handkerchief and wiped off his shoe before handing it to her to wipe her own mouth clean.

"I'm sorry about that. I guess I've had a bit too much tonight." She was so not making her case that she was capable of driving to the hotel.

Thank God for the water Minny gave her. She swished a little around in her mouth and, as ladylike as she could, spit it out. In the bottom of her purse, she found a container of mints. After popping two in her mouth, she felt better, minus the embarrassment.

"So let me drive you to the hotel," he volunteered.

"How do I know you're not drunk yourself?"

"Honey, I haven't drunk more than my limit. You can go ask Minny if you don't trust me. She knows me." He stuffed the used bandana in his back pocket.

"Breathe on me," she demanded.

"What?" he asked, clearly confused at her unusual request.

"Let me smell your breath. I will determine if you're safe enough to drive."

He leaned down, just inches from her face, his mouth open, and let out a hot breath. A chill ran down her spine, and she could have blamed it on the cool night, but just a few minutes ago, she was overheating—so it was all him.

"You smell like beer," she concluded after inhaling his hot, intoxicating breath.

"I never said I didn't drink a beer or two. I said I'm not drunk. I know my limit, and I know I can drive you a lot farther than a mile down the road."

She thought about it. She was over her limit and knew better than to drive even an inch from the bar. She knew nothing about this man, but he did look like a guy who didn't have to resort to lying to get what he wanted.

She was still taking her time to mull over her options when he cupped the back of her neck and brought her in for a sweltering kiss. His tongue snaked between her lips before she had time to register what was happening. She tried pulling away because who did he think he was, but she couldn't—or at least, she didn't want to. He tasted of hot beer. Musky cologne mixed with sweat tickled her senses. It took all her strength not to wrap her arms around his broad shoulders, bring him closer, and run her hands under his shirt so she could touch skin.

It took even more strength not to do a little tasting herself.

Chapter Two

The kiss was over way too quickly. Tex took a step back while she gulped oxygen and tried not to fumble her next words. While his kissing was pretty hot, much like the rest of him, she couldn't let him off too easily. She had a reputation to uphold, and no man—hunk or otherwise—got by with planting one on her without permission.

"What was that?" Okay, maybe that came out a little breathy and not all tough as she'd planned.

"Don't tell me a woman like you has to ask that question."

"Don't be a smart-ass. I mean, why did you do it? Why did you kiss me?"

Yay—she actually sounded fairly composed and not like someone who would be considered drunk by any law enforcement.

"Besides you being the best damn thing I've seen in Patience in a long time, I did it because you looked like you needed me up close and personal to know I'm not drunk. So while I would love to stand out here and argue with you, I have someplace I need to be."

Where he was headed this late at night was none of her business. Even though he'd just invaded her mouth, he didn't owe her an explanation of who he was going to see or why he was going to see them. "Well, since I didn't bite your tongue when I had good reason to, you can tell me a little bit more about yourself."

He crossed his arms, and one corner of his mouth turned up into a half grin that made her think maybe he found her more amusing than annoying, which was the complete opposite expression she got from most people she met. She was a very capable woman, and while most men found her attractive, they didn't find her cute and amusing by any means. Most men expected her to look pretty and say all the right things, but where was the fun in that? She did things her way, and maybe that was why she was still single.

"Okay, Liza, here's the rundown. I run my own business. I drive a Ford because, well, my first truck was a Ford, and once I started with a Ford, I could never go back. It just goes against everything Southern. I love my mama, and I'm single, so don't go thinking you're going to have some crazy wife or girlfriend stalking you because we kissed or because I gave you a ride to the hotel."

"Why is it I think you just described every other man in Patience? What's your last name?"

"Avery. Why?"

"Because that is something personal, not so generic, and I have a feeling you are the only Tex Avery in town."

"Does that mean you trust me?"

"That means you can drive me to the hotel. Don't confuse that with trust. I just think you can probably get me there a lot safer than I can. Men are very untrustworthy."

"Says who?"

"History, that's who. Brad cheated on Jen, Bill did it to Hillary, and Leroy Anderson kissed my ex-best friend when I was in sixth grade."

He laughed. "I'm surprised a boy named Leroy could get even one girl, let alone two." He pulled his keys out of his front jeans pocket and twirled them around his finger.

Tex guided her to none other than a soft-gray, four-door Ford truck.

"I thought when I heard my granddaddy talk like it was a sin because another man drove a different make of vehicle, it was just that…talk. But you are serious?"

"Absolutely. People around here take that kind of offense seriously. Believe me, you don't ever want to be caught even thinking of switching sides." He opened her door and waited for her to climb in.

Because she wasn't completely drunk, she hauled herself up with minimal help from Tex. He touched the small of her back to make sure she didn't slip, and a hum shot all the way to her core. She didn't even want to think of the ways her body would respond if he touched bare skin. After he closed her inside, she took a steady breath. The more air she inhaled, the more her body reacted to him and the scent his cologne left lingering inside the truck.

He slid in behind the steering wheel and brought his truck to life. It was loud and big—and very sexy. It was a real man's vehicle, not like the compact car Greg poked around in.

"So why are you here? In Patience, I mean?"

"To be honest…a cheating asshole and a best friend."

"I take it the best friend was sleeping with the ex?"

She waved her hand. "Oh no, not that. Thank God. I found my boyfriend screwing one of his patients because, apparently, I'm cold and boring in bed. Well, I would be a little more enthusiastic if his cock was longer than a whopping two inches." Did she really have to add that last part?

He laughed again before saying in a much deeper voice, "Cold and boring doesn't look like you, sweetheart." Tex ran his gaze up and down her body.

She didn't mind because looking was where it stopped. He could look at her, and she could like it. "How do you know?"

"A man can look at a woman and tell."

While she knew she was always a good lover, hearing another man say he thought she would be was nice. Not that she had any plans to let Tex find out firsthand just how good a lover she could be. "Greg didn't think so."

She'd been with her share of men, and even though she never found what she was looking for in a partner— that connection she was sure she was supposed to feel— she did have some wonderful sex, and she'd never had any complaints before her relationship with Greg.

"He's an asshole. Greg knows jack shit." He stressed the latter. "How does your best friend fit in to Patience?"

"Anna grew up here and recently moved back after being away for over a decade."

"Why don't you call her, and I can drop you by her place? The Town's Inn is clean and, as far as I know, a good place to sleep, but I'm sure your friend will be happy to see you."

Calling Anna should have been the first thing Liza did when she got to town, but she needed a night to think and regroup. She'd already talked to a kickass bartender and was on the brink of spilling her guts to a sexy stranger. She'd just talked to Anna earlier that morning, and Liza had told her she would probably be coming to visit in the next week, so already being in town was going to be a surprise. "No, I'm going to call her in the morning. She doesn't know about Greg, and she is so happy right now about the remodeling of her coffee shop and bookstore. I don't want to take her away from that to come take pity on me. I'll feel better tomorrow."

And she would. Greg would not steal one more day from her. She was here to support Anna and the big deal happening in her life. Anna didn't need Liza showing up looking a mess and being all needy.

"I don't claim to understand everything about women, but I've come to realize over the years that they tend to always drop everything for a good friend. I'm sure if you called her, her shop would be the farthest thing from her mind," he pointed out.

"That's what I don't want. Anna deserves this. I won't be the person to take even a minute of that away."

He nodded and seemed, for the time, to accept her refusal to call the only person she knew in the small town. "What did you do to the cheating ex? After your little incident with Jefferson, you don't strike me as the type of woman to take anything lying down."

She almost smiled at the memory and the feeling she had right before she opened Greg's door. She felt sexy. "I walked into his office and heard a lot of moaning and heavy breathing, so I turned on the light, and there they were. One of his patients had him pressed against the wall, one leg wrapped around his waist. I think you get the picture." She settled back on the bench seat, not caring that her sweater dress was riding up, revealing more leg than she normally would show.

"And?" he asked.

"And what more do you want to know?"

"I know you just didn't quietly shut the door and let them finish. If that's the case, I will be highly disappointed in you, Liza."

What could she say? She knew she would end up regretting the way she handled Greg and Kathy. "I thought about going all crazy-like on the woman, but it wasn't her fault. Apparently, they met when he was treating her, but when treating her turned into sleeping with her, she found another nurse practitioner. She didn't even know he had a girlfriend. As for Greg—well, I honestly was too shocked and almost numb to really lay into him like I should've. I left his office, went to our apartment, threw some things in a suitcase, and hightailed it here. I needed to get as far away from him as I could."

"Now you're here," he said, sounding a little too happy.

"Now I'm here," she agreed.

"I know you said you didn't, but are you sure you don't want me to call your friend for you?"

"No, I don't want to bug her this late at night. Plus, she has this rat bastard fiancé, and I'm in no mood to deal with him tonight. I am too weak. I want to feel refreshed and ready to do battle when I finally meet him." She could feel her blood pressure rising just thinking of Jake.

"Wow. You just love all kinds of men, don't you? Remind me to never piss you off."

"Jake deserves it. He thinks because he knows how to catch and hit a baseball, it gives him a free pass. He, too, is a cheating asshole. My friend might have forgiven him, but I haven't. I've talked to him only once, and he hung up on me. He won't get the chance to do that again."

"Are you talking about Jake Lawrence?" Tex asked.

"Yeah. You know him?"

****

This woman was something, and Tex honestly feared for Jake's safety. Liza had strong feelings for his friend and not the strong feelings a man wanted from a woman like her. "You can say that. I sometimes do jobs for him."

"He's a rat bastard, isn't he?"

What was Tex supposed to say? A while back, maybe Jake had been a bastard, along with some other things, but he was none of those now. He'd turned his life around since finding Anna again, which meant Liza was the friend Anna kept referring to. He'd heard Anna mention she had a friend coming in the next couple of weeks, and if he remembered correctly, every time Anna mentioned Liza coming to Patience, Jake cringed.

"Jake had some problems a few years ago, but he really is just a good ole boy. You might change your mind when you meet him."

"I doubt it. Men are who they are because of history. They do what they know, and there is no changing it. All men are destined to cheat."

He was sure she wasn't making sense anymore or she was talking way over his head. Anna had mentioned Liza was a therapist and lived in Linden where Anna moved when she suddenly left Patience after they graduated from high school. But he was pretty sure Liza was hurt because of her ex-boyfriend's stupid move, and therefore, she was generalizing all men and putting them in the same pot. She probably wouldn't even remember half the things she said by tomorrow.

He pulled into the Town's Inn parking lot. She reached over on the bench seat to grab the biggest purse he'd ever seen.

"Wait, don't go yet. I need to know if you're okay."

"I'm fine, really. I'm tired all of a sudden and just want a hot bath and bed."

He was certain that if he didn't already have hot images running through his mind after her telling him she would be hot in the bedroom, he for damn sure did now. He saw her stripping down to nothing but a black bra and panties, then bending over to run her bath. She was pulling her hair up in one of those high ponytails women wore, then unsnapping her lacy bra—because Liza was anything but plain—and then sliding her matching panties down her nice legs.

His cock was pulsing behind his zipper. *Time to get it together, because the last thing this woman needs is another man coming on to her tonight.*

"Let me run in and tell Ms. Lulu you need a room. Damn, we forgot your bags. You want me to run back to your car and grab them for you?" he asked, looking for any reason to keep her in his truck.

"No, that's fine. I'm sure they have a robe or something I can wear for the night. I will call Anna tomorrow and have her get my stuff for me, then take me back so I can get my car. Thanks for the offer, though."

"Okay, if you say so. I'll be back in a sec." He leaped out of the truck and jogged to the front entrance. Ms. Lulu gave him a questionable look, as if wondering why he was getting a hotel room instead of just taking his date back to his place. After figuring out his explanation of Liza being new in town and just needing a room for the night wasn't changing Ms. Lulu's suspicions, he gave up. After all, he wasn't known as the celibate kind, and, boy, did the hotel owner love town gossip. She knew about all the cheating men and women who came in and out of her hotel. It wouldn't surprise Tex if she was single-handedly responsible for the rising divorce rate.

Maybe Liza was right. Maybe everybody cheated at one time or another. That was the exact reason he was never going to have a serious relationship.

Tex came out waving a key in his hand. After opening the passenger-side door, he helped Liza out of the truck and took it upon himself to walk her to room 113. He didn't want to leave, and she must have felt something similar because they both stood there a minute, not saying a word and staring at the door. A sort of anticipation hung in the air like the fresh scent of her perfume.

He was used to women asking him to come in, but Liza wasn't going to do that. She was in man-hating mode, and he was no exception.

"Well, I guess I'm going to go. I promised my mom I would swing by before heading home."

"It's, like, almost eleven. Won't she be in bed?"

"No, probably not. She's a night owl." He found himself strangely nervous. "It was nice to meet you, and I'm sure I'll be seeing you around." He leaned in and gave her a small kiss on her cheek. It was gentle compared to the sudden, but worth it, kiss he'd given her earlier.

She turned her back on him and entered her room. He whistled all the way back to his truck.

****

Liza leaned against the hotel door. "What was that?"

Tex had looked as if he wanted to ravish her right then and there. She was supposed to despise all men right now. Ever since the blue-green-eyed devil showed up out of nowhere, all that logic had gone out the window.

The thought crossed her mind to come out and ask him what he was thinking, but he struck her as a person who told the God's honest truth. She didn't think she was prepared for that. What if he said he wanted to come inside her room and have wild and crazy sex with her? Would she let him? In her state, probably so.

She praised herself for having some restraint. That was something to be damn proud of, considering she was semi-drunk and had just found her ex banging another woman. No one would have blamed her for inviting Tex inside for a night of unattached sex.

Why was she relieved he was going to see his mom instead of meeting some tanned blonde ten years her junior?

Instead, she hadn't given him another look after he kissed her cheek and told her good night. She took a scalding bath and planned on sleeping for a full eight hours. She decided she didn't need the night to bawl her eyes out over Greg. If he couldn't appreciate the strong woman she was, then so be it.

Tomorrow she would wake and expect herself to get up and start a better day.

****

"Good God, Jake, why in the hell are we carrying a washing machine up a flight of stairs?" Tex groaned. Killing his back and legs carrying a washer upstairs, in a bookstore of all places, made no sense. "Why does a bookstore need a washer and dryer?"

"You must be blind or stupid as hell. You haven't noticed the coffee shop you've been putting cabinets in for the past couple of weeks," Jake answered.

Tex did know a coffee shop was on the first floor of the bookstore. Jake and Anna had hired him a couple of months ago to help with the remodel. No way could Jake and Anna have done all the work without it taking way too long. Anna was itching to have her baby complete and open for business. According to Jake, the shop had been a dream of hers for some time.

Having work was good for Tex. He was a man who liked to stay busy. His life felt like a mess most days, and between Avery Landscaping and the remodel, the work kept him sane.

"You don't pay my ass enough to be doing all this shit. Where's your brother?"

They took a small break. Tex didn't want to admit that if he didn't, one of his arms was bound to fall off. Plus, he had a feeling Jake's knee was acting up and he needed the breather more than Tex did. He noticed all morning that Jake had been unsuccessfully trying to hide that he was in pain. Several years ago, while playing for the Atlanta Rockets, Jake had ended up with a bad knee injury during a game. He had been one hell of a baseball player, still was when they played during the summers on a local softball team. Watching Jake spiral out of control after his career ended and his mom died had been difficult. He'd gone from being an overly confident ballplayer who knew he was one of the best to a man who enjoyed fighting every biker he came across in Ollie's. Tex was glad to see his friend get his life back together.

They leaned the washer on the steps with both of them holding it upright. "Why don't you stop complaining, and I'll buy you a beer at Ollie's tonight."

A beer wasn't worth the damn washer, but Tex liked to jerk Jake's chain every now and then. He and Jake, along with Anna, had gone through school together. He wasn't as close to Jake as he was to Jake's younger brother, Bradley. That was mostly because Tex and Bradley liked the same things—women. Bradley was a ladies' man, and he and Tex had quite the stories to tell. Recently, though, things had started to change.

"I'm only doing this for Anna. I could never turn a pretty woman down, especially that one. She could ask me to rob a bank, and I wouldn't think twice about it."

Jake locked his gaze on Tex. "Anna is my woman."

Tex refused to think of it as a sign of jealousy, because he was happy with his life. Wasn't he? Of course he was. He had all the women he wanted, although none of them as classy, sweet, and sexy as Anna, and because she would deny being sexy, that made her all the more irresistible, but he wasn't going there. If he made another comment about Anna, Jake would for sure kick his ass or let the washer crush him.

He'd watched a baseball game with Anna before she and Jake were engaged, and while he would never openly admit it, he'd seen the look Jake gave him that night from across the bar. Jake had wanted to kick his ass then, and he for sure would now. Nevertheless, Tex just couldn't stop himself. He apparently had a death wish. "I thought she would've beaten me here this morning. I've been getting used to seeing her."

"You better watch yourself, Avery. You think I've forgotten about that little kiss. Well, I haven't. You keep your thoughts away from my wife."

"She's not your wife yet, man. I can still try to

change her mind, let her know what a real man feels like. I have a lot more where that kiss came from."

Jake picked that moment to let go of the washer. Since Tex was on the downward end, it took everything he had to keep it from tumbling onto him. The muscles in his arms and legs burned. Did he really have to piss off the man holding the equal part of this big-ass machine?

Jake took back his part of the washer. "I let you stand up straight that night you decided to kiss her. I won't make that mistake again."

Tex chuckled. "I know she's your woman. It's just so easy to piss you off. There's no need to be so territorial." Truth be told, if he had a woman who came close to Anna, he would be damn territorial himself.

What was up with him? Why was he thinking of a relationship and women who only fit in relationships? A woman who was out to have a good time, no strings attached, was what he usually looked for. Those women he could handle in his life. They didn't require too much out of him or expect anything other than a roll in the sack. If he was feeling lonely one night, maybe they would have dinner, but that was all he had to give. He had a good thing going. He didn't need to invest in something that would eventually end. He also didn't need some crying babe mumbling on about how he broke her heart.

They finally got the washer up the stairs. The dryer could wait until later in the day. Maybe Bradley or one of the other men helping work on the shop would be around to lend a hand. Tex was about to ask if Anna had finally picked out her paint colors when a feminine voice drifted up the stairs.

"Looks like your woman's here. I dare you to go all

caveman on her," he said to Jake.

Jake hollered down the stairs, "Up here, sweetness," followed by, "Shut up, smart-ass," to Tex.

Tex would love to see Anna put Jake in his place if she knew he was staking his claim to her. She loved Jake and only had eyes for him, but she wasn't one to allow any man to dominate her. At first, he thought she had just been hanging out with Em, her very vocal best friend from high school, too much, but he'd soon realized that was the way Anna was made. Back in high school, she'd been shy and mostly stood back in a crowd, trying not to draw too much attention to herself, but since coming back to Patience, she'd become a strong woman who didn't take any shit. Tex admired that. She'd grown up over the past eleven years, and whatever had held her back before was no longer an issue.

Anna walked in the door like a fresh breeze, bringing the scent of vanilla with her. He was sure there was some technical name for the scent, but to him, it was plain ole vanilla. She was dressed in jeans and a New York Sparks T-shirt layered over a white, long-sleeved tee.

"Oh shit, Anna. You know I don't like that shirt. I thought we decided you wouldn't wear it in public. It's something that should only be worn while cleaning the house, if even then." Jake pointed to Anna's choice of clothing.

"You decided, I didn't. I'm just showing my support. I've already told you that just because I'm marrying a former Atlanta player doesn't mean I will abandon my team. When you marry me, you have to take the Sparks, too. You will not be telling me what I can and cannot wear, Jake Lawrence. Don't think for one second that just because I'm a woman that I will be the only one doing all the cleaning."

"I hope Texas kills any chance of them going to the World Series. Do you have to wear it in public? I mean, it's really embarrassing. Everybody's probably already talking about it."

Tex noticed that Jake left out the part about doing the cleaning. He knew Jake *wasn't* the kind of guy who dominated women. Jake was probably picking his battle for the day. The most important one at the moment was a T-shirt.

"Oh, please, get over yourself. Nobody cares anymore. You're just jealous because Atlanta stunk this year and blew all chances of making it to the playoffs."

"Now, that was low. I'm going to have to monitor how much time you spend with Em. She is rubbing off on you in a bad way. Dissing a man's team is just wrong."

"Well then, you better shut up, or I will wear my Jax Dalton shirt to bed tonight and let him keep me warm," Anna shot back.

"That's a hell no. If anyone is going to warm you, it will be me. Not some old shortstop who plays for a shit-ass team and who just needs to retire already."

Tex listened to the *happy* couple go back and forth about as simple a thing as a baseball shirt.

"Tex, don't ever decide to marry a woman who supports another baseball team." Jake sounded only mildly annoyed, which was something considering he hated everything to do with New York.

Most residents in Patience lived and breathed the Atlanta Rockets and despised New York. Tex guessed it was only because the Sparks almost always went to the playoffs, like this year and the year before. He enjoyed watching the game and loved playing even more. He didn't care who was playing. Not that he would admit that to the older men, who would disown him.

"I love New York," Tex replied. That was sure to get another rise out of his friend, who was close to blowing a fuse at the topic and the fact Tex had had one fun night with Anna four months ago.

Jake leaned over and punched Tex's arm. Anna stood there and laughed, causing Tex to do the same. The only person not laughing was Jake.

He'd apparently made one too many comments about the lovely Anna for the day.

They all three worked around the shop for the next hour. Anna stressed over paint samples while Tex examined his work to the kitchen cabinets. Jake did something or another upstairs in the bookstore part of the shop, probably so he didn't have to look at the back of Anna's shirt. As he and Anna discussed the shop and other simple things going on, Tex realized Anna not once brought up Liza. He looked at his watch and wondered if Liza had even gotten out of bed yet. If not, that would explain her not calling Anna by now. He should have gone by the hotel and checked on her, left her aspirin for her hangover or something.

Last night, he'd thought about telling Liza that he knew Anna, but for some reason he held back. It had been stupid, and she would most likely have his head for it later, but he hadn't wanted to talk about anything concerning him for the night. He'd been enjoying Liza's company and the distraction she provided him.

He was fucking losing it, but he couldn't shake that kiss.

What in holy hell had he been thinking? He snorted. He hadn't put much thought into it. She'd been standing there looking cute and slightly tipsy, and he couldn't control his impulse to kiss her.

The need to kiss her again before she disappeared into her hotel room had been there, but he'd held back. Not for him, because he didn't want to hold anything back when it came to Liza, but he knew she didn't need another man coming on to her and, in the end, disappointing her.

He was sure by the sexy expression in her eyes that she would have let him come in with little persuasion. Plenty of other women had given him that same look, and most of the time, he went inside, but that wasn't what Liza needed. For once, he was thinking with the smarter part of his anatomy.

"Hey, Anna, did you know that your friend Liza is in town?" Tex asked.

Anna's head whipped around so fast her ponytail hit her in the face. "She's what? She's in Patience?"

Chapter Three

What in the hell? was Liza's first thought as she came to in a strange hotel room. A minute passed before she remembered why she was wrapped only in a bath towel. Right. Late night, bath, and bed.

She sat upright and shoved her now-dried hair out of her face. The banging at the door didn't stop, and her pounding head wasn't appreciating it. How many glasses of wine had she actually drunk? She thought three, but it could have been four. The space next to her was empty, and she didn't know if she was more relieved or disappointed that the hottie who'd driven her to the hotel wasn't there. Of course, having sex with a complete stranger would have been a mistake, but God, he was fine, and she had no doubt he would be good in bed. Minny knew him, though, and Liza liked to think Minny wouldn't let her get in a truck with Tex if he wasn't at least a decent person.

Some parts of their conversation on the way home from the bar were a little fuzzy, but she couldn't get his face out of her head. He was rugged and handsome in the truest sense of the word. She brought her hand up to her chest. Had she done or said anything stupid to him in the truck? Knowing her and her state, she probably had.

Bang. Bang. "Liza, I know you're in there. Please open up," a voice said from the other side of her hotel door.

She put both feet on the floor and stood. As she made her way to the door, she kicked her boots out of her path. Out of habit, she looked through the peephole, even though she already knew the voice belonged to Anna. Anna was dressed in holey jeans and a sports T-shirt. Pieces of her blonde hair tumbled from her ponytail.

"Why didn't you call me as soon as you got to town?" she demanded when Liza opened the door. She sounded more confused than hurt as she stood holding one suitcase in each hand.

Liza froze, letting the previous day run through her head. "It was late, and I didn't want to bother you. I was going to call you today. Promise."

"According to Tex, you showed up at Ollie's a little after seven or eight. You know me better than that, Liza. You knew I wouldn't be in bed. I admit I do go to bed around ten. Well, it ends up being around eleven after Jake, ya know, but that's only because I'm about to open up a business, and I need to start getting up early. But—"

"Wait! You know Tex?" Did Tex ever say anything about knowing Anna? No, she would have remembered that. "He never mentioned he knew you. Only that he sometimes did work for Jake. Oh God—"

"What?" Anna asked.

She didn't want to get into it about Jake with Anna. Anna knew Liza was wary concerning him due to the way he'd treated her when they were teenagers and the pain it caused Anna for many years. It wasn't until Anna came back for her high school best friend's wedding last summer that she met up with Jake again, discovering she had never stopped loving him. Liza hadn't been surprised, but it still didn't mean she liked it. "It's nothing important. I just can't believe Tex didn't tell me, that's all. What else did he say?"

She didn't want Anna to perhaps know the scene she'd caused at the bar. Some of it was unclear because of the state she'd been in, but it still wasn't the impression she liked to leave.

Had she mentioned Greg cheating on her? Maybe if she did, he hadn't told Anna. Anna looked so happy. She hadn't sounded so chipper or seemed so at peace in a long time. Telling her about Greg would only make her sad and lose the joy comforting her. Liza refused to allow that.

"Nothing, except that he saw you at the bar and some guy named Jefferson was hitting on you, so he intervened. He put two and two together and knew you were the friend I talk endlessly about. Why? Did something else happen? Are you okay?" Anna's voice lowered as her eyebrows drew together in a frown. "Did Tex do anything? If he was disrespectful, I will kick his butt."

Wow, who was this person standing in front of her? "Tex was fine, and nothing worth mentioning happened."

Liza took the suitcases, realizing Anna was still standing outside the room. She moved out of the way so Anna could come inside. "Thanks for bringing my bags. How did you get into my car?"

"You left it unlocked."

"Crap."

"I never lock my car either. I didn't lock the apartment door until Jake practically yelled at me for being so careless."

"Thanks for bringing them. I didn't have anything

to put on, as you can tell."

Liza dropped her bags on the bed and rummaged through them to find something to wear besides the towel she currently wore like a dress. She pulled out a white lacy bra embroidered with black flowers and matching panties. She was feeling sexy, and even though nobody would see her flirty undergarments, they still made her feel good about herself.

"Are you okay, Liza?"

"Why? Do I look that bad?"

"No, I mean you just look sick or something. How about we drive to the diner and get breakfast?"

Grease was not going to make her feel better. Food wasn't high on her list of priorities, but she'd come all this way and hadn't even gotten to talk to Anna. She wanted to know if Anna had made any wedding plans and if she was happy. Liza sensed by their endless phone calls that she was, but she wanted to hear her gush about everything good that was finally happening in her life.

"Let me freshen up a little, and then we can go eat. I also want to see what has you picking Patience over Linden to open your shop." She gave Anna her best innocent smile because they had gone rounds about where Anna would open her shop and the fact Liza was really going to miss her closest friend.

"Don't you start with that. I'm still not too happy you spent an entire night here without calling me as soon as you crossed city limits."

"Uh, yeah, I did do that, didn't I? Let's just chalk it up as me missing our slumber parties."

Anna walked closer and wrapped an arm around Liza's shoulders. "I've missed you, too, Liz," she whispered in her soft, nurturing voice. "You're here now, so let's not waste the time. Go throw something on, and when I say 'throw' something on, I mean pick something quickly and let's go. I don't want to wait an hour for you to pick the perfect top that matches the right jeans that go great with your favorite pair of boots. I'm starving."

"Geez, I forgot how testy you get when you haven't eaten. Give me twenty minutes, tops."

Liza dashed into the bathroom. She was going to need every one of those minutes to put color back in her cheeks and convince her stomach not to puke up more of last night's wine.

"You've got twenty minutes before I'm dragging you outta here," Anna called out.

****

Forty-five minutes later, Liza and Anna sat at a table in C.C.'s Diner. So Liza had gone a little over her twenty-minute limit. Anna was a softy and hadn't followed through with her threat.

Over her sexy panties and bra, Liza wore a soft gray scarf tee that looked amazing with her dark skinny jeans. Instead of boots, she'd chosen ballet flats. They were sensible but dressed up a simple outfit.

"You call that throwing something on?" Anna had asked when Liza stepped out of the bathroom.

"What's wrong with what I have on? You said we were going to a diner. I thought this would be fine, but I can change."

"Seriously, Liza, look at me."

Anna could always appear sexy in jeans and a T-shirt. Liza's style was a little different.

"Why do you always have to outdress me? I swear, between you and Em, I always feel like a plain Jane."

Liza reassured Anna that she was sexy, and then they'd driven to a quaint diner on Main Street.

Liza thought about only ordering coffee, but the aroma of greasy food surprisingly made her stomach growl for something more. She did an overlook of the menu, and when the older woman came back to check on them, she ordered a BLT sandwich and a cup of coffee with lots of cream. Anna ordered a big plate of pancakes with extra butter and extra syrup, crispy bacon, and coffee with cream.

"Are you really going to eat all that?" Liza asked. She wasn't trying to be rude, but it was a lot of food. In the past, Anna had always seemed to be trying the latest diet because she thought she was overweight, which, in fact, was never the case. Anna was curvy, and Liza could only wish for a butt like the one her friend had.

"Most likely. I plan on running this afternoon before our girls' night."

"I wasn't saying anything about your weight, because I think you look really great. Wait, what's this about girls' night?" She remembered Anna telling her that a bunch of women got together every Friday night and did whatever. Liza had girlfriends back home, but she didn't have friends she did something with every week. She was intrigued and eager to meet Anna's Patience friends.

"This Friday we're all going over to Em's house for margaritas and wine. It's usually a good time. You have to come meet everyone." Anna looked so sweet that even if Liza wanted to, she couldn't turn her down.

"Of course I'm coming. I've been hearing about girls' night for months." She couldn't think about alcohol at the moment. Her headache had her thinking about never having another drink. Nevertheless, she needed a night out with some girls, even though she didn't know anyone but Anna.

"Good. Sometimes we meet at Ollie's, but we always seem to run into the men there. That's why we're doing it at Em's tonight."

Liza had only heard about Em and her crazy ideas, but she looked forward to finally meeting her. Em had been a loyal friend to Anna since childhood. Liza liked knowing that Anna hadn't been all alone when she was forced to deal with an abusive stepfather at an early age. Anna was one of the strongest people she knew.

As Anna relayed the directions to Em's house, a waitress placed their food in front of them. Anna's pancakes smelled to die for. Not that Liza's BLT looked bad, because it didn't, but those pancakes had an aroma all their own.

Liza gave Anna a puppy-dog look.

"You want a bite?" Before Liza could say anything, Anna was already handing over her fork.

"Next time, I'm going to have to go for those." Liza put the fork in her mouth and experienced heaven. Never had she tasted anything better.

She gave Anna her fork back and started to eat her own food. She drank all her coffee and ordered a refill. Coffee was her best friend. In the mornings, it was sometimes better than sex. Or maybe she was just having shitty sex.

A bell dinged above the front entrance. She turned to look, and there he was in all his handsome glory.

He wore jeans with a pullover and scuffed work boots. She expected him to have a hat on for some reason. Maybe because a man like Tex looked as though he would have a ball cap or cowboy hat on at all times. Standing by the counter, he ran a hand over his short hair.

The woman behind the counter turned a deep shade of red and shyly smiled, a twinkle in her eye when Tex spoke to her. She walked with pep in her step to the back while he took a seat on one of the stools at the counter.

Liza didn't know much about him, but she knew enough to guess that women falling all over him were part of the norm.

He didn't look too smug about making the waitress blush—in fact, he looked kind of lost. When she saw him last night, he'd looked full of life, eager to have fun. He knew what he wanted, and he went for it, not regretting his actions later. At least, that's how he'd been last night when he took her by surprise and put his tongue in her mouth. Right now, he almost looked helpless and depleted. A sadness she couldn't explain washed over her.

Anna called him over to their table. He made his way through the growing crowd of people and edged in next to Liza, taking most of the empty space in the booth. His thigh couldn't help but rub against hers, and her breath caught. Her reaction to him last night had not been because of the wine she consumed, but a clear connection.

He picked a fry off her plate and popped it in his mouth. She didn't mind. He could take anything he wanted from her.

"What brings you ladies out?" He gave Anna a flirty smile but turned to smile and stare right through Liza.

She locked eyes with him and couldn't will herself to turn away. She wondered if he'd thought about her after he left last night, because she certainly thought about him. He must have entered her dreams sometime during the night. Otherwise, why else would she have woken to him being one of her first thoughts? Her body longed for another one of his kisses, which was inappropriate because they were in a public place. She also didn't need a guy in her life. Especially one who didn't mind flirting and clearly had the look of a ladies' man.

She hadn't felt this attraction in a long time, and that was sad because she'd been in a serious relationship for over a year. What did that say about her and her relationships with men?

"A girl has got to eat. What are you doing here?" she said, trying to sound unaffected by his presence and failing miserably. A lot of thoughts swarmed through her head, inappropriate thoughts to have when sitting across the table from her best friend having breakfast.

She started to pick at her napkin, and he laid his hand over the top of hers. Much like last night, a streak of desire shot through her system, followed by a wave of lust. It was actually sweet, and she wondered if he really could feel what she was thinking. Anna gave her a pointed look, and Liza quickly lowered her gaze.

He looked agitated. "My mom wants some damn cupcakes that C.C. only makes this time of year. I think they're pumpkin something or other."

Recognizing his agitation so soon confused her. She could blame it on the fact she was taught to know people and read them, but she didn't believe for one second that was her reason for knowing Tex was not acting like himself.

"Anything C.C. makes is good, so I bet they're wonderful," Anna said before popping in her last bite of pancake. "What are you and the boys doing tonight?"

"Ah…it must be Friday girls' night? It's the only damn time I can hang out with Jake and Tommy. Most nights, I'm stuck with Bradley. Unfortunately, that guy can never leave a pretty lady alone long enough to drink a full beer or play a game of pool with a buddy. I don't know what's in the cards, but I have no doubt it will be good. It will put your Aretha Franklin singing with margaritas to shame." A sweet smile formed as he drummed his fingers on the table.

"I don't care what you and my soon-to-be brother-in-law do, but Jake and Tommy are off-limits," Anna said to Tex. When she was being demanding, her eyes deepened to a different shade of green. She meant business when it came to Jake. "I don't want to feel responsible for Em trying to kill any one of you," she added with a playful smile. The way Anna talked about Em, Liza didn't doubt that Em was likely to kill anyone who came between her and her husband, Tommy.

"Jake won't do anything more than have a beer or two and lose a game of pool. He's so wrapped up in you that he can't even have a conversation without you being a part of it. You have nothing to worry about."

She liked that Tex was reassuring Anna, even though she didn't need it. Liza knew Anna believed in her relationship with Jake. She was glad Anna felt that, but it didn't mean Liza trusted Jake completely. He needed to prove himself to her before she stopped thinking of him as anything but a rat bastard.

She'd never thought about it before, but she wanted someone to love her so much that she was on their mind all the time. Obviously, she wasn't on Greg's mind, or he wouldn't have been having an affair with Kathy for who knew how long.

Liza was now sure she'd never really loved him. She was creeping up in age, and she just thought it was time to have love in her life. The only problem was she forced love instead of letting love find her. A mistake she knew better than to make. Enough couples had come to her after committing that very same error.

"Hey, Tex, your cupcakes are ready," the older woman who waited on her and Anna hollered out while holding up a medium-sized box with the diner's logo printed on the top.

"I better get these to my mom. Anna, I'll see you back at the shop in about an hour. I thank God you've finally picked a paint color. Liza, it was nice to see you again. I'm sure I'll be seeing you around."

She searched his face to see if he was being honest, and she thought she saw it. He looked genuine, and she liked that about him. He might be a big country-boy flirt, but he wasn't one to play around. What he said, he meant, even though he hadn't mentioned knowing Anna.

She was definitely going to confront him about that when they were alone. And she did want him alone again.

He rose from the table and gave them both a quick kiss on the cheek before walking out the door and giving Liza the perfect view of his well-shaped butt. She liked to think he'd put a little bit more passion in the kiss he gave to her.

Just keep living in fantasyland, Liza.

"Why would Tex be seeing you at the coffee shop and bookstore and thankful you picked a paint color?" she asked.

"Jake hired him to help out. Jake and I wanted it to

be something we created together, but it turned out to be too much work, so Jake hired Tex. It's great because we can open a lot sooner than we first thought."

Liza was learning more and more about Tex Avery.

She insisted on paying their bill since she hadn't called Anna the night before, and Anna took her to get her car at the bar. Anna never mentioned the looks Liza had kept giving Tex or the way Tex's hand fit nicely over hers. She gave Anna a big hug before making plans to meet at Em's around seven that night. Liza couldn't wait to meet everyone. Only bummer was the men were not allowed at a girls' night, meaning she had absolutely no way of running into Tex again. She headed back to her hotel room to take a nap or watch terrible daytime television until it was time to get ready for girls' night.

****

Liza,

Sorry to have to do this through an email, but it needs to be done, nevertheless. It is my job to inform you that because of staffing issues, we have to let you go as an employee. You have always done exceptional work here, and because of that, we will be happy to help you in any way we can to find employment elsewhere. I hope you have a nice vacation.

John

Liza slammed her laptop closed. She'd read what few words were there over and over again until they blurred together. How was she being fired? What had she done to deserve this? The email was short and simple, and that hurt because she'd worked her ass off for that practice. There were no staffing issues. It had to be some kind of joke.

After college, she'd started working at the office as

an appointment scheduler and continued in that position until she got her master's. She'd then done her post-degree internship, and after passing the licensing exam, she'd started working full time as a family and marriage counselor. If they were going to fire anyone, it should have been someone who worked there a lot less than she had. She loved her patients and gave them everything she had every day. In some small way, she liked to think she helped make a difference in their lives. They needed her, and she wouldn't be there for them anymore.

Something wasn't adding up.

Greg.

She didn't know why, but his name popped into her head like a light switch suddenly turned on, brightly shining on her situation. He had something to do with this. She just knew it. He was good buddies with John, her supervisor, head of all the therapists. Greg had this done to her. What an insecure little prick. He was having an affair with one of his patients, which was a big no-no, and she was the one getting the ax.

She thought about fighting it, but at the moment, she didn't have the energy. Fuck it—for now.

She flopped back on the bed and closed her eyes. Let them have the damn job. She couldn't go back there and work around the cheating asshole anyway. She would find something else. Something a lot better. This would not break her. Nevertheless, she couldn't help but think about all the people who depended on her.

She was not one to tuck her tail between her legs and run when things got tough, but she didn't feel this was worth fighting. Yeah, she loved her patients, and they were the only reason she felt guilty for not demanding the truth in her firing, but right now she needed to focus on her life and finding Liza again.

****

Tex walked into the ranch-style brick home. It was smaller than most of the houses on the street, but he had always loved the house. After his worthless father left them, his mom had worked hard to give him this home, and for that he would forever love the gift she'd given him. A place he knew he could always come back to.

Four years ago he'd decided it was time to move out and find his own place—a house he loved and was proud of—but it was just walls and a block foundation. It was quiet and bare and didn't give him the feeling of security. He only found that when he entered his mom's house.

On most days, he loved coming back here, but today just didn't feel right. He knew when Maggie, his mom's home-health nurse, called him to tell him his mom wanted some damn cupcakes that it was going to be one of *those* days. Well, except for being able to see Liza again so soon. He needed to kiss his mom for putting him in the right place at the right time. If nothing else, being near Liza for those few minutes made today a little better. God, he was starting to think like a female.

The leaves on the trees in the front yard had already begun to change from green to shades of oranges, yellows, and reds and were falling from their branches, blanketing the ground. Tex didn't know why everyone wanted the colorful leaves raked from their yards. He thought they made the place feel homey, but it kept him in business, so he couldn't say too much.

He walked up the sidewalk he had poured himself, one of the first things he did to the fixer-upper when he was old enough to pour concrete and know he could do a good job. After the sidewalk, he'd moved on to building a railing around the porch, something his woodworking teacher taught him. Over the years, when he and his mom could spare the extra cash, he'd completed more work on the house. It was the least he could do to try to repay her for all she'd given him.

The same porch swing hung to his left, a present he'd given his mother on Mother's Day when he was seventeen. It needed a fresh coat of paint, so he would add it to his list of things needing touching up.

He tapped on the door but didn't wait for a response, letting himself into the living room. After all the years he'd spent in this house, it always smelled the same to him. The scent was a mixture of something baking in the oven—which nowadays was probably some type of candle burning if Maggie wasn't in the kitchen supervising actual baking—the perfume his mother had worn since he was a boy, and a little bit of a musty smell. This was home. She was home, except now she was suffering, and he didn't know what to do.

"Mom. Maggie. I'm here with cupcakes." He laid the cupcakes down on the coffee table. He was feeling a little too jittery and told himself he should have switched to decaf an hour ago.

He walked over to the mantel above the fireplace and picked up the small carousel he'd bought his mom for Christmas a couple of years ago. He loved he was able to give her something she cherished as she did.

No matter who it was, she would always show off the small figurine, then hold it in her hands, close to her chest. He didn't know what was so special about it, because he had bought her better, more expensive things, but she loved the carousel.

He placed it back on the mantel when he heard his

mother coming. Until this day, even in her old age, she could put the fear of God in him. He didn't want to get caught with his hand in the cookie jar.

He loved her because she never gave up on him, and so he would never lose hope in her. No matter how far away she went from him, he would try to find a way to assure her he would always be there. He wanted to give her what she had given him his whole life—love and support.

He went to her and put a kiss on her soft, wrinkled cheek. Taking both her arms, he guided her to the recliner she always sat in. "How are you feeling today, Mama?"

"Is that why you're here, just to check up on me?" Pearl waved a hand in front of her face. "I'm fine. Don't you worry about me, honey." She still talked in her soft, fragile voice, but no matter how soft her voice came out, she always made him stop and listen. Growing up, he was a hardheaded boy who did stupid things, and even though his mother was soft-spoken and laid-back, she never—not once—let him slide. She'd spanked his tail more times than he could count, and now he could say he deserved every one of them.

She never compared him to his father, and in fact, she never mentioned the man. He had always thought he got his hardheadedness and wild ways from his father. He didn't want his mother to look at him and be reminded of the man who left her, but she'd only given him a spanking when he needed it and unconditional love.

He squatted in front of her, placing both of her small hands into his much larger ones. He wanted to be able to see who he was talking to. "I'm your son. You can tell me if you're having a bad day. I just want to take care of you." She hadn't forgotten him yet, but it still bothered him that she would one day.

He watched her face change to something harsher than it was only a minute ago. This was when her condition bothered him because she was not herself. She was not his mother at times like this, but yet she still was. He tried to remind himself that wasn't her, but sometimes he couldn't hide his shock. He would never get used to the person she was slowly becoming.

"I know you're my son. What, do you think I'm so stupid I wouldn't know who you are? It is not your job to take care of me. I take care of you, and that is final. You can quit coming over here to just check in. If it's a hardship and you don't want to come and see me, then don't." Pearl sat back in her chair and closed her eyes.

Tex wondered if she thought about what she was saying and knew she wasn't acting like herself. Was she scared? Did she know what was going on? The thought of her scared and confused terrified him. Her feeling alone with a disease she couldn't understand about killed him.

No matter how many books he read late at night when he couldn't sleep, trying to understand what was happening and find any way he could to reassure and make her feel safe, nothing could prepare him for seeing a loving mother turn into the opposite of just that.

He also wondered if her mind was trying to make her search to find the real her—a mother who had never raised her voice to him. She was stern and told it like it was, but she never yelled. He guessed that's why now the disease made it so hard for him to see her do things she normally wouldn't do.

When she didn't open her eyes, Tex announced, "Mama, I brought the cupcakes you wanted." When she opened her eyes and nothing registered, he became concerned. It looked as if she felt nothing.

Maggie hung back, giving Tex time with his mother. He looked to Maggie for help.

"Ms. Avery, you know the cupcakes you wanted C.C. to make for you. The pumpkin ones with cream-cheese frosting?"

No response.

An unmanly lump formed in his chest. This was all happening too fast. He wasn't ready for this. His mom was only in her midfifties. She was older but too young. When Pearl said nothing, he pushed to his feet and took the box into the kitchen. He needed a minute to process the fact his mother didn't remember she'd wanted cupcakes two hours ago.

After entering the kitchen, Maggie laid a hand on his shoulder. "You will get through this, Tex."

Tex liked Maggie. She was around his age and came highly recommended. Her job was to sit with his mother every day. She made sure his mom took all her meds, got a bath, dressed, and ate one good meal. He didn't know how Maggie accomplished that last task because some of the medicines caused Pearl to lose her appetite. His mother hadn't questioned Maggie being there, and Tex was glad because whether she knew it or not, she needed a nurse. Tex needed Maggie. He was also thankful his mother remembered Maggie. He didn't even want to imagine how much harder it would've been on everyone involved if he had to explain to her who Maggie was and that it was okay to trust her on a daily basis.

Sometimes the guilt would set in for not being with

his mother more, but he had to work to help provide for both of them. She had money from her retirement fund, but with her doctor visits, meds, and hiring Maggie full time, he had to step in and cover a lot of the expenses. He didn't mind. It was his turn to take care of her, even if she didn't like it.

"How late do you stay at night?" Tex asked her. He got the feeling his mother shouldn't be left alone anymore. While he tried to come by some nights during the week, he couldn't do it every night. He'd stopped over last night and watched a cupcake baking show with her, which was probably why she was in the mood for cupcakes this morning. The only problem was she didn't remember wanting the cupcakes and might not even remember him coming by to watch the lousy reality show with her.

"I stay until after she eats dinner and takes her night meds. So I probably leave between seven and eight. I get here at seven every morning."

"Aren't you tired? I mean, I love how you take care of her, but that seems like a lot. Don't you have a family?" He wondered if she was single or maybe married. She was curvy with a beautiful face, bold deep-brown eyes, and most importantly, she took great care of his mom.

"All of my family lives in Knight County. When I started staying with Ms. Avery, I hadn't been out of nursing school long and was only concerned with my career. I would, though, like to have a day off during the week or weekend, just so I can see my family and do errands, but I will do whatever you think is right."

Now he really felt like a selfish bastard because while he was going out with the boys, forgetting about his problems and getting away from it all, Maggie never got a break. That had to change. She worked seven days a week. Of course she would want a day off. He only spent a couple of hours every other day with his mother, and he needed a break from the mental part. It only made sense Maggie would need that, too. He felt like shit for not realizing that sooner.

"I'm sorry. I have a feeling she is only going to get worse, and you are going to need a few days off every week."

"I'm okay. I didn't mean this job is too much for me, because it isn't. I—"

"I know you can handle your job. You do a damn fine job, but things are going to get more challenging, and everybody needs time away. Let me see what I can do, and then we can come up with a better schedule."

He took a calming breath and moved to the living room. It was turning late, and he needed to get more work done before he went out with the guys. He needed a cold beer and meaningless talk between men. When had things gotten so out of control? One day he was having innocent fun with different women and hanging with the guys, and now he faced being a responsible adult. He couldn't pinpoint when his life had taken a dramatic turn, and it wasn't in the direction he preferred.

Maybe, before now, he'd lived like a lousy teenager instead of a grown man. Yeah, he did adult things. He had a house and business—those were very adult things to have—but he'd still acted like an adolescent on the daily. Now life was happening, forcing him to be a better man.

His mother sat in her chair, head leaned back, eyes shut. She appeared so peaceful and innocent, but what she was going through wasn't innocent. It was harsh and unfair. Her disease didn't care that she was still young or that she had a son and, at one time, good friends who cared about her and would feel lost without her.

He kneeled on the floor in front of her. "Mom," he said softly, trying not to startle her. The last thing he wanted to do was make her day worse. That would only make Maggie's day suck, and that woman deserved a bonus for what she did on a daily basis. When he got back to his office, he would write her a check. He usually didn't give random bonuses to his employees, but Maggie was different. She took care of the most important person in his life.

His mom popped her eyes open and stared at him. She had such love in her eyes, and it broke him. Scratching a thumbnail across his jaw, he thought about the best way to say goodbye. He didn't want to leave her upset. He wanted their visits to be positive, something they could hold on to when things really got bad.

He spoke softly. "I have to go back to work, but Maggie is here, and if you need me, she will call me. Remember the phone I got you last week? All you have to do is press one, and you can reach me anytime, day or night."

"That's sweet, honey, but I'm fine. I already told you I don't need a cell phone. The house phone works just fine. Why would you want to waste the money?"

"Because the cell phone can fit in your pocket or robe and be with you at all times."

"You make it seem like I'm on lockdown. You're the one you need to be taking care of. When's the last time you had a good home-cooked meal?"

He couldn't tell his mother that Jenny Tate had tried

cooking him homemade lasagna but failed miserably. Those had been some damn crunchy noodles. So he told her a white lie. "It's been a while, Mama." Even though she probably knew, or used to know, he liked to go out with a lot of women, he didn't feel comfortable talking to her about it.

She brought her hand up to his cheek and patted him gently. "Well, I demand you come over for Sunday dinner. Remember when we used to do that after you moved out? I can't even remember why we quit."

Tex remembered. It had been a Sunday night, four months ago. He was running ten minutes behind, and he felt bad because he knew from talking to his mom earlier that day that she was looking forward to having dinner with him. When he arrived, he found her in one of her flowerbeds out front pulling weeds. She didn't even remember having a conversation with him that morning.

He played it off as him dropping by to surprise her with cooking her dinner.

That was the day he'd had the sinking suspicion that something was terribly wrong.

"Why don't you and Maggie come over for dinner this Sunday?" Pearl suggested, smiling. "Maggie, what do you like?"

"Mom, Maggie is going to start having Sundays with her family, and she will only be here a half day on Saturdays."

"When did that happen?"

"About thirty minutes ago. You and I need more time together, and she needs to be with her family. I think it will be good. Why don't I come over and we cook a meal together? Besides, if I want to survive on something other than ramen noodles, I'm going to need you to teach me to cook."

"That sounds good, but, Tex, you listen to me. I am going to be fine. Besides, Maggie and I have a date with the television. My soap opera will be on soon."

He smiled because just when he thought he'd lost her, there she was. His same mother, the mother who never missed an episode of her favorite daytime television show, sat in front of him. He pushed to his feet and kissed the top of her head.

"Tex, you know you're going to have to settle down sometime." She brought a hand up to her mouth to shield it and whispered, "Why don't you ask Maggie out? She's a sweet girl. I could teach you how to cook. Make her a nice meal."

His mother still being capable of caring about him and his happiness filled him with such joy. "I'll think about it, Mama." He nodded to Maggie. Her cheeks flushed as he walked out the front door.

Standing on the porch, he breathed in all the air his lungs would allow. Wow. He didn't know what he was walking into, but he wasn't prepared to see his mom so angry one minute, then try to set him up with a woman the next.

When had she ever tried to set him up with someone? He couldn't remember if she ever had. She was like any other mother and used to make comments about him finding a nice woman to marry and one day give her grandchildren, but that was the extent of it.

Children were not on his radar. He was a single man with enough troubles, and the fact remained his mother would never know if he had kids or not. Why did a guy who never thought about having kids feel sad for his mother and her lack to have and remember having grandchildren in her life?

He couldn't subject a child to his destiny—what could be their destiny. He was not going to be responsible for passing on the disease his mom suffered from every day. So no, kids were out of the question.

Chapter Four

Liza stared at the two sets of photos. One set featured a high, off-the-floor maple table with matching chairs. The other showed a black, sleek, square table with high-back chairs. They were pretty much the same table but in different finishes. "Which one do you really like?" The question Anna wanted everyone to answer before the night was over.

Her friend was at the beginning of stressed-out mode over the remodel and getting the shop ready for business. Liza felt bad she hadn't come sooner to help take on some of the load. She couldn't wait to see the shop and all the work Anna and Tex put into it, and she guessed Jake helped in some *small* way.

"The mustard-colored walls you decided on for the main space will look nice with the black wood. I think they will complement each other, so I choose the black finish," Liza said.

"That's what everyone has said so far. Well, except for Jessie." Anna didn't hide her enthusiasm, and Liza decided it looked good on her.

"How long will it be until the remodel is finished?" A bubbly woman Anna had just introduced as Georgia asked.

Georgia seemed to love vibrant colors and didn't mind dressing in whatever mood she was in. Her blonde, bouncing curls looked almost childlike with the wide orange headband and large flower taking residence on the side of her head. Liza immediately liked the talkative woman and couldn't imagine anyone not being drawn to her innocence and whimsical ways. She was just too sweet not to love.

"Probably another three weeks. All that's left is the painting, setting up the tables and chairs, and all the décor stuff. Em, you're still helping me with that, aren't you?" Anna turned and asked Em, who was just popping the cork on a bottle of blackberry wine.

Yuck. The thought of more wine repulsed Liza. She'd drunk enough last night to fill an entire bottle. *Great.* She was now a boozer because of Greg and her lack of a life.

"Yes, Anna. I've told you a million times. I am going to help you. I have lots of ideas."

Everyone decided to take a seat out on Em's deck, despite a chill in the air. The outdoors didn't bother Liza; fall was her favorite time of year. She loved it when the air turned crisp enough that a light jacket was necessary. She pulled her cropped peacoat close around her to fight off some of the cold.

Em walked over, looking like a waitress down at Ollie's—minus the pink hair—holding a serving tray full of wineglasses and one lonely beer. She looked like a woman who knew how to flaunt what God gave her. She wore a short, low-cut dress that showed off some amazing cleavage and a pair of thigh-high boots. An image of a blonde bombshell in a football commercial came to mind. Liza was as straight as they came, and she still had some attraction to the tanned beauty.

Em wore her platinum-blonde hair straight, reaching the middle of her back. Liza always considered herself very fashionable, but she had a feeling Em took things to a whole different level. She was bold and lively, even in black. Liza decided Em would be a refreshing person to be around and was bound to bring some excitement. She would make her focus on something besides being unemployed and once again single.

"If you don't mind, Em, I would love just a beer."

"When did you start drinking beer?" Anna asked.

"I'm just trying something new. I always drink wine. Plus, you promised margaritas." Liza had been looking forward to the margaritas.

"That's my fault," Em chimed in. "I was supposed to go to the store and pick up the tequila, but I got busy at the hair salon and forgot all about it. Next Friday, though, you will get a margarita. Let me run back inside and grab another beer."

After returning, Em placed the tray down on a nearby table, handed Liza a beer, and sat in the chair next to her.

"This is some tasty wine, Em. Where can I get a bottle?" Georgia asked, already finished with her first glass.

Liza wanted to tell her it wasn't good to suck it dry, that the hangover in the morning would have her regretting it, but she kept her mouth shut. She wouldn't have liked it much if someone told her to calm down, especially someone she just met. Last night, she would have socked anyone who spoke up about her many glasses of wine.

"Mama and I went to the winery over in Knight," Em said.

"I've never been to a winery. How was it? For some reason, I think of a bunch of people just sitting around getting toasted on free wine." Georgia poured herself another glass. None of the other women looked at her funny, so Liza assumed this was normal for Georgia.

"In my case, it was my mama getting tipsy on all the wine. I tried each wine until I found the one I loved, then I stopped and put my glass down. My mama tried every dry, semidry, and sweet wine there was. Luckily, they only give you a small taste. Otherwise, I would have had to carry her out of there."

"That's funny because my mother would never do anything like that. I don't think I've ever seen her drink a glass of wine or anything else with alcohol in it. I would love to see her loosen up a bit," Georgia said.

Anna walked up, took a wineglass from the tray, and found a seat across from Liza and Em. "Georgia, don't believe everything this girl is telling you. I know Mrs. Bradshaw, and she would never get drunk in public. She's only a social drinker."

"You weren't there," Em interrupted. "And she wasn't drunk. She was…let's just say…really happy about life. Don't get me wrong—she would whip my butt if she knew I was telling you guys this."

Jessie, who was Em's sister-in-law and Anna's good friend, joined them. Jessie took her beer bottle and perched herself on the railing. She smiled at Em. "I ought to tell your mama you're going around telling everyone she's a drunk just so she will spank you. Now, that would be hilarious." She laughed.

"Oh, grow up, Jessie," Em scolded.

"See this cold beer? I don't drink wine. It's for lightweights. This beer says I am grown."

Everyone, including Liza, let out a loud laugh. She'd thought it would be strange sitting around with all of

Anna's friends, but it wasn't. She liked them all, and she liked having a girls' night with them.

"So, Liza, how many big bad secrets do you know?" Jessie asked as she placed her beer bottle on the table.

Liza could tell right off the bat Jessie would have rather hung out with the guys than the girls. She could probably outdrink them all and kick their asses at pool at the same time. She was simple but not plain in her faded jeans and pink long-sleeved John Deere shirt. Her straight brunette hair looked to be natural, and even though it was October, she still had a nice, natural tan.

"What do you mean?"

"Anna said you were a therapist. I just thought you would know all kinds of juicy information. I mean, how many cheating spouses do you see? I bet a bunch because men are such assholes."

Liza had kept her firing and cheating boyfriend to herself. Being unemployed and single was still new to her, and she wasn't ready to share those bits of information just yet. She was livid with Greg and what he'd done to her, but on the other hand, she felt liberated. She wasn't scared to be without a job. She just didn't like to fail. Even though none of it was her fault, it still seemed as if she'd failed. And that pissed her off more than what Greg had done.

"I can't say much, but I do know a lot of couples who are trying to work things out in their marriage and see if they should even stay married. And for the record—women cheat, too."

"Not as much as men. I'd bet my next beer on it," Jessie said.

Liza thought about it. "I say it's probably fifty-fifty."

"And you are able to help them?" Georgia asked.

"I try. It's mainly me getting them to ask the right questions and talk to each other. They really do all the work. I'm just there to guide and confront the issues coming between them being happy and having a healthy relationship."

Georgia brought her hands to her chest, covering her heart. "That is so nice that you do that. I think it's amazing. I've never told anyone this, but I think when I was younger, my parents went to therapy. I noticed them fighting a lot, and that wasn't normal in my household. They never said anything, but I started to put two and two together when they had an *appointment*"—Georgia made quotation marks with her fingers—"every Tuesday night. No one talked about it, and after a while, things got better. They've now been married over thirty years."

"That's great they could work things out. I've seen it more times than not where the couple decides to go their separate ways, and it's always hard on the kids."

"And that's her job, not something she does as a hobby on the side," Em said.

"Yeah, it is what I do, and people pay me to help them, but I do get satisfaction out of it at the end of the day. I love what I do."

"And she's very good," Anna pointed out.

It was time to change topics because Liza was liable to lose it at any second. Her job was all she had left, and now that, too, was gone. Of course, switching topics was what she needed to do until Em said, "Maybe she could talk to Tex."

Everyone in the group fell quiet except Liza. She sat up straight in her chair. "Why would Tex need to talk to me?"

Jessie threw her arms in the air. "Good God, Em, do you always have to open your big fat mouth? This is none of your…our business."

"Oh, zip it, Jessie. You have a bigger mouth than I do." Em leaned back in her chair, bringing her wineglass to her lips. "Besides—" She took a sip of wine. "—he needs to talk to someone. Here's Liza, and she's a professional."

"Why would Tex need to talk to me?" Liza asked again.

"Do you know how pissed he would be if he walked in and heard you talking about his situation?" Jessie said.

"What situation?" Liza wished someone would take notice—since she was the professional—and answer her.

"It wouldn't be a situation if he would do something about it."

"What's he supposed to do, Em? Please tell me."

Em held out her arms. "Are you getting my point? Talk about it."

Jessie let out a half laugh. "That's not going to change anything. Now quit butting in."

"Actually"—Liza held up a finger—"talking about it could help him. I need to know what I will actually be helping him with." All sorts of things ran through her mind simultaneously, but one scenario stood out. Since they were just talking about cheating spouses, Tex could be married, but no, she was sure that wasn't it because he did emphasize last night that he was single. However, he could have been married in the past.

"Sorry, Liza, but it's not going to help this," Jessie said.

Liza glanced to Em, whose arms were crossed and lips turned up in a pout. She stuck her tongue out at

Jessie. "Fine, I was just trying to help."

"I know." Jessie's voice was no longer stern but comforting.

Wait. What? And just like that, the discussion was over. The two women were moving on, and Jessie was getting the final say. Liza still didn't know what in the hell was going on.

If Tex—or anybody—needed her, she wanted to help. But Tex...she especially felt the need to be there for him. He'd looked so down this morning when he first strolled into the diner. She'd known then she wanted to help him in some way, even if they only talked.

"How about we move these chairs, turn up Beyoncé, and dance our asses off?" Jessie was already moving the chairs and humming a song as she went.

Liza didn't want to dance. She wanted to know what made Tex tick, what possibly could bring a strong and solid man like him to needing professional help. Moreover, dammit, how did he have the power to draw in a woman who needed to swear off men for a couple of decades?

Everyone else had a second glass of wine except Georgia, who was on her third. Jessie worked on her second beer while Liza sipped her first. Anna was right. She wasn't a beer drinker, but she tolerated it for the sake of not having to drink another glass of wine.

Everyone seemed ready to have some downright fun. Em turned up the radio loud enough for it to blast through the open windows and french doors. All of a sudden, a Beyoncé hit blared through the speakers. Liza had heard it several times and even had it on her playlist. It was a good woman-take-control kind of song. It must be fate, because it was a song she needed to hear. She was a woman who needed to find herself again and take control of her life. She didn't need to be at a practice that didn't appreciate her hard work, and she sure as hell didn't need a man to make her happy and feel complete. She was on her way to find Liza Dyer again, and maybe coming to Patience for a while was just what she needed.

"All right, girls, it's time to shake what the good Lord gave us," Jessie announced, then downed her beer and plunked it on the table with a loud *thud*.

What the hell? The old Liza would let her hair loose and dance her ass off without having to be drunk. In fact, she used to love to dance, but Greg didn't. She wasn't drunk, but she wasn't going to pass on an opportunity to get up and dance. The environment was good. She drained her beer and tried not to make a face before she stood to shake her hips a little.

Tex was still on her mind, but right now she needed to make herself her main focus. Right now, she needed some fun.

"You go, girl," Em screamed as she rubbed up on Jessie.

Before too long, all five of them were dancing and singing. Liza looked over and was shocked to see Anna actually dancing. She wasn't one to embarrass herself in public, but there her friend was, hands up in the air, shaking her tail and singing to the max. Maybe she'd had a little more to drink than Liza. Everyone looked happy, and even though Liza had been through a breakup and lost her job, she, too, was happy. It must have something to do with Patience.

****

"Hey, boys, what can I getcha tonight?" Minny asked all four men.

68

"Beer, please." That was something Tex didn't have to think about, a nice change from the rest of his life. He was tired of thinking about everything, especially his mom. She was getting worse, and he could do nothing about it.

Tomorrow he was going to have to find someone to help Maggie, which left him no choice after making the sudden decision to give her half-day Saturdays and full Sundays off. The poor girl couldn't do it all by herself, and Tex had to work. He guessed he could move back home, but that just didn't hold much appeal, even though it might be his only choice. Right now, he was going to enjoy his beer, and tomorrow he would deal with the deep shit.

His friends ordered beer as well. Minny uncapped all four bottles and set them in front of the men. Tex grabbed his first and guzzled almost half. He was thirsty, and he had been waiting a good long time for a cold one.

With it being a Friday night, the place was at full capacity. People scattered across the bar, the tables, and a few biker-looking men played a game of pool. The clack of balls rang out while Alan Jackson wailed from the jukebox.

"Is something bothering you, man?" Bradley turned to Tex.

It jerked Tex away from his thoughts, forced his gaze from the bottle in front of him and to Bradley's face. He plastered what he hoped was a smile on his face. "Nah, I'm good."

Bradley flashed a wicked grin. "Why don't you quit burning a hole through your beer bottle, and we single guys go find us some women?"

Tex knew the guy was serious as a doornail. Bradley

didn't go anywhere without a woman, and usually Tex was on board with that logic, but not tonight. Why not, he didn't know. He wanted to sit his ass on his barstool and drink as many beers as he could before the night ended. Then he wanted to go home, crawl into bed, and pray that by morning his life would be back to normal.

He could dream.

"I don't see much I like," Tex said. He was telling the God's honest truth.

"What? You're going to turn down a woman for the night? Bradley's right. Something is wrong with you tonight." Jake took a seat right next to him, tossing peanuts into his mouth with one hand and gripping his beer bottle with the other.

"I'm all about women, just not at this moment. Now, can I sit here and drink my beer without getting shit from you guys?"

"You're the one turning over a new leaf. You can't blame us for being shocked," Tommy piped in from the end of the bar.

This was stupid. How was he turning over a new leaf? He just wanted a night out with the guys—which he was now regretting—to sit, drink, and talk about sports. He didn't want to go chasing after a woman for one night of pleasure.

Why didn't he want to find a woman to help him forget for the night? Any other night, having a willing woman at his side would be high on his list, but for some damn reason he didn't feel like it tonight.

Maybe his visit with his mom earlier affected him more than he thought. Seeing two different sides to her was too much for one day, and it was clearly fucking with his mind.

"I know what it is. He's got a thing for Anna's friend Liza." Jake threw a peanut in the air and caught it in his mouth. "Why, I don't know. The woman is plain scary if you ask me. She's a man-hater or something."

Was there any truth to what Jake said? Was he interested in Liza? She was a woman who could set a man on fire, and he couldn't deny the attraction between them when he drove her to the hotel last night and this morning when he saw her and Anna at the diner. He could feel the heat radiating off her.

If he were honest with himself, he would have to admit he wouldn't mind spending some alone time with her. Maybe see if there was any truth to Jake's idea.

She was not some man-hating bitch, as Jake liked to think. She was only like that with Jake, and that had nothing to do with Tex. She could continue thinking Jake was the scum of the earth, but that didn't mean she thought Tex was scum.

"She doesn't hate all men, just you, Lawrence," Tex said as Minny placed another bottle in front of him. Anna must have told Jake about him meeting and driving Liza to the hotel.

"Why hate me? I never did anything to her. I haven't even officially met her. How can she judge me after one two-minute conversation four months ago?"

"I don't know, man, but you are definitely on her crap list."

"Well, shit. I thought after I won Anna over, I would stop having to deal with women who hated me. Now I have to deal with her crazy friend. It just doesn't seem right."

"You better play nice if you want to keep Anna happy. Girls have some secret code or something.

Something about bitches over dickheads."

"Where in the hell did you hear that?" Bradley asked, choking on his beer and looking clueless.

That was shocking since Bradley should know a little bit more about women, having slept with half of Patience. Tex was even sure he'd slept with a married woman or two. It was truly a wonder the guy was still alive.

"I heard it from some woman I met. For some strange reason, she thought we were dating"—which was something Tex didn't do—"and after she found out I had slept with her best friend a couple of months earlier, she informed me of this secret code. Why are women so sensitive?"

Bradley waved Minny over for another beer. "Have you seen Jamie Jones yet? Boy, is she flexible. I've never seen moves like it in my life. I think she's some type of yoga instructor."

"Can't say I have," Tex said. He'd seen her around, and she had approached him, being all giggly, not too long ago, but he just wasn't in the mood. He wasn't in the mood a lot lately.

Maybe he needed to get laid. How long had it been…a couple of weeks maybe? Surely, it hadn't been longer than that.

Bradley got up from his barstool as if ready to make tracks. "Jake, Liza probably hates you because you led Anna to believe you'd been with another woman back when y'all were teenagers and didn't tell her the truth till eleven years later. It was pretty shitty."

"How would you know, jackass? This coming from a man who goes through women like he does his underwear. I don't need any love advice from you. Anna and I are fine now. Liza needs to get over it, and so do you, apparently. I'm getting plain tired of you always bringing up the mistakes I made when I was eighteen years old." Jake spoke with all the love a brother could have and was probably the only one who could get away with calling Bradley a jackass.

"Whoa-ho, bro, I was just sayin'. I won't bring it up again. Gosh, you aren't a little touchy about the topic, are you?" Bradley grabbed the beer Minny just put in front of him and made his way across the bar to a table full of women dressed in short skirts and cleavage shirts.

Tex knew what Jake had done to Anna back when they were teenagers still bothered him. Jake lying to Anna for eleven years by making her think he'd cheated on her was bad and something Tex didn't understand. Anna was a good woman, and he still couldn't believe Jake would let her go like that. There had to be more to the story. The lie had made Anna leave town and not return until Tommy and Em married last June.

"All I know is one day all that running around is going to catch up with him. I wouldn't wish the single life on anyone. I'm happy to finally be tied down and married to Em." Tommy moved over to Bradley's now-unoccupied seat. "I think it's smart of you, Avery, to stay away from the bar women. You're liable to catch something."

Tex laughed. Tommy was probably right. He was glad that in all his sexual years, he'd always practiced safe sex. No matter how uncomfortable "the talk" was with his mom, she'd stressed that and made him promise he would practice safe sex.

Bradley must have said something because the table of girls giggled. "Hey, Minny, will you bring these ladies another round of whatever they're drinking?" he yelled above the booming crowd and jukebox. Minny left the bar and carried a tray of fruity-looking drinks to the table.

Tex cracked a handful of peanuts before tossing them in his mouth. Minny set another beer in front of him, making it his third for the night. He didn't really need it, but what the hell—Tommy was driving.

"What kinda music y'all want on the box?" Tommy asked as he dug in his jeans pockets for spare change.

"How about we drink to Hank Jr. tonight? While you're at it, why don't you throw a little love Alabama's way?" Jake gave Tommy another handful of change.

"All right. They're coming right up." Tommy walked over to the jukebox to play good ole country music.

"So what time does Anna want you home?" It was meant as a joke. Tex was starting to get a beer buzz and enjoying it. Unlike last night, he planned to drink over his limit.

"Anna and I don't put limits on each other. At least I get to go home to a woman every night."

The comment was a lighthearted dig back at him, but it stung a little. He didn't have to have a woman to go home to. He was happy being alone. He had the luxury of taking a woman to bed anytime he wanted—a different woman every other night if that's what he chose.

The dude ambled closer to the bar, but Tex didn't expect the biker guy to stop and talk to him and Jake. He looked as if he belonged to a motorcycle club. The excessive amounts of leather, tattoos, and deep scowl triggered trouble in Tex's mind. Every nerve went on high alert.

"You might want to get your jackass friend over there. Those are our women." He hiked a finger to the pool table where four of his biker friends stood glaring back. "He is getting in our way."

The guy stood closest to Jake, which made the biker talk directly to him. "Did those women come with you?" Jake asked in a level tone, showing no intention of backing down if things happened to get out of control.

"It doesn't matter. We saw them first, so that makes them ours. You best get that motherfucker away, or there will be hell to pay."

"That *motherfucker* is my brother, and if there is going to be any hell to pay, it will not be by your hands. It looks to me like those women are enjoying their time with my brother, more than they would with you shitheads." Jake got up from his barstool and crossed his arms, making him look bigger and stronger.

The pissed-off biker moved in a little closer. "I don't think you want to mess with me, Jake."

Jake looked taken aback.

"You think I don't know who you are? I guess you've forgotten about your wild stage when you would come in here and try to fight my buddies. We haven't forgotten. We would love to kick your ass again."

"Those days are behind me," Jake proudly stated.

Jake had spent a long time trying to put his reckless life back together, and Tex wasn't surprised that Jake wouldn't remember the men and their previous encounters. Tex was not about to let Jake ruin his new life over this jackass.

Life went on around them as if nobody could sense the uproar about to ensue. Tex could feel it, and he was sure Jake felt it, too. Tex stood from his barstool. He placed his hands by his sides, fists clenched, waiting for an opportunity to do something.

"Remove your brother…or else." The biker moved another step closer to Jake.

Jake never backed down. He firmly held his position. "I don't take orders too well. I tend to do what I want when I want."

"I guess that's why you don't play ball anymore. All you are is a washed-up ballplayer who never should have made it in the first place. You and your brother are both pieces of shit." The biker's stern eyes blazed a hole through Jake.

Tex felt the heat radiating off Jake. He had been around him long enough to know Jake was not going to stand there and take the words the biker had just dished out. Jake picked up the beer bottle, the one he'd emptied right before the rude interruption by the biker dude. There was only one other use for it.

Quickly, Tex took the bottle away from Jake, set it on the bar, and turned to come face-to-face with the man twice his size. It happened so fast that he couldn't comprehend everything he was doing. One minute he was taking a bottle away from Jake, and the next minute he was throwing a right hook. It felt good. It felt liberating. He'd been going through so much the last few months he needed to get some things off his chest. Getting in a fight with a worthless asshole helped make up for many things in his life he couldn't change right now.

He had the guy by the shirt and pushed up against the bar. He let go a few more punches, and while he was at it, he picked up the beer bottle he'd just taken out of

Jake's hand and smashed it over the biker's head. Before he knew it, two men were pulling him back, but not before the other asshole made contact with Tex's jaw. Tex went willingly, only because he got what he wanted. He could say he was standing up for a friend, but in truth, he needed to kick some ass. While he couldn't fight what was really going on in his life, he could do something about this.

The owner, Ollie, came out from behind the counter, waving a baseball bat in front of the biker but talking to Tex and his buddies. "I think you boys need to leave for a while. Let things cool off a bit."

"Sorry about this, Ollie," Tommy volunteered after he discovered what was going on. He joined the party and helped Jake pull Tex off the guy.

"No problem. The jerk deserved it. I'll see you guys later."

Bradley was the first to start talking. "Fuck! What in the world happened over there? One minute, I'm about to get the phone number of one of the girls I was sitting with, and the next minute, I look up and see Tex bloodying some guy's nose. What in the fuck happened?" His hands flew in every direction. He was more hyped up than Tex at the moment.

Walking to Tommy's truck in the parking lot, Tex said, "The guy just came up and started talking shit."

"No," Jake corrected, talking to Bradley. "The dude wanted those women you were hanging all over. He wanted us to remove you from the picture."

"Me?" Bradley said, acting innocent. "Those women weren't even with those punks. One of the girls told me that those freaks had been watching them for a while. She said it really scared her, and she was glad when I finally walked over." He looked very proud of himself.

So if Tex thought about it, he'd taken a punch for Jake, Bradley, and the women Bradley was hitting on. His jaw would hurt like a motherfucker after his adrenaline slowed. Right now, he was so amped up he could only feel a light throb. He was definitely going to need ice.

"Tex, thanks for what you did. I know why you did it, but just so you know, I can still fight my own battles," Jake said.

Tex understood. He wouldn't want someone else coming into his fights, but he didn't want to see Jake go back down that dark road again. He liked the new Jake. "I know you still can. I just needed to kick some ass tonight."

"I could tell. Anything you want to talk about?" Jake kind of looked uncomfortable.

Men were not supposed to talk about their feelings, but Jake would for Tex, and that made Tex thankful for his friendship. Tex really hadn't had anyone to talk to. Bradley was usually the one he hung with, but he was too much like a kid, and while he liked Tommy, they'd never had a close relationship. Not like the one he had with Bradley and Jake. Still, that didn't mean he cared to talk about what was really going on in his head and his real reason for wanting to kick that guy's ass.

"I'm good. Just got a lot going on at home."

"Your mom?" Jake asked.

Jake knew a little about Tex's mom, but Tex didn't like to talk about it. In fact, he talked so little about it that people didn't know how bad things were becoming. If they weren't direct friends with his mom, and she didn't have that many left, they really didn't know about her sickness.

At least, he didn't think they did.

"How about we talk about something else? I was getting a beer buzz, and now that's shot to hell. Fucking bastards."

Tommy strolled over, holding a beer in one hand, and offered it to Tex. "Here you go, buddy. It looks like you could use one."

"Thanks, Tommy. How'd you get this?"

"Ollie let me get one last beer. Why don't we leave this place and go sneak in on the women?"

They all took their seats in Tommy's truck since he was the one who'd picked each of them up. Jake sat in the front with Tommy, and Bradley and Tex sat in the back on the short ride to Tommy and Em's house. As Tommy pulled in the driveway, Tex noticed four other cars parked, not counting Em's.

They filed out of the truck before making their way up the sidewalk. Tex envied Tommy and Jake. Tommy came home to an overly loud Em every night and slept in the house they'd bought together. Jake just got a second chance with the only woman he'd ever loved. He didn't like to feel that way because he was happy with his life. He'd never wanted a wife before. Why was he thinking about it now? First, thinking about kids and now, a wife.

Tommy went through the door first, and the rest of the guys followed. The music blared with ear-busting rock and roll. That was a surprise. Usually, the women went for Aretha. Tex could hang with them if this was what they listened to. The band AC/DC rocked the house with "You Shook Me All Night Long." The floor of the living room was scattered with shoes and purses, and Tex heard laughter and loud, jarring singing. He made his way over the clutter and headed toward the noise. Several empty wine bottles and a few beer bottles were found in the kitchen. The french doors leading to the deck were wide open.

Bingo. All five women were jamming out. Em and Jessie rubbed against each other while they held their wine and beer. Anna and Georgia were off in their own world, singing to each other while using their hands as microphones.

Then there was Liza. A confident Liza—the woman he'd thought about most of the day. She was on top of a patio chair, singing at the top of her lungs, her head flung back, and her brown hair whipping in the wind. She let the music move her in ways Tex would have dreams about later. Her butt and hips shifted perfectly in her dark, ass-cupping jeans. She was perfect. He couldn't budge. He didn't want to, because that would cause her to stop dancing, and he sure as hell didn't want that.

He was content to watch her for the rest of his life if possible. While her singing was off-key, her body was right on the mark. The lust he automatically felt with every turn of her hips almost paralyzed him and made his cock swell painfully against the front of his jeans.

He didn't know how much time passed, but she finally noticed all the other men. She stopped swaying to the music and smoothed her disheveled hair. Her gaze ran up and down his hyperaware body, forcing him to react to her in ways that were too private for this audience. His only thought was *hell yeah*.

Chapter Five

Oh, shit. Oh, shit. Four sets of eyes were on her. Well, not only on her. The other women in the room acting a fool didn't seem to matter at the moment. It seemed as if all were looking at the new girl in town, thinking she was some lunatic who danced on chairs and sang high-pitched songs, all made worse because she knew she couldn't sing a note if her life depended on it.

One of the men walked back into the house and turned the music down. She steadied herself by gripping the tabletop and easing off the chair she had decided was a good place to live out her diva moment. Right now, she was shamefully regretting that stupid idea. *Sheesh.*

"Hey," Jessie cried, "I was just feeling it. Turn that back up, Bradley."

"Looked to me you were way past the point of feeling it, baby. I swear I need to start attending the girl parties and leave the boring married men behind."

"What about Tex? He too tame for you now, or is he taking all the bimbos?" Jessie wanted to know, looking oddly annoyed.

"Well, Tex used to be the only one I could stand to hang out with after Jake got smart and proposed to Anna—and I say that in the best way, Anna, my love—but now Tex has gone off and decided he isn't interested in women. Guy's seriously lost it. I guess I should be happy since that just leaves more casseroles for me."

Bradley? Liza ran the name through her head until it hit her that Jake had a younger brother. Man, she'd thought Tex was a hottie. Bradley had to be in a whole different league, and she'd just met him. Not even met him yet, but finally had seen him. His light-blue eyes twinkled as he mentioned Anna and sparred with Jessie. She could already tell he loved the ladies and the ladies loved him right back. His unruly hair would look to some that he was unkempt, but it really only added to his sex appeal. She could admire a fine man when she saw one, and she would have continued looking if it wasn't for her feeling the eyes of someone else watching her.

She moved from hottie number one to hottie number two. Her heart beat double-time when her gaze locked on Tex—as he merely raised a thick, beautifully curved eyebrow at her—and an electric current pulsed between them.

Tex continued to stare at her. "I never said I wasn't interested in women. Let's just say I'm becoming more selective."

Was that a smirk? Why did she think that was a loaded statement? Damn, which bra did she have on? She'd long ago shucked her coat, and she couldn't exactly *feel it*, as Jessie liked to point out, if she was bogged down by a coat. Now she had only her thin scarf tee. She would not look down at her chest, but when Tex's gaze moved from her warm face to her chest, she remembered she'd been feeling sexy that morning and put on her lacy bra. Just great. He could apparently see she was *feeling him*. She wrapped her arms around her chest, only to cause more amusement in his eyes.

Georgia drained her fourth or fifth glass of wine and only missed a step or two to place her glass on the table.

She wore a loose smile and slight befuddlement in her eyes. "What about me, Brad? I'm still single, and I would love to stare at you all night."

Was Georgia flirting with the good-looking charmer? Nobody seemed shocked. Liza had just met Georgia, but even she could tell the bubbly, romantic woman was acting out of character.

Bradley ignored Georgia and her fluttering eyes, not skipping a beat to make quick introductions with Liza. How rude. The least he could do was throw some of that good ole charm her way. She was drunk off her ass, but she seemed like a nice girl who was cute in a childlike way…but still cute.

He spoke slowly, his southern drawl thick as molasses. "And you must be Liza."

Liza focused on the man standing in front of her looking just as sexy as Tex but not having the power to make her oddly blush and dampen her panties. "That's me. I take it you're Jake's younger, more-charming brother."

Bradley belted out a laugh that echoed through the tree-lined backyard. He wiped at his eyes and turned back to look at Jake, who had his arm around Anna. "I thought Tex was slightly overplaying it when he said you would love to cut off Jake's balls, but I see you still have some hatred toward my brother."

So Tex had mentioned her feelings toward Jake to the boys. That should piss her off, because she'd confided in him with the impression that he wasn't close friends with Jake and his brother, but it didn't.

She was thankful to have something other than Tex and his smoldering looks to turn her attention to for a moment. "Hatred is putting it mildly. I've always thought of your brother as a rat bastard. There's no need to look at him differently now."

"Liza," Anna scolded.

"It's fine, honey. Your friend can think of me any way she likes. I don't know if I was a rat bastard because, well, I've never met one, but I was an asshole, and she has every right to be protective of you."

"That isn't what you said at the bar. If I remember correctly, you said she was crazy and needed to get over it," Bradley chimed in.

Liza marched right up to Jake, meeting his gaze. "Crazy, huh? I might be a little crazy because I am protective of my best friend and saw her go deep inside herself because of you and your lies, but hey"—she shrugged—"if that makes me crazy, oh well. You didn't deserve Anna eleven years ago, and you sure as hell don't deserve her now."

This was good. She needed a distraction, and Jake was the perfect person to give it to her. Coming into town, she'd told herself that she wouldn't mind laying all her pent-up anger on him, and now she was. And oh, he deserved it. He'd hurt her friend, and for that, she would never forgive or like him. Still, she wouldn't let that come between her and Anna. Now that she'd said her piece and he knew where they stood, they could get along, for Anna's sake.

"Nice going, you dumbass." Jessie punched Bradley in the arm, causing him to stumble. Liza was sure Jessie could punch him a lot harder if she wanted and lay him out on his ass.

"I was just sayin'. It's not my fault Liza doesn't mind laying into Jake. I haven't seen a woman do that since Anna."

Right on. Liza was happy that Anna hadn't just given in to Jake and his pursuit of her. She'd made him fight for it, and that was something that the Anna she'd first met wouldn't have done. She was stronger and more confident. Anna coming back to Patience was good for her, even though it made Liza sad she was losing a friend.

"Oh God, Tex, what happened to your jaw, and why is your right hand puffing up like a baseball?" Em cried. She ran to him and cupped his face in her hand.

Liza looked from his jaw to his hand, and worry washed over her. She resisted the urge to push Em out of the way and take over the cradling and mothering.

"Come inside so I can get a better look, and I want you boys to tell me what you got yourselves into."

All the men looked to one another, then fell into line right behind Em. She apparently ran a tight ship, and when she spoke, everyone listened.

Em pushed Tex down in a kitchen chair while everyone else took a seat in the open living room. Jake stood by Anna and wrapped his arms around her as she hugged him tightly back. Jessie stood in the middle of the room, and Georgia plopped heavily on the couch, leaving Bradley to take the oversized leather chair.

"Anna, there's a first aid kit in the spare bathroom, under the sink. Liza, will you grab a bag of peas out of the freezer, please?"

"Why in the hell do I need peas? I'm not hungry. I just got punched in the jaw, and now that you've pointed it out, it hurts like a motherfucker." Tex rubbed his jaw with his bruised hand.

Anna left Jake's side and rushed down the hall. Liza, like everyone else, followed Em's instructions. She pulled out the first bag of vegetables she saw, then grabbed a second bag for Tex's hand and thrust them at Em.

"Thanks, hon."

Em gently put the frozen bag to Tex's purple-and-blue jaw while he took the other bag and put it on top of his hand.

"Now that's taken care of, I want some damn answers. Who punched you, and what did you do?" Em demanded. She shot Tex a stare that probably terrified most men.

"Why do you think I did anything? It could have been Tommy, Jake…or most likely, Bradley who did something."

"Don't give me that, Tex Avery. You're the one who has the multicolored jaw and baseball-sized hand. The smell of cheap perfume mixed with beer tells me you guys were at Ollie's. So spill."

"It really wasn't Tex's fault, Em. It was me."

Anna turned to Jake as she walked back into the living room and handed the first aid kit to Em. Her eyes narrowed as she spoke. "Why you?"

"These biker dudes came in—"

"Bikers… Really, Jake? I thought you were past getting in fights with bikers the size of the Undertaker." Em turned the mothering look she was giving Tex to fury.

Liza definitely didn't want to ever piss the woman off.

"It wasn't like that, Em."

"Then please tell us. What was it like? I swear, if you do this to Anna again, I will join Liza in kicking your ass." Em put both hands on her hips. She looked badass in her tall boots and short dress. Liza was mistaken earlier; Em didn't resemble Faith Hill at all. She was more like a kickass Catwoman.

"Em, baby, please calm down. It wasn't Jake who caused the fight. This biker came up to Jake and Tex and demanded Jake remove Bradley from a table of women he and his buddies had their eyes on. Understandably, he refused, which any of us would. The biker didn't like it, and Tex stepped in." Tommy walked from the shadows of the room and kissed Em's cheek.

Liza hadn't noticed him until now. He wasn't as attractive as Bradley and Tex, but he was appealing. He had an easy way about him that made Liza wonder how he and Em ever got together.

He wore a slight mustache and wasn't overweight, but he wasn't fit either. Opposites apparently attracted. Maybe Tommy grounded Em, and Em loosened up Tommy.

"So this is your fault." Jessie faced Bradley and looked to be shooting bullets at him.

Major chemistry was going on there. The heat and intensity rolled off them in waves and warmed the room to another degree.

"Why do you enjoy busting my balls every chance you get? I didn't even know about the losers, and the women were uncomfortable with them. If anything, Tex stuck up for the girls." Bradley got up from the chair and walked to the large window, seeming to stare into the darkness. "I mean it, Jessie. Everything is always my fault. I thought we were cool, but I guess not, because I think you enjoy making me your punching bag."

The room fell quiet. Even Georgia stopped pouring herself yet another glass of wine and stared at the commotion. Bradley stormed out the front door. Yep—

major heat was going on between those two. An explosion of emotions was bound to release when they finally figured it out.

"Everyone needs to calm down. Hey, what happened to the music?" Georgia cried, shaking her hips and spilling a few drops of wine on the light carpet.

"Georgia, honey, please watch the carpet. I can't afford to have it cleaned every time you come over," Em cried.

As if on cue Georgia took her place on the couch and drank her gazillionth glass of blackberry wine.

"What in the hell was that about?" Tex winced.

Liza turned to Jessie. She had always had the urge to step in and try to bring light to a hostile situation, but she felt like an intruder to the close group of friends. She also thought her voice wouldn't be welcome at the moment.

Jessie clasped her hands together as she stared at no one in particular. Maybe Liza was wrong. Maybe Jessie recognized the storm brewing between her and Bradley. Maybe Bradley was the blind one, not Jessie. She might not recognize how strong their attraction was just yet, though.

"I'll go talk to him." Jake planted a kiss on Anna's cheek and made quick strides to the front door.

"No. Jake, wait." Jessie reached out and grabbed Jake's arm. "I'll do it. I'm the one he's mad at. We might as well hash it out now. Whatever it is."

Jake nodded and let Jessie take his place.

"I've never seen him get upset about anything unless it's toward Jake, and that's just being brotherly," Tex volunteered. Besides Jake, Tex most likely knew Bradley the best. They lived the same single lifestyle. Of course, they would prowl the bars together, looking for women.

But now Tex was being selective. That, for some reason, thrilled Liza.

"I don't like him talking to my sister like that," Tommy said.

His raised voice told Liza he cared for his sister. He, too, was protective of someone he loved, and Liza knew all too much about that. She would go to the ends of the earth for her family—that included Anna.

Jake spoke up, running a hand through his shaggy hair. "He and Jessie have a weird relationship. One day they're best friends, shooting pool, drinking a beer together, and the next day, they're fighting over who grew the best crops that season. I don't think they even know how strange they are with each other. Tomorrow they'll be fine."

"I think it's something more. Just a few months ago, Jessie bid on him at the bachelor auction. She looked pretty upset when she lost to some barely legally aged girl. There are feelings going on there that they haven't realized yet or don't want to realize. They are going to have to confront them sooner or later. Otherwise, there will just be more arguments, and they will lose a good friendship." Anna wrapped her arms around Jake and hugged him, as if thankful she'd recognized her feelings for him and was never going to let him go.

"I don't know if I like it," Tommy piped up. His hands were clenched at his sides.

"Well, like it or not, you have to let them work it out for themselves. We are staying out of it," Em informed her husband. She gave him a little nudge and patted him on the butt.

He let out a sigh but didn't say anything else about Jessie and her relationship, or non-relationship, with Jake's brother.

"Well, it looks like you're going to live to fight another day, slugger," Em told Tex while knocking him in the back of the head.

"What the hell, Em? Give a guy a break. That asshole's face could have broken my hand." He raised his hand from the now-thawed peas.

"You want me to kiss it for ya, Tex?"

Everyone turned their attention to Georgia, who seemed shocked by what she'd just asked.

"Crap." She gasped, choking on a little bit of her wine. "Did I just say that out loud?"

"Yeah, honey, you did. How many glasses have you had tonight?" Tex looked first to Liza, then to Anna.

"I don't know. Just a few. I think I need to lie down for a minute. I'm not feeling too good all of a sudden."

"I've already been puked on this week. Jake, Tommy, it's your turn to do the gentlemanly thing."

"Who threw up on you recently, Tex? I thought you were taking a break from women." Jake gave a half smile while Anna took it upon herself to put a pillow under Georgia's head as she stretched out on the couch. Liza covered her with a leopard throw.

Please don't let him tell everyone I acted like a drunken teenager and puked on his boots in Ollie's parking lot.

Tex handed Em her peas back. "I never said I was giving up women. How stupid do you think I am? I said I was just being selective." He strode over to stand a little too close to Liza, and she could feel everyone's curiosity screaming.

"When have you ever cared about the women you were screwing?"

"Jake," Anna scolded. She rose to the tips of her toes so she could follow Em's action and slap him on the back of the head.

"Sorry. I mean sleeping with."

Tex gazed down at Liza, and she, well, she concentrated on the mirror hanging above the couch, which was a terrible idea because she could see Tex and the wide grin he sported.

Great. He hadn't told on her, but everyone saw his clear-as-day intentions. Jake was right. She literally was crazy for feeling any type of attraction to the ladies' man, who apparently didn't mind who he *slept with*…just as long as he was sleeping with someone. It was time for her to make an exit before he made himself any clearer.

"I guess I'll be going. Em, thanks for having me. I have to say that it's been…interesting."

"No prob, chick-a-doo. Next week I promise margaritas."

Anna stood by the front door, holding Liza's coat and purse. "Call me tomorrow, sweetie."

Liza gave her friend a one-armed hug, trying not to look her in the eye. She really didn't want to have Anna judge her since Anna thought Liza was still involved with Greg.

"I promise. I want to see the shop."

"I'll see everyone later." Liza waved and tried running to her car. She didn't want anyone to figure out how terrified she was of Tex and the way he looked at her. She hoped she had a good poker face and hid what she was really thinking.

"Wait." Tex was across the room in record time, and

before Liza realized it, he was gripping her arm. She stood one foot inside and one foot outside. Damn—she was so close. "Can you give me a ride? Tommy picked me up tonight."

"Why don't you get a ride from Jessie?" Anna suggested. "She might need someone to talk to. Speaking of, someone might want to check on the two of them. I haven't heard yelling, but then again, that doesn't mean they're not having a fistfight of their own."

Liza and Tex were the first out the door, followed by the rest, except for poor Georgia. She was out like a light, hair fanned around her round face, and snoring in the most unladylike way.

Tommy walked around the house but came back empty-handed. "No one is out here."

"Jessie's truck is gone," Jake pointed out. "I guess they made up, and she took Bradley home."

"Just great," Tommy spoke up. "I swear, if your brother does anything—"

"Tommy." Em stopped her husband in midsentence. "We decided to let them be. She is not a child, even though you have a hard time believing that. She's a grown woman, and she can take care of herself."

Liza couldn't ignore the fact that Tommy had not agreed to leave Jessie and Bradley be. Em had decided that, but Tommy nodded and backed down. He wasn't fooling Liza. He clearly didn't like the idea of Jessie being anywhere around Bradley. Liza couldn't blame his concern, but if anyone could handle the cocky, woman-loving man, it was Jessie. Liza didn't doubt the woman's ability to put any man in his place.

Funny, most of her friends would have said the same thing about her at one time. Where was that person? She missed her and was pissed she'd lost herself in the year she'd been living with Greg. Her mission now was to find that sure-of-herself woman who was vocal about her expectations in a man and didn't mind being alone. In fact, she sometimes chose being alone over giving her time to some worthless man who sat behind a desk all day and didn't mind living off his daddy's money. Sometimes she just enjoyed sitting in her apartment and reading a steamy romance novel over having to doll up just so she could please a man.

"I guess that ride with Jessie is out of the question. Looks like it's just you and me," Tex announced, looking too happy with the little outcome.

"What about Jake and Anna?" Liza suggested.

She needed to be smart, and the smart thing was to not be in a car alone with Tex again. Last night she'd really had no other option. Well, she could have waited for Minny, but after the lip-lock she'd been too vulnerable to put up much of a fight against Tex and his sexy bedroom eyes.

"Anna's car is a two-seater."

Damn, why hadn't she remembered that? Liza had been the one to push Anna to get the sleek sports car.

"So what do you say? You think you can stand me for one more night?"

Oh yeah, she could stand him for one more night…and one more night after that. In fact, she could do a lot more than just stand him. She had sexual frustrations she could definitely use him for, something no romance novel could help with. No. That was not happening. She needed to get it together because it looked like she was going to be in a car with him, trapped again.

"Okay. Fine, then. Get in." She hoped she sounded more put out and not deep-down ecstatic at being alone with him.

****

"Nice car. It doesn't seem to fit you, though, not to mention that it's way too big for a little thing like you. I have to say it does drive smooth," Tex said.

"I guess I'm not wrapped up in what I drive like Patience boys," Liza shot back while turning to give him a little smile.

Her SUV was stupidly a sensitive subject for her. It represented the person she'd turned into. It screamed practical and boring. At least it came with cool options like a sunroof, but it wasn't a sports car like what Anna drove. Seriously, how had her practical, safe friend ended up with the sports car while she decided to buy a metallic boat? The universe made no sense sometimes. Just because she was now in her thirties and expected to drive the family car didn't mean that was how she was going to run her life. Nope—no more. The new thirty was like twenty-something. Right?

"At least I'm riding in your foreign-made car. I could be stoned for this, lose my business, all my friends. My mom might even disown me."

"Oh, pah-leeze, nobody really cares what you drive. I think me giving you a ride…to where"—she wanted to know—"is not going to matter to the people in Patience. I wouldn't worry too much about your business or your mother's disappointment."

"You're probably right about my mother. She doesn't know the difference between a camper and an SUV. As far back as I can remember, she's driven the same blue station wagon. She literally cried when I

94

threatened to sell it after it left her stranded in Knight."

"What did you do?"

"What any good son would do. I paid a fortune for the parts and fixed it. I can't handle a woman crying."

That touched a chord with her. What was it her mother would say? *You can always tell how a man is going to treat you by the way he treats his mother*?

"Turn at the next stop sign. My mom's house is the third house down on the right," he instructed.

Liza turned onto the right street and counted the houses until she got to the third one. She pulled into the driveway right behind the blue station wagon. They sat for a moment in silence, surrounded by the darkness. The only light visible was from a floodlight perched on the side of the house.

She sat facing forward, afraid of what expression he might hold. She wasn't ready for him to leave yet. After evening her breath, she started counting in her head. *One…two…three…four…*

Even though the seats were large, he still took up the whole thing. He situated himself and turned his body toward her. "Liza, can you look at me, please?"

She was on thirteen when she finally stopped her silly obsession and looked him in the eye. Her eyes were still having a hard time adjusting to the darkness but not enough that she couldn't make out his strong jaw and his lack of shaving, from what she could tell, the last few mornings. The slight stubble covering his face added a sexiness she couldn't put into words.

"Where's your truck?"

"It's at my house. I told my mom I would come over tonight. I'll get it tomorrow."

"Didn't you come here last night, too? You've

talked about your mom but haven't said anything about your father."

A sullen expression fell over his face. "He's not around."

"Where is he?" Okay, she just didn't know when to butt out and keep her mouth shut. Not everyone wanted to reveal their family history, but she couldn't resist because Em and Jessie's discussion earlier still kept her wondering.

"I don't know. He could have another family or be dead for all I know. He left my mom and me when I was six. We haven't seen or heard from him since."

"That had to be hard."

"It is what it is." He shrugged.

It was time for her to shut her trap, even though it went against everything she wanted and was trained to do. She wanted to say more than "that sucks." She wanted to tell him that his dad leaving had to have been hard on him and his mother. That being a young boy growing up without a male influence in the house had to have affected him in more ways than one. But she shut her mouth before she started a therapy session she was sure he wouldn't appreciate or accept.

They had only met the night before, and while he had kissed her and obviously flirted with her back at Em and Tommy's, that didn't justify her butting into his personal life. She was not one of his closest friends, like Em and Jessie. She was just another woman to him. He was known to be a flirt and charming to anyone with breasts, and even though she knew all these things to be true, she wasn't ready for him to get out of her car.

"How's the jaw and hand? I hate to say it, but your jaw is already turning colors. Who won?"

"Won what?"

"The fight."

He covered his heart with both hands, looking offended. "Me, of course. The biker only got a punch in while I got a punch in and cracked a beer bottle over his head."

"You smashed a beer bottle over the top of his head?"

"Yep. The asshole deserved it."

"The one night I go there and need a distraction, I get nothing but myself being the distraction. You and the others go there the very next night, and all hell breaks loose. That's just my luck."

"So you would enjoy watching me in a bar fight?" He gave her a half smile.

"Not you particularly, but I would have loved for anything other than me being the entertainment for the night. Thanks, by the way, for not telling Anna about my ex and the real reason I didn't call her." She stopped and held up a finger to emphasize her next question. "And speaking of last night, why didn't you tell me you knew Anna and were good friends with Jake and are helping remodel her shop? I can't remember everything I said, but I'm pretty sure I made my feelings known about Jake. That would have been a good time for you to mention you knew the best friend I was talking about. I should be totally pissed at you."

"But you're not, are you?"

Now that was hot. His eyes seemed to dance against the moonlight and showed amusement.

"No. But only because you kept my secret about Greg and drove me to the hotel."

"Not for the kiss?"

Thank God for the darkness blanketing the sky. Otherwise, he would be able to see her heated face as she remembered the way his mouth took hers, demanding she give in to him. Well, no more of that. She was now running the show when it came to any man who walked into her life. Not that she thought she and Tex had anything going on, but he was being all confident and flirty. Therefore, she had to take charge and only give what she was willing to let go of.

She angled her body, bringing her right leg up on the seat. "It was just a kiss. Don't get all cocky on me and think you're the best thing that walked on water."

"Me…cocky? I was just asking if you enjoyed the kiss. It did, after all, seal the deal and allow you to let me drive you to the hotel. I have to say it was pretty good. Not even you can deny that."

Okay, she'd said what she said. It was out there now. She felt a tad out of control at the way he held a force over her. "I admit, what I remember, it was okay. Don't think it will happen again, because I'm pretty sure I mentioned last night that I currently hate all men, or at least implied it."

"I thought you were just drunk and that only applied to Brad, Bill, Greg, and some pimple-faced boy named Leroy."

How much had she really revealed? And how badly had she rambled on about cheating men and how all of them were dogs?

"You weren't supposed to be listening to all that. And Leroy did not have pimples. He was actually cute for a middle-school kid. He was even the school's star basketball player."

"If you say so. I guess his parents really just didn't

like him." He chuckled. "Why wouldn't I listen to you? I actually learned a lot about you."

"Like what?"

"You are most likely a celebrity news junkie, and you keep up with politics—at least the scandals. Three glasses of wine is your limit in one night, and for some reason, you tell me about the man you just figured out you never really loved—at least not romantically—instead of your best and only friend in Patience."

Wheeeww. She thought she was a little bit more complex than that. How in the hell had he seen all that in the mile drive to the hotel? It was true. She secretly did love keeping up with what was going on in Hollywood, she followed politics and could handle more than just three glasses of wine in the past, but because she hadn't drunk much lately, three was apparently her limit. The part about her not loving Greg was something new. She still couldn't answer the question and be one hundred percent, because what did that say about her and how blind she was in her own relationship? Better yet, what did it say about how desperate she was to find that connection with another person and be a typical thirty-five-year-old woman?

"How do you know I didn't love Greg? You just met me last night. He could've been the love of my life." She wanted to sound more demanding but failed miserably.

"We both know that's a far stretch. I just don't think you felt anything deep for him, or you would be crying your eyes out on Anna's shoulder while eating straight out of the ice cream carton instead of shaking your perfectly shaped ass on a chair…and *not* crying."

"This coming from a man who's never loved a woman in his life," she shot back, meaning to sting him a little bit.

He shrugged his shoulders. "No, I've never loved a woman other than my mama, but how would you know that? You just met me last night."

"Fine. You got a point, but I did care about Greg. I wouldn't have lived with him if I didn't."

Tipping her head back on the headrest, she closed her eyes for a moment. No, most likely she didn't love Greg in the way she knew love was supposed to be. Maybe that was why he'd found someone else. He could have recognized before she did that he and Liza had a friendship more than a breathtaking love. She just wished he had told her before cheating and lying. That threw the idea of friendship right out the window. Maybe she would still have a job if he had talked with her about his unhappiness. She would have been in shock and upset, but after the shock wore off, she would have come to realize that Greg was right and that their relationship was something that would not bring them to the future they were destined to have.

"Well, honestly, what do I know? I'm just a good old country boy, one who can't tell the difference between love and lust."

If that just didn't say it all. When it came to love, Tex was not a man to take seriously. But for some crazy reason he saw something in her that she'd been too afraid to admit to even herself.

"Thanks for the ride, Liza. I'll probably be at the shop sometime tomorrow. I have a few finishing touches to do to the cabinets. Maybe start painting, depending how much we can get done." He opened his door and stepped out, leaving her feeling alone because the space he filled was now empty.

"It was the least I could do since you made sure I was safe last night." She wanted to reach over and lay her hand on his arm, but she talked herself out of it. It would have been a bad idea.

He leaned his head back inside the car before shutting the door. "Just so you know—I really want to kiss you right now."

"Then why don't you?"

When did she start acting crazy?

"I wouldn't be able to stop it from going to a lot more than just kissing. You're not ready for me yet, honey."

"It could be me who you should be scared of. I *know* you're not ready for what I have to offer."

"I guess we'll just see, then, won't we?"

Chapter Six

Liza had long ago yanked off her *I'm all talked out* mask and now stared at the popcorn ceiling. At least she'd packed the mask. Otherwise, the lamppost brightly burning outside her room would have prevented her from getting the sleep she managed to get. Of course, the room she rented would have a bright light shining in it. That was going to have to change. She stared at the clock sitting on the nightstand by her bed and cursed aloud. Seriously, it was only seven o'clock?

She got out of her lumpy hotel bed when it became clear that sleeping was not an option. Maybe reading the erotic romance novel the night before hadn't been the best of ideas. She'd known her favorite erotic romance author would deliver yet another hero she would fall in love with. She hadn't expected to see Tex as that hero in her dreams.

That was two nights in a row Tex had entered her mind when she was sleeping, leaving an intense picture of just how sexy he was when he decided to go a day or two without shaving. The first night she could handle because she'd been too drunk to let it keep her awake, and she'd only seen his face. Last night, on the other hand, had definitely been sexual. Her dreams would be a positive thing, considering her lack of a sex life at the moment, but she awakened every time his hands touched her or his mouth tasted her. It was damn frustrating, and her mood went from being aggravated she hadn't gotten her eight full hours of sleep to plain PMS, except without the period. Painkillers weren't going to help her this time. What she needed was sex, and that was out of the question.

She threw her hair in a loose ponytail and padded over to the four-cup coffeepot, starting her morning routine. Coffee—news—shower. A routine felt good, except she was in a hotel in another town and had nothing needing immediate attention. If she were back at home on a Saturday, she would still be sleeping between her six-hundred-thread-count sheets. She would probably wake at around eight because she didn't like to sleep her day away. She would make her coffee and drink her first cup alone because Greg liked to run a couple of miles in the mornings. Later that night, they would go to a movie or maybe have dinner. They would end the day snuggled with a blanket on the couch, watching reality television.

How pathetic. Saturdays were for going out for cocktails with friends, maybe seeing a band play at a local club, or staying up late eating pizza in bed and having an all-night sex marathon.

Now that would be a Saturday.

Just because she was in her thirties didn't mean she had to suddenly change her ways and become a bore.

The good thing about the small coffeepot was it didn't take long to brew. She added several creamer cups and even more sugar packets. She tested it and decided it would do. She made a mental note to buy better coffee than provided in the rooms and hazelnut creamer. As long as she had her morning caffeine fix, she could make it through any day.

She propped herself on her bed and flipped on the television. She finally found a news station, and when she decided nothing drastic had changed in the world since yesterday, she turned it off and drained her cup.

She let the water in the shower heat, and when it reached the scalding temperature she desired, she stepped in and let the spray wash away her sleepiness.

When she was done, she concluded that she looked and felt better. She chose a warm sweater and jeans to wear. To dress it up a tad, she added dangly earrings. She'd had the same haircut for the past year, and the brunette color she wore straight every day was starting to bore her. She wanted something different, something fun. She did a once-over in the mirror and decided she looked pretty damn good.

There was somewhere she felt drawn to be. She had been pondering all morning if it was a good idea, and after not talking herself out of the crazy idea, she knew she could not go. So she was going to go against herself and just do it.

****

After a couple of minutes driving into town, she passed what looked like a newish jumbo sign that read *Home to Jake Lawrence, number twenty-five.*

"Ughhh," she groaned.

Patience resembled so much of Linden. They were both small towns filled with the same people everyone had known since they were born. That was the reason she'd felt so out of place last night after the guys showed up. Anna and the others had gone all through school together and had been intertwined in each other's lives forever…except for the eleven years when Anna lived in Linden. Still, Anna had a connection with those people, and it made Liza happy she'd found those bonds again, but at the same time it made her feel disconnected from Anna's life.

She loved the small-town feel and the sense of family it brought. Most folks in her hometown looked at her and thought she was out of place because she dressed a little differently or went for dating men who wore suits and ties over the wrangler-wearing men who worked the land. But she was a southern girl at heart. She knew all the words to Billy Ray Cyrus' "Achy Breaky Heart" and could sing it off-key like the rest of them.

She didn't mean to drive a little slower than the speed limit when she turned down the same streets she had the night before, but she really wasn't ready to come face-to-face with Tex again. So why in the hell was she going to his mom's house?

As she'd done the night before, she counted the houses and turned into the driveway leading to Tex's mom's. A Ford Focus sat in the driveway. Liza didn't remember seeing it there last night.

The yard, covered in colorful leaves, looked like a Tennessee postcard.

She stepped out of her car, and a gust of wind welcomed her. She inhaled while walking down the sidewalk. She hoped they were awake. It was after nine. Didn't older people get up at, like, six in the morning? What if Tex wasn't even there? What if someone else had already taken him back to his truck, probably whoever drove the red car? She wasn't going to know unless she knocked on the door. She opened the screen and knocked. Nothing happened. She knocked a little harder and waited a few seconds. She heard the turn of a deadbolt, and there he was.

The man who had been in her dreams now stood in front of her, looking as if he'd just gotten out of the shower. The scent of his soap and shaving cream instantly surrounded her.

Damn, he'd shaved.

She stared at his fresh cheeks and jaw. *Do not kiss his hurt jaw and make it feel all better.* She didn't know if she was thankful or not that he wore jogging pants and not a towel. She forced her gaze back to his face.

"Let me guess? You can't get enough of me, can you?" He looked a lot bigger in the doorway.

His strong, hard body should intimidate her, but it did the opposite. She wanted to pull him out of his mother's house because, well, his mother probably wouldn't approve of what she really had in mind, and roughly throw him against the brick while lingering kisses that started at his brow ended somewhere between the droplets of water sliding down his chest and his incredible flat stomach. She could do a lot more to him, but it was daylight, she was new in town, and she didn't want to have to defend her reputation everywhere she went for however long she was there.

"There you go being cocky again. You're pretty sure of yourself, aren't you, Avery?"

"How many times do I have to tell you I'm not cocky? I just state the obvious, and the obvious is that you're knocking on my door before noon. Not that I'm complaining, but still, I have to wonder."

She felt his gaze like a touch. He was making it obvious he was taking a full-on look at her. "If you should know, I—" Liza tried to glance over Tex's shoulder when a woman's voice drifted outside.

"Tex, are you finished in the bathroom?" the woman

called out.

He turned his head, and through the narrow opening, Liza saw a brunette who looked to be in her early twenties standing in the living room.

"Yeah, Maggie, go ahead. I'll be in, in just a minute."

Liza forced herself not to let her emotions take over. If she got too worked up, it would just prove to her and Tex that having a woman in his mother's house at nine in the morning bothered her. She was most likely the owner of the Ford parked in front of her. Tex said he only drove Ford vehicles because of some stupid southern law, so maybe he only went for women who drove the same brand of vehicle. No, now she was being plain ignorant, stupid, and crazy. So Tex calling a woman late last night for a booty call should not matter to her one bit. But boy, was she screwed, because it did.

"I'm sorry. I didn't know you had company. I'll just…I'll let you get back to whatever you need to get back to." She applauded herself for only half stumbling through that.

"Why rush off? You never said why you came by. It had to be something for you to make me your first stop today."

"How do you know you're my first stop? I could've been all over Patience this morning. I could…"

Tex crossed his arms across his chest and stood tall. "Come on, Liza, you don't think I know this town? I've lived here my entire life. I know nothing opens before nine on Saturdays. Marge doesn't even open the diner until after nine. Saturdays in Patience are considered a time to sleep in and reward oneself for a week of hard work. So don't give me the runaround. Just tell me why you're here."

"Don't you need to get back to your lady friend?" she asked, trying to sound unaffected at the fact that he had a lady friend.

"Is that why you're itching to get away from me? Jealous?"

Now he was being cocky, because the full-size grin spreading across his face told her nothing but that. Flustered, she replied, "No, I'm not jealous. You've got to be kidding. Why would I have any reason to be jealous of your more *selective* friend?"

"So you are green. You just don't think you have a reason to be, and it totally pisses you off. Am I right?"

"When did you become so irritating? I came here to see if you needed a ride back to your truck, okay? Stop thinking it means anything more. Now that I know you already have someone to take you, I will just go." She started to walk away, but she was turning over a new leaf. The old Liza would just say what she was thinking, no matter what. "I do have one question."

He stepped out onto the porch, letting the screen door slam behind him. "Shoot."

"Why did you say you wanted to kiss me last night when you already had plans to have another woman lined up?"

"I said I wanted to kiss you because I wanted to kiss you. As for Maggie, well, she's a nice girl, and she's here a lot, but we have no romantic connection. So whatever is running through your head right now is not true."

"Nothing is running through my head."

"You want to know how I can tell you're at least a little upset about another woman being here?"

"I'd love to," she flatly stated.

"Your hazel eyes get a little darker, almost scary, and your stare is more lethal. Any sane man would back down when those two changes happen."

Was he right? A little Italian ran through her blood, so she knew she could have a very bad temper if she let it go that far. But did her eyes go dark and her stare turn dangerous? She decided to dismiss him, because she didn't like that he could read her so clearly and so fast.

"You can try to say I haven't known you long enough to pick up on that, but I know a lot more about you than you think. I thought we established that last night. How about you come in and have a cup of coffee while I put on more clothes? Then you can drive me home because, as you predicted, I do need a ride to my house. It'll save me from having to call one of my men."

"Okay, fine." She smoothly walked back toward the front door, refusing to stomp and let him know just how flustered she was.

He held the door open for her, then followed. The warmth from his body had her wanting to ravish him all over again.

A small woman who had to be Tex's mom came from a hallway and moved into the living room. "Tex, son, you're letting all the warm air out. Have I not taught you anything about keeping the light bill down? It's wasteful to just throw all your hard-earned money out the door." Even though she meant business and was clearly giving her son a lecture, she spoke softly and oddly sweetly.

"Sorry, Mama. It's all Liza's fault."

Liza quickly glared in Tex's direction. "Me? You're the one holding the door open when you could have easily come outside."

"But you're the one I was holding the door open for. See? Your fault."

"You're so infuriating. I'm beginning to seriously regret my decision to ask if you needed a ride."

"Tex Avery, I did not raise you to blame a woman. You need to apologize to Liza. It sounds like she was only trying to help, and you are being disrespectful in my house."

Liza liked this woman. Any woman who stood no more than five feet three and could keep the man towering over her in line was strong-willed and didn't let anything get in her way. *Way to go, Ms. Avery.*

Liza kept her arms crossed and smiled sweetly at Tex. "Well?"

He looked ready to argue but turned his head away from his mother's gaze and focused on Liza. A slow smile spread across his face. "I'm sorry, Liza. My mama is right. She's always right."

She quickly glanced away because his sharp gaze was doing all kinds of things to her insides and worse—her girly parts. Not a good feeling to have in his mother's house.

"Now that is all cleared up, what is this about you needing a ride? Where is your truck?" his mother asked.

"It's at my house. Tommy picked me up last night, then Liza brought me here. I was going to call one of the guys to pick me up this morning."

"What about Maggie or me? One of us would have been happy to drive you home. There was no reason for Liza to get up this early and come all the way over here."

Tex had both his fists clenched at his side. "Mama, you haven't driven a car in almost a year, and it's pointless for Maggie to have to leave since she just got here."

Liza noticed Tex's aggravation.

His mother waved a frail hand in the air. "I bet I still could."

He dropped the subject.

"We haven't been formally introduced, Ms. Avery. I'm Liza, as you already know, but it's nice to meet you." She tried to break the sudden silence.

"Oh, dear, please call me Pearl."

"You have a lovely home, Pearl. Your front yard makes me think of a Tennessee postcard."

Things started to feel lighter, and more importantly, Tex seemed looser. She didn't understand why that was important to her, but it was. He looked upset, and it didn't sit well with her.

"Not much has changed since Tex was a boy. He's done most of the work, you know. He can do about anything."

"I can see. Have you been over to see the coffee shop and bookstore he's helping remodel for my friend Anna? I'm going by there today to see it for the first time."

Pearl turned to her son. "I didn't know you were doing any remodeling. What about the landscaping business? Has something happened to it?"

Tex's shoulders went stiff. What was it about his mother that made him change his demeanor? Did she really not know about him helping with the remodel?

Tex looked to Liza as if upset with her. As if she had done something wrong. "No, the landscaping business is fine. A buddy of mine asked if I could help with his fiancée's coffee shop and bookstore, and I said yes."

"Why haven't you mentioned it? Which buddy? I didn't know any of your friends were getting married."

"Jake."

"Josie Lawrence's oldest? I thought he was off playing baseball. I remember the day she found out he was being drafted. She called every person in Patience to tell them the good news."

"Jake doesn't play ball anymore. He was injured a few years ago. Now he's back in Patience."

"That's terrible. That boy must feel lost since losing his mom and dad and then his career. Next time I see him, I'm going to invite him and his fiancée over for dinner." She clasped her hands together and smiled.

Now Liza was totally confused. Pearl seemed not to know anything that happened in Tex's life. Liza knew Jake was popular in the town. The rat bastard had a sign with his name in big letters on it just over the city limits.

"I will tell him, Mama. I'm sure he and Anna will appreciate that. I'm going to change my clothes. I've got to go check on my men, and I will be back later." Tex kissed his mother on the cheek before exiting the room.

"You sure know how to put your son in his place, Pearl. I need to take lessons, not that I'm planning to do anything with your son…" She was totally messing this up. "He can just be so irritating sometimes."

"I know, dear. Believe me, I know. He's also a good boy. He got into his fair share of trouble growing up, but I refused to let him become like one of those hoodlums I taught in school. I tried my best to teach him to be respectful. I like to think I did right by him, that he grew up from that boy and learned how to be a good man."

"I haven't known him long, but so far, if you can get past his cockiness, he is a good person. I think you did a fine job."

"How long have you known Tex?"

Now, that was tricky. Liza didn't want Pearl to think she and Tex had some type of relationship, but how was she supposed to explain why she was dropping Tex off at her house and then picking him up the next morning?

"I met him two nights ago." She figured it best to keep it simple. "My friend Anna, who is engaged to Jake, is friends with Tex."

Pearl walked over to the mantel above the fireplace. She seemed to accept Liza's response and leave it at that. "You see this, dear? My Tex gave me this when he was just a teenager."

"It's very pretty." The figurine was small and appeared inexpensive, but the look in Pearl's eyes told Liza the carousel was priceless.

"Yes, it is." Pearl set it gently back on the mantel and moved to sit in a rose-colored chair.

Most of the furniture in the house looked outdated, but in some way it fit perfectly. The rose colors mixed with hunter greens matched the woman's gentleness and kindness. A gold-framed mirror hung over the couch with hummingbirds and butterflies surrounding it. Pictures of Tex were scattered on end tables and hung across walls. Some when he was a baby and others when he was in high school. Even in his younger days, he was handsome. His chestnut hair was much longer than now, but the same beautiful eyes stared back at her.

The woman she accused of coming over for a booty call walked into the room, carrying a glass of orange juice and a small plastic cup with several pills. "Pearl, you need to take your medicine. I brought you juice since you hate water."

"Thank you, Maggie. You remember everything." Pearl tipped the cup of pills and swallowed them with the juice.

Maggie hadn't noticed Liza standing in the room. Maggie's attention was only on Tex's mother. Pearl smiled at Maggie, and Liza sensed both women thought the world of each other.

Maggie turned to take the glass back to the kitchen when she stopped in her tracks. "I'm sorry. I didn't know anyone else was here."

"I'm Liza, a friend of Tex's." She held out her hand.

Maggie's cheeks flushed as she shook Liza's outstretched hand. "It's nice to meet you, Liza."

Tex strolled into the room wearing the same jeans and shirt he had on the night before, but he still looked smoking hot.

"Maggie, can I talk to you in the kitchen for a minute?" he asked quietly.

Liza wasn't invited to the kitchen, so she found a seat on the couch. She could make out some parts of Tex and Maggie's conversation but really wasn't trying to snoop. Tex said something about being back before she left and that she didn't have to return until Monday. Maggie had to be some type of nurse, but why did Ms. Avery need a nurse? She looked to be in good health as far as Liza could tell. Some things were a little off, but that didn't require a full-time nurse, did it?

"They think they're being discreet, but I know they're talking about me," Pearl spoke up.

Liza started to say something that maybe would help Pearl in some way, but then Tex and Maggie came back in the room.

Tex got down on his knees in front of his mother's chair and held both of her small hands in his much larger ones. It was a sight that could cause tears for even the strongest of people. Liza refused to be emotional over a man loving his mother.

He spoke much more softly than usual. "Mama, I'm leaving for a while, but I will be back around one o'clock. I'll bring by some movies and takeout food."

"Why are you spending every night here? I thought you bought your own place because you were ready to leave me. There is no reason for you to feel obligated to sleep on my couch every night." Pearl leaned her head on the back cushion and closed her eyes.

He stared a hole in the floor. Liza thought about leaving mother and son alone with whatever was going on between them, but she planted her feet, hoping to remain unseen by both Tex and Pearl. She couldn't help but notice Pearl's blank expression and Tex's firing glare.

She didn't know how long the room stayed quiet. She looked to the kitchen and thought about slipping away to find Maggie. Maggie seemed to have a strong bond with Pearl, and maybe Liza would be able to help. She heard dishes clanking in the kitchen, so she tiptoed toward the sound.

The living room was small, but the kitchen was even smaller. A wooden table that would barely seat four people was placed in the corner. The cabinets were situated in an L-shape, and between the stove and fridge was little counter space. She guessed they didn't need much space when Tex was growing up since they'd been the only two who lived there.

It wasn't like the house she grew up in. Her house had always been bursting with people when she and her sister invited friends over every day after school and sometimes for dinner, too. She felt sorry for Tex and his lack of having a real family, a family that included a father. Maybe if his father had stuck around, he would have a sister or brother.

Maggie loaded dishes into a portable dishwasher that stood by the back door.

"Maggie?"

The woman jumped as if she hadn't heard Liza enter the room. She put both hands up to her chest, and Liza couldn't ignore the bright shade of red she turned. Oh, how she understood that feeling all too well recently, but a man was responsible for her severe case of blushing.

"I didn't mean to startle you. It's just something is going on out there, and I just thought, well, I don't know exactly what I thought you could do."

"What's wrong?"

Liza kept her voice low, not wanting Tex to hear her talking about him and his mother. "That's it, I don't know. Pearl was fine, then she raised her voice and said some hurtful things to Tex. Her behavior seemed to change so suddenly. I can tell you have a way with her and Tex. I guess I just thought you would be the best person to help, if help is even needed."

Maggie bit her bottom lip, looking at the floor before meeting Liza's gaze. "I don't know about that. I mean, I love what I do here, but I wouldn't say I have a way with Pearl—and certainly not Tex." When she said Tex's name, her face turned a deeper shade of red.

"I beg to differ. I saw you with her. Her face lit up when you came in the room. And for Tex, well, I haven't known him very long, but I know he cares about his mom. So if you make her happy, then that means something to him."

Maggie turned back to filling the dishwasher.

"That's nice of you to say."

"It's what I see. I can usually read people pretty well."

Maggie turned back to face Liza. "How can you tell all that when you just met me and Pearl?"

"I guess I've done it for so long that I just got really good at it. I'm a family therapist. So I can usually tell what I'm dealing with when the person or persons come into the room. Sometimes, I am surprised, and it teaches me not to judge so quickly, but I know when I see a kind person. You are one of those people."

A half smile lifted on Maggie's face, and that made Liza feel really good. One minute Maggie looked as if she were ready to bolt from the room, as if Liza were some kind of crazy stalker, and the next minute she was almost cracking a full smile.

"You can tell me to mind my own business, but I'm nosy by nature, so I can't help but ask. What do you do here?"

Maggie's bold eyes grew even larger. She looked like a deer caught in the headlights. "I...uh..."

"You ready, Liza?" Tex growled as he stormed into the kitchen.

His question came across as being a demand. Even though Liza didn't do well when it came to someone demanding her to do anything, she let it go because something in his expression told her he was troubled. Probably about the situation happening in the living room.

Blushing, Maggie cleared her throat. "If you need me to stay until my regular time, I don't mind."

"No, you need a few days off. You told me that yesterday. So you will leave here at one."

117

Maggie appeared startled at Tex's comment and embarrassed when she glanced at Liza. "I didn't mean I couldn't handle my job. I just asked for a day off in the future. You don't have to start letting me off so soon if it's going to be a problem."

"I know you can do your fucking job—"

"Tex." Liza cut in. She would not stand by and let him terrify the poor woman.

He glared at her but lowered his tone. Squeezing the bridge of his nose, he looked at the linoleum floor. "I'm sorry, Maggie. I didn't mean to blow up at you. You didn't deserve it. You've been nothing but nice to my mom. It was a good idea to give you the time off because you need it. We all need a day off during the week to unwind. Hell, I go out every Friday night while you sit here with my own mother." He bitterly laughed. "How lame is that?"

"I love taking care of Pearl. She has always been kind to me. I know things are hard, but she loves you very much. Because of your mother, I probably know more about you than most of your girlfriends do…not that you have multiple girlfriends or anything. It's just…" Maggie trailed off, blushing a color of red that Liza didn't even know the name of.

Tex put a hand up. "I get it. I have to do some work stuff, but I will be back here around one. If you can, will you stay until I get here?"

"Of course."

"Thanks." He turned to Liza and gestured back toward the living room. "You ready?"

****

Liza and Tex climbed inside her car, shutting out the early morning chill. The sun shone brightly through her windshield, so Liza leaned over Tex to open her glove box and retrieve her sunglasses. Her arm brushed his thigh, and she stilled. He went motionless and looked at where her arm lay. She quickly grabbed her glasses and moved her arm and hand away from harm's way.

She had thousands of questions to ask him as they sat in his mom's driveway. Like why didn't his mother know about his friends or business, why did she fall silent in just a moment's time, and why was Maggie needed to sit with her? She didn't have to draw conclusions to know something was clearly wrong with Pearl.

"Are you going to start the car?" he asked with a small chuckle.

She must have been in her thinking mode, and when that cap was on, she blocked out the rest of the world. Her coworkers would say that was what made her good with her patients. When she committed to helping someone, they got her undivided attention. She would catch herself recalling their conversations and thinking of suggestions for their next session.

She turned over the ignition, slowly backed out of the driveway, and pulled out onto the street, suddenly remembering she didn't know where Tex lived.

Before she could ask, he motioned for her to turn left, then right, then onto Cherry Street.

"I'm the last house on the left." He motioned to his short driveway.

She didn't know what she expected, but it wasn't this. The sage-green and brick house with cedar posts was an average size on an average lot, but the landscaping was impressive. The two rocking chairs on the front porch made it picture perfect.

"This is nice and so not what I expected."

"What? You expected me to live in some frat house with beer cans all over the yard?" He laughed.

His deep laugh was nice to hear, especially after the scene at his mom's house. He'd seemed so sad her heart literally ached for him, but she ached over something she knew nothing about, and that irritated her. She wanted to know—yeah, she knew it was none of her business—but it would bug her to no end if she didn't get some information. Maybe she just craved anything to get her mind off her own problems and life changes. She had shared private things with him, and even though she'd been drunk, it still counted.

"No, I just didn't expect this. It's nice…really nice."

"Thanks."

"I love the landscaping. I guess this is some of your handiwork?"

"I couldn't have my yard lookin' a dump. I needed to promote the business, and why not advertise my own house?"

"Smart."

"I would ask you in, but I'm only going in to change into clean clothes and head to the office. If I didn't say so earlier, thanks for the ride."

"You offered a half-ass thanks, and that was only because your mother forced you. Which, by the way, I don't appreciate you trying to throw me under the bus with her."

"I figured she would be more forgiving to company. Me, now, she will still whip my butt."

"I doubt that. I do have to say I like the way she puts you in your place. I like a woman who is strong and doesn't let any man, son or otherwise, get in her way."

He kind of shuffled his feet on the floorboard and rubbed his hands up and down his thighs. Liza could tell the conversation had moved to the uncomfortable stage again. The heat in her car was on medium-high, but she could swear she felt a chill.

"What happened back there, Tex?" She paused and lowered her voice. "I mean, what happened with your mother?"

As soon as the words came out, she knew he didn't perceive them in the way they were intended. His eyes turned a dangerous blue, dropping the green shading altogether. Ah, the color change to deep blue meant anger or some other intense emotion.

"What do you mean?" His voice came out stern, and the last thing she wanted to do was start a fight.

"It looked like your mother was lost there for a minute or two. She was pretty hard on you. From your reaction, I'm guessing she's not normally like that."

"You don't know shit, Liza. Don't think because I give you a ride one day and you give me one the next, that makes us friends. It doesn't. I don't need you snooping in my family business."

"Soooo you can ask questions about my life and go as far as to tell me I never loved the boyfriend I lived with for over a year. You say you know me so well and have no problem forcing your opinions about my life, but I can't be a little interested in yours?"

She waited for a response, but he said nothing. She stared at his tight fists. Fine. If he didn't want to talk, that had to be okay with her, but it hurt a little because she'd shared so much with him, things that she should have gone to Anna about. That's where she needed to be. She needed to confide in Anna. She could no longer trust that

Tex wouldn't turn on her and tell all of Patience about her ex and her getting drunk at Ollie's.

"You're the one who forced your problems on me. I couldn't shut you up that first night. Still, I wonder why you haven't told Anna, your supposed best friend, about your boyfriend. I didn't ask for you to spill your guts to me," he roared.

"You know what, Tex? You're right. I did drunkenly tell you about Greg. Sorry I saw you with your mom and how you looked when she raised her voice to you, and I felt—"

"Felt what…pity? I don't want your help, and I sure as hell don't want your pity."

"You just looked upset back there, and I can't feel pity for you when I don't know why I should. In my experience, it helps if you talk about it."

"Who the fuck asked for your help? I don't need your counseling and psychobabble."

She couldn't stop her mouth from falling open in shock at his bluntness and tone with her. "My mistake for trying to help. I have to ask you. Why did you kiss me that first night and badly want to last night if all I've been to you is a whiny woman you just want to get rid of? Now, get out of my car."

He sat for a minute, his chest heaving, before he opened his door. "Just because we shared something that barely resembled a kiss doesn't mean I want your input." He slammed the door and stalked to his front porch.

She expected him to maybe apologize or at least turn back before he noticeably slammed his front door. He did neither. Him saying they were not friends nor appreciating her input stung, but what bothered her most was that he hadn't even acknowledged their kiss. It was more than just something that barely happened. She'd been somewhat drunk, but she'd felt their chemistry. The sensation was strong every time they were in the same room.

"Well, screw him," she sputtered aloud. She wasn't going to let any man ruin her visit with Anna. She'd come to Patience because she needed her loyal friend's shoulder and to be supportive of the opening of the coffee shop and bookstore. Forget Tex. He was just a blip on her radar, someone she barely knew. Now her attention was going to be on Anna and having some overdue girl time.

Chapter Seven

Liza found Anna's shop in no time at all. She knew it was on a side street, beside a realtor office on the corner. She drove past it once and followed Main Street until she realized she was heading toward the rural part of Patience. After turning around in someone's driveway and heading back to town, she saw the sign reading *Garrett Tillman Realty*. The office building sat on the corner of Main and Spring Streets.

The grayish-blue siding stood out first to her. She had to laugh because blue had always been Anna's favorite color, which Liza knew was only because the Sparks' colors were blue and gray. She took a narrow alley past the shop and parked in the back. An older model van and a white truck with *Avery Landscaping* printed on the door were also parked there. It wasn't Tex's truck, because she'd just left his house.

The house was stunning and seemed like the perfect building for a coffee shop and bookstore. It had a welcoming vibe. The shiny white shutters stood out against the blue. The two-story house's porch reached from one side of the building to the other. Two rocking chairs sat on the porch. The second story had a balcony that also went from one side of the house to the other. Shrubs, flowers, and plants that Liza knew nothing about surrounded the house, and a single decorative lamppost was situated on one corner of the yard. A few pumpkins took residence on the front step. She wanted to cry because Anna was finally getting her wish.

Liza brought her hand up to knock on the door when it flew open, and a young, shaggy-haired boy who didn't look old enough to be out of school came rushing out, holding a couple of gallons of paint. She could either jump out of the way or be trampled.

"Oh, I'm sorry, ma'am. I wasn't expecting anyone to be standing here."

Had he really just called her ma'am? That was it—she was officially getting old. She was old enough to be the boy's mother if she'd had him at the age of sixteen.

"It's okay. You've got work to do."

"Well, yeah. Tex wants me to finish painting the upstairs bathrooms today."

"Since you're on the clock, why not slow down a bit? You'll get more money that way…if you know what I mean." She felt a tad awful for telling the boy to slack off on the job, but taking something away from Tex felt good.

"I can't do that. I have a job to do. It's up to me to get it done as soon as I can. It's not just Tex. Ms. Kelly is very excited to open her shop."

She took one look at the kid and realized he seemed to deserve it. He was a young man, working on a Saturday morning. In her eyes that defined responsibility and was deserving of a few more dollars.

"Well then, I better let you get back to work. It was nice meeting you…" She held out her hand.

"Kyle." He set one of the paint cans down and shook her hand. His palm was sweaty, and by the color spreading down his neck, she wondered if she made him nervous.

"It's nice to meet you, too. I'm Liza, a friend of Anna's. I'm sure she appreciates all the work you are doing."

He nodded, picked up the paint can, and rushed down the front steps.

She walked through the door and waited before calling out to Anna. She couldn't decide what to look at first. Was it the custom-built staircase, the fireplace flanked by two dark wood bookcases in need of a few coats of paint, or was it the gorgeous, naturally scarred wooden floors? People paid a lot of money for floors that looked like that. The only thing that negatively stood out was the canary-yellow walls and balloon border. Surely, that was not one of Anna's ideas gone bad.

Liza heard footsteps coming down the stairs.

"Liza, when did you get here?" Anna asked, sounding surprisingly cheerful, considering it was before noon.

"I just got here. I woke up early this morning and couldn't wait to see the shop. It's amazing, Anna."

Anna pulled her hair from its ponytail, fixed some loose strands, and then put it back up in its rightful place. Instead of her usual hoodie and blue jeans, she wore a chunky white sweater and dark jeans tucked into Ugg knockoffs, and the only reason Liza knew that was because she knew Anna would never pay the expensive price tag. She would just go to the local shopping center and get a boot that resembled the same for less than thirty dollars. Liza liked that Anna was natural and not so caught up in the trends. Anna liked what she liked, and that was all there was to it. Liza still wanted to dress her friend up in a fitted sweater dress with a chunky belt so her curves would stand out. Some tall boots wouldn't hurt either. Yeah—like Anna would ever go for that.

"You think so? I mean, I love it, but I couldn't wait for you to see it and tell me what you think. You've listened to me more than anyone about what I would love for it to look like. I knew you would know if it was looking like I've always envisioned it."

"I think it's more than what you first envisioned. Look at this place. It's huge. There's so much you can do. But the next thing I would do is get rid of these yellow walls and balloon border. That was definitely not in the vision."

Anna laughed. "It was previously used as a child's consignment shop. I guess the previous owners used very childlike colors. I imagine it would be cute for a kid, but for a coffee shop and bookstore—no way. I'm really glad I picked the mustard color for the walls. I think it's going to bring in the warm feeling I want."

"I do, too. The black tables and leather chairs you already have, then throw in some oranges, browns, and greens into the lounging part. But that's just me. I don't know much about décor."

"You know me. That's exactly how I see it in my mind. Tex put in the distressed-looking black cabinets and countertops last week. We just have to paint the kitchen, and it will be ready to stock. Then we'll add the finishing touches."

Liza followed Anna into the kitchen. It opened to the living room and dining room. A counter separated the kitchen from the sitting area. Liza imagined there would be barstools lined down the counter. They entered the actual kitchen. Placed in the middle of the space were an island and sink, while black cabinets with nickel knobs lined the walls. The countertops were empty at the moment, but when it was time to open, she knew kitchen gadgets would be scattered all over the place. Liza was not a cook and wasn't interested in learning. Her microwave worked just fine, and takeout was always an option, even in small towns.

"Anna, I know you love books and everything that goes into that, but do you know how to make different kinds of coffee, muffins, coffee cakes, and whatever other things coffee houses carry?" she asked. Surely her friend had thought this through. Anna could cook slightly better than Liza, but they were not five-star meals.

"Yeah, that was my first thought, too. The bookstore is my thing. The coffee and cakes are just a bonus to draw the people in. I want to create a place where people feel at home. They drink their coffee, eat a muffin, and check out the new releases."

"That still doesn't explain what you're going to do about the coffee-shop part. Do you have any ideas who is going to run that? You can't do everything."

"I met this girl, Jill, back when Em was getting married. She works at the hair salon right now, washing hair and sweeping the floors, but she's ready for something more challenging. I mean, washing other people's hair all day has to be boring. She came by soon after we started the renovations, and we got to talking. Before she moved back to Patience, she worked at a coffee shop when she was in college. I offered her the job, and she eagerly accepted. She will mostly be in charge of the coffee shop, making the menus and coming up with the types of coffee we will serve. She's putting together a list of all the equipment we need, and one day next week we're going shopping."

"If she went to college, why is she washing people's hair?"

"Something happened. I don't really know what it was, but I know she never finished school."

"Is Jill going to do it all by herself? What are your hours?" Even though Anna and Jill were very capable women, Liza worried if that would be enough.

"Open at eight thirty Monday through Friday and close at six at night. Saturdays and Sundays we will open at nine and close at five. We'll see how that goes for a while, and if we need to change it, we will."

"That still seems like a lot of work for just you and Jill to do by yourselves. I don't doubt you for one minute, but those kinds of hours will exhaust you in no time."

"I've already put an ad in the *Patience Gazette*. I've gotten a few responses from teenagers looking for after-school work and weekends. Since there aren't a lot of part-time job opportunities in Patience, I was hoping for this kind of applicant. I've talked to a few girls who I think would be responsible, but I still have a few weeks to decide. Other than that, it's just me, Jill, and Jake, even though he's not too happy about it."

"And why in the hell not?"

"Don't start, Liza. I've heard your opinion of Jake since I brought him up all those years ago, and while I'll admit I didn't make him sound very promising, all that has changed. We are no longer eighteen-year-old kids who act before we think. We wasted so much time being hurt and angry when in truth he should've never lied, and I shouldn't have run or broken up with him in the first place—"

"I'm sorry I brought it up. It's just I saw how hurt you were when we first met, and I guess when I hear his name or see him, it makes me see your face again. You seem happy now, and I don't want anything to mess that up for you."

"Thank you, Liz."

"At least I'm doing something right for a change. It doesn't make the past several days a complete bust."

"Why? What's happened?" Anna asked, eyes narrowed.

Liza threw up her hands and started to pace the open room. She stopped at the fireplace mantel and wiped a finger along the peeling paint. "Where do I even start to answer that?"

"Why not at the very beginning?" Anna gently said.

"Well, for starters, Greg was screwing around behind my back, and I don't even know if I feel betrayed by it because I don't know if I even loved him. Then I lose my job because of a false staffing issue. Then I come here and…I don't know. It seems like my life is changing every minute of every day, and I'm just trying to catch up."

Anna walked to Liza and held out a hand. Liza took it, and for the first time since seeing Anna again, she felt that sisterly bond they'd always had. She liked having her friend's love and support. That was just the way they were, except it was usually Liza comforting Anna. Not that Liza regretted anything she and Anna went through, and Lord knew Anna needed a shoulder to cry on. Knowing Anna was there, no questions asked, when she needed a shoulder or hand, as it may be, was a nice feeling. If she stayed in Linden and needed Anna for anything, Anna would be on the road within the hour.

"Why didn't you tell me about this?"

"I don't really know. I guess I didn't want to take

away from how happy you are and your moment. You deserve all this." Liza held her hands out to gesture at the future coffee shop and bookstore. "Plus, I just needed a day or two to let everything sink in."

"Don't you ever think that way again. I don't know if I should grab you again and hug the life out of you or be mad that you've been dealing with all this on your own when I could've been helping you through it."

"I know that now. I should've called you Thursday night when I came into town instead of going to that stupid bar and spilling my guts to everyone who would talk to me."

"You told Jefferson before me?"

"Lord, no. I was too busy trying to stop my ears from bleeding over his cheesy pickup lines. I talked to Minny, and well, then I ended up telling Tex when he was driving me to my hotel. I only told them about Greg cheating, not about me losing my job. I didn't find that out until Friday afternoon."

"I can see why you talked to Minny. She's a good listener. And the way I heard it is that she was really good to Jake when he was going through a hard time, but Tex. What made you open up to him? Don't get me wrong— I like Tex and all, but he doesn't strike me as the listening type. In fact, I sometimes think he blocks out the talking part and skips straight to the horizontal part."

That was not what Liza wanted to hear, but it was time for her to face facts. Tex was a dog just like Brad, Bill, Leroy…and Greg. Why would she ever think he would be any different? Because he drove her to a hotel when she was drunk instead of trying to get in her panties, or that he flirted with her after girls' night and said he wanted to kiss her? That meant nothing.

Especially to a sexual being like Tex Avery.

"I had too much to drink. You know I just start rambling when I've drunk past my limit. What can I say?" She shrugged. "He just happened to be the one driving the truck."

"Are you sure it wasn't more than that?" Anna raised her eyebrows.

"Of course not. I can't help it that I keep running into him," Liza said a little too quickly.

"If you say so, but I felt major sparks flying at the diner yesterday morning. Then last night, you two couldn't go two seconds without looking at the other. I mean, you've probably spent more time with him than me. I can't help but ask."

"I'm sorry, Anna. I didn't realize—"

"I'm kidding, Liz. Just be careful with Tex. You have been through a lot lately. I would just hate to see you hurt."

"Now where have I heard that before?" Liza asked, smiling.

"I think I've probably heard it from you a time or two."

"Don't worry about me, Anna. I just need more girl time and to throw myself into something, anything, and how lucky I am to have a friend who happens to be opening a very cool coffee shop and bookstore that could use the extra hands."

"I haven't asked how long you plan to stay."

"Well, I have no boyfriend or job to go back to, so I don't know…forever?"

"I would love that, but let's not start looking for a house just yet. Once things calm down, you will feel differently, believe me. It took me eleven years to figure out where I was supposed to be, and it just happened to be the same place I started."

"You said you will be opening in about three weeks?"

"I hope to be."

"I'll stay until then. I want to see this place full of people and watch you take in the fact that you finally did it. You made your dream come true."

"Now I'm really going to cry." Anna used the sleeve of her sweater to carefully wipe her eyes. "I'm so excited. Where are you going to stay? You can't stay at a hotel the whole time. I wish the apartment was bigger, but it's just a studio. There is always my childhood home, but—"

"No, I couldn't stay there. I might not have ever seen the place, but after our many conversations about it, it's like, in a way, I have terrible memories of that house myself. I will be fine at the hotel. I just need to switch rooms, or I will never get any sleep."

"What's wrong with your room?"

"There's a light that shines right through my window. I tried using my eye mask, but it still kept me up." Okay, that wasn't all that kept her up, but she would not be having any more dreams about Tex. She didn't even want to think about him during the day. What he said to her earlier was uncalled for and way past disrespectful.

"I'm sure Ms. Lulu wouldn't mind switching your rooms. I don't imagine there are a lot of guests staying there right now anyway."

Her mind jumped back to her fight with Tex. Just who did he think he was saying she knew shit and had no right snooping? She was not snooping. Snooping would indicate she was trying to get information behind his back. She was flat-out asking him about his mother and if he needed to talk. What was the harm in that?

She couldn't help that she jumped right in when she recognized a problem. For so long she'd been helping people talk through their problems in life. She'd even held back with him because she didn't want to come across as trying to be his therapist, and what had he done? He'd accused her of trying to counsel him.

"Are you listening to me, Liza?"

She regretted letting him talk her into getting into his big truck. Yeah, she was vulnerable, but she couldn't deny the kiss—ohhhh, the kiss that was barely there, according to him. *Well, see if he gets another one.* He'd sneaked up on her when her defenses were down, but nope, not going to happen again because she didn't plan to be in the same place as Tex while she was in town. That was most likely an unrealistic goal since he was working at the shop, the shop she'd just agreed to help with, so if she had to see him, she would just keep her distance.

All sparks of electricity and tingling sensations that hummed through her body were not happening again. She could turn off her attraction for the asshole if she wanted to.

And she wanted to.

"Liza!"

She came back to reality and realized she had her thinking cap on again. "I'm sorry. What were you saying?"

"Take the thinking cap off and focus on the real conversation, not the one going on in your head."

"How did you know?"

Anna chuckled. "I've known you way too long for you to ask me a question like that. Believe me, I know when you're in deep thought. What or who had your mind running endlessly?"

Liza decided to tell a white lie. "I'm thinking about Greg and my job. I loved my job and my patients. What am I going to do?"

"There are plenty of practices that would be lucky to have you on staff. What about your own dream?" Anna looked as if she were keeping a juicy secret.

"What dream?"

"The dream of opening your own practice. Remember the night we were having one of our slumber parties with my aunt, and I told y'all I wanted to open a bookstore? You said then that you would love to open your own practice so you could run the show and make sure the patients were getting what they deserved."

"That was just talk. I don't know the first thing about starting my own practice. Let's just focus on your dream for now since you actually know what you're doing. We'll worry about my employment later, okay?"

"For now," Anna agreed. "I don't want you worrying about Greg. I know exactly what you need. Just give me a minute to make a phone call." She left the room and walked to the back of the shop.

Liza heard Anna talking, but she couldn't make out what she was saying. She wondered what Anna had in mind to help her forget about Greg and her job problems. Was it really Greg she needed help forgetting? Was he really the reason she felt like eating a whole carton of cookie dough ice cream?

"Everything's set. Let's go."

Kyle walked down the stairs, and it hit Liza that she

hadn't even noticed him come back in.

"Kyle, I'm leaving for a bit, but Tex is on his way, and Jake will be over this afternoon. If you need anything, call me," Anna said.

"I will. It was nice meeting you, Liza," Kyle, who looked to be sixteen years old, yelled out as Liza and Anna exited through the door.

Just her luck, she was making an impression on guys twice her junior, but the men her age were complete jackasses. She should have a heart-to-heart with Kyle and tell him up front what women need, break the cycle and not be the lying asshole women want to smother in their sleep.

****

Painting detailed trim wasn't the job for a man who wanted to be destructive, but it had to be done whether he was in the mood for it or not. So there he was, painting the fireplace mantel. He wouldn't be able to paint the rest of the trim downstairs until they started painting the walls. He was glad Anna had finally picked a color.

Kyle, a young kid who usually worked for him on the weekends doing yards, was working upstairs. He'd recruited Kyle to help with the painting after Anna and Jake hired him to help with the remodel. Good was an understatement when describing Kyle. He came from a single mother who was trying to raise him and his two younger siblings. Tex guessed things had to be tight at home, so he always kept the boy busy, secretly paying him a dollar more than the other kids working for him. The other two boys, who worked once or twice a week during the summers, only needed the money to fill their tanks and take their girls on dates. They didn't really need the money like Kyle did. He probably used his money to buy groceries or pay the electric bill. The kid didn't even have a car. For the first month after starting the job, he'd walked or ridden a bike to the shop. Tex wouldn't have it, so he let him drive an older model Ford he was thinking of trading in for a better work truck. Nobody said anything in front of Tex, but he knew there was talk behind his back that Kyle was a suck-up and got whatever he wanted. Tex put a stop to that and told the other punks that if they worked as hard as Kyle did, they might actually earn something other than a paycheck.

Tex held a soft spot for the boy because his situation hit too close to home. He, too, had been raised by a single mother who luckily had only one child to worry about. Tex felt bad that he hadn't been more like Kyle. Maybe if he were, his mother would have had it a lot easier than she did.

This morning, he felt bad for Kyle for a different reason than his family situation. He was taking a blunt hit to Tex's frustrations. Tex thought the kid would have the regular-sized bathroom painted by now, but he hadn't. Kyle had said he got to the shop an hour late because his mom was sick, and he had to take his sisters to the babysitter's for the day. Tex wasn't mad about that, but he was mad the bathroom wasn't finished. To make matters worse, he really didn't know if he was even mad about the damn bathroom.

Earlier, he'd stomped and cursed his way out of Liza's car, then almost broken his own front door, slamming it with such force. Only a couple of framed pictures had fallen to the floor, scratching the wall. He was lucky that was all his tantrum had damaged. He could have taken a baseball bat to half his house. But since he only had a big-screen television he could really cause damage to, he'd instead stalked to his bedroom, slammed that door like he was a teenager, and fallen on his bed, inhaling several breaths and letting them out slowly.

The last time he remembered being that mad was when he'd found out his mom was sick. He had drunkenly blocked out most of that week, but that wasn't an option right now. Right now, he had to worry about keeping his business afloat, get the damn painting done, apologize to Kyle, and somehow deal with Liza.

He was screwed.

He stilled his hand, because her mouth had fallen open, and her eyes had gone wide with fire when he said she knew fuck and he didn't need her psycho mumbo jumbo. It was true, but he didn't have to say it exactly that way, nor did he have to make fun of her profession. He didn't doubt she was good at what she did. She was a strong woman who could do anything, but he didn't believe in sitting in a room with a stranger and telling them all about what he was feeling.

He plopped the paintbrush down on the lid of the paint can and rubbed the top of his head. What had he been thinking? Kissing her at Ollie's was something he should have never done. She'd needed a ride because of the glasses of wine she'd put away, but he didn't have to kiss her to persuade her. No, he'd done that because nothing could have kept him from kissing her at that moment. It about killed him to have to make the kiss so short. What he'd really wanted to do was shove her up against the dirty building, mess up her perfectly placed hair, and run kisses from her forehead to where her dress veered, revealing a small amount of cleavage, and still, that would not have been enough to satisfy his craving for her.

Why was this one woman getting in his head and driving him crazy with a pounding headache and hard-on? Any other time, he would just screw whomever he wanted, and if he felt like doing it again, he would. If not, he would just move on with his life. Oh God, he was a real dick.

The front door opened, and in walked Jake, holding a bottle of water. Just what he wanted—company.

" 'Sup, Avery? I didn't think you were coming over today," Jake said with an easy smile.

Oh, this was even better, company who was all smiles and grins, who had a perfect life with a perfect woman.

Nodding, Tex picked up his paintbrush and dipped it in the milky-colored paint. "I just needed to come in and make sure Kyle was okay. What time is it?" He ran the brush along the wood.

Jake glanced down at his watch. "Twelve thirty."

Fuck. He wanted to get the mantel painted, and that was not going to happen because he spent most of the time thinking about Liza and what a fucking asshole he'd been to her. He thought about calling and asking to see if Maggie could stay a little longer, but this was his life now.

"I got some other stuff I got to take care of today. Can you keep an eye on Kyle? He's a good kid, but I've been kind of hard on him today. I don't want him staying here half the night to try to prove something to me."

"Yeah, that's no problem. I was planning on ordering us a pizza today and making it a man's working day since Anna bailed."

"What kind of day?"

"Man's day. I knew Kyle would be here, and I just thought he and I could crank Aerosmith, eat some pizza, and maybe work a little. Anna and I were originally supposed to go over to Knight and look at this big furniture outlet, but she canceled because Liza needed a spa day or some shit. I don't know about these women sometimes. I mean, they just spent last night together. Do they really need to rally the troops around Liza and spend the entire afternoon at Cut & Curls? But—" He shrugged and tossed back his water. "—I guess I shouldn't complain too much because I get out of picking between two leather couches that look exactly the same but somehow sit completely differently, and I get to spend the day eating and drinking."

"Don't ask me. I can't begin to understand what goes on in a woman's head."

Jake chuckled. "Is that why you've decided to become more selective with your women?"

"I was drunk and had just gotten in a bar fight. You can't believe everything I said last night."

"Whatever, Avery. You weren't even close to feeling buzzed before we left Ollie's. So what's up with the change?"

"Didn't we just have this damn conversation last night? Yes, I still like women and still plan to get laid on a regular basis. No, I'm not into Liza or any other woman at the moment, so can you please let it go? And while you're at it, tell the others, too. Fuck, I will put an ad in the *Gazette*, telling the whole town that even though I'm done sleeping with bar chicks every night of the week, I am still the same woman-loving Tex Avery."

Jake drew back. "Whoa, man, chill. I was just pulling your chain. Kyle deserves a free lunch and a raise if this is what he's had to put up with all morning."

Tex tossed the paintbrush down on the lid. "I'm sorry. It's just been one of those mornings. I just need to stay away from people for the rest of the day if I want to keep my employees and friends."

"I get it. Back in the summer, I had the same look you do and had the same crappy attitude to go along with it. Bradley showed up one day and started smarting off his mouth as only my brother can. One comment led to another until we were both rolling around in the grass. If it wasn't for Tommy breaking it up when he did, Bradley's face and my right hand would've looked like yours does right now."

Jake and Bradley had gotten into a lot of fights over the years, but it had been a while since they let things get too out of hand. Nowadays, it was more Bradley saying something out of line to Jake, usually about Anna, and Jake doing nothing more than threatening to kick his brother's ass.

"It's been a while since I've seen one of those good old Lawrence fights. What did the kid say that time to put you over the edge?"

"Well, I'm sure that won't be our last, and you will live to see another one. The thing is that Bradley's probably deserved ninety percent of those punches, but that day he didn't."

"So why not?"

"Because Bradley might act like a big kid most of the time, but he was right. He saw right through me and bluntly told me to get over myself and do something about it. After that, I have to admit things started to get better for me."

Tex crossed his arms. "Is there a reason you're

telling me all this? Because it seriously seems out of left field."

"I know you have a lot of personal stuff going on." When Tex growled, Jake held up a hand. "I get it, and like I said last night, I'm here if you need me. I know what I went through is not the same as what you're going through now, but I will say that I, too, made a change in my life, and it was the best damn thing I ever did. The bar chicks are way overrated. A real woman, like Anna, is the complete package. I'm not stupid, Tex. I know you spend more time working than hanging out with my brother. Everyone last night saw the way you and Liza acted around each other. Now, in my opinion, the woman is just plain scary and someone all men should fear, but I know how Anna feels about her. Anna doesn't just give her time to anyone. That tells me there is something good about Liza. If I were you, I would get over myself and do something about it before Kyle quits and I lose a hard worker I actually enjoy having around."

"I'm happy everything worked out with you and Anna, but y'all have a connection or some shit women like to say when they're talking about their soul mate. Everyone knew you two were meant to be together back in high school. I don't have that with anyone, especially not with Liza. After this morning, I would be surprised if she ever talks to me again."

Jake sighed. "Oh shit. What did you do, and is this going to cause trouble with me and Anna?"

"Why would it cause problems with you and Anna?"

"Because you and I are friends, Anna is protective of Liza, and if you do anything to her, it will be like me doing something to her. I know it sounds crazy and messed up, but like I said before, I don't understand women."

"Don't worry, I'll fix it. I'll just give her some of this Avery charm, and I'll be back in her good graces in no time." Tex forced himself to smile.

"If you say so, but it will take a lot more than flattery to get you off Liza's crap list. Believe me, I've been on it since the day Anna met her. Having her lay into you every time she sees you is not a good thing. She might look like one of those cute little Maltese dogs, but she really is a Rottweiler with sharp, pointed teeth."

Tex laughed. "I'll keep that in mind." He pulled out his wallet and took out a twenty. "Give this to Kyle and tell him to put some gas in the truck. And make him leave before four. His mom is sick, and he needs to be home with her and get his sisters from the babysitter's."

"Man, that can't be good—his mom being sick and all. Things are hard enough for them as it is. He's a good kid. Better than either one of us was at his age."

"Tell me about it. I'll see you Monday morning."

Tex left the shop and drove to what he was sure was the last running video store in the country. A comedy would be good, but he doubted his mom would enjoy *The Hangover*, so he went for second best, a Paul Newman flick. He checked out *Butch Cassidy and the Sundance Kid* and headed back through town. He'd just order a pizza for dinner later in the evening. He avoided looking over at Cut & Curls when he first drove by, but now that he was coming back through town, he couldn't stop his head from turning to see if he spotted Liza's car. The metallic SUV sat parked right in front of the building.

Jake had said Liza needed to be in the company of girls today. Did that mean she'd told Anna about this morning? Anna was for sure going to give him an earful the next time she saw him. He deserved much more because he wasn't taught to speak to any woman the way he'd talked to Liza. He was upset with his mom, well, not at his mom, but at the disease taking her away from him. He didn't have anywhere to place the blame because who could he yell at? It wasn't his mom's fault she was dealt this. So who was he supposed to take his anger out on? Liza had just happened to be there, and he'd tried to make things light in the car ride back to his house, but she'd had to ask about his mom and the scene at the house. He hadn't wanted to talk about it with her, but she just had to know. She wanted him to say it aloud, and he wasn't ready for that. If he said it, it would make it real, and he liked living in denial.

He drove past Cut & Curls and put on a brave face as he drove toward his mom's house. He had to do this. He had no choice but to be present and give his mother anything she wanted.

Chapter Eight

"You guys really don't have to do this. I'm fine. Nothing a gallon of ice cream can't fix," Liza said while Em pushed her into a chair and turned her around so she faced the mirror.

Anna laughed. "Ice cream is not the answer. You keep doing that, and you'll end up twenty pounds heavier and having to run a mile or two a day to lose the weight."

"How many times do I have to tell you, Anna, you look great? You never needed to lose anything," Liza scolded.

"I know I looked fine, but I did need to lose a couple of pounds. In fact, I don't mind running now. It frees my mind and allows me to think clearly. I guess you can say it's my *me time*."

"I can find better things to do in my free time besides sweating and huffing my way around a boring track." Em shook her head, as if she found it inconceivable that someone would actually enjoy working out.

"Like what?" Anna asked.

"Like sex. Sex can make you very relaxed, and if you do it right, it will even give you a workout." Em ran her hands through Liza's wet hair. "Now, how do you want it, Liza?"

While Anna laughed at Em's dead-serious remark, Liza thought about her hair. She'd said she was going to start being herself again. If she was going to change, she needed to change everything. Well, not her clothes, because the way she dressed had never changed over the years. She kept up with most fashions and added her personal style to everything she wore, but her hair, that was something she could change.

"How about we add highlights?"

"What color are you thinking?"

"How about red?" she asked, then doubted herself. "Or do you think that's too much?"

Em smiled. "Red would be perfect. You'll look like a little sex kitten. If Greg was here, he would take one look at you and kick his own ass for running around on you."

Liza felt deceitful for letting Anna and Em think her bad mood was due to Greg and her losing her job. The job stung, but Greg not so much. She was angry with him, but it wasn't enough to put her down in the dumps. No, she was bring-out-the-ballbuster angry and in the process of swearing off all men because of Tex.

"Red is very brave of you," Anna said while flipping through a celebrity magazine.

Em looked at her. "Says the woman who went from brunette to blonde."

"I needed a change. I was a brunette in Patience. I needed something different when I went to Linden. Red or any other colors that can be found on the American flag would have been too much of a change for me, so I went with common blonde."

"Well, you're back in Patience. Have you ever thought of going back to a natural brunette?" Em rubbed her hands together.

"Not right now, so don't get too excited." Anna pointed to Em. "I love my hair. I might surprise Jake one day and change it. I know the color of my hair doesn't matter to him, but he sometimes brings up how my hair was brown back in high school. It would probably bring us back in time if I changed it."

Em mixed her coloring products in a bowl. "Just like a man to think brown and chestnut are the same color, but I think it would be sexy."

Anna tossed her a look and laughed. "Is sex all you think about?"

Em shrugged. "Most of the time."

Liza and Anna laughed as the bell above the door jingled, and in walked Jessie, wearing overalls and a baseball cap. She pulled her hat off and threw it on the counter at one of the stations before flopping down in a chair and tossing her head back.

"What's your deal, sister-in-law?" Em asked.

Jessie raised her head and groaned. "Men. I swear they think women can't do anything. They are just jealous because they hate to admit the fact that we just might do something better than them. I can't take it anymore. I do more on the farm than Tommy and Dad put together, and what do they do? They treat me like a five-year-old. I know what I'm doing."

Em pulled out several pieces of foil. "Which one was it this time, Mr. Earl or my husband?"

"Both. I get up this morning, and since it's Saturday, Dad hadn't left yet to open the hardware store. He asks what my plans are for the day, and I tell him we had several more acres of corn to shell. He then informs me I shouldn't be driving the combine because I might break something, and it cost too much for me to go off and mess something up. He suggested that Tommy run the combine, and I do odds and ends around the farm that some city girl could do. I guess Dad thinks that all the corn we have already shelled just magically appeared—because neither he nor Tommy did it. I did, with the help of a few of our workers. Did I break his precious combine? No. I know how to run equipment, damn it." Jessie pulled her ponytail down and propped her boots on the station counter.

Liza knew from growing up in a small rural town that even though the rest of the businesses in Patience looked at Saturdays as a day to sleep in, farming was hard work and long hours. It didn't matter that it was a Saturday morning and the rest of the town was sleeping. They still had a lot of work to get done that day.

"You didn't start a fight with your dad and brother, did you?" Em asked.

"No, Em, you would be proud. I did what they expect women to do. I cooked breakfast with Mama and served it to them before the big men went out to work."

"You know that's not what they think women are for. If that were the case, Tommy and I wouldn't have lasted a week because he might get a frozen pizza one night and a ham sandwich the next. I know your daddy doesn't expect your mama to have three hot meals on the table every day."

"I know. It's just that's how they make me feel sometimes. We are equals when it comes to the farm, but they make me feel like they are doing me a favor by letting me be in business with them."

"Your daddy is just having a hard time with you being a grown woman. Tommy, too. They are very protective when it comes to you. You should have seen Tommy last night after you went outside with Bradley. He was ready to put a hole in the wall. I don't have to tell you that's not like your brother. He is the most laid-back person I know."

"I think Daddy wished he had another son and just tolerates me because Mama would lay into him if he left me out."

"I don't think that's it at all, Jessie." Liza eyed Jessie through the mirror in front of her. "Most daddies have a hard time letting go of their daughters. They don't worry about their sons too much because they look at them as being more like them—strong and protective. When they look at their daughters, they see some man breaking her heart, and all they want to do is take away any hurt you may feel in your life. I don't know your daddy or your mama, but I do know people, and I would bet that is some of how your daddy is feeling."

Jessie sighed but came across as a bit calmer and didn't seem to mind that Liza just stuck her nose in personal business. "He needs to worry about Tommy more than me. Tommy would let Em run all over him before he would ever tell her no. I'm a lot stronger than my brother."

"Hey!" Em protested.

"It's true," Anna added. "Em, don't even try to deny it. I can name more times than I have fingers when Tommy went along with what you wanted because you wanted it."

Em shrugged. "You're probably right."

"Not that I'm complaining, because I couldn't dust or bake one more thing, but why are we having a girls' night in the middle of the day?" Jessie asked.

"It's Liza," Anna said. "She found out her boyfriend was cheating on her and that he is most likely the reason she lost her job."

Jessie exited the room, then came back, opening a can of diet soda. "Sounds just like a man." She made a face of disgust. "Shit, Em, can you please stock the fridge with something besides diet drinks?"

Em grinned before she stuck out her tongue. "Don't go looking if you know that's all I have. And *you* can stock the fridge with anything you like."

Liza hadn't been keen on Anna planning an emergency get-together with Em and Jessie at Cut & Curls. For one, after Anna left Linden, Liza didn't have one specific friend, let alone two or three, she could call when she needed good male-bashing time. Of course, she had girls she went out with occasionally to hit the mall, but most of her time had been with Greg, her family, or work. She'd thought she was fine with that, but after sitting in the salon with a group of women who knew each other, who snipped back and forth, and who had each other's backs, she knew she was missing something.

She looked at Anna and wondered when they had traded places. It didn't seem that long ago when Liza was the one with the confidence with men, friends, and coworkers. Liza could handle it all. She could be her own best friend in a crowd. Now she felt lost and alone and in need of having someone who had her back. Anna was now the one who seemed comfortable and strong.

She tuned in to Em and Jessie and smiled at the two women who could fight one minute and make up the next. They were best friends and like sisters, and Liza wouldn't doubt that they felt that way long before Em married Jessie's brother. Liza couldn't remember if she and her sister had ever been like that.

Her sister was seven years younger than she was, but

shouldn't they have had some type of playful, sisterly bond? She loved her sister, but they were just two different people who walked two different paths. Her sister always wanted to be a stay-at-home mom and the wife who had dinner cooked and on the table by six every night. That was how their mother was, so it was only natural for Erin to follow. That wasn't Liza. She wanted a family, but she needed a career, too. She wanted it all, and it shouldn't be too much to ask to have it, damn it.

"So what's the story with the boyfriend?" Jessie asked. "I mean, he's already cheated, and you've only been gone…what…two days?"

Liza sighed. "I caught him cheating the day I left to come here. I walked in on him and one of his patients in his office."

Em set a timer to remind her when it was time to rinse Liza's hair. "Isn't that like a big no-no?"

"Yeah, but he said afterward that they felt a connection." Liza made quotation marks with her fingers. "He referred her to someone else. I don't know if that's true or not."

Anna got up from her chair and leaned on the counter beside Liza. "I didn't tell you this when you were seeing Greg, but after y'all started living together, I could see a change in you. You just didn't seem yourself. You acted happy, and you didn't treat me differently or anything, but I sensed something was off."

"I've heard that before."

"From who?" Anna asked.

Crap, she hadn't meant to say that out loud. Could she tell them about Tex? Did she want to? "It's nothing."

Em pointed to a sign above the door. Liza read it. *Everything said between these walls is sacred.*

"That means you can say anything in here and it will stay in here. We won't say a word," Em announced. "Anna had it made for me."

"Because you see that sign every time you walk out those doors. It reminds you to keep your trap shut," Anna said.

"So spill," Jessie said. "I can see you want to."

Liza crossed her arms and let the emotions of this morning wash over her. "Tex."

"What about him?" Anna asked.

She stared at Anna for a long moment. Why was she hiding anything? It wasn't like she'd done anything wrong with Tex. She was trying to help, and he looked as if he could use someone to talk to. What was so wrong with that? She weighed her options and figured if she didn't tell the three women staring at her, begging for any gossip she could dish out, she would say she wasn't going to let Tex ruin her visit with Anna, but she knew he would put a damper on it. She didn't want that. Maybe talking to people who knew Tex would help her understand why he suddenly blew up at her for nothing more than her doing what she did every day.

"He pretty much hit the nail on the head and pointed out that I never really loved Greg."

Anna's eyebrows rose. "And why would he say something like that? You two just met...unless—"

She could feel herself blush. "No, whatever you're thinking, we did not do. He drove me to the hotel, I drove him to his mom's and drove him to his house this morning, but that's it. Now that I've thought about it, the only time I've really talked to him has been in a car."

Em straightened her workstation. "Why did you see him this morning? I don't understand."

"He spent the night at his mom's house. I went there this morning because I knew he didn't have a way to get back home. I offered to give him a ride. I was just trying to be nice."

"I bet you wanted to give him more than just a ride," Em said in her most sexy voice.

"Shut it, Em," Anna scolded.

Liza continued, trying not to think about her and Tex doing anything that pertained to sex. "I met his mom and Maggie, and everything was fine until he blew up at me for no reason."

Jessie asked, "Did he get upset at you about something that had to do with his mother?"

The room was quiet. Liza didn't know if she was missing something. Maybe she had done something that crossed the line with Tex. She should have just kept her big mouth shut. "I noticed at the house that his mom was acting a little different. At one point she yelled at him for nothing. Then she sat in her chair and looked like she was a million miles away. I wanted to help, so I asked about her, and he was not having it. He said he didn't need my counseling."

"Oh," all three women said in unison.

So it was her fault. "What does 'oh' mean?"

"It's just that Tex is protective of his mother." Jessie looked down at her soda. "Tex is a good guy. At first glance, he looks like a charming ladies' man, which he is—don't get me wrong—but he's also private when it comes to his family."

"Everyone knows something is wrong, but he won't come out and say it. Nobody really knows what to do. We just pretty much give him his space. He doesn't talk much about it. At least, I've never heard him," Em added.

Jessie let out a heavy sigh. "Here we go again."

Liza looked around the room. "So he doesn't talk to anyone?"

"I think he has said a few things to Jake, or Jake has asked him if everything is okay. But Jake says he blows it off and changes the subject," Anna said.

"What do you think it is?" Liza asked.

"Don't say it, Em." Jessie's eyes narrowed on Em.

Liza turned to Em, who ignored Jessie. "His mom's sick."

"Fuck it all to hell," Jessie cried. "I give up. You never listen to me anyway."

Em crossed her arms and pointed her stare in Jessie's direction. "What's the big deal? She already suspects something, and he might just talk to her, because he's sure not talking to any of us."

"Sick how?" Liza asked.

Em's once stern expression softened. "That I don't know."

And he wasn't letting anyone else help him. "Does he have any other family around? He told me about his dad, but are there aunts…uncles?"

Em and Anna shook their heads.

"He has no one?" It came out as a whisper. How awful. Her heart ached for him because having a parent who was ill seemed unimaginable to her. "I hate that he's going through this and feels he can't talk to his friends. I wish he wouldn't take his frustrations out on me, though. He was way out of line for bringing up my relationship with Greg and saying that I was snooping into his family business. It might be best if I stay out of his way."

Em walked to the radio, and the soulful voice of

Aretha Franklin filled the shop. "I've known Tex a long time. I bet after he clears his head about whatever set him off this morning, he will be kicking himself over what he said to you, Liza. Tex is a friendly guy. I've never known him to ever hold a grudge or even stay mad at anyone longer than a day. Honestly, I think it's going to be impossible for you two to stay out of each other's way."

"Why do you say that?"

Em laughed as she swayed to the music. "Because I saw the way y'all looked at each other last night. You wanted to claw my eyes out for even touching him."

"I swear I did not." Liza had no other choice but to lie to Em. "I will admit we did kiss once, but I was a little drunk, and it was quick, more of a reassurance than a spark. We are obviously two sexual beings who are single and don't mind flirting with each other, but after this morning, I'm giving him his space."

"If you say so, Liz, but I know you, and you might not want to, but you definitely have a spark with Tex," Anna said.

The timer rang, so Em and Liza walked to the sink. Em turned on the water and checked the warmth with her hand.

Jessie stood, looked in the mirror, put her hair back in a ponytail, and looped it through the back of her hat. "Sorry to duck out before the big reveal, but I have to take care of some stuff."

"Like what?" Em asked her sister-in-law with a raised brow. "Don't be mad at me."

"This has nothing do with you and your big mouth. I'm going home, kicking Tommy out of the combine, and doing what I planned to do this morning. I'm a part of the farm, and the men are just going to have

155

to get used to it. Thanks for the chat. I'll see y'all later." Jessie unlocked the door and pushed it open.

"I'll call Tommy and tell him I need him to come to the shop to fix a pipe or something. That will save you from fighting him," Em hollered out over the music.

"No." Jessie waved her hand. "The fight is the best part. I shouldn't have given up so easily this morning. See ya."

Jessie was right. She shouldn't have given up so easily, and neither should Liza have.

She was in town for Anna, and she was bound to see Tex again. Liza was not going to back down from him. She was finished letting a man determine her happiness and life. What she needed was sex, and since she couldn't have sex with Tex, she would just have to have fun with someone else. In the meantime, maybe Jessie was right about another thing. Maybe the fight was the best part.

Still, her heart went out to Tex and how alone he must feel.

****

Tex spent his Sunday afternoon with his mother, having Sunday dinner like the one she'd requested earlier in the week. He hadn't seen his bed in a few nights, and his body screamed for a comfortable place to rest, so his mom waking him by phone at eight that morning and giving him a grocery list was the last thing he needed. While he was at the market, he'd picked up a few other things she liked to have around the house. Because of her lack of appetite, he liked to keep a lot of meal shakes around—along with bread, juice, eggs, sandwich meats, and a couple of frozen dinners.

When he walked in the door, his mom was dressed

in a fashionable sweat suit, her makeup applied, and her hair fixed. She was glowing. She was even doing laundry, and it warmed him to see her doing such normal things.

Tex cooked the country-fried steaks and the mac and cheese. He also heated a can of pork and beans. His mom tossed herself a small salad and put the rolls in the oven. She didn't seem to notice that he did most of the cooking, and one of the purposes of having the dinner was for her to teach him to cook.

They both sat at the same table where she'd forced him to do his homework as a child, had household talks, and had many other family dinners. He'd skipped out on breakfast that morning, so by the time the food was ready, he was starved. His mom poked around at her plate, and he tried not to make it too noticeable that he kept up with her every bite. Overall, he thought she had enough, and he felt as if he'd done something right that day just by making sure she had at least one good meal.

He finished his first plate and was at the stove, scooping more beans on his plate, when she said, "You need to substitute some veggies in your diet and not so many cans of pork and beans." She laughed. "I swear when you were a kid, I tried everything to get you to eat something green, and you fought me tooth and nail. I couldn't even manage a green bean down your throat."

He shook his head and smiled at the memory of his mom trying to do everything, including bribe him with money or ice cream, to get him to eat his greens, but he'd been stubborn and had not once given in. She'd eventually given up and accepted his poor eating habits.

For a moment, as he finished eating and they both cleared the table, it felt as if nothing had changed. That nothing *was* changing.

He was full and satisfied with how the day ended. That was until his mother turned on the television and skipped to her favorite channel. It was well known for its "ripped from the headlines" movies. He sighed and couldn't bring himself to complain because he was too damn happy with being there and seeing her so content and full of life. He got comfortable on the couch, threw his scuffed work boots on the coffee table, and propped a pillow behind his head.

They caught the first movie thirty minutes into the story, but his mother still seemed to know the plot, and it didn't take him long to figure out some asshole was cheating on his pregnant wife with his secretary, who happened to be ten years younger than him and who wound up getting pregnant herself. The second movie was even more predictable than the first, and his mom must have felt the same way, or she was just tired because when he looked up halfway through it, she was soundly sleeping in her chair.

The sun had not yet set, and he itched to be outdoors. He caught the screen door before it slammed and quietly put it in place.

Sometimes, his mom's neighbor put a couple of horses in her field behind the house, and it had been a while since he walked the fence. The neighbor probably did it, but at the moment the chore gave him something to do besides wander around the backyard throwing sticks. Much as he expected, everything was as it should be. He dragged off a few branches that had fallen from a recent storm and tossed them into a brush pile he planned to burn. He made a few mental notes of things he was going to have to fix when spring rolled around—the porch swing needed repair, and the trim and shutters needed a fresh coat of paint.

He could probably spare some guys to come out over the next couple of weeks and get a lot of the work done, but when it came to his personal stuff, he liked to do the work himself.

As he started back inside the house, something seemed off and missing. He looked around, trying to figure out what it was. Everything to the eye looked exactly the way it had for the past couple of months. A normal porch with rocking chairs, something that most Patience residents had. That was when it hit him. Something was missing, and he felt stupid for not realizing it sooner. Flowers, mums especially, were absent. They were his mother's favorite. She had not come by his work to pick any up, and he was too absent to remember or realize that she had not gotten any this year. He could go out with the guys most Friday nights, but he couldn't spare the time to make sure his mom had her favorite flowers.

He shook his head and mentally beat himself up as he went back inside to check on her. She was still snoozing.

He drove to his house, took a shower, grabbed a change of clothes, and thought about grabbing his pillow, but he didn't want it to look too obvious that he was spending another night there.

Not too long ago, he would be spending a Sunday working around his house, catching up on bills, or cozying up with a woman, but now his Sunday nights were guaranteed to be a night full of watching his mom's beloved television program.

The friendships portrayed on the show were what he

wished for his mom. She needed some of her old friends, women who could understand her and have things in common with her. At one time, Ms. Edna and his mother had been very close. How, Tex didn't know. Edna wasn't the sweet-old-woman type like his mother, but she was always good to them, and he couldn't help but wonder when she'd quit coming around. Probably about the same time all the others quit. For a month after her diagnosis, Pearl had isolated herself from the world because she felt embarrassed. After a while, her friends had quit calling and given her the space she wanted. His mother needed to get out of the house for a while. She needed a friend who wasn't Maggie.

He locked his house and headed back toward his mom's. On the drive, his mind kept going to Liza and yesterday morning. He'd been a jackass to her and in the wrong, but he wasn't used to letting anyone in when it came to his family. It was in her nature to try to help— he understood that—but that wasn't what he wanted. He wanted to be able to get in her car and have a normal conversation, maybe flirt a little. Instead, he'd smarted off to her and said a lot of things he knew he was going to pay for. He hated the thought of being on her crap list, because by looking at Jake, the newest and longest member, it was near impossible to get off it. He liked Liza, and he wouldn't mind getting to know her better, but he couldn't do that if she refused to speak to him.

He was going to have to apologize. The urge to head to the Town's Inn so he could do just that was there, but he wanted to get back to his mother. They had a good time together, and he wasn't ready to let it go yet. No, soon he would tell Liza he'd been out of line and get her to see why he'd said the things he had. Right now, though, he had a marathon to watch with the most beautiful woman in the world.

Chapter Nine

"What can I get you, doll?" Marge asked. It was the same woman who'd waited on her and Anna her second day in town.

Liza eyed her menu. The pancakes Anna ordered the last time sounded wonderful, but she decided on something healthier and more appropriate for lunchtime. "A chef salad and a soft drink sounds good, Marge."

The owner of the diner scribbled down her order and hurried behind the counter. She looked to be in her early fifties, and even though she worked around fried food all day, she still took the time to put herself together. She was a very pretty lady, dressed in trouser pants and a black V-neck shirt. Her long red hair was loosely braided down her back. She had friendly green eyes and a warm, caring smile.

Liza had spent the entire day before with Anna. Since Anna had decided a girls' day was necessary on Saturday, she and Jake never made it to the furniture outlet in Knight, so she and Liza went. Jake looked relieved he didn't have to go.

They laughed, and she caught Anna up on what was going on with some of the people she sometimes hung out with in Linden. Liza drove just in case they needed to haul anything, and while she regretted buying her large SUV, it did come in handy because Anna found a couple of large pictures that were on sale and would look good anywhere in the shop. They wouldn't have been able to haul everything home if they were in Anna's little sports car.

That night, she had dinner with Anna and Jake, and while spending any time with Jake wasn't high on her priority list, she did it for Anna. Liza was proud of herself for being the perfect guest, except for the few death stares she gave him across the table. Hey, she didn't claim to be perfect. But Jake never engaged with her. He was surprisingly friendly to her, considering she'd gone off on him in front of all his friends a couple of nights before. She also couldn't ignore the fact that Anna looked truly in love with him.

She had gone two days not thinking of Greg, but when she saw Anna and Jake together, the betrayal hit her all over again. However, it was different somehow. It wasn't so much about Greg as it was the fact she had lost herself for a while.

Today, Anna had to deal with the business part of the shop and start ordering books for the bookstore. Liza would only be in the way and somewhat useless, so she decided to catch up on sleep in her new hotel room. When she realized she had no other choice but to go out for food, she'd ended up at the diner.

Unlike most, she didn't mind eating alone. She was content observing the people around her, and she liked to play a game with herself of trying to figure out what they were thinking based on their expressions and body language. It was so a therapist thing, and she knew it, but she didn't mind admitting it.

Another waitress brought her salad and soda to her. "Why are you eating alone?"

Liza turned her head away from observing a young

mother with a toddler who looked just like her. Jessie plopped down in the seat across from her, slurping from a straw.

"Anna had some bookstore business to take care of today, and I had to eat. You want some?" Liza pushed her plate toward Jessie, who picked up a crouton, dabbed it in ranch dressing, and popped it into her mouth. "Is that all you want?"

Jessie licked her fingers. "I'm having plates put together to go."

"Plates?"

Jessie looked annoyed. "For me, Daddy, and Tommy. They're at the hardware store and sent me over to pick up food."

"Are you still having problems with them not seeing you as an independent woman who can run a tractor?" Liza asked lightly but was curious. She could tell it truly bothered Jessie that her dad and brother didn't seem to see her as an equal. Liza would rather talk to Jessie about her family drama instead of staring at the woman and her little girl, feeling jealous.

She couldn't explain why she was drawn to them specifically, because she had never looked at a mother and child and felt she was missing something. Nevertheless, something had struck her hard as she sat at her table, faced with a woman who had to be younger than her twenty-eight-year-old sister was, and feeling that her life was lacking.

"Oh, they let me drive the tractor. It's the combine they have issues with, along with other work they think I can't handle." Jessie looked at Liza as if she actually knew the difference between the two pieces of farm equipment. "Nothing's changed, but I don't expect it to, at least not anytime soon." She shrugged. "I just don't let it get to me too much. Plus, when they're not around, I do what I want."

"Have you ever tried talking to them about how you feel?"

Jessie laughed. "You're kiddin' me, right? They are two of the most stubborn men I know. Don't let Tommy fool you because he seems so laid-back and doesn't say much. He's just as hardheaded as any other man. My daddy is the same way. There's no talking to them and making them see any other way but their way. My daddy listens to my mama, and Tommy pretty much does whatever Em says, but that's as far as they budge."

"I don't know your daddy, or Tommy for that matter, but I did see the way your brother acted the other night when Bradley said what he did to you. He loves you. I think he would listen if you talked to him."

A waitress came by and refilled Liza's soda and Jessie's sweet tea. Liza thanked her while Jessie asked her about her son. Just the way Liza knew almost everyone in Linden, Jessie probably knew everyone in Patience, and if she didn't, Liza wouldn't doubt that Jessie would talk to them anyway.

Jessie was friendly, and under her tough-girl persona she was sweet and considerate, not that Liza would ever tell her that to her face. While that would be a compliment to most people, to Jessie it would not. She and Jessie were different in many ways, such as the way they dressed. Jessie was dressed in overalls again, with her ponytail pulled through a ball cap, and Liza was wearing the jeans that made her butt look good. They also shared similarities. They had something to prove to the world. Liza, too, understood how important it was to come off as strong and confident.

Jessie tore pieces off a napkin. "Tommy is only like that when it comes to guys. He's very protective. I'm just glad he didn't do anything."

"What do you mean?"

"Until recently, I tended to hang with the guys more than the girls. Girls' night is a new thing, something we started doing after Anna moved back home. Tommy wasn't too thrilled I hung out at Ollie's and drank with his buddies while I beat them at pool. I mean, he has some pretty hot friends. You put Jake, Bradley, and Tex in a room together, and the masculinity just hangs. Women of all ages tend to flock to them." Jessie paused and then quickly added, "Not that I've ever done anything with Jake. He has always been Anna's, and we have been nothing but friends."

"I guess I can see how that would make Tommy uncomfortable." Liza tried not to think why it bothered her that Jessie didn't say she and Tex never did anything.

She was well informed in the short time she had spent in the small town that Tex was known for charming the panties right off every woman. That shouldn't matter because she had already decided sex with Tex was not an option. So why did the thought of Jessie and Tex being together bother her?

Let it go. It doesn't matter.

"I started to understand, so I began hanging out with other guys I went to school with and even some I know in Knight. I still play on the softball team, but I can't help that there is not an all-women's team, and I love the sport too much to not play because of my brother."

Liza couldn't stop herself from bringing up the question she already knew the answer to. "But you still hang out with Bradley?"

Jessie crossed her arms. "I mean, we see each other around because we have the same friends, and we sometimes can't help but push each other's buttons, but we've known each other a long time."

Liza was pushing it, but either Jessie really didn't know, or she was trying to hide what was really going on between her and Bradley. "You don't think it's more than that between you two? You did leave together the other night."

"Well"—Jessie actually blushed—"he needed a ride home. For some reason, I always tend to be his personal driver. We're friends at the end of the day, no matter what happens." She went back to fidgeting with the napkin and not looking Liza in the eye. "I guess there is a little something there that makes us pretty tight. We flirt with each other because that's just our nature, and we fight because he can be a jackass and I can be stubborn like my dad and brother. I don't know…"

Liza took a drink from her glass and gave Jessie a moment to think about what she didn't know.

Jessie smirked. "Soooo, have you and Tex made it to the bedroom yet?"

Liza let her change the subject because she didn't know Jessie well enough to pry any more than she already had. Liza didn't like talking about her nonexistent sex life in a public place filled with townspeople enjoying their lunch.

"I don't plan on sleeping with Tex."

"And why is that? He's hot."

"I think it's best if I let Tex be. You said so yourself."

"I didn't mean it like that. I don't know…it's just—

"

"You feel for him," Liza suggested.

"Yeah, I guess."

"I get it, Jessie. You don't want some outsider coming in and making things worse for him. You're a good friend."

"I know you wouldn't make things worse. I just feel the need to protect him."

"I will never do anything to hurt him. I like to talk, but if he doesn't want to, then that has to be okay, even though I don't think it's very healthy for him to keep things bottled up."

Jessie smiled. "You want to do more than just talk. You want him, and you want him bad."

Liza laughed. "Okay. I won't deny I'm attracted to him, but he has a lot going on. It would only complicate our lives. For one, if I do have sex, and that is a big if—" She lowered her voice as people walked past their table. "—I really don't think it should be with anybody that has close ties with all of you guys. It will just make things awkward."

"There is a great sports bar in Knight. I bet we can find some pretty hot guys there right now since the World Series is about to start. You know anything about baseball? You start talking about sports, and the guys will come running."

"I know enough. I am friends with Anna. But that's not necessary. I really just need some time without a man around. I lost a little of myself when I was with Greg. I don't want to rush into anything. Thanks, though."

"I get that, but maybe getting back to you is you needing to put yourself out there and have some innocent, no-strings-attached sex with a hot guy." Jessie sipped at her drink. "Just a thought."

She let Jessie's words sink in, and maybe the woman had a point. She didn't know anymore, but she was not going to pass up any opportunities to live. A woman walking slowly across the street caught her eye. Something seemed familiar about the elderly woman carrying a paper bag in each hand.

Jessie turned around to peer out the front windows of the diner. "Whatcha looking at?"

"Do you see that woman? She looks familiar to me for some reason."

"Me, too. Oh God, I think it's Ms. Avery. What is she doing?" Jessie's eyes went wide.

"I don't know, but those bags look too heavy for her to carry wherever she's going. Why is she walking?"

"Most of the time she's with Maggie or Tex when she's in town. I should call Tex." Jessie dug in her front pocket, then pulled out a cell phone.

Liza stood and grabbed her purse. "I'll take her home. I think Tex is at the shop working with Jake. I have nothing else to do today."

"Are you sure?" Jessie asked.

"Yeah. Thanks for sitting with me for a while."

"Let me give you Tex's cell number just in case you need him." Jessie called out the digits while Liza put them into her phone. "I'll see you Friday night?"

"Yeah, Friday night."

Liza went to the counter and handed her ticket to the same woman who refilled her and Jessie's drinks. She paid and put a few extra dollars in the tip jar. Marge called out Jessie's order, and Jessie was already in line with her money in hand. They said their goodbyes, and Liza walked into the breezy air.

She knew it was going to be chilly and windy, but she couldn't bring herself to put her recently done hair in a ponytail. She loved the vibrant red highlights and felt sexy showing them off. She pulled her coat a little tighter around herself and ran across the street, not caring that other cars had to wait. Pearl was on a park bench in front of the courthouse when Liza reached her. Since it was cold, Liza was thankful the woman was dressed in a warm coat and scarf. If only she'd remembered her own scarf.

"Pearl."

The woman looked up from placing her bags on the pavement beside her feet. "Yes, dear?"

"I don't know if you remember me. I am a friend of Tex's. I met you the other morning at your house." Saying she was a friend of Tex's was the only explanation she could come up with for knowing her son.

Pearl's stare turned blank.

"I'm Liza. I came by your house Saturday morning to give Tex a ride home." Liza didn't think Pearl remembered at all.

Tex's mom still looked confused but waved it off. "Yes, I remember. I don't know why that boy continues sleeping on my couch, but I do love him being around. Just don't tell him I said so, or he will never leave." Pearl winked.

"I won't." Liza pointed to the grocery bags. "You have a lot of stuff there."

"I needed to pick up a few things at the market. I didn't realize until after I bought all this that I had to carry it all the way home. It's no fun getting old. Stay young as long as you can."

Liza smiled and sat down. "I'm afraid I'm already

getting old. It has recently hit me that I'm thirty-five years old, and I expect you not to reveal that to anyone." She winked as she asked Pearl to keep her secret. "I just don't know where my life has gone, to tell you the truth."

Pearl kindly patted her on the hand. "Oh, honey, you are far from being old. What are they saying nowadays? Something about thirty being the new twenty-something? You have nothing to fret about. Your life is every day, and you have lived through it. Now, if you have appreciated it, I don't know, but if you haven't, it's time you do. Don't take anything for granted when it comes to your family and friends."

Liza nodded. "May I take you home?"

"I'm sure a nice girl like you has better things to do than drive an old lady around. I'll be fine. I just needed to rest a minute. I could use the fresh air."

"Honestly, you would be giving me something to do. I'm visiting Patience, and the friend I'm here to see is handling some business. You would be doing me a favor and getting me out of my hotel room."

"Then I would appreciate the ride."

Liza hurried to try to pick up both of the grocery bags, but Pearl snatched one out of her hands. Must be a pride thing and not something she associated with women. Most of the time old men had a problem with accepting help and realizing they weren't as strong as they'd been twenty years ago.

She and Pearl walked across the street and put the bags in the back seat of Liza's car. She pulled out of the tight spot in front of the diner and drove the short distance to Pearl's small ranch house.

Pearl let Liza carry both paper bags into the house. Liza noticed that Tex's mom looked tired. She couldn't leave Pearl, and for some reason, she didn't want to.

As Pearl unlocked the front door, she asked, "Would you please have some tea with me…"

"Liza." Liza was officially becoming worried. She was suddenly glad she'd found Pearl when she did. "I would love to, thank you."

Liza followed her into the kitchen with the sun shining through the window above the sink, making the room bright. She set the bags on the counter and began unpacking them while Pearl opened a small canister decorated with roosters. She pulled out a couple of tea bags and put some water on the stove.

"Just leave those bags there, honey. I will get to them after we've had our tea." Pearl opened the cupboard and pulled down two teacups.

Liza pulled out a half gallon of milk and a carton of orange juice. "Pearl—"

A gallon of milk was already in the refrigerator.

Pearl sat at the table as the water boiled. "Are you close with your parents? Are you an only child?"

Liza continued unpacking the second bag. She pulled out a loaf of bread, bananas, and a box of granola bars. "I am. They are wonderful parents to my younger sister and me. My dad owns an insurance firm, and my mom takes care of the household and does volunteer work. I guess you could say growing up, I was closer to my mom because she was there when I got home from school and was active in all my school activities while my dad had to work long hours. Now that I'm older, I'm more a daddy's girl while my sister is more like my mother."

Liza took the bananas out of the plastic bag and set them on the counter. She took the bread and bars and walked them to the pantry. Inside was a breadbox. When she opened it, she found a full loaf of bread already there, too. It seemed odd to her since Pearl lived alone and bread only lasted a week or so before going stale. She placed the new loaf on top of the breadbox, slid the granola bars beside a couple of boxes of mac and cheese, and noticed five other boxes of the same granola bars in the pantry.

First, the milk and now the bread and granola bars. Alarm bells went off in her head, and it took a lot of willpower not to say anything, but she had heard Tex loud and clear. She was staying out of his family business.

"You didn't have to put my groceries away. My son has finally found a good girl."

"Oh, I'm not Tex's girl. We just met."

Liza could read the shock showing on Tex's mother's face. Liza realized that what she just said didn't come out the way she meant it, and Pearl probably had all kinds of thoughts running wild through her head.

"I mean, we met through a friend I'm here visiting. He just needed a ride the other night," she quickly added.

Pearl looked disappointed. "That's too bad, because Tex needs a girl like you. I've been trying to get him to ask Maggie out, but I know she isn't his type. She is sensitive and somewhat shy. He would be too much for her, but I think you would be a good match for him." Pearl removed the hot water and poured it over the tea bags in the two cups.

Liza sat at the table and concentrated on her tea. *A good match for Tex?* First, with Jessie, and now, his own mother was trying to hook them up. Did she have a big sign on her head that read *In Need of a Man* in big bold letters?

"I can't help to be blunt and ask how you would know that. I mean, you just met me," Liza questioned. She was curious about Pearl's observation of her personality.

"I really don't know. You have a way about you that resembles a strong, capable woman who wouldn't let any man run all over her. My Tex needs that kind of woman in his life to keep him in line. I've had the job of doing it for thirty years, and I love my son, but he needs to quit running around with these floozies, grow up, and think about having a family."

Liza was flattered at the kind words. It was something she didn't know she needed to hear, but after Pearl described her in a way she hadn't thought of herself in a good while, she knew she needed to realize that about herself again. She was not some weak girl who ran and hid when things got a little tough. No, she would stand tall and fight when something was worth fighting for, and her finding herself in Patience was something to strive for.

"I don't know if *strong* is an accurate word to describe me right now. I'm kind of at a crossroads, and my life seems out of sorts. I certainly don't feel strong."

"I would disagree, sweetie."

They both sat and drank their tea while Pearl bragged about her son, and Liza enjoyed the stories. Tex throwing up as a kid on his first roller-coaster ride, him bringing home his first bad report card, Pearl making him sit at the kitchen table every night and study his spelling words until he was eventually the best speller in his second-grade class, and him refusing to this day to eat any type of vegetable. They were the small things that made Tex the man he was today.

She liked the way Pearl saw her son. It was the way a mother should look at her child—knowing he was in no way perfect and sometimes not agreeing with his lifestyle but loving him endlessly. Pearl put her expectations aside and only wanted Tex happy with his life.

Liza couldn't help wondering how her mother would describe her. Would she say she was strong and capable? Would Mom be proud of her and her decision to have a career and be happily single before she settled on a guy she really didn't love? She liked to think her mom would say and think all of those things, but a little doubt creeped in. She never doubted that her mother loved her, but she also knew her mother had expectations when it came to Liza's life.

Liza wasn't one to have regrets, because in some way, those experiences shaped her into the person she was right now. Even though she wasn't completely happy with the person she was at this moment, she knew she would get there. She would look back on this moment, sitting with Pearl, and know their conversation helped give her a new perspective and made her feel empowered.

While she was talking and laughing with Pearl, she sensed someone else in the room with them.

"What are you girls doing?"

Liza turned in her chair, and Pearl just looked up from her cup. Tex towered above them.

"Honey, what are you doing here? I thought you would be working today since it's so nice outside." Pearl stood and gave her son a kiss on his stubbled cheek, then pushed him into the seat next to Liza.

"Jessie called me and said you were in town today. I thought I would drop by and make sure you got home okay. Why didn't you call me, and where in the hell is Maggie?"

Liza felt inadequate that she wasn't good enough to sit with his mother for an hour or two, but she disregarded it. She was there today because she'd been the only person to help at the time, and she was glad she had because she was able to get to know the woman who raised and loved the man she couldn't seem to get out of her head.

"Maggie called this morning. She's sick with some stomach virus. I told her to stay home and call me in the morning. She sounded awful. I hope she gets better, but if not, I want you to go see if she needs anything," Pearl insisted, clearly accepting Maggie into her life.

"Why didn't she call me?" Tex demanded.

"Because she doesn't have to. She is here for me, and therefore, you are out of it, son. So don't go raising your voice at me." Pearl sounded strong and capable.

Tex let out an incoherent mutter, then closed his mouth. He was a smart man. "I'm sorry, Mama. I didn't mean to raise my voice. I just wished I knew you were going to be alone today and walking to the market—it's too chilly out there to be walking that far. Why didn't you call me if you needed to go somewhere?"

"I am not dead, Tex. I needed a few things at the store, so I went to get them. It's no big deal. Liza saw me and volunteered to bring me home. We've had a nice chat while drinking our tea. You want some?"

Tex made a disgusted face. "I'll pass."

He looked to Liza, and she noticed the way his eyes crinkled a little when he smiled. She could tell he hadn't been sleeping.

"Thanks for bringing her home," he said in a much lower voice.

She could feel his gaze like a touch. A tic started in his jaw. She looked down at her tea, breaking eye contact, but she could still feel him. He had a presence, and it was making a major impact on her system right now.

Time to leave.

Liza stood. "Pearl, thanks for the conversation and tea. I had a lovely time. If Maggie is still sick anytime this week, maybe I could come over and hang out."

Okay, this was not staying out of Tex's personal business, but she enjoyed the company. And when Anna was working, it would give Liza something to do besides sit in her room watching terrible reality television.

To most, hanging with a woman old enough to be her mother wouldn't be considered having fun and finding herself, but she wasn't one to be put in a box. She did have fun with Pearl. Therefore, there was no reason not to visit her more while she was in town. Pearl represented something stable in her when everything else was out of control. She needed that and welcomed it from a wonderful lady. Who cared that it happened to be from the mother of the man she had a few dreams about and felt wildly attracted to?

"Honey, I would love that." Pearl beamed. "Write your number on that dry-erase board hanging on the fridge, and I'll give you a call."

She grinned and quickly wrote down her number. She added her name above it because for some reason she felt Pearl needed it. She put her cup in the sink and gave Pearl a hug. "Thanks again for today."

"Me, too. And Liza?"

Liza stopped in the doorway and looked at Pearl while she tried avoiding Tex. "Yes?"

Pearl smiled. "Don't forget what I said concerning you and my son. I have a feeling about this one."

All the blood drained from Liza's face, and Tex's eyes grew wide.

Tex now knew he was one of the topics of their conversation. Even though she hadn't brought him up, this was just great. She was still mad at him for all of the hurtful things he'd said to her Saturday morning when she'd really been trying to help.

She kept a steady stride all the way to her car and was proud of herself for being able to put one foot in front of the other after Pearl's huge comment. She hated to break it to Pearl that there was not, and would not be, anything between Liza and her son. It was officially time to get Tex out of her mind. How she was going to do that, she didn't know.

****

As Tex drove back to Anna's shop, he was thankful he'd driven the short distance into town more times than he could count in his life, because his brain wasn't functioning properly and his mind was running rampant. After making sure everything was okay with his mom and reminding her to use her cell if she needed him, he made tracks back to his truck. What had his mom meant when she said *don't forget about what I said about you and my son* to Liza?

When he saw Liza's car parked in the driveway, he'd thought the opportunity to apologize had finally presented itself. He would have been stupid to tell her he was out of line in front of his mom, because she would want to know why he was apologizing, and then her knowing would only cause *two* women to be mad at him. He'd planned to follow her outside to thank her once again for picking up his mom and then work the apology into the conversation, but after his mom's departing comment, his feet had been planted to the floor. Letting her exit out the door had been his only choice, and considering the way she rushed out of the room, she'd been just as eager to walk away from him.

Had Liza staked out his mom to try to get information out of her after Tex blew up at her? Was she really that desperate to abandon her own issues and seek his? He didn't know that much about Liza, but he knew that wasn't her style. She'd really just happened to see his mom and genuinely wanted to give her a ride home…and for offering to come back for another visit—he didn't know what to think about that. Nevertheless, his mom had seemed to enjoy her time with Liza. It thrilled him to see her excited about anything. He was just thinking that his mother needed friends, and right now that friend happened to be a sexy little woman who must have allowed Em to play with her hair. He shouldn't be too picky.

He turned right onto Spring Street and was about to pull in front of the coffee shop and bookstore when his cell phone buzzed in his pocket. He awkwardly pulled it out and looked at the screen displaying Mikah's number—a man who'd worked for him for several years and who he'd recently promoted to job foreman when taking on the remodel job for Anna and Jake.

He hit Send as he put the truck in park. "Talk to me, Mik."

Tex listened and cursed under his breath. "I'll take

care of it. It's not your fault. I forgot to tell you I talked to Edna last week. Thanks for calling. Yeah, I know. She frightens me a little, too."

Between the remodel, Avery Landscaping, and his mom, he had too much going on. He had never forgotten to follow through with a customer before, and worse, it was Edna. All he needed was another angry woman.

What he needed was a vacation, or better yet, a good distraction, not something that would only add to his out-of-control life but would give him something to look forward to. He laughed as he got out of his truck. Edna could wait…for the moment he was enjoying the slide show playing through his head. Liza and distraction replayed over and over again. God, the woman was always on his mind, and he was tired of only trying to imagine how wild and free she would be. It was time to get the real picture.

Chapter Ten

Liza spent the next hour at the walking track with Anna. It was somewhat isolated and peacefully quiet. Anna had always said it was like a sanctuary she could go to, to clear her head and feel better when she left. Liza also knew the track held strong memories for Anna and Jake of their old and new relationship.

Anna had loaned Liza a pair of tennis shoes to wear. Otherwise, she would've had to walk in her ballet flats. Liza walked while Anna ran one lap around the track, then they spent the rest of the time walking together and talking. She told Anna about finding Tex's mom in front of the courthouse earlier that day and how she'd had a surprisingly good time drinking tea. She left out the parts about enjoying the stories Pearl told her regarding Tex and that Pearl thought she would be a good match for her son.

Anna didn't seem too surprised when Liza told her that Pearl said she seemed like a strong and capable woman. Anna just laughed and said, "That is a given, Liz."

After she and Anna ended their walk, Liza returned to her hotel room for a hot shower. She finished up quickly. She turned off the bathroom light and was drying her hair with a towel when a knock sounded at the door. She looked out the peephole and saw Georgia. Because it was a woman at the door, she decided she didn't need to put on a robe. And really, what man would be standing outside her door at eight o'clock at night? Who did she think she was? Some high school girl whose heart thumped at the thought that her first love was coming to sneak her out of her room to go to the park and lie under the stars, dreaming of their future?

She opened the door. "Georgia, what's up?"

Cheerfully, Georgia said, "I hope I'm not bothering you. I was just hoping we could talk."

Liza stepped back and waved her inside. "No, of course not. I was just about to flip through the television stations and open a carton of mint chocolate ice cream. I'm all ears."

Georgia sat on the bed and straightened her pumpkin-colored cardigan. "I know we just met the other night, and, well, I probably made a bad impression, considering I drank too much wine and was told I made some unladylike comments to the guys, but I guess not knowing you will make it easier for me to talk. Before I got toasted, I know you said that you were a therapist and that you helped a lot of couples with their relationships."

Liza threw the towel she was drying her hair with on the dresser and sat beside Georgia.

"I am. But I don't only help couples. I have, or had"—she corrected herself since she currently didn't have any patients—"patients who wanted help for other things like depression, losing a job and having a hard time dealing with the change…even people who just needed someone to talk to and shine a light on their life, help make things clearer."

"That's what I'm hoping you can do for me. Shine a light, I mean."

"First, I need to know what's going on."

Georgia's cheeks turned a rosy color. "I want a man."

"Do you have a certain man in mind, or do you mean *a* man?"

She nodded. "I have a man I like, but he doesn't seem to notice, or if he does, I have no effect on him. I see him every day, which sounds like a good thing, but it only makes me want him more. I can't take it anymore. Do I just put myself out there and tell him how I feel, or do I continue longing for someone who doesn't see me in a sexual way?"

Liza thought it over and found it crazy that Georgia had come to her for relationship advice, but then Georgia didn't know about Greg and his cheating. Liza had kept it to herself during girls' night.

"Have you thought about putting distance between you two?" she asked.

"That's kind of hard to do when he's your boss."

Liza swallowed. "Your boss? Don't you work for Garrett Tillman?"

She had heard about Garrett from Anna. At one time, he'd had her childhood home listed and had been trying to sell it but instead made a stupid deal with Jake and let him rent it out. The way Anna described Garrett, he didn't seem like Georgia's type. She had a sense of humor, always cheerful, and loved colorful clothes. According to Anna, Garrett's decorating style consisted of all beige, and Liza had seen firsthand because Anna and Jake were living in Garrett's apartment behind his realty office. Anna had said he was a shy man who mostly kept to himself.

"Yeah. You think I'm crazy, don't you?"

"No. I've never met Garrett. I have only heard about

him through Anna. He sounds like a nice guy who needs some serious decorating help."

Georgia laughed. "I tried to bring some color into the office, adding a couple of pillows and a striped area rug, but he just mumbled. He can sell a house, but there is no way he could stage it."

"So Garrett doesn't notice that you are feeling a little more than the boss-and-employee relationship?"

"I honestly think he finds me annoying, but I'm good with the clients, and I caught on pretty quickly when he hired me. So no, he doesn't see me in any way except being some obnoxious woman he has to put up with on a daily basis." Georgia groaned as she buried her face in her hands.

"I think you're being too hard on yourself. He wouldn't keep you on the payroll if you got on his nerves and he couldn't stand you. You're a strong and capable woman. Maybe he doesn't know how to handle that."

"That is so grade school. I thought boys were supposed to grow up to be men."

Liza shook her head and laughed. "Honey, I might be a licensed therapist, but that doesn't mean I fully understand why a man does what he does. They can be intoxicating one minute and total jackasses the next." She got up from the bed, went to the small mini-fridge, and pulled out a carton of ice cream. She grabbed two plastic spoons and offered one to Georgia.

Georgia hesitated, but Liza insisted. "Go on. Ice cream can cure everything except having a bigger waistline."

They both sat and ate right out of the carton.

Georgia licked her spoon. "Love is supposed to be overwhelming, crazy about someone, highest form of emotion. Why wouldn't Garrett want to experience that?"

"Sweetie, that's how you feel about love, but not everyone thinks it's a pure high of emotion. If you are lucky and it is that way, it usually never lasts."

"I don't believe that. I think love can be amazing with the right person, and if it's real, it will last. I really think that if you love someone, you would do everything in your power to be with that person. Love is a very powerful thing."

"I like you, Georgia. You are not cynical about love even when you have feelings for a man who may not share those same feelings. I wish I was more like that, but I'm thinking I might not have been the right person for you to talk to. I'm honestly not too good when it comes to my own relationships. I have no right to give you an ounce of advice at this moment."

"I think there is something you can help me with, though," Georgia said, looking hopeful.

"I'll try my best. Shoot."

"I think I am cursed because men don't see me as a sexual being. I do desire very much to be. They seem to like me well enough, but because I don't dress the sex-kitten way or because I am overly talkative, they never look at me as being more than an entertaining friend. I know I could never be you, but I want a man to be attracted to me."

Liza looked down at her pajamas. "Like me? Look at me, Georgia. I'm dressed in candy-cane pajama pants when it's not even Christmas, with a plain white T-shirt. My hair is wet, and by morning, I will look like something out of *The Exorcist*. You don't want to be me, believe me."

"But even in your pajamas you look sexy. When I've seen you around town this week, you always look so put together. I love the way you dress. It screams confidence. Me, on the other hand, I dress like I could join the circus."

Liza burst out laughing. "You do not. I love the way you dress, too. You are just being yourself, and I've been told that carries presence. You are nice, sweet, funny to no end, and some man is going to look at you and fall madly, crazily in love with you. You just wait."

"But I want to be a sex kitten, or at least close to one. I want Garrett, but if not him, I want a man to look at me and say 'wow.' "

"Don't try to change, Georgia. You are a wonderful person all by yourself. One day, a man is going to realize that." Liza knew firsthand about changing for a man. Telling Georgia not to follow in her footsteps was the best advice she could dish out.

"You think so?" Georgia asked.

"Yes, I honestly do."

Liza gave Georgia a hug goodbye. She was happy to see that she made a difference. Georgia looked better leaving than she had when she first arrived. She was so innocent and pure, and Liza hoped she wouldn't be too disappointed if Garrett never came around. Someone would—the woman was too damn sweet to never find the crazy-about-you love she desired.

After Liza put her ice cream back in the freezer, she propped her pillows behind her back and made herself comfortable on the bed, deciding to read a little before going to sleep. Maybe she wanted to because she never went a day without reading a few pages. Or was it because she hoped the book would bring more good dreams about Tex?

She hadn't even read a full page when a loud knocking pierced her thoughts, making her flinch and drop her book. "Who in the world?" she muttered.

She threw off her covers and trampled to the door. She unclasped the chain and yanked it open. "Tex," she said, stunned because he was the last person she expected to see standing outside her door.

His gaze dropped, and slowly, he brought it back up to meet hers. Maybe she should have looked through the peephole, then she would have known she needed the robe since it was indeed a man this time. Her pajamas were not in any way sexy, but she did have on a white shirt without a bra. She cleared her throat and refused to wrap her arms around her chest so he could no longer see her nipples were hard.

"Is there a reason you're here? Because last time we talked, you made it very clear that we are not friends. That you, in no capacity, want me to *counsel* you, which I was not doing."

"I brought you this." He held out a pot of golden flowers, which she couldn't believe she hadn't seen the instant she opened the door.

"Mums? You brought me a plant? Why?"

"I guess it's my way of apologizing. They have always been my mother's favorite, and since y'all had a good time, well, I just thought you would like them."

"Thank you, but you know I'm currently staying at a hotel. What am I supposed to do with it?"

"They like a lot of sunshine, so I suggest sitting them outside your door."

She brought them to her nose to smell. "I'll do that. Thanks, but you didn't have to bring it to me tonight. It has to be after ten."

"I just left my mom's and decided to stop by before I went home."

She nodded and held her tongue. Not knowing if Pearl was okay had nagged at her all afternoon. When she said nothing, he turned to walk away.

She heard herself ask, "Do you want to come in?"

He stopped in his tracks and spun around. He looked tired and beaten. His jaw still a little discolored from the punch he'd taken didn't help matters any. Without saying anything, he walked toward her. She stepped back as he entered, gazing at his profile. He was one glorious-looking man.

She watched as he glanced around the room. "You never seen a hotel room before?" she asked with a slight laugh.

"I have, but not a Town's Inn room."

She shook her head and didn't hide that she didn't believe him for a second.

"What, you don't believe me?" he asked.

"I've heard things about you. I just find it hard to believe a man with your type of reputation has never taken a girl to the local hotel. I've seen your mom's house. It's not big enough for you to quietly sneak a girl in and out of your window without her hearing."

He arched one brow. "And what exactly *have* you heard?"

"Just that up until now you have not been very selective with who you've been with, and that between you and Bradley, you pretty much have serviced the entire town of Patience."

"Ouch. You don't hold back much, do you?"

She shrugged. "I just tell it like it is."

"I like that about you, Liza. I was that guy, I guess, for a long while, but I'm just not looking for the occasional hookup anymore." His eyes went dark.

Oh. God. Why did that admission seem to relieve her in a big way? The temperature in the room felt warmer. She forced herself to meet his eyes squarely, eyes that sparkled with lust and desire. She swallowed the lump in her throat. "What are you looking for?" she bravely asked.

He slowly walked to her, and though she knew she should have moved, she didn't want to. She was not going to back down from Tex. Before she realized it, and realized how close he was, she could feel his body heat combining with hers. He had a wicked look in his eye, and the juncture of her thighs began to spasm.

He planted his lips on hers, and his mouth took over like a man who knew exactly what he was doing. He rubbed, then slipped his tongue between her trembling lips. She started to protest, then relaxed into it as she heard a low groan rumble from his chest. That was enough to make her lose what little control she possessed.

Mmmm. God, yes. Now, this was kissing. She couldn't get enough of his touch, his scent. Slipping her fingers under his T-shirt, she explored the hardness of his back. Still, that was not enough. She needed so much more. Eagerly, she pulled at his shirt until he broke free of her lips, and together they tugged the shirt over his head. Her fingers splayed over the dark hair that fanned across his chest. *Damn...*

His hands roamed her back, her ass. The bulge hardening against her thigh had her hungering for more. She started to move against his thighs, but he braced both of his hands firmly on her waist and held her back. That was okay for now, because just kissing him was that good.

"Shit," he whispered between kisses.

He pushed her against the wall just behind the front door. With him lining kisses down her throat, all she could do was press her body into his and sigh. She missed his mouth on hers, but the things he was making her feel with the kisses he was laying on her neck, the slopes of her shoulders, and right between her aching breasts were more than enough to satisfy her.

He cursed again as he tugged at her pants, not seeming distracted by the red-and-white Christmas candy. She leaned her head back against the wall, closed her eyes, and let him pull them all the way to the floor. She was literally going insane. She wanted him urgently kissing her lips while he kissed softly down her quivering stomach. If only he could give both areas the same attention at the same time. Finding a little strength, she stepped out of her pants.

"Now, how did I know you would be wearing lace?" A grin split his face.

He slowly traced the outline of her panties, drifting downward to her thighs, sending little tingles up her legs. She quivered under his touch, and that seemed to make him want to touch her more. She didn't complain.

Dropping to his knees, he kissed a trail down her stomach, only stopping to lightly kiss the lacy fabric covering her mound. She was way past the point of being ready. *Ohhhh...* This was how it was supposed to feel with a strong, masculine man. Him on his knees in front of her, kissing and licking, sometimes even biting at her flesh, made her feel like a goddess.

"I take it you like lace." She sighed, stifling a moan.

His voice was deep, and his breath warmed her skin. "The first time I saw you, I knew you wore sexy panties. I haven't thought about much else."

She went from bracing her hands on his shoulders to threading them through his hair, knowing that clinging to him for support was her only way of staying on two feet. At the same time she drew in a shaky breath, he eased one finger inside her, caressing hot spots to drive her wild while his tongue licked her inner thigh. Her head flew back against the wall as deep pleasure rippled through her. All her thoughts jumbled as one, but she didn't need to think. She only needed to feel, and God, was she doing that. Afraid of her own volume, she bit down on her bottom lip.

"Don't hold back on me now, Liza. The rooms around you are unoccupied. I checked. So feel free to scream. In fact, I demand you to."

He captured her with his mouth, and with that, she let go of any insecurities she had. With every lick and tug, she found herself lost in a pleasurable high of sensation. She moaned deeply, and it rumbled through her head, but she was sure she was not only thinking it but actually making the pleasurable sounds, because the more *oohhhs* and *ahhhs* she let escape as she moved to the rhythm his fingers and mouth set, the harder he kept up with his deep ministrations.

"Ohhh…God, Tex, I'm almost there."

With both of his hands, he pushed her ass forward, bringing her closer. "Oh hell, honey." He groaned, and she could feel his lips move against her as well as his warmth.

Her orgasm came hard, and she found herself crying

out, digging her nails into his shoulders, and welcoming the sensations that ripped through her. She felt limp and weak but exhilarated. Okay, this was probably not her smartest move, but she didn't care anymore. The old Liza would have put herself out there and just asked for what she wanted. No—that was not her at all. She would *take* what she wanted, and right now she wanted the man releasing a wave of heat through her.

Grasping his head in her hands, she brought him to his feet. He shadowed the room as he towered over her. She licked her lips as she tugged him down until his mouth was on hers.

He deepened the kiss as he pressed one hand against the wall next to her head. She felt pleasantly trapped.

She didn't appreciate being bossed around very well, and she hadn't met a man yet who would take charge and match her in the bedroom.

She knew Tex was a man to be reckoned with the first time he took it upon himself to kiss her, but it wasn't until tonight, showing up at her door, holding a potted flower, looking sad and beaten up by the world, that she realized she was in major trouble when anything concerning him was involved.

She walked toward the bed, and once he sat down, she lightly slapped her hand to his chest and pushed him onto his back. Freely, she worked her way up his body, running soft kisses up his hard stomach, kissing both his shoulders, up one side of his neck, and stopping before she brought her lips down to his. Gazing at him, she unbuttoned his jeans and slipped her hand inside.

"Holy shit, Liza." He gasped.

Giving him a playful smile, she continued stroking him. His eyes slammed shut as he came up off the bed.

She felt powerful, and that was something she hadn't experienced in a long time.

He grabbed her wrist and forced her away. She eyed him, confused but thinking maybe he wasn't ready for things to end just yet. Maybe he had other plans for her. The very idea sent shivers down her spine.

His eyes opened, and he leaned his forehead up until it touched hers and their lips were tantalizingly close but still not touching—and that was a problem for her.

"This has to stop," he rasped.

She stared down at him. "What do you mean it has to stop? Isn't this why you came here tonight?"

He gently pushed her off his lap. She sat on the bed, too mad to care that she was bare from the waist down. He was silent as he stood and started to button his jeans.

Had she missed something? "Well?" She expected him to give her some kind of explanation.

"No, it isn't why I came here tonight. I came here to apologize for being an ass the other morning. I had no intention of sleeping with you."

She held out both hands, palms up. "Then what was all this about? Because I know for damn sure it wasn't all me. You're the one who kissed me, among other things." She wasn't shy about sex—she loved sex and, therefore, didn't mind talking about it with him.

"I didn't mean to do that." He tugged his shirt over his head. "I shouldn't have done that. I just couldn't control myself. You asked me in. Your pajamas shouldn't be considered sexy, but the candy canes did something for me, and I only wanted to see, then taste what was under them."

"So I'm just someone you could play with for the night. What, you didn't have any bar chicks on call for the night, so you decided I would be available to get you off?" She walked past him, slipped back into her panties, and decided to forgo the pants…only because she was still wearing her nightshirt.

He raked his hands through his messy hair. "Dammit, Liza, you know it isn't like that. I already told you I didn't plan this, and I told you I'm no longer that guy. I've changed."

She rolled her eyes and let out a laugh. "Whatever. Men don't change. Especially men like you. Just go." She waved him off. "And next time you need the attention of a woman, don't go out of your way to find me. I will not be played."

"For fucking sake—I am not some Hollywood movie star, and I know nothing about politics. My name is not Leroy, and I'm nothing like your dick of an ex-boyfriend, so don't go comparing me to him. I have never played a woman. Just because I've been with a lot of women doesn't mean I was an asshole to them and didn't respect them or didn't give them exactly what they wanted. The women I've been with understand how things are, and most of them are only looking for a good time, no strings attached. As for tonight, I got nothing but a major hard-on because of how sexy you are. You're the one who got serviced and all the attention."

This man was intolerable, and she didn't for one minute think he was innocent in all his years of sleeping around. He'd probably broken a lot of promises and many women's hearts. Well, she didn't care because he was no longer on her radar. He was right. She did have one mind-blowing orgasm, but if he expected her to thank him, he was greatly mistaken. She would not feel humiliated because she offered herself to a man who was eager to leave her naked and wanting to spend the night having hot and bothered sex.

She rose a little straighter, crossed her arms, and stood her ground. "I hope you don't expect a thank you, because you aren't the only man who has given me an orgasm."

He laughed, and that infuriated her even more.

"I don't want to get into this with you right now. I have my reasons for stopping before things happened that we couldn't change. I don't know what else to say."

Apparently, he wasn't the man she'd thought he was—a man who could match her in the bedroom and challenge her mentally as well as physically. Nope, Tex was not that guy. That guy probably only existed in her racy romance novels. Those men were just a fantasy of what she really wanted in life.

"I guess that's it, then. Thanks for the flower. Hopefully, I won't kill it." The idea struck her, but she wouldn't feel right taking her frustrations out on a pot of innocent mums.

He opened the door and was about to walk through it, but he stopped. Liza's heart raced. Was he changing his mind? Did he want her no matter what was holding him back?

"Don't forget they need a lot of sunlight." He shut the door behind him.

She stood there for several minutes, trying to figure out what the hell had just happened. That's all he had to say, to remind her to keep a damn flower in the sun. What a night.

She put herself out there by demanding what she needed, and he stopped her. Why would a man who had been with plenty of women in the past just stop all of a sudden? If Tex didn't want her, that didn't mean she wouldn't find another nice, attractive guy to go out with while she was in town. She didn't want to make Anna think she had to entertain her every day and night. She would enjoy going out with a friend, drink some wine, maybe have a little sex.

"Ugh," she groaned as she settled back into bed. She glanced at her book on the floor and groaned even louder. It looked like another sleepless night.

Chapter Eleven

"What in the hell does he have on?" Liza asked over her coffee cup. She was looking at Jake as he slapped paint on the open downstairs room.

Anna chuckled. "A bet gone wrong."

"It must have been some kind of bet to get Jake in a Sparks T-shirt. Didn't he play for Alabama or something?"

"Alabama? Come on, Liz. Haven't I taught you anything about baseball? He played for the Atlanta Rockets. Atlanta. Rockets. Alabama doesn't even have a major league team, for God's sake." Her friend looked about ready to send her to the wolves because she didn't know about a damn baseball team.

"Well, what's with the shirt? Did New York win the World Series or something?" Liza was proud that she remembered the World Series and that it usually took place this time of year.

Anna, on the other hand, wasn't impressed. "What. Am I. Going to do with you? Game one of the World Series isn't until this Friday. But we did win the AL Championship and are in the World Series"—Anna pointed to Jake, who didn't look happy at the moment—"which is why Jake has to wear a New York shirt for the entire day."

"What if New York lost? What would you have to do?"

"I would have to replace my New York Sparks license plate with a Boston one."

Liza knew all too well about the rivalry between New York and Boston. Anna was usually pissed for days if New York lost any of those games. "He plays dirty, huh?"

"He really hates New York, but I wasn't worried. I have faith in my boys." Anna shrugged and leaned back in her cozy leather chair. "You should have come over last night after our walk to watch the game. It was actually pretty entertaining with Jake pacing back and forth in front of the television while cursing at it. I loved it."

Liza took another sip of her coffee before sitting on the table that separated her and Anna. "Now that you mention it, I had a pretty entertaining evening myself."

Anna's eyes grew wide. "Do tell."

"It started with Georgia coming by and ended with Tex leaving me hot and bothered holding a plant."

"What? Why did Georgia stop by? Is she all right?"

"Yeah, she just wanted to talk about men." Liza would have said more, but she thought what she and Georgia discussed was private and not meant to share even with the closest of friends.

"Talk?" Anna questioned.

"Yeah…talk."

Anna didn't push for anything further, as if knowing Liza wasn't going to tell her anything more.

"Did you not hear me say Tex and me being hot and bothered in the same sentence?" That *was* juicy information Liza was dying to let out.

Ever since showing up at the shop that morning, she had been itching to confide in Anna about her night with

Tex. But of course, Jake was around, and Anna was in no mood to talk until her second cup of coffee. She had long ago learned how to deal with Anna and her mornings. She didn't want to talk about baseball when all she really was thinking about was Tex's hands running up and down her body, his mouth on her.

"I did, but I thought you were mad at Tex? What changed between yesterday afternoon and last night to make you hot for him?"

"He came by to apologize and bring me a pot of mums. He looked so tired that I stupidly asked if he wanted to come inside. He obviously did, and I really don't know when things got so out of control. I mean, I was literally out of control, Anna. One minute, he was telling me he was looking for more than the occasional hookup, and the next minute, he has me pressed against the wall, tugging my pants down to my ankles. It's probably because I was feeling like I was lacking since Greg cheated on me, but last night, being with Tex, I felt powerful." Her cheeks flushed at the memory. She unwrapped the scarf around her neck and laid it on her lap.

Anna gave her a look. "Can't say I didn't see that coming. So how was it? He apparently didn't spend the night, or you wouldn't be all bothered right now."

"We didn't have sex," Liza said a little loud. She looked at Jake and was relieved when he never glanced their way.

"I thought you just said—"

"I never meant we had sex…at least, not literally."

Anna nodded, seeming to get her drift. "Why not? It seems there's been a buildup to y'all hooking up. Everyone can see the way you two look at each other, and the way you describe last night, it sounds pretty intense. I didn't think Tex would turn you down for a minute. Wait…did you turn him down?"

And that was where her problems lay. She'd been in that hotel room ready to let her past go, but he hadn't. He'd flat out turned her down. Well, she couldn't say it didn't sting a little, but it wasn't going to get her down.

"Oh, I was already primed and ready. He could have asked me to do anything, and I would have done it, but I wasn't expecting him to say *we can't do this*. He's been with hundreds of women, but for some reason, I'm not good enough." She again looked in Jake's direction, who was still thankfully minding his own business.

"That doesn't sound like Tex."

"You're telling me." Liza groaned. She remembered the moment he pushed her off his lap.

"Did he tell you why?"

"He said some bullshit about us not being able to take anything back. I didn't want to take any of it back. I was ready to experience and have fun in Patience. Tex wasn't. At least I got an orgasm out of it."

Anna laughed. "Yeah, I guess you can put that on the positive side."

Twenty minutes later, Liza insisted Anna show her the rest of the shop. It always seemed as if her personal problems were getting in her way of seeing more than just the downstairs. She wanted to see the bookstore part of the shop. Liza, too, shared a love for reading and could spend hours looking through a bookstore. While she desired more of the erotic romance novels and Anna enjoyed the low-key sensual stories, they both could relate to each other on what it felt like being captivated by an author's tale of lovers.

Liza followed her friend up the staircase to the second floor. She looked at Anna and could only smile. "Wow! It feels like another world up here. It's perfect. You've actually done it. I'm so proud of you."

"I haven't done it yet. As you can see, the shelves are still empty."

"Still." Liza stared at the dark-stained shelving that seemed to go on forever. "It's pretty awesome. How did you even accomplish this look? Didn't you say the previous owners had some kind of children's store here? Where did the shelves come from?"

"That was all Jake and Tex. The upstairs was one of the main reasons we had to hire Tex. Jake couldn't have done this by himself. I swear if he hadn't always wanted to be a baseball player, he totally could get into the remodeling business. He has the skill."

"I'll have to give him that, I guess," Liza admitted. "What's this room over here?" She walked toward one of the other rooms.

"This is going to be the children's library. I thought, after settling into things, I could offer a story time once a week—give the stay-at-home moms and dads a reason to get out of the house and mingle with other parents. Remember Ms. Langley, the librarian in Linden?"

Liza nodded. "Of course."

"She always did things for the kids, and I remember thinking that was a special idea. I guess I tucked it away for future reference."

The kids' room was almost finished. The walls were a basic khaki color with low-to-the-ground white bookcases. Two small wooden tables and chairs sat under the window, and a yellow rug circled the center of the room.

"One of my sister's best friends is a really good artist. I bet I could call and ask her to draw some kind of artwork on the walls," Liza volunteered.

"I thought about letting the kids draw pictures and then me framing and hanging them around the room. It's cheap and personal. What do you think?"

"I like that idea."

"And this over here"—Anna pulled on Liza's arm to move her to the room right beside the kids' room—"is my office." She held out her hands as if she were making some big reveal.

"Uh, Anna, there is nothing in here."

"There will be. I have to focus on everything else right now, but I will get to it. That's not the point, though. I'm finally getting my office."

In the early years, when Anna would talk about opening her own bookstore but then decided people were going to need coffee to drink while reading, she would always describe her office. It never changed. What Liza stared at now was not what Anna had been describing over the years. The walls were baby blue, and only a few storage boxes lay on the hardwood flooring that stretched through the entire house.

Liza smiled. "Yes, you are, honey. You definitely are getting your office."

****

It was late Friday afternoon, and Tex was trying to sneak through the back door of the coffee shop before Bradley showed up to ask what time he was coming by to pick him up for guys' night out. Most of the time they would alternate, always making sure they had a designated driver, but tonight the guys were joining the girls at Ollie's to watch the big game. Tommy and Em would ride together, Jake and Anna would ride together, so that left him and Bradley odd men out. Tex had been ignoring his buddy's calls all day, already knowing why he was calling. Bradley always tried to skip on his turn of playing the safe driver because it meant that he actually had to hang with the boys all night and not venture out back with a blonde, but he also didn't like the responsibility. Well, Bradley was going to have to hitch a ride with Jessie or Georgia for all Tex cared, because Tex was not going to Ollie's.

Maggie called him earlier to tell him that his mom was having a good day and it would probably be okay for him to stay home for the night if he wanted. He didn't have to see himself in the mirror to know he looked like death. Maggie had seen it, his mom had asked if he had been eating and sleeping, and for the last couple of days, Anna had been telling him to cut out an hour or two early so he could get some rest. Except for the lumpy couch, he felt relaxed at his mom's, probably because he knew he could get to her if needed.

Tuesday night, he'd come to the realization that he needed his bed. He'd had every intention of driving straight there after he left his mom's that night, but for some damn reason, he took a left instead of a right and wound up at the Town's Inn.

Tex took a chance on Liza being awake, but it wouldn't have mattered if she wasn't. He had already made the decision to see her. He told her the truth when he said he didn't go there to sleep with her. He said his visit was to apologize, but that wasn't all it could have been.

He'd *needed* to see her, and that only led to him nearly sleeping with her. He already knew how well that would have turned out. She had just been cheated on, she was Anna's best friend, and she would want him to talk to her, something he had no intention of doing with anyone.

"Where are you going?"

Tex didn't stop opening his driver's-side door. "Calling it a day. I'll see you tomorrow morning."

"You're not coming to Ollie's tonight?" Anna asked.

"I'm pretty beat. Getting old sucks."

"We're the same age, Tex. Are you calling me old?" Anna feigned an innocent smile.

She was so damn cute with her ponytail coming loose and allowing tendrils to fall across her face, freckled with mustard-yellow paint.

"I guess I didn't think about that before I said it, huh?" He chuckled. Anna had always been able to do that to him. She could be spitting mad, and still, he couldn't help but smile or laugh at her. He should have grabbed her before Jake weaseled his way back in, but he knew that would have never happened because Anna belonged to Jake. Jake's life was better with Anna in it.

"I'll forgive you if you come out with us tonight. How can you miss game one? Tex, it's the World Series. You are my Sparks partner. You have to be there to help me torture Jake," she begged.

Little did she know she was his weakness when it came to any woman other than his mother. He loved and respected the hell out of her—as a friend, of course—and she could get anything she wanted from him. He looked to the ground, hiding his grin because he couldn't let her know she suckered him in that fast.

"Come on, Tex. You know I will be the only one

cheering for New York in the whole bar. Em doesn't know squat about baseball, Jake will be betting against me, and while I've taught Liza well, she still doesn't hold the same passion as you and I do for the game." Her catlike eyes pleaded with him. "I need you there, pleeeease."

"Fine, but I'm not promising I'll stay the entire game."

"Deal." She kissed him on the cheek.

****

Liza waited on bringing up the fact, but she had to do something before Anna was completely down to nubs. "Girl, you've got to lay off your fingernails. Here"—she pushed the tin of peanuts—"bite on these for a while."

Her friend looked tense. "I mean, come on, our ace is working on three days' rest, and we're getting killed with the home-run ball."

It was an hour and a half into the game, and most people sitting around the table had long ago tuned Anna out, except for Tex. He seemed to share the same tense mood, but baseball didn't appear to dictate his. He was clearly in a foul mood for a whole different reason.

Em and Tommy now sat at the bar, and Bradley and the woman he'd come with were at the pool tables. Georgia had decided not to come out, and no one knew where the hell Jessie was. So that left Liza slowly sipping her glass of wine, trying to keep her mind and eyes off Tex. She'd known it was a very good possibility she would see him tonight, but she'd at least thought Georgia or Em would keep her busy.

She was not so lucky.

Jake looked way too smug and cocky. "What can I

say, sweetness? Your team just really isn't that good."

Anna cut her gaze to Jake, and because he was a smart man, he backed off.

"I'm going to put a few quarters in the jukebox."

"I swear if that man wasn't so sexy, he would be sleeping in a room right next to yours tonight, Liz."

"The rooms around me are unoccupied," she said before she could stop herself. She was bored. What could she say?

Tex choked on his beer, and Liza smiled because it was the reaction she was hoping for. She wanted him to remember their *almost* night together, picture her in her lacy panties, and die of a major hard-on. He might have thought she felt uncomfortable with him there—being a constant reminder that she'd pretty much asked him to have sex with her—but it would take more than that to humiliate her.

He knew that just last week, she'd caught her boyfriend screwing one of his patients.

So she'd let her guard down, had been willing to sleep with him, and he'd turned her away. That was all she needed to know. She could make him rethink playing her just by being her sexy self.

"Tex, want to play a game of pool with me?" The twenty-something who'd come with Bradley ran her hands through Tex's hair.

Who came with one man and hit on another while her date was in the bathroom? These were the types of women Tex went for? Blondie here was screw-worthy but not her? So be it. She should feel relieved that Tex had stopped things when he did.

He barely glanced the woman's way. "Sorry, Leah, but I promised Anna I would watch the game. I'm sure

Bradley will be out of the bathroom in a second."

Leah looked down at Anna with loathing. "Doesn't she have her own man?"

"Don't you?" Anna fired back.

"Bradley and I are just having fun. I'm not tied to a man."

"Why doesn't that surprise me?" Anna laughed without an ounce of humor.

"And what is that supposed to mean? You think because you got Jake to propose to you all of a sudden that he actually pined for you all those years? Why don't you ask him about the fun we had together?"

Liza was proud of Anna because, unlike Liza, she kept her cool. If the backhanded comment upset Anna, she didn't let it show.

"If that makes you feel important, I will. Have fun with my future brother-in-law, because tomorrow you will never hear from him again."

Way to go, Anna!

Leah crossed her arms and achieved the look of making her breasts seem bigger.

Liza couldn't help but laugh.

"And you think you have any control over who Bradley sees? Don't tell me you're screwing Bradley on the side. Maybe I was wrong about you. Maybe you're not as straitlaced as I thought."

"Girrrl, I'm going to let you walk away from my table just because it's the end of a commercial break and I don't want to miss my game, but if you ever come around me mouthing off again about things you obviously know nothing about, I won't hesitate to show you how disgusted women like you really make me." Anna shooed her away. "Now go. My friends and I have a game to watch." She turned her attention back to the television as if Leah didn't exist.

With a scrunched-up nose, Leah stomped back to the pool tables.

Liza directed her attention to Tex, who was looking at her with a grin on his face. She smiled back and felt the electricity that seemed to connect them whenever they were in the same room. How could she be so attracted to a man who for some reason wanted her but at the same time didn't want her? Her mind went to Georgia, and she realized they had a lot in common at the moment.

Jake came back to the table, holding two beers. He handed one to Tex, who thanked him before tipping it to take a drink. "What did I miss?"

When neither Anna nor Tex answered, Liza did. "Just one of Tex and your brother's bar bunnies running her mouth." She stopped to take a drink. "And according to her, she was also one of yours at one time."

Liza and Anna both watched Jake.

"One of mine? I've never been with Leah."

Anna nodded, as if to say *that is settled*. "Good."

Tex shot a gaze at her, and she couldn't help but notice how dark and dangerous he looked. It was as if her comment hurt him in some way. His shoulders stiffened. "And Leah is not one of my bar bunnies either."

"Well, she sure acted like it. Besides, I'm sure you've had plenty just like her."

"You jealous, sweetheart?"

He was daring her to admit she wanted him again, but she was not jealous. She just stated a fact. It was a fact that needed pointing out since one of his women looked at her friend with disgust because Anna was getting all of Tex's attention and she wasn't.

"Please, I just don't see what men see in women like that. What's the appeal?" She was talking aloud but looking at Tex. "Can't y'all see women like Leah are only skin deep and only out to stake their claim? They just want to let the rest of Patience know they've bagged one of the hottest men in town."

"You think I'm hot?" Tex asked sarcastically.

"I was referring to Bradley," Liza said dryly.

Jake burst out laughing. Anna didn't seem to notice the conversation going on around her anymore. Tex leaned back in his chair, stretching out his long legs. He was sitting directly across from her, but because of the small table, his legs rubbed against hers. She didn't move, not wanting to acknowledge how close he was to her.

"What makes you think men like me and Bradley aren't out for the same thing? Maybe we like everyone in town to know that we've been with the homecoming queen and prom queen both."

"There's no way Blondie was homecoming queen."

"Yep," Tex and Jake both confirmed.

"But just for your information, I've never been with her," Tex went on to say. "She mostly hangs with Bradley."

"You don't have to tell me anything." A weight had been lifted off her chest at learning Tex had standards.

Maybe he'd told her the truth the other night. Maybe he was trying to change and look for someone he could have something real with. *Oh. God.* That's why he turned her down. He was looking for someone to have a future with, and he knew she was not that person. For one, she was only visiting. Secondly, she wasn't interested in a relationship this early after a breakup. She was really only interested in sex. Finally, she'd found a man who seemed to understand her needs in the bedroom, and he had just gone off and changed his whole life.

"Liza?" A man wearing a firefighter uniform approached the table.

That got Anna's attention as well as Jake and Tex's.

"Yeahhhh?" She had never seen the guy before, but since it was a Friday night and a big game was on, the bar was pretty crowded.

"I hope you don't mind, but Bradley sent me over to talk to you. I haven't been able to stop looking at you all night."

Tex let out a sarcastic laugh while Anna smiled and nudged her with her elbow. Liza admired his good looks. Filling out his dark-blue uniform was a broad chest and nicely toned biceps. His wide smile matched his friendly blue eyes. Immediately, she was drawn to his charm.

"How can I turn a guy down that says things like that? Last time I was in here, all I found were some very bad pickup lines. It's nice to hear a man who knows how to actually flatter a woman. Why don't you sit down...?"

He held out his hand, and she took it in hers. "Jason Saunders."

She already knew he was a firefighter, and by the patch on his sleeve, he worked or volunteered for the Patience Fire Department.

"So why, out of all these women in here tonight, am I the one you couldn't take your eyes off of?" She cast him a playful smile. She used to love flirting with men, especially men who came in the package of a uniform. They were the best.

Most men were surprised by her bluntness and lack of shyness, but Jason didn't seem to be. It was as if he expected it from her. "You're different. There are a lot of beautiful women in here, but none have the confidence you have."

"And how would you know that?"

"Because most of these women feel they have to wear short skirts and low-cut shirts to attract a man. You know you're sexy and can attract a man in a whole different way. I bet you look sexy in your most unsexiest pajamas."

"Only if you have a thing for Christmas candy," Tex muttered, but it turned out to be loud enough for everyone at the table to stop and look at him. "Ouch, dammit." He rubbed his leg and stared at Anna glaring a warning at him to zip it.

Liza was kind of taken aback at Jason's compliment. She always had confidence and knew how to own her clothing and make it work for her, but it was nice to hear a man say she was pretty without trying to be a Leah or all the other scantily clad women crowding the bar. Not that she was the only woman in the bar who didn't show her boobs. Anna was dressed in her usual jeans and sports shirt. Em did have on a snug dress that showed her curves, but Liza was starting to figure out that Em didn't dress seductively to draw attention to herself. It was just her personality. And who could judge that? Liza had opted for skinny jeans tucked into brown boots with a silky blue cami and cardigan. Since she had new highlights and a slight trim to her hair, she'd decided to add big, bouncing curls. She'd also made her eyes look a little smokier than usual. When she left her hotel room that night, she'd felt sexy again. Jason confirming that only made her night better.

She playfully swatted at his arm. "I know you're just being nice."

"Just honest." He was charming and genuine. "So I take it you're here visiting Anna and Jake?"

"Just Anna." She heard Jake laugh and was glad he found her hatred toward him amusing. "I had to come be a part of her grand opening of the coffee shop and bookstore." She turned to Anna. "Something has just hit me. Have you decided on a name? Because 'coffee shop and bookstore' doesn't do it justice."

"I'm having a hard time with that part. I need some major help."

"Maybe you could have a naming party," Jason suggested.

"A what?" Liza and Anna both asked.

"One of my sisters is pregnant, and when she couldn't come up with a boy's name, her friends threw a naming party. I don't know exactly how it works, but according to my sister, everyone at the party put a name in a basket, then my sister went through each name until she found one she liked." He shrugged. "I don't know. It might help."

"I like that," Anna said. "Thanks, Jason."

"I've heard a lot of people say how excited they are to have a bookstore in town. Right now, everyone has to drive to Knight," he told Anna.

Liza was happy Anna was actually listening and not screaming at the television again.

"We're pretty excited, too. We're going to have an open house in a couple of weeks, just to let everyone in town see the place and hopefully like it enough to shop there. You should come," Anna insisted.

"Only if you like wine," Jake cut in. "My fiancée informed me that beer isn't fancy enough for her big reveal."

Anna kissed Jake. "You'll live."

"You just get off work, man?" Jake pointed his beer to Jason.

"Yeah. We're short on volunteers, so that has me and the other three paid firefighters having to pull a few extra shifts. I got off at seven tonight and thought I would stop by to have a beer and watch a few innings of the game before heading home to sleep for twenty-four hours—that is unless Liza agrees to go out with me tomorrow night." He glanced her way and flashed a quick, charming smile.

Minny stopped by the table and set a drink in front of Tex. He must have signaled for her sometime during the conversation. Instead of the beer he had been drinking for most of the night, Minny gave him something stronger in a glass and on ice. He turned it up and wiped his mouth with the back of his hand.

"Aren't you here to visit Anna? Don't you think it would be rude to spend all your time with someone else?" Tex sounded irritated at her for some reason.

"I'm here to visit Anna and enjoy Patience." She met his gaze evenly. She wasn't going to back down from him, especially since he was the one being rude.

"I understand if you can't. I know you're here for Anna, but you can't blame a man for trying," Jason said.

Before Liza could say anything, Tex opened his big mouth again. "Aren't you married?"

Now *that* got Liza's attention, and Tex knew it would since she had been a victim of a cheating man. Her eyes pleaded for Jason to say that Tex was drunk and didn't know what he was talking about.

Jason had sat there and taken Tex's little comments, dealt with his stares, but this time, she noticed his shoulders stiffen. "I'm divorced."

Tex acted surprised. "That's right, she left you."

"Chill, man. I think Minny needs to cut you off before you get into another bar brawl," Jake said.

"No, it's fine, Jake. For some reason, Tex has a problem with me tonight," Jason said.

"I just think Liza needs to know what she's getting into. Besides, it's public knowledge that your wife left town to get away from you."

"You really don't know what happened. That's between me and Sarah."

What in the hell is going on here? She knew Tex was close to being drunk off his ass, but he sounded angry. Testosterone pulsed around the table. She could pick out Tex's musky, manly smell over all the other men at the table. Heat rolled off him in waves. He had acted pleasant until Jason came over to the table. From then on, Tex had made it clear he didn't approve.

"Well, after you go out with this one"—Tex pointed to Liza—"she will want to know all about your problems and try to help with them. So just be warned that she is very vocal."

Liza put a hand up to stop Tex from saying another word. "Jason, do you want to take me out tomorrow night?"

"Yes." He didn't look one bit rattled by Tex's little hissy fit.

"Then it looks like we'll be going on a date." Liza put her cell number into his phone, then kissed him on the cheek. It was the least she could do after the crap Tex pulled. "Call me after you wake up tomorrow, and we can decide what we want to do."

"I'll do that. See you tomorrow." He told Jake and Anna goodbye but probably felt it was best to ignore Tex, because he didn't say a word as he shrugged past him. He did stop by the bar to say hey to Tommy before leaving.

Liza leaned back in her chair and shot dagger looks at Tex. "What in the hell is your problem? There was no reason to bring up his divorce. Those are personal things—you of all people know about that. There was no reason for you to be so rude to him." Now that Jason was gone, Liza could act as pissed as she wanted.

He rolled his eyes before he straightened and grabbed his glass. "I thought you should know he isn't who he claims. He can come over here and say all the right things, but there is a reason his wife left. I thought you had a right to know before you went out with him."

"Those are the types of things people talk about on a date. But, oh, you've never actually been on one of those, have you? You just like to screw 'em and leave 'em."

"Liza, it's time to calm it down," Anna hissed.

Liza didn't care that once again she was making a scene in the local bar. Tex was out of line, and she wanted to know why.

"No. I want to know why Tex is being an asshole. Jealous?" she asked with a confident smile.

"Why would I be jealous of Jason? He's a divorced man who works too much. What would I get out of being jealous of him?"

"You really don't like that I'm going on a date with him, do you?"

"You do what you want, Liza. I don't have a say in the matter."

"You did last night, but you let me go. Now you have to deal with the fact that another man finds me attractive and wants to show me a good time around Patience for as long as I'm here."

She bent over to pick her purse up off the peanut-covered floor. Tex reached out and grabbed her arm to stop her from walking away. Anna and Jake were still sitting at the table.

"I can't do this with you, Liza," he growled.

"Then let me go. I like you, Tex, and at one time I thought we would have some fun together. For some reason, though, you stopped that from happening. I will not feel ashamed because I put myself out there, but I am putting myself out there again. Jason is a nice guy." She jerked her arm away from his grip. She was about to let the conversation go but had the urge to add, "And at least Jason tried to have a relationship. Yeah, it might've ended in divorce, but he tried. It's more than I can say about some men." She let that sink in for Tex before she spoke to Anna. "I'm going to go after I talk to Em. Call me tomorrow?"

"Be careful, Liz." Anna blew her a kiss.

Liza walked past Tex, but she could still feel the tingles running up her arm where he had touched her. Her breasts, thighs, and stomach clenched at the thought of what that man could do to her. Whatever he was doing to her.

Chapter Twelve

Liza ran her hands through her hair and smiled. God, it was good to get back to feeling more like herself, the person she was longing to be, but while she was satisfied with her decision to put red highlights in her hair, the change wasn't enough—she needed more. She would be lying if she said going out with Jason didn't sound like a great solution to her funk.

A soft tap sounded on her hotel door. She liked a man who was on time.

After she opened the door, he looked her up and down. He was an interesting mix. While he was charming and kind and didn't seem to be the type of man who would ever make a woman feel uncomfortable, he also didn't mind showing a woman he found her attractive.

His dark denim jeans hugged his muscular legs that were probably a result of his firefighter job. The light blue in his shirt matched the color of his eyes. She couldn't help taking a minute to soak it all in.

"You look beautiful," he said.

"You don't look bad yourself."

One corner of his mouth turned up. "Shall we go?"

She grabbed her coat off the bed. He stepped into the room and helped her into it.

"Thank you."

"Mums?" he asked, pointing to the flowers on her

dresser.

"A gift from Tex."

One unruly eyebrow rose. "Gift?" He seemed amused.

Crap. "More like an apology plant. He did something really stupid."

"Something like last night?"

"Well, he did act like an ass last night, but the plant is for another time." Her face heated at the memory of the night he'd showed up at her door. "You ready?" She was glad when he nodded.

After just going through two red lights, they pulled into a Mexican restaurant parking lot. "I hope this is okay. We could have driven to Knight if you preferred. They have a lot more options."

"No, this is perfect. I'm too hungry to drive thirty minutes, then have to wait another thirty minutes for a table."

A host with cat ears and painted-on whiskers showed them to their table.

She looked at him, and he whispered, "Halloween." She'd forgotten Anna told her Patience was celebrating Halloween on Saturday instead of Monday since the kids would have school.

His hand brushed her back as he pulled out her chair.

"You are quite the gentleman. First, with the compliments, then helping me into my coat, and now, pulling out my chair. I don't know what to think about all this."

"I grew up with a sister. Being a gentleman was one thing she required. She might've been younger, but when I got old enough to date, she made sure I knew how to treat a lady."

She nodded. "I say you have a good sister."

After the margaritas arrived, they settled into easy conversation. "So tell me about your sister. I know last night you mentioned that she is—or was pregnant."

"I think Julia told me this morning she is now thirty-one weeks. So in about two months, I will have a nephew. I'm looking forward to it, but I don't know about all the crying." He laughed. "I doubt his and my schedules are going to match well. When I'm going to be home after working twenty-four hours straight and need the sleep, he will pick that time to whine all night. I'm not looking forward to that."

"So you and your sister live together?"

"Yeah. She moved back to town a couple of months ago."

He turned his focus down to his drink, and Liza knew there was more to the story. She wanted to ask but didn't want Tex to be right. Maybe she should let it go.

"She was married to the love of her life. He died five months ago, so I talked her into coming home. I bought my parents' home when they moved to Florida several years back. I helped her pack, and now we are back under one roof together. It was strange for a while, but we've found a way to work around each other. Plus, she needs me there. She can't go through all this by herself."

The love he had for his sister paralyzed Liza. She liked to see a man treat his family with respect and love them through anything. How was this guy still single?

The waitress came by, offering them another round of drinks, but they declined. Jason asked for sweet tea, and Liza settled for water.

She squeezed a lemon into her water. "I'm sorry about Tex last night. I don't know what got into him."

"You really don't know?"

She had the sneaking suspicion he knew what was wrong with Tex. "Why? Do you?"

"It's simple…he likes you."

She held back a snort. "He does not like me." *If he did, he would have slept with me when he brought me the mums*.

"A guy knows when another man is jealous."

"You sound like you're speaking from experience."

He laughed. "Let's just leave it at a man knows."

"I won't pretend to know what goes on in a guy's head, because if I did, I would be a very wealthy woman."

Jason dropped the subject of Tex and his absurd behavior, choosing to ask about her work and family, and she gave him the highlights. She made sure to leave out being a disappointment to her mom because she wasn't the housewife type and about finding Greg with another woman. Some things were not meant to share on a first date.

After leaving the restaurant, they walked a couple of doors down to an ice cream shop. It was almost too cold for ice cream, but she enjoyed the company, and he seemed to as well. He pulled into the Town's Inn parking lot a little after ten.

They stood outside her door as she searched her purse for the keycard. "Thanks for dinner," she said.

"I hate to end the night so early, but I promised Julia I would paint the nursery tomorrow since I'm off."

"When do you go back on call?"

"Monday at seven in the morning."

"Then I understand you having to get home. Maybe we could do this again when you're not at work or on brother duty."

He grinned. "I get off Tuesday morning. I would like to take you out to dinner again."

"Won't you be tired? We could wait until Wednesday or another night. It really will be fine."

"No, I want to see you again, and Wednesday is too long."

"Okay, Tuesday it is. I'll talk to you later." She leaned in and kissed him on the cheek.

He jogged back to his truck but waved before he got inside. She shut herself inside her room, away from the cold. First went her high heels, then her coat. Jason was handsome, charming, and really a good guy, so why wasn't she disappointed when he cut the night short?

****

Liza got to Anna's shop half an hour earlier than she'd told Em to meet her. Notebook in hand, she walked around Anna's bare office and jotted down remarks. She thought back to all her conversations with Anna about her one-day dream office. But now the office was a reality and looking nothing like Anna's vision. Liza wanted to change that, and when she asked Em what she thought at Ollie's the other night, she'd been all too eager to help. Together they were going to paint, decorate, and do whatever necessary to give their friend her dream office.

Liza was starting her second page of notes when Em breezed through the door holding two travel mugs.

"I hope that's coffee?" Liza asked desperately.

"Thought you could use it. Eight in the morning is awful early for someone who had a big date the night before."

Liza took the travel mug Em offered and gulped half

of it down before answering. "I actually, for the first time since being here, had eight full hours of sleep. I think I was just exhausted, and finally, my body just gave out. Before last night, I thought I was going to have to ask Anna if she had any sleeping pills."

"Was the date with Jason that bad?" Em was her usual delightful self.

"Jason was great. He promised his sister he would help her with the baby's room today, so he had to cut the night early. I think he works a lot. I couldn't really be too upset that he needed sleep."

"It's so sad about Julia. I couldn't imagine losing Tommy and having a baby without him around." Em's voice colored with concern. "Did he say how she's doing?"

"He didn't really say, but I imagine she can't be doing that good. He seems committed to helping her through it, though. The way he talked about her was really sweet."

"So I see you've been making notes." Em pointed to Liza's spiral notebook. "What do you have in mind?"

Liza moved around the room and showed Em what she was thinking. Em jumped in and suggested they face the desk toward the doorway and put some type of cabinet or bookshelf behind it. In a little over an hour, they had the basis of what the room would look like. The walls would be sage green. A black desk would sit in front of a distressed cabinet and bookshelf. Some type of armchair would be off in the corner with a couple of blankets so Anna could curl up on cold nights and read or just enjoy a cup of tea while she looked over the books and inventory.

Liza and Em walked back to their cars. Liza had

hoped they went unnoticed by Anna, who was right next door in her and Jake's apartment.

"You sure she doesn't know about us meeting here?" Liza asked.

"No. I told Jake to keep her occupied."

"You told Jake what we were doing." Liza made it clear she didn't think that was a good idea.

"I had to. Who else did you think left the door unlocked for us?"

She hadn't really questioned that, but now that Em brought it up, someone did have to let them in.

"I guess you have a point." As much as Liza hated to admit it, Jake being in on the plan could work to their advantage.

Em volunteered to pick Liza up the next morning to start on their to-do list since the hair salon was closed on Mondays. Em knew her way around Knight, so she drove.

Liza was about to get into her car when she remembered the other thing she wanted to talk to her about. "Hey, Em."

Em stopped by her car. "Yeah?"

"What do you think about planning a naming party for Anna? Jason suggested it since Anna is having a hard time coming up with a name for this." She motioned to the shop. "He said his sister had one because she needed help coming up with a name for her baby. He said something to Anna about it Friday, and she seemed to love the idea."

Em opened her car door and then tossed her purse and keys inside. "That's a unique idea. I love it."

"I was thinking we need to have it pretty soon. I'm getting tired of calling it a shop or coffee shop and bookstore. What do you think about next Sunday afternoon?"

"Sounds good, girlie. I'll come up with a list of people to invite, and we can go from there."

"It will be fun." Liza waved. "I'll see ya tomorrow," she added before slipping into her car.

****

Liza woke Tuesday morning to her cell phone shrilling next to her ear. She rubbed her eyes and glanced at the clock sitting beside her phone on the bedside table. Seven a.m.? Who would call so early in the morning? She didn't recognize the number flashing on the screen, but it was a local number.

She hit send and put her cell to her ear. "Hello?"

"Honey, did I wake you? I forget sometimes that you young folks don't get up like us old ones. You go back to sleep and call me when you get up."

Liza knew immediately that Pearl was on the other end of the line. Her soft voice gave it away. She cleared her throat and tried to sound more awake. "No, I was just getting up. How are you, Pearl? Is there something you need? Is Maggie still sick?"

"I'm doing well. Maggie is not sick, but I called her this morning and told her to spend the day pampering herself. Ever since she got over that bug, she's looked so tired. There's no reason for her to drive all the way to Patience just to hang out with me."

Liza wondered if Tex knew about this. She doubted it. "Are you sure that's a good idea?" She didn't *know* if Pearl knew who Maggie was and why she was there. Liza didn't know exactly why Maggie was there either.

"I think it's a wonderful idea because I have something else in mind today." Excitement rang in

Pearl's voice. "I just have to be home before my soap comes on."

"What do you have in mind?"

"I want you and me to have a day out doing woman things. My treat. What do you say?"

How could Liza turn such a sincere offer down? "Give me an hour, and I'll be over."

She hung up the phone and made her coffee. It was way too early, considering she'd stayed up past midnight searching the internet for ideas for Anna's office surprise. They'd bought the paint from the hardware store Tommy and Jessie's family owned. In Knight, they'd found the perfect desk and swivel chair to match. They'd also come across a beige corduroy chair at the same furniture outlet she and Anna went to last week. Em was going to have Tommy haul the furniture on his flatbed truck and keep it in her garage until they were ready to set everything up. They surprisingly had made a lot of ground, but a lot more needed doing.

She planned to go to Knight tomorrow to check out more places Em recommended, and as much as she hated it, she needed to ask Jake a favor. She would do that later, before her date with Jason, because right now she was spending the day with Pearl and actually looking forward to it.

A little before nine, she pulled into Pearl's driveway. She thought she might see Tex's truck there, but it wasn't. Probably a good thing. His being there would only complicate things and ruin her and his mother's day out. He most likely wouldn't agree with Pearl insisting that Maggie stay home while she spent time with Liza. Well, who cared what Tex thought? She was looking forward to her girls' day with Pearl. As long as Pearl had a good time, that was all that mattered.

Pearl came out her front door the same time Liza put the car in park. Liza got out to help her into the car. "You look nice."

Pearl was dressed in a pants suit with an animal-print silk scarf, and gold dangly earrings hung from her ears. She carried a large handbag, causing Liza to smile because she was guilty of the same thing. Her motto was that a woman could never carry enough stuff. Pearl even wore a light foundation with a touch of blush applied to her cheeks. She was a very pretty woman, and Liza only imagined that she'd been a real beauty back in the day. It was a wonder she never remarried after Tex's father skipped town.

"I was thinking we could have breakfast at the diner first. I'm starving, and the coffee I drank an hour ago is gone. Unless you've already eaten?" Liza said.

"I was thinking the same thing. After we fill our stomachs, I want us to go to Cut & Curls." It sounded like Pearl already had the day planned.

"Then I say we better get started." Liza backed out of the driveway and navigated through the streets until she was back on Main Street.

They had to park at the courthouse and walk across the street to C.C.'s, but Pearl didn't seem to mind. In fact, she seemed to enjoy the fresh air and cool morning.

Pearl picked at her plate while Liza ate every bite of her fluffy pancakes. She noticed that after Pearl pushed her plate away, she took out a pill organizer from her purse and took two or three different pills. Most elderly folks took medications, but she was curious only because Tex refused to tell her anything about his mom. Pearl would only allow Liza to pay the bill if she could leave the tip. Liza agreed.

Cut & Curls was just a few buildings down from the diner, so they walked.

"Liza, Ms. Avery, what are y'all doing here?" Em hollered out above Otis Redding tearing it up on the radio. "Ms. Avery, didn't Ms. Edna just do your hair a couple of weeks ago?"

"She did, but I thought she could come up with something different. I'm in need of a change."

Em looked shocked. "Edna is in the storage room going through our supplies right now. She should be finished in a couple of minutes. Why don't you take a seat and look through these books? You might find what you're looking for."

"Thank you."

Liza took Em off to the side. "Just don't let Edna do something too crazy. I don't want to make Tex madder at me than he already is. If I bring his mom home looking hot, he will have a conniption fit."

"Don't worry. It has been a long time since Edna has done something other than the respected over-fifty ladies' haircut. Where is Maggie?"

Liza told her the story about Pearl calling her that morning and asking if she wanted to spend the day together. "I couldn't say no. She is such a nice person, and I do like hanging out with her. I told her to call me anytime Maggie couldn't be around."

"Does Tex know?" Em asked.

"I don't think so, but I haven't asked either. Luckily, we haven't run into him. I figure we're pretty safe in here."

Em lowered her voice. "Do you think you should call him? I mean, what if he stops by the house and Pearl isn't there? You want to talk about a conniption fit. He'll blow a gasket if he finds out you took his mother out without running it by him first."

"Pearl is not a puppy, Em. She needed to get out of that house for a day. Have you seen her? She put makeup on and everything."

"Just don't say I didn't warn you."

Liza was draping her coat on the back of a chair when who she perceived was Edna walked from the back of the shop. She had to be around the same age as Pearl. She was tying a cape around her faded flowered top when she noticed Pearl sitting in a vacant chair.

"Pearl, what you doing here? You're not scheduled for another cut till after Thanksgiving."

Pearl abandoned her chair and the book she was flipping through. "Just spending the day with Tex's new girlfriend."

Liza felt the blood drain from her face. She stumbled over her own feet when the fragile woman pulled her to her side. Liza looked to Em, pleading for help, but Em looked to be just as shocked and, for the first time, at a loss for words.

Edna frowned. "You must be why that boy is so distracted that he forgot about my leaves and dropping me a new load of mulch last Friday. I guess my plans for working around the yard Saturday could be changed for the sake of two lovebirds."

Liza cleared her throat, plastered on an awkward grin, and held out her hand to the scary woman. "I'm Liza. I'm a friend of Anna's." She hoped Pearl didn't notice she left out the part of being Tex's girlfriend. It was too strange to say aloud, and she liked Pearl, but not enough to say she and her son were lovebirds.

Edna's expression softened a bit but quickly changed back to looking unpleasant. "You from New York or something?" She ran her gaze up and down Liza's appropriate outfit.

Liza told herself that the woman was important to Anna. With anyone else who would have dismissed her, she would have given some smart-ass comment, but she held her tongue. Anna so owed her for this. "No, I live in Linden. Anna has told me so much about you and the fond memories from when she was a child. You must be so happy she is back in Patience."

Anna's onetime neighbor grunted. "I'm surprised she is fond of anything concerning her childhood or finds anything good in it."

"Well, I know for a fact she's fond of her memories of you."

Edna quickly turned her attention from Liza to Pearl. "Pearl, would you like me to go ahead and trim your hair?"

"What did you mean when you said Tex has been distracted?" Pearl asked Edna.

"I phoned him a week in advance and requested he come out and drop a load of mulch so I could cover the beds around my house. When I got home last Tuesday afternoon, it was obvious he forgot. I called his office and must have lit a fire under one of his employees, because when I was getting ready to leave for work this morning, he was pulling down my driveway. He probably has too much on his plate. Hopefully, the rain will hold off so I can get out in the yard this weekend."

Pearl dug through her handbag. It took several minutes for her to find what she was looking for. She pulled out a cell phone. "I'll call him and tell him to mulch those beds for you. You shouldn't be out there doing all that work alone. My boy can find the time to at least do that for you since he put you off. I just knew there was something going on with Avery Landscaping."

Liza felt bad for Tex. Edna obviously didn't care that he was running himself thin between the coffee shop and bookstore, keeping up with his landscaping customers, and sleeping on his mother's couch every night. She wanted to defend him, but to do that, she would have to bring it to Pearl's attention that she was part of the reason her son was so tired. He'd most likely forgotten about Edna because on the Tuesday he was supposed to work on her yard, he was too busy taking care of his mom after Liza found her walking around town.

It hit Liza that if Pearl called Tex, he would find out she was not at home and not with Maggie. She sighed in relief when Edna grabbed the phone from Pearl's hands.

"You'll do no such thing. I like working in my yard. If I wanted him to mulch my beds, I would have told him to. Now quit being silly and tell me if you want me to do your hair or not."

"Liza, honey, will you hand me that hair-styling book?" Pearl pointed to the chair she'd sat in before Edna came into the room. Liza gave her the book, and Pearl opened it to a dog-eared page.

"Can you do this?" She held the book up for Edna.

Edna looked over her glasses. "You sure you want me to do that?"

"Yes. Can you do it?"

"Woman, I've been doing hair for thirty-plus years. Sit down in this chair while I go get the color ready." She looked to Em. "Grab her a cape."

Liza reached for the book on Edna's workstation. There were only two pictures, and since one of them was of a sixteen-year-old girl with long blonde hair, Liza figured the picture on the next page was what Pearl had in mind. She stared at it while Em wrapped a cape around Pearl's neck. She wanted this? Liza thought they were going to Cut & Curls for Pearl to get a trimmed version of what she already had—not something totally different. Tex was going to kill her.

Edna came back into the room, stirring the color mixture. "This is semipermanent, but still, you need to be sure, Pearl."

"I'm sure, Edna. I was also going to see if Liza and I could have a mani and pedi."

Liza spoke up. "You don't need to do that, Pearl."

"Yes, I do. Didn't we decide to have a girls' day?" Pearl asked.

"We did."

"All right, then." Pearl's smile reflected in the mirror in front of her, and the gesture warmed Liza to know she was in some way responsible for putting it there.

While a woman named Katherine applied a deep purple color to her nails, Liza watched and waited for Edna to finish with Pearl's hair. For the past hour, she'd tried to not look panicked, but Tex giving her one of his pointed stares while reminding her to stay out of his business replayed over and over in her head. She was really not in the mood to go round two or three with him.

Em gave her several sympathetic smiles as Pearl went on and on to every woman in the shop how she was so proud that Tex finally found a good girl to date. Liza internally groaned, but Pearl looked so damn happy she couldn't remind her of their past conversation over tea—that she and her son were not a couple. She wasn't sure they were friends. That even if Tex hadn't turned her down the other night, they still wouldn't have any type of future. In fact, she had dinner plans with Jason that night.

"What do you think, Liza? Is it too much?" Pearl asked as Edna twirled the chair around.

Pearl beamed. Liza nibbled on the inside of her cheek because she was nervous. She really wanted to give Pearl the reaction she expected. When she looked up from blowing her nails, she was amazed. Pearl looked five to ten years younger. Her once gray hair had light-brown highlights running through it. Edna must have given her a slight trim because her bangs swept to one side, right above her brow, with the rest of her hair just as short as it was before. Instead of what Liza liked to refer to as the "old lady" haircut, Pearl's hair now had layers that framed her oval face.

Liza left her chair, forgetting about her wet nails and bare feet. She grabbed Pearl's hand and squeezed it. "You look stunning."

Pearl lightly squeezed back. "Thank you, dear. Now let me get some color on my nails, and we can head to our next destination for the day."

"What about your pedicure?"

"I'll wait. It'll give us a reason to get together another day. Plus, I want us to hit the Casual Dress. I want to start going back to church."

Edna removed Pearl's cape. "It's not even noon. You have more than enough time to get a pedicure and go by the dress shop before it closes at four."

"Edna, you know I have to get home before two to

watch my soap."

"You need to get a DVR, Ms. Avery," Em told her.

"A what?" Pearl looked at Em as if she were speaking another language.

"DVR," Em said again. "It allows you to record your shows, then go back to fast forward, rewind, or even pause through them. You can even record several shows at once."

Pearl was sold. "Liza, when we get home, we're calling to order me one of those DVRs."

Liza nodded before laughing.

After spending another thirty minutes at Cut & Curls, they walked the short distance to a women's clothing store. It was in the stretch of buildings between the diner and hardware store. After Pearl found a couple of shirts, two pairs of dress shoes with small heels, and four fall-colored tops, Liza had Pearl home five minutes before her daytime show started. Pearl asked her to stay, but Liza wasn't that much into soap operas. Liza promised to tell Tex that he needed to order her a DVR so she wouldn't have to be home by a certain time every day. She gave her word, knowing full well she didn't have any idea when she would see Tex again. Nevertheless, when she made a promise, she intended to keep it, so she would have to call him before her date with Jason and deal with him being a smart-ass.

Speaking of her date, Jason had called when she and Pearl were picking out shoes, but planning a date with one man while the mother of another man thought she was dating her son was rude. She'd ignored his call until after leaving Pearl's house. He mentioned them having dinner and maybe seeing a movie in Knight.

Before she could think about her date, she had to do

something she had been dreading all day, ask Jake for a favor—and, boy, was he going to love her needing him to do something for her, but for Anna, Liza would do just about anything.

Chapter Thirteen

"You took my mother out?" Tex demanded.

"Hi to you, too."

Damn. Liza stood in front of him, looking too damn fine for a woman who was headed to Bradley's for the night to watch a baseball game—because that's where Anna was, and surely, that was where Liza was going to be. Her snug, long-sleeved navy dress hugged every one of her curves, and God, the heels she wore, a color matching her ivory skin, were high enough to make her almost eye level with him. Her legs looked long and lean, and he wished they were wrapped around him at that very moment.

Why hadn't he slept with her when he had the chance? Right—he'd been on an off day, having a conscience and thinking before acting. What was it with this woman? Why couldn't he just sleep with her and get her out of his system? Would that really be that bad? Yes, it would, because Liza wouldn't just want sex. She would want him to reveal things about his life that he wasn't ready to face. He liked living in denial. Denial was good for him right now. He didn't want Liza getting in his head and making him realize how alone he really was in the world. She would know how pathetic he was because it bothered him more than it should have that his mother changed her hair and wanted to go back to church.

"Hi. Now, why did you feel the need to go behind my back and change my mother? I thought I made it perfectly clear I wanted you to stay out of my business."

Liza's eyebrows rose, and okay, she looked as if she could spit nails. "Change your mother? What are you, five years old? I didn't change anything. Your mother called me. She asked me to take her out for the day, and because I actually like her, I agreed. Not everything revolves around you, Tex. Pearl has a right to change her hair color if she wants. I happen to think she looks beautiful, and if you would take the time to see how happy she is right now, you wouldn't be interrupting my night to yell at me for something so ridiculous. Find a life, a bar slut, anything. Just stop finding reasons to show up at my door whenever you feel like it, because I do have a life."

He laughed. "Don't flatter yourself, sweetheart. I don't get up in the morning and start thinking of ways to see you. Besides, what social life do you have in Patience that makes you dress like that?" He gestured to her attire as his nonthinking body part got hard.

She let go of the door and, with a smug grin, crossed her arms. "I have a date."

The swell of her breasts left him with the urge to reach out and pull her close to him so he could feel them pressed against his chest. What was that she said? "With who?"

"Jason. This will actually be our second date. Unlike you, he doesn't growl like some rabid dog every time he sees me."

Jason? Second date? She'd flirted with Jason at Ollie's Friday night, but he just chalked it up as her trying to show him what he was missing. He never expected her to actually take Saunders up on his lame offer. The end of that night, he'd tried to block all of it from his mind, so maybe he hadn't allowed himself to be aware of the fact that Liza really did like Jason. Was he jealous? Hell, no.

"Where's he taking you? The diner for a cherry float?"

"Now who's getting into whose business?"

Okay, he was technically butting into her life while keeping her at a safe distance, but this was different…how, he didn't know, it just was. She was new to town and didn't know the locals like he did. He knew Saunders was a decent guy, but Liza didn't know that. For all she knew, he could be a serial killer who chopped his dates up after their second date.

"What do you really know about your date?"

"You're still crossing into my business, buddy." Her tone spoke volumes. He sensed she was losing patience with him and his obvious indication that Jason was a bad guy.

He was reaching for straws, but something inside him broke, and he didn't care anymore. "Just tell me what you know, Liza. He has a past with women."

"And you don't?" she shot back. "It's common knowledge, the many women you've been with. Now, if that is not a past with women, I don't know what is. Jason is a good guy, and you know it. Why are you so against him and me going out and having a little fun? You turned me down, Tex. Do you not get that?" She used her index finger to tap her temple. "I put myself out there, and against my better judgment, I was willing to sleep with you, but you left. You lost your chance, so now I am going out with a nice guy who finds me attractive and nice to talk to. He will be here soon, so you need to leave. Oh, and by the way, your mom wants you to order her a DVR from the satellite company."

"Let me guess," he growled. "You gave her that idea, too."

"No, that was all Em and Edna. Pearl just wanted me to tell you since she thinks I am your girl."

That took him aback. For a moment, he stared at her blankly. "What's that supposed to mean? Why would she think that?"

"I have no idea. When we had tea last week, she thought we were a thing. I told her we just met and that I'm in town for Anna. She looked disappointed but went on to say that I would be good for you. She realized Maggie is not your type."

"At least she finally figured that part out. She was embarrassing Maggie every time she brought up the notion we should go to dinner. I like Maggie, but only because she is good to my mom." He didn't know what to think about the rest of the conversation she'd had with Liza.

Did his mom really think Liza would be the perfect woman for him? For most of his life, his mom had overlooked his wandering ways when it came to the opposite sex. She knew he didn't date but still seemed to have women around when he needed one. It had been just recently that she took an interest in who he spent time with. Now his mom had it in her head that he and Liza had a thing for each other. *Great*. He didn't want to confuse her and get her hopes up. He thought her talking endlessly about her day out with Liza was just her being happy to get out of the house and spend the day with someone other than him and Maggie. Not that his mom didn't enjoy having Maggie around—he knew she did—but it had to be refreshing to be around another person. She was becoming attached to Liza, and he didn't have the heart to tell her that Liza had no interest in him. Or was it him who didn't have any interest? He really didn't know anymore.

"What did you say to her today to make her think we are a couple?" He stopped, then added, "Did you tell her about last week?"

She rolled her eyes. "Yeah, Tex, that's me. I told her you showed up at my door looking like death because you have slept on her couch almost every night I've been here. Then when I asked you to come in and take a break from thinking about her or working every second of the day, you pleasured me with your mouth but in the end played me like a fool, because you are no longer interested in the occasional roll in the hay, and that's all I would be to you. Yeah, that's exactly what I did." She started to slam the door, but he blocked it with his body.

He didn't want to think, to feel, to need her the way he did.

He inhaled a deep breath, then released it slowly. "Is that why you think I left you half-naked in bed?"

Her strong stance weakened a bit. He seemed to have had just as intense of an effect on her as she did on him.

"What else am I supposed to think?"

"The last thing I wanted to do was leave you." Every inch of her was nice to look at, but he settled on her eyes and watched as she bit her lower lip, feeling it clear to his groin. "I mean, look at you, Liza. I would have to be half-blind to not want to stay with you in that bed twenty-four hours, and I don't mean to sleep." He motioned toward the bed but never let his gaze leave the depths of hers.

She threw her hands in the air. "Why are you doing this, Tex?"

"Doing what?" he asked, confused. "Telling you the truth?"

"No. Why are you here, once again, saying all the right things but not meaning a damn one of them? I really don't get you."

Why did she not see he was trying to be a decent guy? The kind of guy she deserved to be with. Liza was everything opposite of what he usually found in his company. She was strong and confident and didn't rely on the compliments of a man to make her feel competent and worthy. She didn't need him, and while she was only in town for a short time, she didn't need to be bogged down by the likes of him and his currently messed-up situation.

"I'm not trying to jerk you around. I honestly mean every word, and I think you know it. I know you've noticed when we're in the same room, we always seem drawn together. We are electric. We would be electric in bed together."

"Again, why are you saying these things to me now? You keep forgetting a very important part in all your big talk—you walked out on me."

"I'm here now."

He stepped into her space, and when she didn't retreat, he reached for her hand. Bringing her fingers to his lips, he brushed a kiss across them. It was an odd gesture by him because it seemed so intimate. Why he was taking things slow with her, he didn't know, because slow was not what was in his mind. He wanted things hard and fast, and after he had her that way, he might have the patience to give her body the attention it so deserved.

His hands ached to run the length of her body. He longed to cup her ass, to bring her closer and show her the full extent of his desire for her. She needed to know he was not bullshitting her, that he wanted everything about her, except her expectations. That's why he was taking things slow. It hit him—he kept her an arm's length so she would finally realize she was too good for him.

Her eyelids fell shut. He stared at her for a short time and could have groaned aloud because the scene was almost erotic.

"Uh-mm."

Liza's eyes flashed open, and Tex turned around at the sound of someone clearing their throat. Jason. He blew out a quiet, irritated breath. Just what he wanted—an interruption.

Jason looked reasonably calm while holding a bunch of mismatched flowers. "Am I interrupting?"

"Jason." Liza cleared her throat and looked at Tex. "I have a date to get to. You need to leave."

He stared into her eyes, searching for regret in what they were feeling and maybe about to do if lover boy hadn't showed up, but all he saw in the hazel depths was heat and longing. Seeing that wanting on her face assured him that what was going on between them would not be a one-night affair. Who was he kidding? Once he got inside her, he knew he would want more. God, when was the last time someone needed him like that? Never. In his thirty years, he'd never witnessed a woman with so much desire for him in her eyes. It was a longing that went way past just being sexual.

But there would be a time for them to finish what they had been setting up the past week and a half. He nodded and realized he still held her hand tightly in his. He squeezed it before he let it fall to her side.

When he turned from Liza, he stopped at Jason. "Man, I want to tell you I'm sorry about the other night at Ollie's. I was out of line bringing up Sarah, what must have been a difficult time for the both of you...and clearly personal. I hope we can write it up as me being drunk and—"

"Jealous," Jason said.

"No, I was going to say having a stressful week."

Jason grinned, probably not believing a word Tex said. "If you say so, Tex. Don't worry about it. I've been an ass before myself."

"Thanks, Saunders."

Tex walked the short distance to his truck, leaving Liza and Jason to their date. That was, if Jason hadn't seen what was going on in Liza's doorway and still wanted to see her. Tex sure as hell wouldn't want to go out with a woman who had eyes for another man.

****

"How long have you been standing there?" Liza asked.

"Usually, when someone asks that question, it means they have something to hide." Jason smiled. He seemed pretty calm, not the reaction Liza expected.

"I know how that must have looked. Tex showed up to yell at me for taking his mom out today."

"He seems to show up a lot, huh? I heard about you and Ms. Avery hitting the town today. Did y'all have fun? Kenny's wife said Ms. Avery looks years younger."

"Who's Kenny?"

"He's a firefighter I work with. His wife said she saw you and Pearl at Cut & Curls. He also heard y'all were going to Casual Dress."

"She called me this morning and asked if I would take her around. I like spending time with her, but I was still back in time to get ready for our date. I *am* ready for our date. Let me grab my purse, and we can go." She talked a mile a minute, trying to make him understand what actually happened.

"Kenny's wife also heard Pearl telling everyone that you and Tex are seeing each other."

"I can explain that. See—"

Jason shook his head. "You don't have to explain yourself to me, Liza. I like you and was looking forward to getting to know you better, but we are not serious. I won't come between two people who look at each other the way you and Tex do or try to make you feel bad about it." He held out the colorful array of flowers. "Take these."

She accepted them and still felt the need to explain. "I barely know Tex. We are not a thing. Besides his need to flirt with me, there is nothing going on between us. We can still go out tonight. You are not standing in the way of anything."

"Tex is a good guy. I've known him a long time. I've seen him with a lot of women but never have seen him try to stake his claim to one. I honestly didn't think he ever would. There is something about you—and hell, I can't really blame the guy. You should call him."

She opened her mouth to disagree, but he was already walking away. After shutting the door, she knocked her head against it several times. Jason had every right to lash out, yell, or at least throw the flowers in her face. She hadn't expected him to kindly remove himself from the picture and encourage her to go out with Tex. Who did that? The perfect guy, that's who.

He was right. They had only gone on one date, and nothing was holding them together. He was an attractive man who was so kind and understanding, but he was not Tex.

Damn Tex.

A kicking sound came from the bottom of her door. She opened it and stepped back. "How did I know it would be you?"

Tex's body rubbed against hers as he stepped into the room. Her body liked the feel of him, even if it was only a light touch, and her senses liked the scent she had grown to recognize as only his.

"I don't know the answer to that. How did you know I would come back after Saunders left…because I did know he would cancel your date after he saw us together?"

"I guess you're happy now?"

"I won't lie to you. Yes, I am thrilled you didn't go out with him tonight."

She shrugged. "I can't really be mad at you. For some reason, all logic leaves my brain when you come around. I don't like it."

"I love that I get to you." He sat down on the edge of the bed, tugging her with him, bringing her between his legs. "Let's do something Thursday night." His fingers slightly stroked the palm of her hand.

"But you're here now."

"Are you saying what I think you're saying?" He raised his eyebrows.

"Maybe we should just give in and finally do *this*."

"Why, Ms. Dyer, are you telling me I'm only good for a quick roll in the hay? I think I at least deserve dinner before you take advantage of me."

"You're such a smart-ass." She tried to sound annoyed, but the smile she let show gave her intent away.

"So is that a yes to dinner…and possible sex?"

"I don't know. What would everyone around town think if I went out with two different guys in the same week?"

"Nobody knows you in town. You'll have to come up with a better excuse than that."

"What makes you think I'm trying to come up with a reason not to go on a date with you? It's a very good possibility that I simply don't *want* to go out with you."

She liked watching him squirm a bit. He needed to know she didn't give in easily and that if he wanted a second chance with her, he had to actually beg.

"It's not fun being played, is it?" she asked.

"How many times do I have to tell you I was not playing you? Damn it, Liza, I like you. I want to cook you dinner Thursday night. I would suggest tomorrow, but my mom decided she needs to start going back to church, which means I have to start going back. I'm trying here, but you can't seem to let my judgment call go—"

"I'll let you cook me dinner, Tex," she whispered near his ear, followed by kissing his cheek.

"God, woman, why do you have to be so difficult sometimes?"

"I just wanted assurance that you meant it."

"Be at my house at six."

"It's a date."

****

Liza told herself she was only wearing dusty-pink, see-through panties with matching bra under her favorite pair of denim jeans and new orange off-the-shoulder top because she needed to do laundry. But who was she kidding? She wanted Tex to crave her body as he stripped every stitch of clothing from her, using only his teeth.

She had no doubt he would be an amazing lover when they finally got together. It felt as if she had been waiting for months to be in his bed, but in reality, it had only been a couple of weeks since she first laid eyes on him and knew she was in deep trouble. They were both used to getting what they wanted, and when they finally got together, things were bound to be intense.

The quick drive to Tex's home was only partly due to her lead foot on the accelerator.

She reapplied her lipstick and checked her hair a last time before stepping out of her car.

He opened the door as she walked onto the porch. She tried not to gawk at his presence and the way he made her stomach drop to her knees. The fact he could do this to her with only a flash of his seductive smile was unfair.

He looked her up and down, and a grin spread across his stubbled face. "You look amazing." Touching her hair, he said, "I love the red."

"Em did it."

"It seems to fit you more. It gives you a sexy siren look." He took her coat and hung it on one of the several hooks in the entryway. Under the hooks were a pair of scuffed work boots and brown loafers. The dress shoes were unexpected, but he did say he had to take his mom to Wednesday-night Bible study.

"Something smells wonderful." The room smelled of garlic bread, and her stomach growled in response.

"I hope you like spaghetti. I just finished tossing a salad, and the bread is in the oven."

She followed him to the living room. It was typical for a man living alone—beige sectional, a wide-screen television, and *Sports Illustrated* and gardening magazines on the coffee table. A few pictures of him and his mom sat on the mantel above the fireplace. Her heart went out to him because something big was happening with Pearl, and she wanted him to trust her with it.

"I could eat anything right now. I got so caught up shopping today that I forgot to eat lunch." She took in the room. "Your house is nice, not exactly what I expected."

"How is that?"

"I guess I pictured milk crates for end tables and plaid, hand-me-down furniture. I like the different shades of blues, creams, and deep browns you combined. You did good."

"I can't take all the credit. Except for the flat-screen, my mom did everything else before—" He stopped midsentence and cleared his throat.

She didn't let the opportunity pass. "Before what?"

"Just before I got really busy with the remodel. It takes a lot of my time, and I don't really have time to go shopping with her. I told her that instead of worrying about my place, she should do a little updating to her own. She needs to start with getting a more comfortable couch."

Before she knew she was talking aloud, it was too late to stop. "I could help. I mean, I have free time and enjoy the challenge. I could take your mom shopping if you like."

His expression turned soft and warm while his eyes were the perfect mixture of green and sapphire. "You don't have to do that."

She punched his arm and nearly knocked him off balance. "I know I don't have to. I want to. I like spending time with your mom, and I think she really liked getting out of the house the other day. I know you have your reasons for not liking her decision to change a few things about herself, but she really was beaming the whole day. I wish you could have been there. If you had, maybe you wouldn't be so mad at me."

"I'm not mad at you, Liza."

"Since when?" she asked, shocked and relieved.

"Since I picked her up for church last night and saw how beautiful she looked. Church has never been my thing, but I didn't really mind it because she was so happy. I didn't even mind when she wanted to stay after the service to chitchat with the ladies' class. I guess I should thank you for giving her a day like Tuesday. I even called today to have a serviceman come out and install the damn DVR. She's already planning for next week and told me to tell my girlfriend to expect a call from her."

She stood frozen as the word *girlfriend* settled in her mind. The comment was meant to be carefree and not so serious, but there was something very serious about the way he said it.

They were saved by the timer going off in the kitchen. "You ready to eat?"

He held his hand out, and she gladly took it.

Tex escorted her to a kitchen chair, then he waited

on her. He pulled out all the stops for the evening. She let the wine linger for a bit on her tongue and realized she'd had the same wine before—recently.

"I had Minny get us a bottle. I know nothing about wine, and you seemed to like this kind."

She smiled sweetly because he had taken the time to think of her when planning their date.

They sat across from each other and fell into easy conversation. She asked about his landscaping business and how he learned to build and remodel things. She was amazed that he'd taught himself, starting with simple things around his mother's house, then moved from there. He told her about the Patience softball league and playing the outfield.

"So what about your family?" he asked.

"I grew up in a normal household, I guess. My mom is a homemaker, my dad works in insurance, and my sister has decided to follow in my mom's footsteps, having a family, the white picket fence, and all." She picked at a piece of garlic bread, trying not to show her emotions regarding her family and her mother wanting her to be something else.

She failed because he asked, "Why do I feel there is more to the happy-family routine? And don't say it's nothing."

Damn. He could read her better than she thought.

"Sometimes, it's hard growing up in a small town, much like Patience, and everyone expects you to marry and have two or three kids before the age of thirty. Most of the girls I went to high school with are engaged or married to their high school sweethearts. I don't let it get to me for the most part, but every now and then, I wonder if something is wrong with me, because I'm nothing like what people expect. I guess that's why I stayed with Greg for so long. When I was with him, I felt like the daughter my mom wanted me to be. Don't get me wrong—my mom is one of my biggest fans and always supported me through college and my need to have a fulfilling career, but sometimes she lets it slip and asks when I'm going to get married or when I'm going to give her another grandchild. My dad, however, seems to understand how career-minded I am."

Had she revealed too much, too fast? Showing her vulnerability about her age and lack of family was not like her. She felt as if a weight had been lifted off her shoulders.

"You have to do what makes you happy. It doesn't matter what anyone else thinks about your life. You can't be something you're not. I don't want you to be anyone else." His voice was so gentle and honest.

"I know that's true. Nevertheless, even though I have a career and don't plan to give it up, I still want a family. I want love in my life."

"Then you will have those things," he said simply. "You are one of the most self-assured women I've ever met, and if you want something bad enough, I don't doubt you will get it in the end. Is it possible that you are reading into your mom's comments all wrong? My mom has started trying to set me up, and now she thinks I'm dating you. That doesn't mean I think she isn't proud of me and the life I carved for myself. She just wants me happy, and I guess—" He pursed his lips. "—to know that I will be taken care of."

She thought about what he said. Had she secretly been accusing her mom of not being proud of her because she, herself, wasn't satisfied with her life? Could it be possible she was using her mom as an excuse, a reason to take a second look at her life and choices? She took a sip of her wine and shrugged. "Maybe. I don't know. I never thought of it that way. I just automatically take her suggestions as her wanting something more for me, like she isn't proud of the woman I am right now."

"I don't know your mom. I just don't like you being so hard on yourself."

"Thanks."

He stood and started to clear the table.

Being there with him, sharing a meal and conversation, seemed normal. Even though she'd said more than she intended to him, or anyone else for that matter, she didn't mind that she'd told him about her feelings toward her mom.

His jeans fit his ass perfectly, and she couldn't stop the slight tingle between her thighs. She didn't find it fair that he had seen her almost naked and she hadn't yet seen him. They were going to have to change that.

She didn't want to interrupt him because he looked sexy being all domestic, but she had to ask. "Why don't you trust me?"

He stopped loading the dishwasher. "What do you mean?" He wiped his hands on a dishrag and leaned back on the counter, his ankles crossed.

"I've not held back once with you. You know about my family, Greg…me losing my job. I've told you a lot more than you've confided in me. Most people find it easy to talk to a therapist, not that I want you to look at me that way, because we are something else completely. I just don't get why you can't talk to me, give me something."

"My life is complicated, Liza."

"Everybody's life is complicated, Tex."

"I can't."

She had asked him several times about his situation, and every time, he refused to open up to her. He didn't want to talk about it, at least not with her, and according to Anna, he hadn't talked about it with anyone. She guessed that was what bothered her most. He denied the people around him the privilege of helping him, deciding to go at it alone. She didn't know why it was so important to her that she be the one he finally opened up to. It just was.

As bad as it was for her to say, she said it. "Okay. But you're going to have to talk to someone sometime. You look plain tired, and I know you have been so preoccupied that you've forgotten about at least one customer's yard. You can't keep sleeping on your mom's couch, worrying about her twenty-four hours a day, and running two businesses. You need help."

"I knew Edna would go off blabbing her mouth. She told my mom, didn't she?"

"Maybe."

"I bet she was freaking out. She already has it in her mind that I'm struggling with Avery Landscaping. I keep reassuring her I have everything taken care of, but when people go off and say things to her…like Edna…it throws her back in to asking me a million questions."

"I wouldn't worry about it. She wanted to call you, but Edna told her it wasn't necessary. She seemed to let it go, but you still need to come to the realization that you're going to need help sometime."

"Maggie is around, and I'm there the rest of the time. That's the best I can do right now." He raked his hands through his hair. "What is it you want from me,

Liza?"

She left her chair and closed the distance between them. God, he smelled good. "I want you to let me be there for you." Did she really just admit that? Things were moving a lot faster than she was prepared for. What happened to just dinner and sex? When did personal stuff come into play?

"Can we just let this be what it is for now?"

"And what is that?"

"Two people who are wildly attracted to each other and seem to like spending time together," he whispered, eyes growing wide. "Okay. I know I don't have a lot to offer a woman like you, but it's all I can do for now."

With him trapped against the counter, she wrapped her arms around his neck and nestled in between his strong thighs. For once, she was in control and could decide what happened next. Her hands fisted in his T-shirt to draw him closer.

As his grin faded, he stared back at her with such need that the air suddenly became sexually charged, taking her breath away. He seemed to look right through her. Any other time she would have found that unsettling, but not with Tex.

He must have read her mind. He lifted her shirt, baring the skin between her belly button and jeans that sat low on her hips. "You have to be the sexiest woman I've ever had my hands on." He positioned his hands on her waist, his touch making her feel warm and tingly inside. Judging by the bulge pressing against the front of his jeans, he was as excited to be with her as she was to be with him.

"What's up with Patience boys and your corny pickup lines?" she whispered against his lips.

"I don't have to resort to pickup lines to have you, sweetheart."

"You think you're that good, huh?" His mouth became her primary focus. She wanted to crush her lips to his but enjoyed the moment and anticipation of finally having him. And boy, did she want him. She didn't know if she had ever felt such a sexual connection with another man.

His eyes went dark. "Why don't you let me show you how good I really am?" He tugged on her bottom lip with his teeth. "I have to kiss you."

She leaned up and captured his mouth with her own. Warm beer intertwined with her red wine. Tex's kiss moved through her entire body. Sinking into it, she let herself feel every sensation.

She had come to know from previous sexually based encounters with Tex that he was easy to be with. Her body seemed to take over, moving against his. It was only natural to press her breasts against his chest, run her fingers through his hair. His hands traveled from her waist to cup her ass, which, of course, meant that in front, she was grinding against the hardness behind his zipper. *Oh. Wow.*

He pulled back, and they gazed at each other. No words were spoken—just deep emotions that only a look could tell. She was getting that look. Tex had obviously reached his breaking point and wanted to have her right there in the kitchen. She hoped he was reading her looks as her being all in for it.

Chapter Fourteen

He switched places with her, his hands settling on her waist again as he easily lifted her onto the counter. His eyes looked wild as they swept over her. First, his hands slid down her sides, across her stomach, followed by the intensity of his gaze. Everywhere he touched, then looked, left heat searing through her body. She immediately wrapped her legs around his waist, putting direct pressure against his growing erection.

He claimed her mouth, making her swallow a moan—not knowing if it was his or her own or a little of both of them.

He tugged on her bottom lip, breathing in a husky voice. "How is this for good?" His hands traced the seams of her jeans running the inside part of her thighs.

She gripped him, forcing him to take the kiss in a harder, more fervent way. He tilted his head one way and then the other to satisfy the hunger that they both seemed overcome with.

With her hands under his shirt, she scraped her nails across the small of his back. She loved the quiver she caused across his skin. When he broke the kiss and bit his way gently down her neck, she, too, trembled.

"That's gooood," she part moaned, part whispered as she tilted her head to give him better access.

Her fingers skimmed to the front of his jeans where she hurriedly unbuttoned them and was reaching for the zipper when his hand caught her by the wrist.

He never stopped the biting and licking ministrations but moved to the other side of her neck. "I love it when you let me know how you feel."

Her lids fell shut. This was really going to happen. No more playing games with endless flirting, no overthinking, and more importantly, no interruptions. A lump of anticipation threatened to choke her. She inhaled deeply, then let it out slowly with the unzipping of his pants.

He sighed. "Shit."

She held her arms high as he pulled her shirt over her head and tossed it in the sink.

A small moan escaped between his lips when he laid eyes on her breasts, only covered with thin pink lace. She felt exhilarated to know she turned him on. He tugged on her bra straps until they fell from her shoulders. She arched her back, pushing her breasts to him. It was more than just wanting; she needed his touch.

"Please." At this point, she wasn't against begging. As long as she was relieved of the ache settled in her breasts, she didn't care.

"Please what?" He kissed down her throat, her chest, and stopped *just* before he met lace. "What do you want me to do, Liza?"

"Touch me," she pleaded.

His hands started at her neck, pressing slightly to her pulse. "Here?"

She shook her head.

His fingers glided downward until they reached the heart hammering in her chest. "What about here?"

She was reduced to one-word answers. "Lower."

Along with voicing her plea, she begged with her

eyes until both of his hands cupped her breasts, gently squeezing them in his palms. Her eyes fell shut again. One of his thumbs rubbed over the thin lace covering her nipple while his other hand cupped the side of her face, and he went back to kissing his way down her face, neck, throat, and then he planted quick but painstaking kisses along her shoulder. He bent down, *finally* replacing his thumb with the warmth of his mouth. Oh, she was thankful for not wearing a padded bra.

It was a shock. Her eyes flew open. "Tex." A hum shot from her breasts to her inner thighs. Who was she kidding? This was not enough. She needed more of him.

She slipped her hands into his boxer briefs and stroked him slowly.

Sweat formed on his brow. "God, sweetheart…" His voice cracked. "Not here."

She didn't stop touching him. Instead, she tugged at his jeans. "Here is just as good a place as any."

His hands took both of her wrists and held them above her head. She wiggled against him, making them both suffer in a pleasure she hadn't known was even possible. "Hey," she cried.

"Let's go to the bedroom."

She had to admit that was a much better idea. Still, no matter how close the bedroom was, it wasn't close enough.

"Wrap your arms around my neck and keep your legs locked around my waist."

He lifted her off the counter, and she held him tightly. Liquid heat surged below as he jostled her up and down, making their way to his room.

He placed her on her feet when they entered the pitch-black bedroom. Her knees felt wobbly and threatened to give way. Luckily, she stayed upright. He turned on a lamp, and a soft light filled the room. The biggest bed she had ever seen took up most of the space. Only a small nightstand and chest of drawers made of the same chunky wood were able to fit in the room.

He held out his hand, and she gladly took it. "Now, where were we?"

"I think you were about to do this…" With her hands on his broad shoulders, she pulled him down until their lips met. The passionate kiss was not something she was used to. She wanted to experience every sensation, need, and pleasure with him. "Then I think I was about to do this…" She tugged, with his help, his shirt up his chest and over his head.

Ahhh…what a nice chest he had. She splayed her hands across it and watched it rise and fall with every breath he heaved. She took her time exploring, kissing, nibbling. His eyes glazed in desire, fueling the fire within her. "Take your pants off."

He toed off his shoes, then socks before dropping his jeans. She knew he would be a sight, but she wasn't prepared for how she would feel when she saw him for the first time. The glow of the bedside lamp only heightened his body. "You're beautiful," she said.

He laughed before giving her one of his sexy smirks.

"What?" She feigned a smile.

"A man is not beautiful…that is all you."

"Beautiful is the only way I know to describe you. You have this ruggedly handsome thing going on, broad chest, working-man hands, which I love, cocky—" She smiled. "—but still with a charming smile. And you have the most captivating, perfect mixture of light-green and blue eyes, except when you're upset and aroused. Then they go very deep. *That*, to me, is the definition of beautiful."

He looked flattered but didn't say so. Instead, he told her to take off her shoes, and she was more than willing to comply. After the shoes, she started unbuttoning her jeans, but then he stopped her.

"I want to do that," he said.

She dropped her arms to her sides and watched as he slowly unbuttoned her pants, then unzipped them. He had seen her half-naked before, but this felt different. This was slow and intense.

He helped her out of her jeans and threw them to the side with his own clothes. Standing there in nothing but her underwear should have felt strange since she had only been with Greg for the past year with a dry spell before that, but being with Tex seemed natural. There was nothing uneasy about it. He looked at her as if she was the only woman he wanted to be with, and she believed she was the only woman on his mind.

"Get comfortable on the bed," he instructed.

She usually didn't take well to someone telling her what to do in any part of her life, but she didn't care so much with Tex. This was what she had been wanting, a man to take charge and meet her every need. She wanted to feel every sensation.

Liza scooted back on the bed until she reached the fluffy white pillows, then waited for him to tell her what to do next.

He crawled up her body but didn't allow his body to fully press against hers.

"I need to feel you, Tex." She wrapped her hands around his back and brought them skin to skin. "I want to know you're here with me." She was so caught in every one of his touches setting off a tingling sensation that spread the length of her body.

He lowered himself onto her, one knee nudged between her thighs. His kisses started with him running his tongue over her lips. When he began peppering kisses down her neck and throat, making sure to caress every one of her sensitive spots, she lost all train of thought. It was as if he knew every place on her body that would send her plummeting over the edge.

She instantly threw her head back, thrusting her breasts forward when he kissed the valley between. "Take it off." She spoke hurriedly and impatiently. She really wanted to savor him and let him show every part of her body the attention he had given her mouth and neck, but at the same time she needed to feel his mouth on her…and him deep inside her.

He thankfully unhooked her bra.

"Now that is what I call beautiful." He stared at her while cupping the curve of her breasts. Lust and passion burning in his eyes. "You sure know how to drive a man crazy."

"Right now, I just want to drive you crazy."

His eyes met hers. "That, you are doing, sweetheart."

He flicked, then tugged on her taut peak. He applied just enough force that she could feel it clear to her thighs.

"Lift up for me."

She did, and he stripped her of her panties. He lowered himself back onto her, looking at her as he put one hand on the bed to prop himself up and skim his other hand down the curve of her hip to the inside of her thigh. She couldn't control her sudden gasp when his fingers drifted over her most sensitive part.

"Ohhh," she moaned.

He started with his fingers teasing her, driving her to the edge. She didn't know what she wanted him to do more, because she wanted him to do everything. He slipped one finger, then two, inside her, finding her sweet spot.

"Ohhh…oh God," she cried out. She had no choice but to thrust at his hand, harder and harder.

His mouth found hers, taking in every one of her cries. His tongue mated with hers, and he bit her bottom lip, slightly tugging it with his teeth. Had she ever felt so much passion?

He stopped kissing her and pulled back. "You're so ready, baby."

"Just don't stop."

"Come for me, Liza." He demanded her to give herself to him, and she loved it.

She shook her head against the pillow. "I don't want to yet." God how she wanted to feel the release, but at the same time, she didn't want it to end. The way he smelled, tasted, and oh God, the way he made her feel was something she wanted to hang on to for as long as she could.

An inner battle raged on inside of her. She didn't want to let go and free herself of the ache settling inside of her body, but she also wanted to give over the power and let him control the situation.

"Stop trying to hold on, dammit." His fingers went deeper. "Come for me," he repeated more sternly.

That was all it took. She could no longer hold out. Her orgasm hit her with the force of a tsunami, causing her hips to come off the bed. When she fell back, Tex leaned in and, with his mouth covering hers, took possession with one powerful thrust of his tongue.

"I need you inside me…now."

"That's good, honey, because I want to bury myself deep inside you."

She eagerly tugged at his black boxer briefs.

"Someone's in a hurry." Amusement played in his eyes, but he couldn't hide the need he also felt.

Her stomach fluttered, because she was the one he needed. He wanted her, even if it was possible that he only wanted her for that one night. "Yes, so pull them down."

"Yes, ma'am." He rolled off her long enough to pull them down his legs and toss them like a rag to the floor.

"Don't call me ma'am," she told him. In her eyes, it was like calling her old, and that was something she didn't want to have to think of at the moment. Right now, she wanted to focus on Tex—only Tex. The other parts of her life, the parts that reminded her she was only getting older and still hadn't reached the success of finding a partner and raising a family, she had no interest in thinking about right now.

"Why not?" he asked.

"Because it reminds me that I am only getting older."

"There is nothing old about you." He placed a kiss on each of her breasts. "I meant what I said earlier. You are the sexiest woman I've ever had my hands on." His breath was hot against her neck.

Eyes closed, she leaned her head back and drew in whatever air was available as he slowly entered her. *That's what I'm talking about.* She spread her legs farther apart.

He positioned himself, and they both groaned as he

sank deeper. "Good?" he asked.

She gave him a simple nod. She had no words to describe how good it really felt. Her heart pounded wildly in her chest while the rest of her body relished in every glorious inch of him. She'd never felt so connected to someone. Even though it scared the hell out of her, it also felt exhilarating.

Their eyes met in the dim light as his hands gripped her hips and delivered the most mind-blowing thrusts. They were slow and sensual, making her feel beautiful and, most importantly, wanted. He wanted her. She could see it in the way he took things slow to make sure she was comfortable and not in any type of pain, the way he kissed her, the way he made sure her pleasure came before his.

She bit her bottom lip, trying to hold back her emotions but wondering what the point in that was. They were alone in Tex's house, and he was making her feel amazing. Why would she try to hide that? "Oh, wow." She sighed.

"Still feel good, baby?"

Did she like that he called her baby? It seemed more intimate, like something more than just casual sex. And it was just sex—that's all it could be between them. She wondered what he thought about that. He did keep her at arm's length when he all but admitted he really just wanted to give in and let the flirting and the jealousy he felt turn into something more.

"Uhhh." All previous thoughts escaped her mind. She filled with the desire and sensations he set off in her body, like warm honey running through her veins with every movement. That fast, they tuned in to each other's bodies. "Really…really good." She leaned up while he leaned in to kiss her.

He set the pace, and she followed, meeting every one of his thrusts. She loved his warmth covering her body. His head fell back. Such a strong man losing every bit of control was an amazing sight. It felt even better because he was lost in the depths of lust because of her. The way she was gripping his back, she was probably leaving nail marks as he continued to rock into her.

"Almost…there, Tex." She wanted him to know he didn't have to demand her to finish.

"Me, too. Oh…shit." He thrust into her one last time, doing them both in.

He fell onto her chest, and she welcomed him. She wrapped her arms around his back and lightly rubbed over the marks she had just engraved there. She felt his heart thumping in his chest…it matched hers. Were there even words for what they just did? If there were, she couldn't find them. After they both caught a breath, Tex rolled onto one side, bringing Liza with him so she would remain pressed against him. She reached down the length of the bed, pulled up the heavy, cream-colored comforter, and spread it across their bodies. She was no prude, but she had to face it—she was getting older, coupled with already being several years older than Tex. Even the most confident woman had her doubts about what a man would think concerning her body when he wasn't caught up in the lust.

He rubbed his hands over her arms. "Cold?"

She snuggled close to him. "I'm good now."

"Don't get too comfortable. I'm not through with you yet." His voice dropped, utterly deep and way beyond sexy. He draped one arm across her stomach.

Liza felt weak, her muscles loose and relaxed. She

let her eyes flutter closed. Just a minute. She just needed a minute to get herself together.

****

Tex never thought he would be the guy who watched a woman sleep in his arms and actually take some kind of joy in it. The only other time he'd almost fallen asleep with a woman resting beside him was spring break his senior year. He and some buddies had driven to Panama City for a week. While there, he'd met with a local girl who thought he was twenty-one. After too much underage drinking, he'd woken up on the beach with a major headache and the girl.

What did that say about him? He was now thirty years old and had never once had a *real* relationship. A relationship where he actually wanted to date the same woman for more than a month and have her sleep over, wearing his ragged T-shirt, and him wanting something other than sex from her. Had he ever just simply needed a woman because he couldn't see himself living without her?

He and Liza had been playing the back-and-forth game for weeks now. It was more like him thinking one thing and then doing the complete opposite. They'd finally pushed the bullshit aside and just enjoyed each other. How long that was going to last he didn't know, and honestly, he didn't want to waste time thinking about it.

Her breathing reached an even point as she fell deeper into slumber, sounding like a melody playing in his head. He strained to look over his shoulder at the bedside clock; it read ten nineteen. For almost an hour he had been watching her rest. It seemed like just minutes ago he looked down and noticed she'd fallen asleep on

265

him. He could watch and hold her for the remainder of his life, and still, it wouldn't seem like forever to him. Watching her gave him time to take in her beauty and get to know the body he enjoyed pleasuring so much.

She thought she was fucking old.

Whoever had put that thought in her head deserved to have their ass kicked. He couldn't stop touching her. Her hair wasn't as perfect as she usually kept it, but it brought back a reminder of running his fingers through it and loving the texture as it slid between them. Her cheeks flushed pink from their lovemaking. Her hands were supple and cool to his scarred and callused ones. They were complete opposites, but for the last couple of weeks, she in some way was the only thing that made sense in his life. It kept coming back to her, and that scared the living daylights out of him.

He thought about waking her with a few touches, a couple of kisses here and there, but couldn't bring himself to do it. While he needed to be back inside her warmth, showing her just how beautiful she really was, she looked too peaceful to wake.

He couldn't ignore the fact he was close to exhaustion himself. In the past week, he'd slept on his mom's couch three times, which meant he'd gotten a minimum of four or five good hours of rest. The remaining hours of the night he'd felt restless and found himself checking on his mother more and more while she slept. The one night he did sleep in his bed, he'd been only home long enough to strip to his boxers and throw himself on his bed, too tired to even pull back the covers.

Liza was right. Before long, he was going to have to come to terms with the fact that he couldn't do it by himself. He had the option of not pursuing more remodeling jobs after the coffee shop and bookstore was complete, but he liked the challenge and satisfaction he felt after creating something with his bare hands. Plus, it would keep him busy through the winter. Any extra money he could make only made his mom's life better. There had to be something else he could do, but he was starting to feel too bogged down.

With Liza sleeping in his arms, him holding her a little tighter, he closed his eyes.

Tex woke with a jolt when he heard his mom's ringtone. He checked the clock and found that he had only just drifted to sleep. God, he was tired.

"Tex?" Liza rubbed the sleep from her eyes. "Who is that?"

He kissed her forehead. "It's my mom. Go back to sleep."

"No, I'm awake." She sat up, bringing the comforter up to her chest. "Is she okay? Aren't you going to answer it?" she asked as he was already bringing the phone to his ear.

"Mom, is everything okay? Are you okay?"

He expected to hear his mother's soft voice through the phone. Instead, it was Maggie. His stomach dropped. *Something has happened, and I wasn't there.* "What is it, Maggie? What's wrong with my mom, and why are you there this late at night?" He knew she'd left his mom's house a little before six that night, because it was his idea that she leave a little earlier since he was going to hang out there before his date with Liza.

"I don't care that she didn't want you to call me. You did the right thing, Maggie." He stepped into his jeans as he continued to listen to Maggie. "Can you stay there until I get there? I'm on my way now."

"Of course," Maggie calmly spoke through the phone.

Tex slipped the phone into his front jeans pocket. He was rummaging through his dresser drawer for a clean shirt when Liza asked what was wrong. "It's my mom. She called Maggie an hour ago because she couldn't stop vomiting." He looked in the direction of the bed to find Liza searching on the floor for her clothes. "What are you doing? It's late. Go back to sleep."

She had already slipped into the panties he'd enjoyed stripping her of earlier and was putting one leg in her pants. She glared at him. "I'm going with you."

"You don't have to do that, Liza. I can handle it." He sat on the edge of the bed and slid on his tennis shoes.

"I want to. If I stay behind, I will only worry about her...and you. Please let me. I won't say or do anything if you don't want me to. Just let me be there."

The simple sentiment combined with the look in her eyes moved even a guy like him. Desire and fear grew tight in his chest. The first he was becoming familiar with when it came to Liza, but the second was new for him. Why fear? Was it because, along with the flirting, things had changed between them, had become intense in a way he had no experience with?

He wanted to tell her to crawl back between his warm sheets and ignore his mom needing him, because if he had a choice in the matter, he would not want to think and see what was becoming more real every day. Why would she want to go and witness what he tried to keep behind closed doors? She wasn't stupid. She knew he was hiding something big from her.

He wanted to tell her to stay at his house, but she wasn't going to listen to him. She was already pulling the

T-shirt he wore earlier that night over her head and stepping into her shoes. If he didn't let her go with him, she would just follow him in her own car.

"All right," he said.

Five minutes later, Tex pulled into his mother's driveway, making sure not to block Maggie in. He grabbed Liza's hand when she slid across the bench seat and got out on his side of the truck.

When they entered the house, the only sound he heard was Maggie barely talking above a whisper to his mom, who was reclined in her chair. Maggie sat in a kitchen chair that she must have placed there. She rubbed a hand over his mother's arm while his mother gripped a washcloth in one hand and a plastic cup with a straw in the other. Her hair was brushed away from her face, making her paleness more noticeable.

As her medication changed, her upset stomach happened more frequently. His heart broke for her, and he felt physically ill because he was helpless. He couldn't do one damn thing for her. Yeah, he could worry himself to an early grave by sitting by her bed and praying to a god he hadn't talked to in so long he didn't even know how anymore. He could give her the best care he could physically and financially give and come rushing every time he heard her favorite song play on his cell phone, but it would never be enough. There was no way to fix the problem.

Maggie rose from her chair when she saw Tex, followed by Liza, come through the front door. He took her spot, grabbed the cup from his mom's hand, and replaced it with his own hand. "Mom, how are you feeling?"

She gave him a weak smile. "I'm fine, honey. I told

Maggie not to call you. I knew you were cooking dinner for Liza tonight." She wiped her mouth with the cool washcloth. "How did it go? Was she impressed?"

"Why did you do that, Mama?"

"Why did I do what, honey?"

"Why didn't you call me when you started to feel bad? I don't care what I'm doing. You have to call me when something doesn't feel right. Maggie lives too far away to drive over this late at night. You should've called me."

"I really didn't mind, Tex," Maggie said.

He heaved a tired sigh. "I know that, and I appreciate you coming so late, but I'm less than ten minutes away." He didn't want to sound stern with Maggie, because she was always too damn kind to him. He'd snapped at her enough times that she should have punched him or quit, but she was dedicated to his mom. There was nothing she wouldn't do for Pearl.

"Don't be upset with Maggie, Tex," his mother told him.

"I'm not mad at her." He stared at his mom and couldn't believe what he was about to admit to her. "I'm more upset with you." He felt lower than dirt for saying such a thing, but it was the truth. She should have called him.

He had a right to be angry about that, didn't he?

She squeezed his hand. "I know, but I didn't want to interrupt your night with Liza. You seemed so excited earlier. I couldn't bring myself to ruin it for you. So I give you permission to be mad at me for tonight. After that, you need to get over it and understand that I just want you happy. It has been a long time since I've seen the kind of smile that girl over there brings to your handsome face."

He didn't know she had seen Liza standing just inside the door. She was behind him as his mom went on and on about the strong effect she had on him. While inwardly groaning, he couldn't bring himself to turn and face her as she now knew just how excited he'd been to see her that night.

He cleared his throat. "Maggie, thank you." Saying it aloud was important. He pulled his wallet from his back pocket and pulled out all the money he had on him. "Take this."

Maggie shook her head, then lowered her voice. "You already pay me."

He didn't know if there was a sweeter person on earth. "Not for the middle of the night, I don't." He thrust the money into her hand. "Put it in your pocket."

Finally giving in, she accepted the cash. She went to the other side of his mom's recliner and leaned down to give her a hug. "I'll see you tomorrow morning, Pearl."

"Why don't you come in after noon?" Tex told her. "I was planning to take half a day off tomorrow. I'll be here in the morning."

"Okay, if you insist." Maggie grabbed her purse from the edge of the couch and smiled shyly at Liza as she passed.

"Liza, come inside and tell me if my son did good tonight," his mom said.

Liza walked up behind him and laid a hand on his shoulder, giving him a slight squeeze. "You should be proud of him, Pearl. He cooked and cleaned the kitchen. He was perfect."

She thought he was perfect?

"So y'all had a good night?"

Tex couldn't resist. He looked up at Liza, who was blushing as she smiled at him. They did have a good night, and he was thinking just that right then.

"We did," Liza finally said. "What about you? Because it doesn't sound like you had a very good night. Are you still feeling sick? Do you want me to get you something?"

"I'm fine, dear."

Even though she was saying the words, Tex knew his mom was not fine. Her face turned a little green, and he could see her swallowing repeatedly. He reached down to grab the basin Maggie had sitting on the floor by his chair, but Liza was already holding it out to him. His mom threw up a little, probably due to the water she'd been sipping.

"Pearl, why don't you let me take you to the bathroom to splash some cool water on your face?" Liza asked.

He had a feeling Liza couldn't stand in the background, as she'd said. She was a doer. He thought he would smart off to her, reminding her that she was sticking her nose in his business, but he didn't mind that she wanted to help right then. Maybe it was because taking his mom to the bathroom to vomit made him want to throw up, too. He had read that it was called sympathy vomiting or something.

"I'd like that."

He and Liza helped his mom out of her chair. Liza mouthed, "Is this all right?"

He nodded. Even though it was after the fact, he liked that Liza respected him enough to at least make sure he was fine with her stepping in to help. He watched as she guided his mom down the hall to the bathroom.

Liza was never trying to be nosy and counsel him. It had been such a dumbass thing for him to say in the first place. Her trying to help was just who she was, and she couldn't turn that part of herself off. If she didn't care so much about other people's happiness, she wouldn't be who she was, and that would be a shame, because he liked her. She could be stubborn and one never to allow him to get away with anything, but he really cared for her. So much so that his heart squeezed a little tighter in his chest.

Having her just one time would not be enough—he would just want her more, and that was something he didn't know if he could deal with. Her being in town for a short time was a good thing. She deserved better than him. He couldn't offer anything but disappointment.

****

Liza found a clean washcloth in Pearl's bathroom closet. She wet it with warm water and handed it to Pearl so she could wipe her face. The woman gladly took it. "How does that feel?" Liza asked.

"I think I'm about to get sick again." Pearl put the cloth to her mouth.

Getting down on the floor to use the toilet would've been too difficult for Pearl when she got sick, so she held Pearl's hair in a small ponytail and made it possible for her to use the sink if she felt the need.

"False alarm."

"You want to sit down for a minute? Just to make sure your stomach has settled," Liza suggested.

Pearl eased herself to a sitting position on the closed toilet lid. "I must come across as a mess. Maggie brushed my hair away from my face. I bet it looks like a rat's nest, doesn't it?"

"No. You're a little pale, but other than that, you look lovely. Look at me. I know I could appear better. We are two peas in a pod." As soon as Liza pointed out her out-of-control hair and oversized T-shirt, she regretted it. She hoped Pearl didn't question why she was wearing a shirt that almost went to her knees. That would not be a fun conversation.

"We have to get our hair fixed together for the wedding. Promise me we will go together," Pearl said.

"What wedding?"

"Your wedding, silly. I wish you and my son would pick a date already. There are a million things we need to do. I promise not to be one of those overbearing mothers-in-law, but I would like to help you plan some of it."

Liza's jaw fell open. Was she dreaming? Had she fallen asleep and missed something as significant as someone proposing to her? Was it possible that Pearl had interpreted Tex and Liza going on a date as them getting married?

When Pearl mentioned how happy Tex was about their date, her body had turned all warm and tingly inside. She was happy because she made him happy. He looked so tired. So she felt like she accomplished something by making his life a little better.

"What makes you think we're getting married?"

The woman laughed. "Tex said he loved you, silly. He told me not to tell, but he also let it slip that you are pregnant." She whispered the word *pregnant* as if it were a big secret.

Okay, now Liza felt faint and sick. Married? Love? Pregnant? They'd just had sex without a condom. She was going to have to discuss that with Tex later, but right now she was confused, and she clearly wasn't the only one.

"He what?" Liza asked when she got past the pregnant remark and moved on to the *love you* part. Somehow that seemed like the biggest shocker.

"Don't be mad at him. He's a good man, but even a good man can be scared of change. I think he just needed me to tell him it is okay to feel so strongly about someone. I know you haven't known each other very long, but he really loves you, Liza, and I know you love him, too."

Liza's chest tightened. Things were starting to click for her. She'd had a gut feeling about Pearl since the first time she met her, but without any confirmation, she didn't want to think it was true. She cared about Pearl, and imagining Tex's mother going through such a difficult time was hard for her. How did Tex feel? What a stupid question. He'd clearly been struggling with something, and he told her more than once he didn't want her involved.

"My son makes you happy, doesn't he?" Pearl still focused on the love, marriage, and baby idea.

Liza was happy at the moment. She was worried about Pearl, but before Tex's phone rang, she had fallen asleep very happy and satisfied. He could be impossible at times, but he also made her feel alive and sexy. "He does."

Pearl let the subject drop and told Liza she wanted to go lie down. Liza made sure Pearl got into her bed okay, then asked if she needed anything before she turned out the light. Pearl's only request was "Just make him happy." Liza nodded. She didn't have the heart to tell Pearl that love, marriage, and anything else were not going to happen between her and Tex.

She didn't mind that Pearl was probably falling asleep with thoughts of wedding flowers, dresses, and baby names for her future grandchildren. If that's what made her happy for the night, so be it.

Chapter Fifteen

Tex sat in his mom's living room, flipping through an old photo album. Liza had fallen asleep on the couch. For the past hour and a half, he'd sat in his mom's chair, content to watch her chest rise and fall with every breath.

The album he'd noticed on the small bookcase in the corner of the room was filled with snapshots of him and his mom and even some of him with his friends from school over the years. He was riding his first bike without training wheels, splashing in the ocean at around age ten, and a couple of his little-league pictures were in no particular order. There were pictures of him and his mom on the day of his senior prom and him with her crying at his high school graduation. His childhood seemed like a lifetime ago. They were good times, but he had taken them for granted. He had no clue things could change so suddenly.

He stared back at his mother's elegant features and longed for her to stay with him in the moment. He'd always admired her strong and resilient nature. She was the best woman he knew, hands down, and he couldn't see the fairness in her deserving an uncontrollable disease.

She was too good. The selfish part of him wondered why he had to face this. The thought made him feel like the weak man he was becoming. He was handling everything all wrong. His friends, employees, Liza,

Maggie, and even his mother deserved better. He shouldn't have said he was angry when she failed to call him. She only wanted him happy. She obviously saw straight through his façade.

When he'd seen her earlier that day, he told her about Liza coming over for dinner. In some way, he'd wanted to include her. He'd asked her what he should cook, and she'd said something easy so he couldn't mess it up. A part of him had wanted her opinion, but the other part just wanted to see her excited about something, and she seemed to really like Liza.

"Tex?" Liza brought herself to a sitting position, brushed her hair away from her face with her hand, and then wrapped herself tightly in the throw blanket.

He laid the album on the floor.

Apparently, Liza read the look on his face, and when their gazes locked, she got up from the couch, the blanket still wrapped around her, and settled on his lap. She peered down at him. "I just want to let you know I'm here if you need me."

"Alzheimer's." What else was there to say? The word *Alzheimer's* was strong enough to stand on its own. It told someone everything they needed to know.

She laid her head on his chest. He loved the way she comforted him and made him feel hope when loneliness and sadness were all he'd felt for the past few months. With his arms wrapped around her, he knew he couldn't do this alone anymore, and she was willing to be the person he leaned on.

"I know," she whispered into his neck.

He was glad she didn't meet his eyes. She probably avoided looking him in the eye because she knew how hard it was for him to admit something so personal.

She pressed her palm to his chest, as if lending him some of her strength. "Talk to me."

He appreciated how she cared enough to try to get him to open up, but he wasn't one to lean on others. It had always been him and his mom. Other than his dad abandoning them, he'd lived a good childhood. Until now, he hadn't had to face the hard facts of life. He had once considered himself lucky because he hadn't had to go through losing two parents and a dream of a career like Jake.

He wasn't ready to talk about the disease destroying his family. Confirming his mom was sick and not going to get any better was bad enough.

"I've already told you I can't."

"You can, Tex. You're a lot stronger than you feel right now. Please trust me with your feelings." She made it sound so simple, but to him, it was the opposite.

"Why do you care so much?" He didn't mean to sound so gruff. "I didn't mean it like that." She didn't deserve his harshness when all she wanted to do was be there for him and his mother.

"You have a right to be any way you want. Nothing you do or say will push me away. I'm here when you're ready."

A giant lump formed in his chest, but he tried his damnedest to swallow it. His eyes filled with moisture, and he inwardly cursed the sign of weakness. He didn't know how he'd gotten so lucky to have this woman come into his life, but he would find a way to talk to God and thank Him for creating such a pure and honest person. She'd been nothing but honest with him from the very beginning.

Yeah—she'd been drunk and probably more open

with him than she normally would have been if she hadn't consumed a bottle of wine, but the first time he met her, she had been nothing if not true to her feelings. When he'd left her that night, he knew she was a tough but equally vulnerable woman. She was a loyal friend to a fault, grouped all men in the same category as her bastard of an ex-boyfriend—which he was determined to change—and she hated Jake with a passion. Those were some pretty personal details about her life, except for her feelings toward Jake, and she didn't have to tell him any of it. Since then, he'd only gotten to know her better and knew where she stood in her life.

She was not going to sit back and wait for a man to get his shit together. She'd made that point the night she took Saunders up on his offer.

What did she know about him? That he only drove a Ford for some southern-boy reason, or better yet, she knew he loved women and had many over the years. It was a wonder she even talked to him.

He looked down at her and watched as she rubbed a piece of the front of his shirt between her fingers. "How can you do that?"

"Do what?"

"Be so patient with me? I mean, I've told you every other way that I don't want to talk about what's going on. I even demanded you not to counsel me. I apologize for that, by the way."

"I don't take demands very well."

He couldn't see her eyes but could picture her smiling while rolling them at him. He chuckled. "I've noticed." His voice turned serious again. "But really…I want to know how you can be so understanding when it comes to the important stuff." He needed to know. For some strange reason, it was important to him.

"I don't know. Maybe it's because I have to be for the job I do, or maybe it's just because I can see how much you're suffering, and I want to help you in some way."

He knit his brow and couldn't believe he hadn't asked her sooner. "Why did you become a therapist? I guess I've always thought people with a traumatic experience were the ones who went down the road of being one." Why he thought that, he didn't know.

"Like I said before, I come from loving parents. When I was growing up, I liked to watch people—I still do. I felt a yearning to fix their problems or at least try to figure them out. It was either me being a therapist or a country songwriter." She shrugged. "I did have friends with divorced parents and dysfunctional families. That could have played some type of role in my decision."

"Do you miss it?"

"I haven't had time yet. I imagine when I go back home, I'll start to miss my patients. I know you probably don't believe in going to therapy, but I have to think that I do some good. I catch myself worrying about the people who've been coming to see me for a couple of years. I don't want them to think I've abandoned them by my own choosing."

"When did I say I didn't believe in what you do?" He couldn't remember ever telling her that what she did didn't help others.

"It's pretty much how I took it when you yelled at me the morning I took you home. I believe you said you didn't need my counseling and psychobabble."

Shit—shit—shit. He'd said some pretty awful things to her that morning, but he was so out of his mind that he couldn't remember everything he said or how he said it. Liza apparently remembered. "I'm sorry for that. I was mad at what you saw, but I never dismissed what you do for people. I can tell you are good at your job and that you help and care about the people who rely on you. Just ignore everything I said that day."

"So I guess I can forget about you telling me we're not friends?"

He winced. "I did say that, too, didn't I?"

"Yeah, you did."

"I say we are more than friends now." As soon as the words came out, he wondered if he should have said them. They were something. Were they friends, a step up, or just people who had sex with nothing more involved? He doubted the last part because he'd never had sex with anyone and felt the way he did after being with Liza. What they did was not casual and unemotional. He cared about her pleasure more than his own. He wanted her to feel everything he felt. Everyone said they had a connection, and he hadn't understood what a connection even was until he was with her.

"I like being more than friends with you," she said.

A grin started in his chest and traveled to his mouth. He liked what was going on between them, even if he didn't totally understand it and was scared of what she did to him.

The room fell silent again. Tex felt stronger and more capable with her just being next to him—or on top of him, as it were. She tucked her head under his chin and laid it there for several minutes.

He leaned his head back to rest on the chair and stared at the reflection the soft light from the lamp beside him made on the ceiling. After pulling in a deep breath and expelling it slowly, he said, "I don't know where to start."

"Wherever you like," she told him.

"It started with small things—her forgetting the right words to use, which was only odd because she was a schoolteacher. It moved from there to her forgetting names of people she'd just met a day or two prior and forgetting where she put things. I once found her reading glasses in the freezer, and when I made a joke about it and thought she would say she just got busy putting the groceries away or was on the phone and had been wondering where she'd laid them, she looked totally confused. She had no memory of ever having them or knowing that she was missing them." He didn't want to stop because if he did, he was certain he would never be able to bring the subject up again. "I finally insisted she see a doctor when I found the door unlocked after she'd gone to bed." He swallowed hard. "She tried to play it off as her just getting older, but I could tell she was scared, too."

"How long ago was that?" Liza asked.

"She was diagnosed this past summer. She had to retire from a job she loved. How is that fair?" His chest felt as if it would explode with the painful memory of sitting next to his mother in a cold, sterile room while a doctor told her she had Alzheimer's.

He stupidly associated the disease with aging. He'd taken a date many years ago to see *The Notebook* on the big screen, so he obviously knew it wasn't going to be as bad on his mother because she wasn't as bad off as the woman in the movie. At the time, she only had a hard time remembering simple things compared to what Hollywood portrayed. A thought an ignorant man would have. Months later he learned Alzheimer's was a progressive disease. It was only going to get worse until it eventually reached the point she wouldn't even know he was her son. Eventually, he would just become a stranger to her. The thought saddened him and had him tightening his hold on Liza.

She sat up straight and met his gaze. "It's not fair to her or you."

He gave a bitter laugh. "Me? Who cares how I feel. My mom is all that matters. It pisses me off, sure, but I don't have a right to feel wrecked over it. I don't have time to know what to feel about it." Except he did have feelings about the world that was ever changing. Thinking of himself when his mom was the one living out her days in confusion and sometimes alone in her own mind was plum selfish.

"Oh, honey," she soothed. "Of course you have a right to feel. This is not only affecting your mom, but it's changing your life, too. I know your mom worries about how you are feeling and only wants you happy. Do you know what she told me tonight when we were in the bathroom?"

"What?"

"She said she wished we would do her a favor and pick a date for our wedding."

"Our what?" he choked out, not able to control the blatant shock that registered on his face.

Her face turned a shade of pink as she was probably remembering what he would consider an uncomfortable conversation. "That, too, was my first thought." She stopped and seemed to mull over her next words. "But after I got past you loving me, wanting to marry me...and me carrying your child, I realized that your mom wants all those things for you, so she created the idea herself."

He wanted to stop her midsentence after the word *love* and ask what the hell she was talking about, but he instead let her finish. Denying several parts of that sentence seemed unimportant.

"She wanted to make sure I know you are a good man but that even you can be afraid of change." She took his face in her hands. "Her exact words to me were 'I think he just needed me to tell him it is okay to feel so strongly about someone.' " She pressed her lips to his forehead. "I admit I was like, *what in the hell*, but what she said really touched me. I didn't know why until right now. It's like she was using me to tell you it's okay to feel, to be concerned and ask for help."

Tex wasn't used to talking about the deep shit, the stuff that ate him up with guilt, but hell, maybe he wanted to tell her and hope at least one person understood.

Still, his voice dropped an octave. "I feel so damn guilty for having a reaction. I'm not the one suffering with a disease that will eventually kill me." He'd never said that part aloud. What was making him lose hours of sleep and something he'd never revealed to anyone was finally out there. Letting someone else in made his mom's outcome seem more real, not that he needed to be reminded of how real it was.

"You are suffering, Tex. Do you not get that what happens to your mom also happens to you?"

He'd read the pamphlets from the doctor's office and knew what Liza was saying to him. Her words were nice to hear, but he didn't believe them.

When he didn't say anything, she got up from his

lap, threw the blanket on the couch, and stood before him. "I will not listen to you belittle your right to have an emotion. Be pissed and hurt. Hell, be angry at your mom—just feel something. You cannot bottle everything inside and expect yourself to carry on."

He took a breath and told himself not to raise his voice. "Why would I be mad at my mom? It's not her fault."

"You're right. It's not her fault, but it is a normal reaction and emotion to have. What if it were you? What if you had cancer and it was too far advanced for treatment?"

Her eyes turned watery. It was as if he were the one who was sick and she was living through it with him. He could see her heart ache for him in a way he'd never witnessed.

"Don't you think your mom would feel everything you were feeling, and maybe more, because after you were gone, she would be left alone with the memories? I know she would, because she loves you more than anything in her life." Her eyes pleaded for him to understand. "You have a right to feel her pain and your own."

He patted his knee. "I miss you." She relented and joined him in the chair again. He hugged her close and just breathed the scent he was becoming so familiar with. When he could bring himself to speak, he murmured, "Thank you."

She kissed the side of his neck in a way that felt more than just sexual. "I will listen to you, be your friend and lover if that's what you need. Don't thank me for doing what I honestly want to do."

They didn't say anything for a long while.

Was he mad at his mom for being sick? He didn't want to believe he blamed her for anything. Not even when his dad left did he say it was in any way her fault. He was telling the truth about not having time to analyze his every emotion. When he wasn't thinking about work or the only family he had, he was sleeping, which just thinking about made his eyelids fall shut.

"Do you want me to take you back to my place so you can get some shut-eye?" he asked.

She burrowed her head into his chest and sighed. "I don't want to go anywhere."

That was good, because he didn't want her to go anywhere. He needed her to be there with him, to help him deal. Her warmth against him was enough to get him through anything for the night. "Okay. Do you want to stretch out on the couch?"

"Am I too heavy for you?" She shifted in his lap.

He grabbed her by the waist before she could get away. "No, you feel perfect against me. I was suggesting the couch so you could stretch out and be more comfortable. But if you want to stay like this"—he motioned vaguely to their bodies—"it's all right by me."

"Then I would rather us stay like this." She stopped and wrinkled her brows. "What if your mom comes in here? What will she think if I'm sitting in your lap, asleep?"

"I say we'll be fine. She already thinks we're getting married and having our first kid. You sitting in my lap is nothing compared to me getting you pregnant before I marry you."

"You do know she'll be telling everyone in Patience. Everyone already thinks we're dating because your mother announced it at Cut & Curls."

Okay, that might end up being a situation he would have to set straight for Liza's benefit. He couldn't have the whole nosy town whispering behind her back, saying whatever people said when another woman was pregnant before walking down the aisle. Anyone with any sense could figure out she hadn't been in Patience long enough to know she was carrying his baby, but they might think she was carrying another man's child while she went on a couple of dates with two local men. Oh boy!

"I'll talk to Mama in the morning. Maybe I can make her understand." He wasn't sure it would work.

"Understand *what* exactly?" She sounded a little skeptical.

She kept her gaze far away from his. "Uh…that there's no wedding or baby…and—" He swallowed. "—that we are not in love." As soon as the words left his mouth, it was as if they didn't carry any weight. That he forced no conviction in what he was saying and supposed to believe. "I will tell her that we're dating—casually, that is—if you want to see me after tonight."

His heart pounded. What was probably seconds seemed like hours before she said, "We can do that."

He breathed easier after she simply agreed to see him again. He craved her kiss, longed to trap her beneath him and have her beg him to sink deep, deep inside of her. He found her voice filled with concern and support echoing through his head comforting. So much uncertainty surrounded his life, but he was positive he wasn't ready to let Liza go. No, not yet.

"Are you and the girls going to Ollie's tomorrow night?" Usually, on Friday nights the men and women got together separately, but sometimes they all just hung together.

Most of the time, he preferred to just hang out with the guys because he was seeing less and less of them as they found their women. Well, except for Bradley. Tex could always count on that guy to have a beer and shoot a game of pool with him, but he wanted a reason to be near Liza. Saturday was too long of a damn wait. She might have been pressed against his body, but he couldn't have her the way he wanted in his mother's house. For now, he had to be content to just painfully hold her. Even though he was touching her, it really wasn't in the way he needed.

"We are," she said.

"We could ride together if you want. Afterward, we could go back to my place." He tried not to sound so desperate to be with her, but he couldn't control the tone of his voice.

"I would, but I told Georgia we would ride together."

He was disappointed. "Okay…well, we'll see each other there." He hoped he would see a lot of her after girls' night.

"That sounds—" She yawned. "—good."

He reached over to the table and switched off the lamp. All was quiet and somewhat peaceful. "Get some rest, sweetheart." He tucked her under his chin.

Exhaustion took him over. He was weary down to his bones. It was funny, because after spending many nights cramped on his mother's couch and only wanting his king-size bed, right then, he didn't want anything other than Liza close to him. The small recliner felt like the best thing he could lay his head on.

****

Liza hadn't talked to Anna much in the last week.

She was busier than she thought she would be, working on Anna's office and seeing Tex the last couple of nights, but Anna was stretched thin herself, and Liza didn't take it personally that they hadn't hung out as much.

"Where in the hell have you been? I decided if I didn't hear from you today, I was going to check your room to make sure you weren't dead. Did you not get my text messages last night?" Anna demanded when Liza walked through the door of the coffee shop and bookstore.

Liza didn't think she'd ever heard Anna cuss, and yes, she had gotten all seven of Anna's messages. They were a play-by-play of the entire last game of the World Series, which the Sparks won. "Uh…I've been…" She couldn't very well tell about her and Em taking secret trips to Knight to buy things for her office. Instead, she decided to fill her in about her and Tex. "Actually, I've been on a couple of dates."

"With Jason?" Anna's face seemed to soften. At least she didn't look as if she could strangle Liza for not sharing her same passion for America's pastime.

Liza liked staring at the men in their uniforms, but Anna was crazy to the point that Liza thought she could be a feature on one of those secret obsession shows about people who liked eating chalk and laundry detergent.

Well, maybe Anna wasn't that loony, but she still scared Liza when a game was tied and it was bottom of the ninth.

"One of them was with him."

Anna's eyes narrowed.

"We went out Saturday night, but…Tex and I spent the night together last night."

Anna blinked. "What?"

"You knew it was bound to happen," Liza reminded her. "You said we were building up to finally sleeping with each other."

Anna sat in one of the easy chairs in front of the fireplace. Liza followed.

"Whew, I guess I'm just a little shocked, because last I saw you, Jason was asking you out while Tex acted all jealous and caveman-like. I figured he would join Jake on your crap list."

Liza laughed. "I'm glad you finally find humor in my and Jake's lack of a relationship."

Anna shrugged. "I've decided to stay out of it. You both are headstrong people. I can't tell either one of you anything, so I'm just letting y'all work it out." She stopped and turned serious. "But one day, Liza, you're going to have to forgive him."

"Okay," she agreed, but she obviously wasn't selling it, because Anna just glared at her. "I will…honestly…eventually."

Anna dropped it. "So how did you go from Jason to Tex in less than a week?"

Wow. She didn't like how that sounded out loud. "I'm awful, aren't I?" She felt bad about the way she'd treated Jason. He was a nice guy who loved his family, served his community, and knew how to make a woman feel special. He didn't deserve what she and Tex had done to him. She knew Tex liked her, and while she wasn't trying to make Tex regret walking out on her, maybe deep down she wanted him jealous.

"You are not awful. It wasn't like Jason was your boyfriend or anything. How did he take it?" Anna winced.

"He was actually pretty cool about the whole thing.

He knew Tex was jealous, and he said he didn't want to be the man in the middle of two people who have something. I really feel bad because he is a good guy, a guy that any woman would be lucky to spend an evening with." Maybe it was best she and Jason hadn't gone out on a second date. "He seems like the type of guy who is ready to settle down. I can't be that woman for obvious reasons."

"And what about Tex?" Anna questioned.

"What about him?"

"You don't think Tex is ready to find the right woman and settle down? I can tell he's changed. I can see him married with kids."

She didn't want to tell her friend about Pearl. Anna would keep whatever was said between them to herself, but Liza didn't feel right talking about something so personal as Tex and his family. It wasn't her story to tell, and she knew how to keep her mouth shut. Even though she craved to tell Anna how freaked out she'd been when Pearl said Tex loved her and wanted to marry her.

It wasn't true, of course, but she couldn't help but wonder what being loved by Tex Avery would feel like. While she was thinking about being loved by him, she let herself go further with the fantasy and wondered if he would ever want to be married with a couple of kids. She was being silly, but it was just her mind trying to figure him out. She knew what Pearl wanted, but did he want those same things one day?

"I don't know what he wants," Liza admitted. "He doesn't like to talk about himself."

"I know that." Anna nodded. "I also know that there's a lot more to him than he likes to show. I don't think he even knows how good of a guy he is."

She could hear and see the concern and love Anna had for Tex. Liza knew it wasn't anything sexual, because for some crazy reason, she was totally in love with Jake. Still, something jumped in Liza's stomach at the thought of another woman being *something* in his life. "How did you and Tex become so close? I know y'all both love baseball, but you seem to really care about him."

"Back in the summer, he kissed me," Anna said, as if it were nothing.

Liza could feel all the blood drain from her face. Why was she just hearing about this? She hadn't talked to Anna much when she first came back to Patience. They'd exchanged a few emails and talked on the phone a couple of times, but she didn't remember Anna ever saying anything about kissing anyone other than Jake.

Anna must have seen the shock on Liza's face because she quickly added, "Don't worry. It was just him trying to get a rise out of Jake. It was just a peck on the mouth. I promise."

Liza waved her off. "I'm not worried." She hoped she sounded convincing. "I just can't believe you didn't tell me. Jake must have been pissed. Was there a fight?" She could tell in the few times she'd seen Jake with Anna that he was protective of her and at one time, according to Anna, had loved to get into fights. She imagined it didn't go well for Tex when he overstepped Jake's boundaries.

"Actually, Jake let it go. Tex still likes to remind Jake of it. Only to push his buttons."

"Men are confusing," Liza pointed out. "If they were women, there would be major hair pulling and bitch-slapping."

"So are y'all going to see each other again?" Anna raised an eyebrow.

"We'll see each other tonight at Ollie's."

Anna offered a dry look. "That's not what I meant."

Liza caved. If she couldn't gush to her dear friend, who could she talk to? "I hope we have more alone time, if that's what you're asking."

"Tonight?"

"Maybe, but I don't want to talk about that right now. I'm here to help you with whatever you need." She smiled. "I don't know if you know this, but you are having your opening in a week."

"Jill should be here anytime to finalize the menu and make sure the kitchen is ready, but you could put some of the books that came in on the bookshelves."

Liza was more than happy to help. "Show me the way."

The shop was quiet. The upstairs was finished, except for the books displayed on the shelves Jake and Tex built. Liza was still in awe of what they did with their own two hands. She had to give Jake credit; he was talented at many things.

She needed to get Jake alone that night to make sure he delivered Anna's surprise on time. Coming through for them was important. If he did, she might start to like him…just a little.

Tex was at Avery Landscaping because he had to catch up on paperwork at his office and mentioned maybe taking the time to repaint the porch swing at his mom's. She was disappointed, but it was probably best if she planned to get anything done. He would be a good distraction, but she needed to work.

She couldn't believe he'd confided in her. She'd

practically begged him to trust her, but she never expected him to feel the way he did. Her heart went out to him. How could he think he didn't have a right to be scared or mad? She wished she could take away the pain he was drowning himself in. When she talked to her patients who experienced gut-wrenching losses, she had similar thoughts. A child losing their parent way too young or a woman faced with the pain after being beaten or sexually abused—those were the things that really got to her and had her thinking of her work after hours.

After listening to Tex pour his soul to her, she wanted nothing other than the ability to take his suffering and make it her own.

She almost brought up the night before when they drove back to his house, but luckily, she caught the words before they left her mouth and thought better of it. He wouldn't appreciate her bringing it up again and might even have been a little embarrassed. She wouldn't be surprised if last night was the first time he'd ever said the word *Alzheimer's*. He'd said it as if he was still trying to believe it himself.

"How's it going, sweetheart?"

Liza jumped at the male voice. She turned and saw Tex standing in the doorway. "God—you scared ten years off my life."

He towered over her, causing her to look up at him. When she thought he would tease her for jumping out of her skin, he just simply said, "I thought you would be happy to see me." His voice was somewhat seductive.

"I thought you were working at the office all day."

"I was hungry." Something in his voice told her it wasn't food he was hungry for.

She swallowed. "Did you go to the diner?"

He shook his head. "No."

Her eyebrows rose as he looked at her as if he could ravish her at any second. "Are you going to the diner?"

He again shook his head and dragged her up to him, bringing them only inches apart. "I have to have you again," he rasped in her ear.

Her heart raced as shivers ran up her spine. She didn't know tattered blue jeans and scuffed boots could look so sexy, but then again, she was finding Tex could wear anything or nothing and still do ungodly things to her insides. A very naughty grin took residence on his unshaven face, and that was it. She lost all logic and just went with what she felt and needed, and what she needed stood in front of her, ready to give her what she so desperately craved.

Chapter Sixteen

She kissed him as if her entire being relied on it.

He pulled back a minute to catch his breath. His gaze swept over her face, and when he stopped at her mouth, she knew they were on the same page. Capturing her mouth again, he lifted his hands to her face and deepened the kiss. She met him with every thrust of his tongue as moisture surged below. Desire filled her chest, the small of her back, and the sensation stretched to her inner thighs.

His hands roamed her back, her ass, but that still didn't seem like enough. His bulge pressed against her thigh, and she hungered for him. Kissing was good. Touching was even better, but body on body was what she craved.

Was she really going to do this in Anna's shop? God, she wanted to, but she just couldn't. Taking a step back, she tried to catch her breath. "We can't do this…here."

"Why not?" He planted soft kisses down her neck, making her automatically tilt her head to the side. "You know you can't resist me."

"What if someone comes up here?" She breathed deeply. His kisses went from one side of her neck to the other, his hands slipped under her shirt, and his fingers almost scorched her stomach. "What if Anna catches us?"

He stopped kissing her long enough to say, "Anna and Jill are occupied downstairs. I snuck up here without them ever knowing. Quit thinking and just go with it."

When she was in college, she loved having sex in public places. She chalked it up as being a naïve college student who thought she was invisible. At the time, it was exciting. The thought of being caught only thrilled her more and put her over the edge. Of course, being caught by Anna would make her feel more embarrassed than exhilarated. However, Anna had said she would be busy with Jill for a while. Maybe if they were quick...and quiet... No, neither was capable of that.

She reached down and pressed her hand to the bulge she hungered for, and she went liquid with lust when his breath caught in his throat. She couldn't stop from giving him a heated kiss, a kiss that curled her toes.

They were both panting. She lifted her arms, then stopped kissing him long enough to let him rip her shirt over her head. He let out a groan at the sight of another one of her lacy bras. Hearing his reaction quickened her own breath and forced her to speed the process of getting them naked.

"You sure do wear expensive lingerie well." His breathing sounded heavier than usual.

She didn't even want to know how he knew what brand of lingerie she had on. Jealousy overcame her when she thought of him with other women—women like Leah. Even though he said he was never actually with Leah, she knew he had been with a lot of women just like her.

She pushed it from her mind, because at that moment, she was the woman he was with. After unhooking her bra, she let it fall to the floor.

"I've never seen anything more beautiful than you right now," he whispered. He said it as if he were seeing her for the first time. She ached for him to touch her, but first, they needed to lose more clothing.

Her hands went to his waistband, hurriedly undoing his jeans and lowering the zipper. He must have felt the same way, because they both toed off their shoes and got rid of their jeans. He tugged off his boxer briefs while she slipped out of her panties. She was self-conscious when he studied her body.

What did he think about her standing before him completely vulnerable? Would he look at her and instantly notice her flaws, compare her to the twenty-somethings he usually went for?

"What's wrong?" he asked, his voice soft and comforting.

She considered ignoring him or giving him some lame excuse she hadn't even thought of yet, but something in his eyes told her he would see right through her and know she was lying through her teeth. "I guess…I guess I'm just realizing that you've probably never been with a woman my age before."

"What in the hell is that supposed to mean?" His tone went from soft to practically yelling. "What is up with you and your age?" He lowered his voice. "How old are you, Liza?"

She glared at him. Did he not know the rule of never asking a woman her age? Of course, he probably only hung out with women just old enough to drink, which made them tell anyone who would listen how old they were.

He just glared back. "How old?"

Oh, what the hell. "Thirty-five." She was trying to

sound proud but wasn't feeling it.

"Well, good Lord, I figured you'd be in an old people's home by now," he said sarcastically.

She let out a breath and spoke softly. "You know what I mean." When he stared at her, looking dumbfounded, she added, "You have to see that most of the women you've been with in the past are barely over the age of twenty. Take Leah, for instance. What is she…twenty-one…twenty-two?"

His nostrils flared. It was a mood she was becoming used to since she made him that way more times than not.

"How do you know who I've been with?" he asked.

She didn't say anything because she didn't know. They never talked about past lovers…besides her and Greg.

"That's right, honey. You don't know. So quit thinking the worst of me and start giving me a little damn credit. I don't sleep with women who aren't even old enough to order a glass of wine. I like women. I've never denied that. I've been with quite a few, but I imagine you've been with more men than just Greg. Have you ever thought that maybe I don't feel good enough for you?"

She gasped. "How could you feel that way?"

"For one, you've been in a serious relationship. Even though Greg was an ass, you still thought you loved him. Maybe I think you compare me to him. And secondly, look at you." He extended his arms and let his gaze wander over her naked body. "You are an amazing woman who is smart, sassy, most of the time confident, and absolutely the most gorgeous woman I've ever been with. That right there is enough to make any man question what he has to offer you."

"I didn't mean to make you sound shallow or anything because you're not. However, you can't ignore the facts, and the fact is I'm older than you. Have you ever been with a woman my age before?"

"Five years. We're really going to stand here and make a big freaking deal because you *just* happened to be born five years before me? Come on, Liza, give me a break." He ran his hand through his hair and paced the room.

He looked like a god. Her eyes couldn't focus on anything other than his naked body. In truth, she'd never met someone with that kind of sheer masculinity and sex appeal.

"Just answer the question," she said with enough force that he turned to look at her. "Have you been with a woman older than you?"

"No, I haven't, but that doesn't mean I have something against it. Most of the women my age and older are either married or engaged. I like spending time with a woman I can actually have a grown-up conversation with. I like being with you." He stopped and seemed to gather himself. When he spoke again, his words were unhurried. "Do you want to be with me, Liza? Do you want to be with me—right now?"

She walked around the space and started to gather her clothes. "You don't get it." She pulled her shirt over her head and reached for her pants when he caught the hem of her shirt and drew her close.

"Tell me what I don't get. I don't know if it's because I'm a slow southern boy or because I'm clueless when it comes to classy women, but I'm at a loss right now, Liza. I need you to help me here."

She didn't feel inclined to discuss that particular

topic with him. He knew she was sensitive about her age and that her mother was in some way disappointed in her picking a career over having a family. That was more than enough of herself to give away. "I don't trust you. I don't know that when you look at me…like this," she said, gesturing to her body, "that you don't compare me to a woman like Leah. I am no fool, Tex."

"Trust me? I haven't even looked at another woman since you got here. As a matter of fact, I haven't been with a woman other than you in the last two months." He stopped and put his hands on his hips. "If I'm not mistaken, you're the one who's had eyes for another man. Have you forgotten about Saunders? Quit using your age as an excuse to keep me away. It's dumb, and you're above that."

Knowing he hadn't been with another woman in two months shouldn't have affected her as much as it did, but a sense of relief settled over her.

"I'm not using anything as an excuse." She didn't think. "I bet you've not thought about how I might feel? I say no, or you would try to at least understand." She pulled away from him, grabbed for her panties and pants, and put them on. If she was going to talk to him anymore, she needed clothes on. "Can you put your clothes back on, please?"

He snatched and tugged at his T-shirt and jeans. "Now," he said when he was fully dressed, "are you going to talk to me?"

"I want to be married," she blurted out. She didn't dare to look him in the eye, because usually, talking about any type of commitment caused a man to turn pale and faint on the spot. Just the night before, he could barely say they were dating. "I'm thirty-five years old,

Tex."

"I know. We've already discussed that to the ground."

"Do you know what it means to be in your midthirties and not have children yet?" She still avoided making eye contact.

"No, I haven't thought much about it."

"If I want kids, I need to have them in the next couple of years. Otherwise, there will be health risks I really don't want to take." She sent him a sideways glance because she was too chicken to face him directly. "I have lost my job, found my boyfriend with one of his patients, which means I am not in a committed relationship, and kids aren't even in the picture right now. I spent a year of my life with Greg and got nothing but loss."

"I do understand all of that, Liza, but what I don't get is how any of that refers to you questioning the way you look or you thinking you're too old for me."

"When I think about those other women, I realize I am not in my twenties anymore. I don't have my whole life in front of me, because my life is happening right now. Since I'm not young and as fit anymore, I also know I have many flaws." She stopped and stood tall. "I know I can hold my own, and I don't usually let such things get to me, but something about us makes me take a harder look at myself." She gave a stern nod. "I don't like what you do to me, Tex."

"Oh, baby, you should never question yourself. I mean it when I tell you that you are beautiful." He took both of her hands and placed them on his hips while he planted both of his strong hands on hers. "I like what I do to you." He paused and lowered his voice. "I like what you do to me, too."

He gently squeezed her sides as he softly kissed her lips. It was such an intimate gesture, and she had never felt closer to him. What was going on? She didn't know what to feel. He hadn't run from the room when she mentioned marriage and kids. Not that she was referring to him when she talked about having a family...because she wasn't.

The kiss was over before it started. She suddenly regretted bringing up her feelings and ruining the moment. If she had kept her big mouth shut, who knew where they would be right now. Would he still be kissing the sensitive spots on her neck and breasts, or kissing farther down her body until she reached a more sensitive spot between her legs, or, God...would he finally bury himself deep inside her again? Even though they had been together just last night, it felt like forever.

She needed to have him again. So being disappointed was an understatement when he picked that moment to leave.

He dropped his hands from her waist. "I better go and let you get back to work."

"I'll see you tonight." She tried not to sound disappointed. He was fully dressed and leaving her hot and bothered once again. *This was my own damn fault.*

****

Tex sat at the bar at Ollie's, nursing a beer, loving the way it felt going down. It was Friday night, and the place was filling with locals wanting to let loose after a workweek.

His mind was in a whole other place than what was going on around him. A song about beer drinking blaring at a high volume, the clacking of billiard balls on the pool tables, and the laughing between friends were in the far back of his mind.

He couldn't believe how open and honest he'd been with Liza last night. Things had become intimate, and it had nothing to do with sex. He really liked her and knew sex wasn't enough for him. His relationship with her scared the shit out of him because he was pretty sure he wanted more.

She'd made it more than clear that she wanted something lasting. She wanted marriage, kids, the whole nine yards, and that wasn't him on so many levels. He could never be what she needed. It wasn't as if she would be sticking around very much longer, and just the thought of her leaving also scared the living daylights out of him.

After last night, seeing her take special care with his mom, he knew things were changing. She had slipped into his life, and surprisingly, he was starting to like it. He liked that she wanted to spend time with his mom, knew his family secret, and wasn't freaked out. Not that he thought she would bolt if she knew his mom was sick and he was so angry. She, in some way, understood him. Much like his mom, Liza was a tough woman. He needed someone in his life who would give as much as he dished out. Liza could do that in spades.

He couldn't deny the sex between them was incredible as well. He was messed up if he thought he could resist being with her again, because their strong connection was part of the reason he'd pulled into the shop when he saw her car parked in front.

"What's going on, man?" Jake asked as he approached the bar.

The interruption jerked Tex from his thoughts,

forcing his gaze from the bottle in front of him to his friend's face. "Just waiting on you assholes." He tipped his beer to Jake and Bradley, who was coming through the door. "What took you so long? I'm already on my second beer."

"Anna and I had to pick Bradley up. For some reason, he took special care in what he wore tonight. He had Anna pick out the damn shirt he's wearing. I swear he's becoming more like a woman every day," Jake said. Minny set a beer in front of him without him having to ask for it. "Something wrong? You looked like you were thinking about something pretty deep when I walked up."

Tex brushed him off. "I'm good." He took a pull of his beer. "So what about those Sparks?" he asked with a fat grin. He could literally see steam coming from Jake's ears. "I bet Anna's living on cloud nine and making your life a living hell."

Jake grunted. "I don't want to talk about it."

Tex laughed. He wished he'd been a fly on the wall as Jake watched Anna's precious ball team—and Jake's most hated baseball team—win the World Series. However, he'd been busy pleasuring and at the same time being swept away by Liza. His night had been well spent if he didn't count his mom throwing up most of the night and thinking he and Liza were getting married, expecting their first kid. He could have done away with that part of the night, but unfortunately, that was a part of his life now.

"You want to shoot a game of pool?" Jake asked.

Jake looked at Anna joining Jessie at a table. Tex couldn't help but feel a tug-of-war within himself. On one hand, he knew he wasn't built for a lasting relationship, but the other part of him, the side of him that seemed to be taking over, felt he was missing out on something pretty incredible.

Where in the hell was Liza? She was supposed to be there by now.

He grabbed his beer. "Let's get a table before they're all taken."

****

Liza left the coffee shop and bookstore after five, and now, a couple of hours later, she sat at a table with Anna, Georgia, and Jessie. After Tex left the shop, she'd tried to keep her mind busy with endless chitchat with Anna while they worked. It felt good to be doing something again.

"Georgia, honey, don't you think you should slow it down a little?" Jessie asked, as Georgia drank glass after glass of wine. "You've only been here for an hour and a half, and you're already on your third glass."

Jessie rarely stopped anyone from having a good time, but Liza was starting to realize that Georgia's drinking was more than just her having a good time. Something much deeper was going on.

"Yeah, why don't you switch to water? I can have Minny bring you a glass," Anna suggested.

Georgia took another sip of her wine, ignoring their concern. "I'm fine," she said without even a stutter. Out of the blue and way off topic, she asked, "Do you guys think I'm sexy?"

Jessie threw her head back and laughed while Anna gave Jessie a pointed look, then brought her concern back to Georgia.

"I'm serious," Georgia said.

After Jessie received Anna's firm glare, she

straightened in her chair and cleared her throat. "Why would you ask that, Georgia? Where is this coming from?"

"Is there something wrong with me, something that is a major turnoff to all Patience men?"

Liza reached out and squeezed Georgia's hand. "Sweetie, I thought we'd already discussed this. You are an amazing woman. If he can't see that, then I say screw 'im."

Anna looked from Liza to Georgia. "Who is the *he* we're talking about?"

Georgia let out a breath. "Garrett."

Jessie gave the reaction Liza expected—complete shock and horror. Anna must have expected it because she stared at Jessie before she could comment or give another belting laugh.

Georgia was a good, sweet person who didn't deserve to feel this wrapped up over a guy who obviously didn't appreciate the woman she was. She was too good for him.

"Garrett…Garrett Tillman?" Anna finally asked. "Are we talking about your boss?"

Georgia nodded.

"Don't let Garrett make you question how sexy you are, and most definitely don't let him make you feel bad about yourself. I'm with Liza. If he doesn't appreciate you, then let him be," Jessie added.

Jessie's matter-of-fact tone and point-blank wisdom on the subject suggested she was speaking from experience.

Liza looked up, and damn if she didn't find herself staring right at Tex's ass. He leaned over the pool table, about to take a shot. "That is some ass," she murmured.

She thought the girls wouldn't hear her, as they were still trying to lighten Georgia's spirits and get her to put down the wineglass, but she wasn't so lucky.

"Which ass are we looking at?" Anna asked.

Liza tried to cover herself. "I, uh, was just saying in general."

"Don't give us that," Anna said. "You're staring at Tex, aren't you?"

What the hell? "What if I am?"

"Then good." Anna nodded. "You've already admitted y'all have been together. Why would you deny lusting after him from across the room?"

"You slept with Tex?" Jessie asked a little too loudly.

God, she hoped Georgia didn't decide to pipe up.

"Well, since Anna blabbed it, I guess I can't lie about it now, can I?" She stopped, then added, "Oh, and I also got naked with him in the bookstore," because she wanted to see the shock on the girls' faces, especially Anna's.

Jessie lifted her hand to offer Liza a high five. "Nice."

Liza returned the clap.

"You what?" Anna's eyes about popped out of her head.

"What can I say?" Liza shrugged before taking a drink of her wine. "He showed up, you were busy downstairs, and I just decided to go with it."

"Wow," Jessie said.

"You had sex with Tex while I was downstairs with Jill?" Anna said. "This was today?"

"Yes, and we didn't have sex." She didn't want to tell everyone at the table she'd gotten a jolt of self-confidence issues and put a damper on what could have been a perfect afternoon of hot, spontaneous sex.

"I don't know what I'm going to do with you." Anna chuckled.

In one ear, she listened to Jessie and Anna talk about how proud they were of her because she was taking her life back, that she was actually having fun in Patience. Anna sounded as if she was actually happy that Liza had almost slept with Tex in the shop. A high-pitched squeal made her stomach drop as the woman came into view. *Don't let yourself go there, Liza.*

She tried to ignore the attractive blonde continuously touching Tex's arm and failing at making it look subtle. With every laugh, touch, and flirty look, the woman was trying to stake her claim to Tex.

She and Tex weren't necessarily dating, but they had plenty of moments to qualify as something. Just a few hours ago, he was being sweet and saying all the right things. She couldn't help thinking that maybe he was going back to his old way and not meaning it when he said he wanted to see her again. If that was true, then he was proving her logic correct when she said men don't change. She plastered on a fake smile as she listened to Jessie talk about her latest lousy date.

From there, Jessie asked, "So do I need to bring anything to this naming party?"

"I thought about making a pitcher of fruit tea and picking up one of those meat-and-cheese platters at the grocery," Anna added.

"You will not be bringing tea and platters, missy." Liza took her gaze off of Tex. She was appalled that Anna would even suggest such a thing. "This party is for you, and we will not have you trying to plan it. Besides, aren't you and Jake going to some bed-and-breakfast tomorrow morning?"

Anna shrugged. "Oh, how did I forget about that?"

"Where are you two lovebirds going?" Jessie asked.

"Jake surprised me with a stay at a little bed-and-breakfast for the night. It's kind of a small getaway before we get so busy with the shop."

"That's so sweet," Georgia chimed in on cue.

"Let me talk to Em again, and I will call you if we need anything else," Liza said to Jessie.

"Me, too," Georgia insisted. "Let me know, too."

"Oh, Tex, why don't you and I go back to your place?"

Anna, Jessie, Georgia, and Liza all abandoned their conversation, turned, looked up, and came to attention at the overly loud woman wanting every woman in the place to know Tex was off-limits.

"Carly," Anna said with disgust.

The blonde she now knew as Carly rubbed her fingers up and down Tex's arm while he turned up his beer. He took Carly's hand and removed it from his body. Liza should have been relieved that he acted as if he didn't have any interest in the other woman, but she still didn't like that another woman was touching her man.

Where in the hell did that come from? Tex was not *her* man. He was just a man she found wildly attractive, who she had a soft spot for, and who pushed all her buttons in bed. He could never be more than that.

"Who's Carly?" Liza asked, trying to sound nonchalant.

"Just a woman who attaches herself to any man who will actually have her. Last summer, her focus was on

Jake, and now, it seems since Jake is with me, she's moved to Tex. What a bitch," Anna said.

Liza's thoughts exactly. Even though she and Tex only had one great night of sex, they'd shared more than just what they did in bed. She couldn't deny their connection. She sure as hell planned to have more than just one night with him. Carly was wildly mistaken if she thought she would be the one going home with him.

When he caught her peeking at him, one side of his mouth turned up. *Play it cool. Don't let him know you're jealous.* She gave him a wave and knew she was trying too hard to prove her point. Anyone would be able to tell she was being as fake as Santa Claus.

He handed his pool stick to Bradley and sauntered toward her table. Her breath caught in her throat as he walked closer. The heat coming from his gaze could be felt in her thighs.

"Ladies," he said as he approached them.

"I see Carly is trying to catch you," Jessie bluntly said.

Tex grunted. "I don't want to get caught…at least, not by a woman like her."

"Does she know that?" Anna asked.

"I think she finally got the point." He turned to Liza. "Can I talk to you for a minute?" He reached out to take her hand.

She looked at Anna, who shooed her away. She took the hand he offered and let him lead her outside.

"What's up?" she asked cheerfully.

"I just want to make sure we're okay."

"Why wouldn't we be?"

"I want you to know that there is nothing going on with me and Carly. She came up to me, not the other way around."

"You don't have to explain yourself, Tex. You and I are not in a committed relationship. You can do what you please."

He took her hand and brushed his lips over her knuckles, making her nipples instantly hard. She could have moaned at the simple gesture, but somehow she held back.

"I am doing what I please. I don't want any other woman but you." He still held her hands, and she could see the depth of his eyes.

She lost all control. Before she could talk herself out of it, she gripped the front of his shirt like a lifeline, bringing him closer so his body was just short of touching hers. "I was not jealous," she whispered in the light of the neon signs.

"Yes, you were."

He smirked, and she wanted to slug him. She wanted to kiss him more. Her lips barely brushed his, then she pulled back. With her eyes locked on his, she traced his lips, letting her fingers leave a trail to his strong jaw covered with dark stubble. Leaning close, she licked his throat, over the throb of his Adam's apple. She could never get enough of the way he tasted on her tongue. A hint of sex and spice lingered in her mouth.

She was torturing them both, but he deserved it. "I guess you'll never know," she whispered right before she found her way back to his mouth and gave him a passionate kiss. Urgency built within her, the need for something more. It was a part of her she didn't know she kept hidden away. Her body tingled as his hands roamed over her.

Because she wanted something real with a man, she

should have stopped what she was doing right then. He just wasn't at that spot in his life. She respected that his life was changing every day and it was a challenge just to keep up, but that didn't mean she should sacrifice everything she desired.

Yeah, she should point all that out, but it was a fleeting thought as his kiss swept through her entire body.

He walked her backward until her back reached the concrete block. With one hand pressed against the wall next to her head, he had her feeling pleasantly trapped.

She ignored the scratchiness of the wall digging into her back and welcomed his sturdy body pressed against her. "I want you…now," she said, breathless. Needing to feel bare skin, she tugged his shirt from his waistband.

He was muscled and lean in all the right places. Her hands shook as if she were exploring the hardness of his back for the first time.

"Damn, woman," he rasped before lowering his mouth to resume kissing hers.

They continued kissing until her lips felt weak and swollen. Still she didn't want him to stop. Nothing was better than his touch, taste, smell consuming her.

"I want you, Tex," she repeated. It didn't matter that they were outside a public place where anyone could walk up. The only thought in her head was needing him.

Without a word, he took her by the hand and tugged her across the parking lot. After fishing his keys out of his front pocket, he opened the driver's-side door. With help, she climbed inside with him right behind her.

In seconds, they were pulling out of the parking lot and heading back toward town.

While snuggling close to him, she let her hand move

to the inside of his thigh, and she licked the side of his neck. She loved the quickness of his breath and the strain she felt behind his zipper.

"What you do to me," he started, but he seemed to need a minute to catch his breath. When he spoke again, his voice came out deep and scratchy. "I don't think…you know what you do to me."

"Why don't we go back to your place where you can show me what I do to you?" she whispered close to his ear, still stroking the inside of his leg.

God, she hoped he had a lead foot.

Chapter Seventeen

Tex threw the truck into park after barely pulling into his driveway. He was tempted to take her right there in the cab but figured a couple of more feet wouldn't be that far.

"I'll race you." She was already scooting across the bench seat to the passenger door. Her wearing heels didn't stop her from jumping out of the truck.

He laughed when she stumbled before catching herself as she took a turn in front of the truck.

"No, you don't."

He raced in front of her and caught her by her waist, swinging her legs out from under her before she could reach the porch.

"Hey!"

His hand covered her mouth. "Let's try not to wake my neighbors."

He led her through the front door, making sure she didn't trip or run into anything since he'd forgotten to leave a light on before heading to Ollie's.

Something hard hit the wall behind him. He quickly turned, thinking Liza had walked into it, but instead she was kicking her shoes off and not caring where they landed. After the sexy heels that made her legs look as if they went on forever, she yanked her shirt off and tossed it to the floor. Good Lord, she wasn't wearing a bra. How had he fucking missed that? Moonlight played across her soft flesh.

"You look like an angel," he murmured.

"You going to join me, handsome?" Her fingers worked at the buttons on her pants. Wavy hair framed her angel-like face. Her hazel eyes looked dreamy. One corner of her mouth turned up in a seductive grin.

In less than a minute, he stood before her in nothing. His cock rose to attention as her eyes glazed over. He loved that she wasn't shy when it came to sex. Except when she questioned her age, she was always so sure of herself. With her thin black panties barely covering her, she moved her body freely and bravely toward him.

By the smile on her face, he knew, at least for the night, everything was going to be okay. Nothing outside those doors could hurt them.

He crushed his mouth to hers, kissing her with such passion. The overwhelming feeling running through his veins was new territory for him.

Her mouth was sweet and inviting. With heat searing through him, he pulled back to catch a breath. No matter what he did, he couldn't seem to get enough air to his lungs. He planted kisses down her neck, and every one of her little sighs tightened his chest. Finally, he raked his tongue over one of her nipples and swore the sensation she experienced rippled through him, too.

"Ohhh…" She gripped his shoulders.

Her body moving against his set every one of his nerves on edge. He cupped her ass and found she was wearing a thong. With his mouth never leaving her body, he pushed away her panties and walked her to the couch. The bedroom was too far. He lowered the two of them on the large couch his mom insisted he have and loved the way her body felt like the perfect match to his.

Her breath came in short gasps as he teased her. "Please, Tex."

"I love when I bring you to begging."

"Just get inside me," she demanded, gripping his ass with her hands and forcing him closer.

How could he turn that down? He lost all control and sank deeply into her.

"You feel so good," she whispered.

"Aw…honey, you, too," he growled. There would be time to take things slow, but right now was not one of those times.

He thrust into her as she arched her back. They found a rhythm. With every one of her sighs and soft moans, she egged him on. Something about Liza made him care about her pleasure more than his own. Her needs came first.

She gasped when he pulled out. "What are you doing?"

He grabbed her ankle and balanced it on his shoulder. Then he was inside her with one hard thrust, going even deeper.

"Oh God," she cried.

He continued thrusting into her warm heat until they both were panting. When he felt her orgasm, her inner muscles contracting around him, he gritted his teeth and let himself explode with her.

"I think I'm going to have to beg more often," she said.

"You good?" He pulled her ankle away from his shoulder and placed it back on the couch.

"Uh-huh…really good. But there is something we need to talk about."

He looked down at her, their faces only inches apart.

Even in the semidarkness, everything about her seemed to glisten and glow. She was so sexy. "What's that, honey?"

"We didn't use a condom either time. I'm on the pill and haven't been with anyone since Greg, but he and I always used a condom because he was afraid that the birth control would fail and I would end up pregnant. I'm not worried or anything. I just felt we should at least acknowledge it."

Shit, how could he be so careless? He should have protected her better than that. "I'm safe, and as far as me being with anyone else…" He drew his gaze away. "Like I said before, it's been a couple of months."

He wasn't embarrassed by his previous way with women, because his past was out there and Liza knew, but he didn't want to discuss it either. He wasn't keen on the thought of her being with anyone other than him. Even though those women were before her, in some way he felt as if he'd betrayed her by being with them.

He tilted her chin to him as he focused on her. "Listen, Liza, I can't change the guy I was before, but you have to believe I'm not that guy anymore. As for us not using a condom, you need to know that I've never done that with another woman in my life."

He rolled them over so they were side by side but still locked in an embrace. She peered at him, looking sweet and genuine and touching something deep inside him that he never knew existed.

"I know that. You are a good guy, Tex. I can see that."

The woman made him hope for things he had no business hoping for. Everything in his life still sucked, but somehow, Liza made it bearable. "When are you leaving?" he suddenly asked. His heart thumped loudly in his chest as he waited for her to answer the question that seemed to always hang in the air.

She bit her lip. "I'm not sure yet. Probably two weeks."

"That's soon."

"Well, I want to be around a little after Anna has her opening. But I do eventually have to go home and figure out what I'm going to do with my life."

"Are you going to be able to find another job in Linden? It is a small town, right?" He was still ticked off that her asshole of an ex was so insecure he had her fired from a job she loved and was good at.

"Yeah, but maybe it's a sign for me to open my own dream. I've been watching Anna make her dream a reality. Sometimes it makes me think…"

A spark came to her eyes, a spark he hadn't seen before when she was talking about her job. He leaned in and kissed her forehead. "What is that, sweetheart?"

"It's nothing but a wishful thought." She tensed.

Her dreams were important to him. "No, tell me. I really want to know what makes you happy."

She tugged at a blanket on the back of the couch.

"Cold?" He wrapped the blanket around them, and she nodded. Everything felt so warm and cozy, as if they were the only two people in the world. "Now tell me what makes your entire face light up."

For several minutes, she just stared at his chest while gliding her fingers from one of his shoulders to the other. His body tensed because he was ready to be with her again. But first, there was something she needed to get off her chest. He was determined to make her talk.

"I've always wanted to open my own practice," she

said. "I don't know everything I need to make that happen. I would have to do a lot of research, but it has always been something I've wanted. I want people to feel safe and at home when they see me. People don't open up completely in sterile, boring places."

"That sounds great." He stroked her arm with the tips of his fingers. "Is there anyone you can contact to help you get started?"

She stared at him. "I don't even have a building to get started in. I've lived in Linden my entire life, but do I want to spend the rest of my life there? I don't know. I have a lot more questions than answers."

He always assumed she would leave Patience to go back to her home in Linden. Now she didn't even know if that's where she wanted to go. Somehow, that changed everything. His thoughts raced. "Do you have any other places in mind?" His voice came out just above a whisper.

He'd been convincing himself for so long that he was not built for a lasting relationship. The knowledge of now figuring out how much he really cared for Liza and could see himself with her for longer than a week, or two, or ten confused him.

In the short time he'd known her, he'd found that she was an ideal match for him in every way a woman should be. God, his mother was right. All this time, he'd dismissed his mom's thoughts on what he had with Liza—telling her and himself that what he felt for Liza could only be temporary. After all, she was not a permanent resident of Patience, and he would only be able to see her every couple of weeks. Putting either of them through that kind of torture wouldn't be fair.

"I've always thought I would love to live in a big

city, such as New York City or Chicago, but I really am just a small-town girl at heart. I love the simplicity, and while it can be annoying to have half the town know who you are sleeping with, it can also provide a sense of security to know that if I ever needed anything, there would be several people waiting in line to offer a hand."

"What about Patience?" he blurted out. *Fuck*. Where did that come from? Patience—did he just suggest she pack up her life and move to where he lived?

She hesitated, looked at him for a long moment. "What about it?"

It was too late to take it back now. He should quit being a wimp and let her know what he was thinking. "Patience is a small town. I'm sure Anna would love having you around all the time." Okay, that wasn't exactly what he meant, even though it was partly true.

She stared at him too long. "I guess I do have Anna here." She dropped her hands from his chest.

Shit. "That didn't come out the way I meant it to," he explained. "But Anna is your best friend, and you are always saying how the townspeople in Linden comment on your life. I was just thinking that maybe…you could consider Patience if you are looking for a new home."

Home. Liza would definitely look good in Patience, especially since he would get to see her every day.

She sat up and squirmed away from him. "I guess I could think about it." For some reason, she was saying all the right words but sounded really disappointed.

He brought himself to a sitting position beside her, the big blanket covering them. "Did I say something wrong?"

"No, you didn't say anything."

"Liza, I can tell you are upset. I'm not the best with

words and actually saying what I mean. I can do the flirting thing all day long, but when it comes to the important stuff, I am at a loss." He was wrecked, and that was saying something because he'd never felt this way about a woman.

"What did you mean?" she asked quietly.

The knot forming in his throat threatened to choke him. He could do this. He could give Liza what she'd given him from day one. Honesty. She seemed honest to a fault. While she acted tough in most situations, she was also pure about her emotions and the way she cared about things. Feelings came so easily to her. He wished he had that quality. Being open was important to her and not just because of her job. Offering support when she thought she could help was in her nature.

He took her hands in his and tried his best to get his words right this time. "Anna would not be the only one lucky to have you in Patience. I have started to think of you as an important part of my life."

She stared at him and said nothing in response to what he just revealed.

"Tell me what you're thinking," he finally pleaded.

She gripped his hands. "Uh…I don't know what to think. I guess I just didn't expect you to say anything like that."

"It's true."

He was the type of guy who kept things bottled up for so long, not letting anyone help him, but he didn't mind talking to Liza anymore. After he told her she was important, he felt he could go even further. "Do you think you would want to move to Patience?"

"I guess it's a possibility." Her eyes went wide.

He smiled and let out the breath he'd been holding.

That was all he could ask for. He'd planted the seed, and now he needed to convince her that Patience would be a good home for her. Anna would help him. She knew Liza better than anyone and would know what he would need to do to convince her that staying in town could be a good thing. It could be the best thing.

****

Liza and Tex arrived at Em's house for Anna's naming party a little over an hour before the party was to start. She'd told him he didn't have to come so early, that he could wait until two o'clock like everyone else, but he'd insisted they go together. She liked that he wanted to be there with her.

Not seeing him since yesterday morning had her missing him like crazy, but she'd needed to spend the night in her hotel room, soaking in a hot bath and going over the confession Tex made to her, although she really wanted him in the bathtub with her. They would have to try that one day. She'd been moved, shocked, and confused, along with a million other thoughts and feelings swarming around in her head. On one hand, she'd wanted him to tell her he was going to miss her when she left. So when he brought up the idea of her relocating to Patience, she'd been thrown into left field. What was she going to do?

"Em, I'm still not totally convinced Anna is going to like your baby shower decorations," Liza commented while she and Georgia hung a *Congratulations* banner on the fireplace mantel.

"The shop is her baby." Em continued bustling around the room, placing baby shower centerpieces all over the place. They were very chic and original with their chocolate brown and pink intertwined with blue.

They would look perfect at an actual baby shower, not a party to help name a coffee shop and bookstore.

Jessie kicked back on the couch, drinking a glass of wine because Em had banned beer. She'd said she wanted it to be tasteful. "I think Anna's going to think you're saying she's fat. I mean, there's a fat woman on every one of them."

"It's a pregnant woman, Jessie, and get your damn shoes off my coffee table."

Jessie didn't move. "But she's not pregnant."

Em walked over to the coffee table and shoved Jessie's feet off. "She's going to think it is a unique idea. It's better than just saying congratulations all over the room."

Liza decided it best to let Em have her way and not argue with her. If Anna didn't appreciate the decorations, she could just take it up with Em.

Tex and Tommy emerged from the kitchen.

"Y'all ladies did damn good picking out the furniture for Anna's office." Tex walked over to Liza and kissed her forehead. "Anna is going to love everything."

"Ohhhh," Georgia squealed. "Y'all are so cute."

Liza blushed. Leave it to Georgia to go all sweet and try to turn a simple gesture into some over-the-top romantic thing.

"I hear you two have been hooking up," Em said, as if just talking about the weather.

Tex laughed and shook his head while Tommy added, "Em."

"What?" Em asked, acting all innocent. "Everyone knows. I don't see what the point is in trying to hide it."

"Leave 'em alone. Not everyone likes discussing their love life in front of an audience." Tommy wrapped his arm around Em and pulled her tight.

"Liza's already admitted to them going at it in Anna's—" Jessie started, but the swinging open of the front door saved Liza.

Thank God. She was going to kill Em and Jessie later. Georgia, too, for getting the whole conversation going.

"Oh, Anna, you look so pretty today. It's about time you retired your baseball shirts and jeans. You look so nice in a dress." Em raised a perfectly manicured eyebrow along with the corner of one side of her mouth. "Does this mean you and Jake had a great time?"

"Let the woman get in the house before you start quizzing her about her love life," Tex said.

Em stood away from the door and let Anna, followed by Jake, come in. Em was right. Anna looked hot in her snug chiffon dress made up of colors that had Liza thinking of the ocean. She even wore a pair of trendy wedge pumps. Where in the hell had this sharply dressed friend been hiding? In all of the time she'd been around Anna, she'd never seen her wear anything low cut or showing a small amount of cleavage. If she had known Anna had clothes like that hanging in her closet, Liza would have insisted they share wardrobes.

"How was your trip?" Liza wanted to know.

Em took Anna's purse to her bedroom.

Anna was glowing, so Liza figured it went really well.

"It was amazing. I swear I've never been to such a quaint place in my life. An older woman ran the bed-and-breakfast by herself since her husband died a year ago. She was so lovely and sweet." Jake planted a kiss on Anna's head before she continued, "We were the only couple there, so we pretty much had full run of the place. There was even a lake in the back where we could have a picnic."

"That's so dreamy," Georgia said.

"She gave me a few ideas for the shop. I can't wait to go back," Anna added.

Ten minutes later, Em's mother, Mrs. Bradshaw, came in carrying a boxful of cupcakes. Not long after, Jill showed up with Bradley dragging behind her.

"What's up with all the fat women?" Bradley held up one of Em's centerpieces. "Is this some way to tell us you're pregnant before the actual wedding?" he asked Anna with a wink.

Jake knocked his brother upside his head. "No, she's not pregnant. This is one of Em's extreme decorating ideas. Let's not forget about the penis party." He took a sip of his wine and stuck out his tongue.

"Now that was a party," Bradley said, seeming to think back. "That's the night Anna wanted to come home with me, but you just had to jump in and scoop her up. Maybe if you would have stayed in the background like she wanted, I would be the one to put a ring on her finger." Bradley jumped back, probably anticipating another one of Jake's knocks upside the head.

"You're lucky the women are here. Otherwise, I would be kicking your ass, little brother," Jake threatened.

"Boys," Mrs. Bradshaw scolded. "I know your mother taught you better than to talk like that in front of the ladies. You need to apologize this instant," she demanded with just enough sweetness in her voice.

Jake and Bradley looked sheepish as they shuffled their feet. At the same time, they looked at Em's mother and both said, "Sorry."

"Can we get to the point of why we are here?" Jessie asked. "I'm tired of saying *coffee shop and bookstore*. It's time to give it a name."

Everyone gathered in the living room. Jessie scooted to the end of one side of the couch after Bradley took a seat on the floor beside the couch. Jessie was so head over heels when it came to Bradley. Liza wasn't even sure Jessie recognized how much she cared for him. Georgia sat next to Jessie, Jill sitting beside her. Liza noticed that Georgia hadn't drunk a drop of wine the entire time she'd been around. Mrs. Bradshaw sat in the oversize chair in front of the window, while Em and Tommy sat in two kitchen chairs Tommy and Tex had brought into the room. Em forced Anna and Jake to sit in the center of the room, in front of the coffee table.

Liza sat on the floor, her legs stretched out. She figured Tex would come and sit next to her, but she didn't expect him to sit behind her. As she situated herself between his legs, he wrapped his arms snuggly around her. *Mmmm…*she felt warm and tingly inside. She couldn't help but turn and gaze at his shaven face. He was so handsome.

Em made everyone write down their suggestions, and she put them in a hat. "Okay, Anna, start picking them out." Em placed Tommy's cowboy hat on the coffee table.

Anna rubbed her palms together before drawing the first name. She unfolded the small piece of paper and read aloud, "Happily Ever After."

Em looked to Georgia. "That has to be yours."

"I love it," Anna said with a smile.

"Pick the one with a heart on it," Em said.

"You're not supposed to tell her which one is yours," Mrs. Bradshaw told her daughter. "She's supposed to guess."

"Fiddle-dee-doo." Em waved off her mother's comment. "Go on and pick it."

Anna looked through the hat until she found the piece of paper with a heart. When she opened it, she burst out laughing. "Only you, Em. Only you could come up with a name like this."

"What does it say?" Jessie asked.

Anna tried to keep a straight face. "Foam and Thongs."

"Emilee," Mrs. Bradshaw said with horror. "What kind of name is that?"

"Sounds good to me," Bradley added.

"You know," Em said, "the book thongs they have now instead of the old-fashioned bookmarks. I thought it sounded clever."

"I don't know what the rest of Patience would think about it, but I'll keep it in mind," Anna said, already reaching for another name idea.

"Do you have another one of your thongs on?" Tex whispered close to Liza's ear. His breath was warm and sweet from his glass of blackberry wine. She wanted to kiss him crazy.

"Okay, the next one says *Coffee & Bookstore*." Jake read the name aloud this time. "Who in the hell would suggest that? That's what we call it now."

"I thought it was straight to the point." Bradley nodded. "People will know it offers coffee and books. Why does the name need to be all cutesy and sexual?"

Anna read a couple of more names that Jill and Em's mom put in. Both were cute and mentioned coffee or books in some way. Jessie, Tommy, and Tex didn't put in a name. Jake pulled out a name and handed it to Anna to read. Anna instantly looked at Liza as she read it to herself before announcing it to the room.

"Oh, Liza, 'New Beginnings.' "

"Do you like it?" she asked.

Anna walked on her knees to Liza and wrapped her arms around her. "I do. I really do."

"There should only be one more." Em pulled out the last piece of paper and handed it to Anna to read.

Anna looked at it, then looked to Jake. Tears welled in her eyes as she stared at her lover. Just looking at the love Anna had for Jake had Liza wanting to tear up herself.

It was as if they were in the room alone. "What do you think?" he asked quietly.

Anna wiped at her eyes and nodded.

"What does it say, Anna?" Jessie asked impatiently.

Anna took a minute to gather herself before she finally told everyone Jake's suggestion. "Nora's," she said with glassy eyes. She stared at the piece of paper with the one name on it for a minute.

Everyone in the room fell quiet. Liza looked around the room, noticing all the women wiping at their eyes, all except Jessie. As soon as Anna said the name, Liza knew it was perfect. Putting Anna's mother's name on the front of her shop was a way for Anna to have a little piece of her mom, who died a couple of years ago, with her as she started this new chapter in her life.

Bradley stood from his spot on the floor. "I guess this was a waste of time. Of course she's going to go with Jake's suggestion."

"Well?" Em asked. "Are you going to go with

Nora's?"

Anna nodded. "Yes. I have to. It's too perfect not to. Thank you, everybody, for trying to help. I'm lucky to have such good friends in my life."

All the women, and Bradley, hugged Anna. She thanked everyone again for their support and hard labor. Liza was all warm inside, knowing her best friend had so many good people in her life who cared about her happiness and knew her so well.

She also had to admit that Jake was a part of that group of people who only wanted the best for Anna. Liza inwardly groaned at giving Jake any type of credit, but she couldn't deny he really loved Anna. She still could go rounds with him on a daily basis, though.

The gang broke up. Jessie and Bradley made a beeline to the kitchen to see if Tommy had any beer stashed in the refrigerator. Georgia and Mrs. Bradshaw started discussing the idea of Georgia going back to school to get her real estate license. Jill had dinner plans with her boyfriend, so she had to leave. Liza wished she had a chance to talk to the woman who was going to be an essential part of Anna running a successful business.

Liza went to the restroom, and when she came out, she noticed Tex having a rather intense conversation with Anna. Anna touched his arm and offered a sympathetic smile. Liza was curious but knew Tex and Anna had a close friendship.

She glanced around the room to locate Jake and caught him going out the front door. Making sure nobody was paying attention, she followed him. She didn't want people to think she actually liked Jake.

"Hey, Jake." She closed the door behind her. She was surprised how warm the weather was, considering it was the first part of November.

"Yeah?" He stopped in front of Anna's car. "Oh…Liza."

She swore she could hear him groan at the sight of her. "Will the surprise be here by Friday?" She went straight to the point. "I don't have to tell you how important this is."

"I've already told you every other time you've asked that I've got it covered."

She stood in front of him, glaring, looking for a reason to go all *Liza like* on him, but she couldn't. He didn't even look annoyed at her typical attitude toward him. "You're not the most trustworthy person. Therefore, I will keep pestering you until I see it with my own two eyes."

"You're right. I'm a rat bastard, a jackass, and whatever else you want to call me. Believe me—I've been called it all by Anna. I know you just want to protect her, and I appreciate that. She's lucky to have someone like you in her corner, but I'm not the bad guy, Liza. Yes, I have a past, but who doesn't? I'm lucky to have a second chance with the woman I was destined to be with. I love her—she loves me, and that's all I really care about." He looked at Liza, probably hoping she would say she understood where he was coming from, but when she didn't speak, he added, "Now about you and Em's *big* surprise, it about killed me to make the phone call, and I took a lot of grief from my former agent, but I did it. Not for you and not for Em. I did it for Anna. I will never let her down again."

Liza wished she had some swift comeback like *I'll believe it when I see it* or *you can't teach an old dog new tricks*. But she just nodded. As she walked back to the house, she looked over her shoulder to Jake and smiled when he turned away from her. Maybe there was something good about Jake Lawrence—just maybe he was perfect for her friend. Damn, she didn't *like* liking him.

Em sent a plate of finger foods and cupcakes home with each person. Liza ended up in the truck with Tex. She thought they would be going back to his place since that was where she left her car, but instead, he drove in the opposite direction.

"Where are we going?" she asked.

"I thought we could take a drive, if that's all right with you."

"Yeah, sure."

They drove through the center of Patience. She'd seen a lot of the small town since she'd been there, but as Tex drove slowly, she took the time to notice what the quaint town offered. Maybe it was because he'd planted the crazy idea of her living there in her head, but with a critical eye, she took everything in.

The large red-brick courthouse was the focal point of the town. A small memorial wall stood in the front lawn, naming the soldiers who had called Patience home and lost their lives. An array of red, white, and blue flowers surrounded the stone. Sidewalks lined both sides of the street, leading a path to all the small businesses. A pink, refurbished building sat next to Cut & Curls, called Mrs. Lena's Flowers and Gifts. She'd neglected to see the building before.

Families walked through town, some still in their Sunday best, others dressed more casually. Several boys rode skateboards, poorly avoiding the families enjoying the sunny day. She loved watching families interact with one another—a dad scooping up his small daughter after she tripped over her own two feet, a mother holding hands with the oldest child while gripping her husband's at the same time. Liza smiled at the family and how blessed they seemed.

"What has you grinning?" Tex asked as he drove through the last stoplight before exiting town.

"People," she said simply.

"What about them?"

"I like to watch them when they think no one is paying attention." When he cocked his head, she felt she needed to clarify. "I don't mean in a stalker kind of way. People act more themselves when they think they're alone. The more I know, the better I feel I can do my job." She threw her hands up in the air, laughing. "Okay, it's official—I'm crazy."

She felt content riding down the winding road that led them away from town. Tex showed her his landscaping business and the high school he and the gang had attended, except for Georgia. He was proud of his town, and it showed.

"That's the road Jessie and at one time Tommy lived on." Tex pointed. "They own probably a hundred acres, but they also lease a large amount of land for corn."

"That's a lot," Liza said. "Isn't it just her, Tommy, and their dad who manage it?" She couldn't comprehend how just three people could keep up a place that size.

"They have hired help when they need it. And a couple of miles down this road"—Tex motioned to the next road past Jessie's—"is the Lawrence farm."

"Bradley and Jessie live close to each other." Convenient.

"Anna, too." And just as they rode past Bradley and

Jake's family home, Liza noticed October Road.

She'd heard all about the road Anna was eager to leave. She wasn't even sure Anna visited the place since she moved back to Patience.

"Where are we going?" she finally asked when it seemed they'd driven for some time.

"You'll see" was all Tex said. He whistled to the song playing low on the radio.

She listened. "You like this song?" It was so unexpected.

"You don't?"

She did like the song, but she just hadn't expected him to like a pop tune. "I'm just shocked you're allowed to listen to this type of music in a Ford truck, is all." She feigned an innocent smile.

"You'll come to realize you don't know me as well as you think you do."

She cast a playful grin. "How so?"

He shrugged and returned a playful smile as he pulled onto a twisting road where she didn't see any houses. He stopped at a small gravel area just off the road. "Here we are," he announced.

Chapter Eighteen

Liza looked around the mostly wooded area. "Are we, like…trespassing?"

Tex reached behind his seat and grabbed a blanket. "I don't know, but I've never been caught before."

He led her down a short slope that stopped at a small creek. After spreading the blanket, he grasped her hand and brought her with him until they sat side by side. All was peaceful and simple. She could sit with Tex and not feel she should be doing something else.

Getting out of Linden for a while was good for her. There were no expectations. She could just be Liza.

Tex grinned. "I saw you all friendly with your nemesis."

Crap, she thought she'd been discreet. "Uh…you saw that?"

"Yep."

"Jake is supposed to get us something for Anna's office."

"Must be big for you to ask for Jake's help."

She grunted because, boy, was he telling the truth. "You're telling me. I choked on my own words."

"He's not that bad, Liza. He's been through a lot, and he is head over heels for Anna."

"I guess he's all right. He did come up with a good name." She wiggled her finger at him and added with a stern look, "But don't ever tell him I said so. I like seeing him squirm."

He sealed his lips. "Mum's the word."

They fell into comfortable silence. So much had changed for her in the last several weeks. Greg had cheated, and she'd lost her job. She'd fled to Patience and met some amazing people, along with a guy she had strong feelings for. Was it too soon to feel this way?

"About what you said last night." She wet her lips. "I liked it." From the corner of her eye, she could see him smiling, but she continued to stare at the slow-moving water.

"What did you like?" he whispered.

She thought long and hard before answering. "You were open and honest about what you want. I've felt you've grown to trust me these past few days. I like it."

"I'm only like that with you. What about Patience? Have you given it any thought?" he asked with a hopeful smile.

"It wouldn't be practical for me to just pack up and leave Linden. My family is there."

His body went tense. "I thought you were already thinking of moving?"

She shifted on the blanket. "I did. I don't know if I meant it, though. I could have just been talking. It's time for me to settle down. I'm getting too old to just up and leave the only town I've known."

She glanced in his direction. His jaw had a tic to it.

"Please tell me we're not going back to your age."

"I didn't mean it like that. I'm not proud of my lack of self-confidence, but that's not what this is about. I have to be realistic, and the fact is, I want a family. I want to be one of those families I saw walking down Main Street today. Don't you understand I can't be so careless anymore when it comes to my future?"

"And living here in Patience would be careless? Living here to see where this"—he motioned with his hands between them—"thing we have could lead would mean you would be sacrificing," he bit out.

She turned to face him squarely. "God, no. I don't mean that at all." She cupped his face in her hands. "So much is changing. Moving is something I'm going to have to really think about. I have to make sure that what comes next in my life is good for me. I have to make that decision. I like you, Tex. I'm having fun, and it's more than just sex and sexual tension for me." She gulped back her fear. "I like being with you."

He closed the small space between them. "I like just being with you, too."

They locked gazes. The way he possessed her mind and body made her feel alive.

"Would you care if I kissed you right now?"

She gave him one of her looks, telling him she found the question ridiculous.

With the use of his teeth, he tugged her bottom lip until she felt the overpowering urge to moan. He licked along the sting, his hand gliding up her back. She liked the feel of his fingers sliding up her spine.

As if he couldn't get enough, he pulled her close, holding tight. Maybe it was all in her head, but it was as if he were gripping her, determined not to lose her.

He thrust his tongue into her mouth; his taste roared through her. The kiss wasn't sweet and gentle. She was excited at this fast-paced, bone-melting, seductive way.

He dragged her more-than-willing body until she sat in his lap, her legs straddling him. She dug her fingers into his hair, liking that he was letting it grow out. She grabbed it and forced him not to move. So much of her body craved his touch, but her lips needed all the attention at the moment.

When she was with him, everything felt enhanced. The smell of his aftershave, the feel of his soft sweater between her fingers, the odd sound of silence as the sun set behind the trees, and God, the taste of his mouth as it eagerly moved over hers.

"Do you want to do this?" He pulled back and rubbed the pad of his thumb over her bottom lip. "Out here, I mean?"

Liza had nothing to say in response, too filled with desire and raw need.

Reaching between them, she unbuckled the thin belt circling his waist. She popped the button on his trousers and liked the hitch in his breath. She allowed him to lower his zipper, so not to inflict damage.

He pulled her skirt around her waist, and without him asking, she rose so he could remove her panties.

"Do you want me to use a condom?" he asked.

It touched her that he was trying to protect her.

"I have one in my wallet."

When he started to shift her off his lap, she shook her head. Relief washed over his face. She trusted him with her body.

He freed himself and, with both hands, gripped her waist and slowly lowered her on top of him. She bit her bottom lip as the sensation rippled through her, and she freely gave herself to him. Blinded to all self-control, she could only think about Tex. They were so close. Her heart raced, her breathing became erratic, and she craved more.

She lifted her body as she clung to his chest, then

slowly slid back down. Her head fell back in passion, and when she looked at his face again, his lids were half-closed.

He continued to thrust into her, kissing her lips, swirling his tongue around her neck. "You have to come for me, honey. I can't hold back much longer." He groaned, his breath quickening.

Heat seared through her as they moved together, his mouth finding hers and his tongue pulsing deeper. Pleasure built within her, and then her orgasm hit hard.

After she gave in and released herself in full force, Tex thrust a few more times before cursing under his breath. Little aftershocks of pleasure vibrated through her inner muscles.

"God, woman," he said, voice ragged. "That was…intense."

With her head against his chest, she knew his heart was beating wildly along with hers.

Everything about life seemed clearer. Simple. What she and Tex shared was special. She could see herself in Patience, being with Tex for as long as she felt as she did right then, which she didn't anticipate ending anytime soon. Since the night he told her he wanted to kiss her but knew he wouldn't be able to stop, she'd ached for him.

He made her feel sexy when he wickedly looked at her with his sea-green eyes. When she lost so much and felt like she was a big fat disappointment to her mom, he gave her clarity. Just wrapped in his arms made her feel more alive than ever before. She'd spent a year of her life not loving a man she wanted to marry. With Tex, there was no doubt. *Oh God, I love him.*

A sting and moisture hid behind her eyes as

emotions swept over her.

His body tensed. "Are you okay?"

She pushed aside her sudden realization. He might be all in for her staying around, but he was not ready for her to admit she was falling in love with him. She snuggled close. "I'm just really relaxed."

"Why don't we continue this back at my place?" he suggested.

With his help, she eased off him. He zipped his pants and buckled his belt as she straightened her skirt and watched him slip her panties into his front pocket. She didn't mind going bare; it was just one more thing she didn't have to take off later.

He was sexy in his charcoal-gray trousers and snug V-neck sweater. It was the first time she'd seen him in something other than jeans. "Wait, don't you have to take your mom back to church tonight? What time is it? Are you going to be late?"

"No. Edna's going to pick her up tonight."

"Edna goes to church?" she asked in disbelief.

He laughed. "Surprised?"

"Floored, actually."

"When I saw her this morning, she took me to the side when my mom was talking to the preacher. I thought she was going to lay into me again for forgetting about her yard. Instead, she asked if she could bring my mom to church on Sunday nights but said I had to take her on Sunday mornings and Wednesday nights, and I quote, 'Because it will be good for my ass to be at church.' "

"Sounds like Edna."

"I think my mom will like having her around again. Before my mom got really sick, she and Edna had dinner or did something once a week. I guess they kind of grew apart when my mom continued pushing everyone away. Edna also wants to spend Saturday nights with her."

"I'm glad you're going to let someone help."

"Yeah, well, I think it will be good for my mom to have a friend. Church and having girls' day with you are good for her, but having someone she grew up with will also be good for her, especially when she gets worse."

"How does your mom always remember me?" Liza asked. "You said she forgets the names of people she recently met, but she met me, and she's only forgotten my name once."

"I'm pretty amazed by that, too. I don't really know why, but I remember reading that people with Alzheimer's tend to remember the memorable things. I think because she likes you so much, she somehow just never forgets. You are pretty unforgettable," he added with a grin. "All joking aside, I really can't answer the whys with a lot of things when it comes to this disease. I just try to find joy in the small things and try my best to prepare for the big ones."

She only nodded because she was sure if she said anything, she would definitely let the tears fall.

On the way back to Tex's house, he drove with one hand on the wheel and the other wrapped around her. She couldn't think of a more perfect night.

****

Tex woke to the morning light filtering through his bedroom curtains. His nose filled with the smell of something odd. *Mmmm...grease*. Looking at the rumpled sheets beside him, he discovered Liza wasn't there. He liked that he found it so normal to wake in the morning to food cooking in his kitchen.

Ever since Sunday night, she'd stayed in his bed,

even on Monday when he had to stay with his mother. She insisted on spending the night in her hotel room, but he didn't want her there. Even if he couldn't be with her, he still liked the idea of her curled between his sheets, leaving her scent for him. Like right now, he smelled her on his pillow, on his skin. After being persistent, adding that he did have the Entertainment Channel on his satellite, she was sold.

Last night, when she was finished having dinner with Anna and Em, she'd come home to him. He'd lost all breath when she waltzed through his front door without even knocking. She seemed comfortable in his space, and he loved her there.

He stared at the clock and couldn't believe he'd slept so long on a workday. It had been more days than he cared to count since he'd felt so rested. He stepped into his jogging pants and then walked out of his bedroom to find Liza dressed only in one of his baseball shirts, singing to the radio softly playing and forking pieces of bacon out of a skillet. He stood in the doorway, staring at her in his kitchen. She moved the skillet off the hot burner before removing a baking sheet full of biscuits from the oven. She was reaching to grab a few plates out of the cabinet when she finally caught sight of him.

"Hey, you." She sounded breathy and sexy.

He approached her, allowing his eyes to take in how beautiful she was. Threading his fingers through her rumpled hair, he tilted her head back so he could kiss her deeply. She tasted of the hazelnut creamer she used in her coffee. Creamer he'd made sure he bought so she would have it for her morning coffee.

"Well, I could get used to that," she said when the kiss ended.

"I always aim to please." He kissed her forehead. "What's all this?"

"I thought I would make breakfast."

He reached into the cabinet to get a couple of plates while she poured him a cup of black coffee before topping hers off. "It smells great." They both filled their plates and sat at his small table.

"Are you sure Anna can't get into her office?" She sipped her coffee.

He stood and filled his plate with more home fries and eggs. "Don't worry. Jake told her the knob is broken. She came huffing and puffing to me about it. I told her I would get to it as soon as I could. It seemed to pacify her for the time being. She's going to be so busy the next couple of days preparing Nora's she's not going to have time to worry about her office."

"I hope you're right. We just need to hold her off until Friday night at the opening."

After they finished eating, Tex helped clean the kitchen. It was only fair since she'd cooked such a big breakfast. There wasn't much to clean, because according to Liza, the trick was to clean as she cooked. Women were so smart.

Even though they both had busy days ahead—him splitting his time between Avery Landscaping and Nora's and Liza helping Anna all day—he was still able to talk her into having a quick shower with him.

She swept her hair up in a scrunchie, and it was the first time he had seen her hair pulled off her neck. He itched to touch her as she stood in front of the mirror in his living room, applying lip-gloss, but he knew just touching wouldn't satisfy his desperate need for her. Even if he found himself buried deep inside her, he would still ache for her the rest of the day.

"You make this house feel like a home," he confessed.

She stared at him through the mirror before slowly turning to face him.

He kept his feet planted on the floor, not able to touch her just yet. It was important he said what he wanted to say. "I've lived in the house for four years, and until now, it has always just been a place I sleep. With you here, adding the little touches you do—your clothes on the bedroom floor, the perfume and makeup all over the bathroom counter, you cooking in my kitchen—it has made this place lively, homey."

She walked to him and leaned in for a kiss. She didn't say anything, and she didn't need to. He knew what she was thinking by the way she moved her lips over his.

"I just wanted you to know," he said when the kiss ended.

"Thank you for saying that."

He wanted to share his feelings…and life with her.

****

As soon as Liza walked into Nora's, Anna handed her a big folder. She opened it and started flipping through the pages. "What's all this?"

"I've been doing research and found it will be fairly easy for you to open your own practice." Anna looked very satisfied with herself.

"What are you talking about?"

"All you have to do is obtain liability insurance. You have your master's in marriage and family therapy and are licensed. You should have no problem finding a company to insure you." Anna took the folder from her and searched until she found the paper she wanted. "Read this."

Liza glanced over it, seeing the words— *requirements in Tennessee, master's degree, licensing, and insurance.* "I'm totally lost here, Anna."

"I talked to Tex, and he mentioned you wanting to have your own practice and that you were *maybe* thinking about Patience."

"Tex? When?"

"At the naming party." Anna smiled. "He really cares about you, Liz. I'm sure he wants you to stay. Why didn't you tell me you had decided to follow your dream?"

Liza had had a feeling Tex was up to something when she saw him talking to Anna at the party. "Did Tex ask you to do all this?"

"No. We had a conversation, but the research was all my doing. After we talked, I couldn't wait to try to talk you into sticking around."

Liza knew what their *conversation* was about. Tex wanted her to stay. She could tell in the way his voice cracked when he talked about it. And while she was excited that she was more than just a fling to him, that he wanted to have a relationship with her, it also terrified her. How long was he willing to give her? Did he want a wife? She knew he was scared, but did he feel the urge to be a father one day? Those were questions she hadn't asked, and he hadn't brought up. If she decided to stay, it had to be as much about her as it was about him.

"I don't know what I want."

"Do you love him?" Anna asked softly.

Liza smiled. She needed to say the words aloud. "Yeah, I love him."

Anna squealed, then quickly covered her mouth when Jake walked into the room. Thankfully, he had his earbuds in.

"Have you told him?" Anna asked.

Liza shook her head. "If I told him, he would run for the hills. I know he wants me to move here, but I don't think he's ready to be in love."

"I think he'll surprise you. He loves you, too. Although I don't think he's admitted it to himself yet. When it hits him, it's going to hit hard. Just give him time, Liza."

Liza wanted to give him time to figure out his feelings, but what if his feelings didn't go past her just being important to him? What if he didn't love her back? Just the thought sent a pang to her stomach.

"When did you become so tuned in to the male psyche?" she asked.

Anna laughed and took her by the arm. "Let's just say I've learned from a really good friend."

****

After Liza showered and got ready, she drove to the diner to pick up two large coffees and a box of muffins, then drove a couple of streets over to Pearl's house. She'd slept at Tex's house for the fourth night in a row. He'd said he would be home after Wednesday-night church, but she'd insisted he stay with his mom. She didn't want him to feel that just because they had a thing going he was required to spend every waking minute with her. His mother was important to him; she was also important to Liza. Liza wanted to make Pearl happy, and she knew just what she could do.

She was trying to balance the coffees and muffins when Pearl's front door swung open.

"Ohhh, Liza, how is my favorite future daughter-in-law?" Pearl reached to relieve her of the muffins.

Okay, that was not what she expected. She kissed Pearl on the cheek and followed her to the kitchen. "Is Tex here?" She'd parked behind his truck, but she didn't see or hear him through the house. It could be possible that one of his employees picked him up.

Pearl pointed out the window just above her sink. "He's out back, walking the fence." She opened a drawer and pulled out a notepad and pencil. "What are your favorite colors?"

Liza was taken aback at how random the question was. "Uh…purple and chocolate, I guess."

"What about yellow?"

"I like yellow." She watched as Pearl hurriedly wrote.

"We'll need to get this wedding planned before March…April at the max. Unless you want to be showing when you walk down the aisle, which is perfectly fine," Pearl quickly added.

So they were back to the wedding idea. Liza heard Tex tell his mother no wedding or baby were on the way. Although Pearl might understand that today, it didn't mean she would always remember.

"I don't know…" Liza started to say before Tex saved her by kicking his boots against the house before coming through the back door.

His face lit when he saw her. God, could he make her melt into a million pieces. He went straight to her, laying a kiss on her lips, not caring that his mother beamed at them.

"Ummm…" She looked at him, then looked at his mom.

He seemed to understand and was already aware of what was going on. "I'm sorry," he mouthed.

Liza smiled and nodded. She was shocked the first time Pearl mentioned Tex loving her and wanting to build a life with her, but now she was okay. She was more stunned that Tex wasn't going a little crazy. His mother was planning his wedding to a woman he hadn't even admitted he loved. Who knew what was going through his mind?

He looked at his watch. "Where in the hell is Maggie? She's usually here by seven. It's already after eight."

Liza cleared her throat. "I called and told her to take the day off."

Tex jerked his head toward her. "You did what?"

And Pearl added, "So what are we doing today?" At least she was cheerful about the idea.

First, she needed to calm Tex before answering Pearl. "I thought your mom and I could have another one of our girls' days today."

"Honey, let me freshen up. Don't leave without me," Pearl called over her shoulder as she left the room.

Knowing Pearl liked her as much as she did warmed Liza. Also knowing she was memorable in Pearl's life overjoyed her.

Liza laughed. "Take your time."

"What are you doing?" Tex demanded. "You can't take her out when she's like this." He gnawed on his lower lip, his agitation plain.

Liza gently squeezed his hand. "Trust me."

"She thinks you're pregnant, Liza. I trust you, but how are you going to handle that when she gets chatty with everyone at Cut & Curls again?"

She stared at him. "I wasn't aware you heard about that." But after she thought about it, of course Tex would hear from somebody how his mom went on and on about him finally having a girlfriend.

He waved it off. "This is different. There is a lot more at stake here. By tomorrow morning, everyone will have an opinion about our wedding and give you pointed stares as you walk down Main Street because you picked me of all men to settle down with. Do you honestly want that?"

"I will get her to not say anything."

"How are you going to do that? I haven't seen her this excited since I opened Avery Landscaping. As soon as I opened my eyes this morning, she started asking me questions about the business and if I made enough to take care of you. She went even further to inform me I work too hard and that I'm going to have to slow down and spend more time at home."

"I will make her promise to keep the marriage and baby just between us for a while."

He laughed. "For a while?"

"Okay," she admitted. "I know it's not the most practical thing to do, but you can't keep her under lock and key every time she gets confused. I will get her to understand. Don't worry, you will still be Patience's most eligible bachelor tomorrow."

He gave her one of his glares. He apparently didn't find her joke amusing. Honestly, she felt a little relieved that he didn't. It told her that he was seriously thinking about having a long-term relationship with her if she chose to stay.

Leaning across the table, she gave Tex a kiss meant to relieve his fears. She wanted him to be okay with her popping up and deciding to take his mom out for a couple of hours. She wanted him to know she would always take care of his mother, that she would always take care of him.

"I missed you last night. Was everything good at the house?" he asked.

She grinned. "Are you asking me if you still have a house to go home to?"

"No. I mean did you blow my flat-screen up watching too much *Jersey Shore*?"

"I'll have you know I stayed on the computer until I went to sleep."

"Looking up more stuff for Anna? I thought you and Em had everything covered." He pinched off a piece of a chocolate chip muffin and held it out for her.

She accepted it. "We do." She couldn't tell what she was really looking up until she got used to the idea herself. She had to make sure she was going to be happy.

"Are we still setting up tonight?" he asked.

"It's going to be late since Anna refuses to go to bed like a normal person. Jake promises to keep her distracted. Don't even say it," she quickly added, assuming Tex was about to make some swift comment.

With a cocky grin on his face, he said, "I can't wait to be with you tonight."

She fluttered her eyelashes. "You know you can't have me anytime you want."

"Says who?" His voice went deep and sexy. It vibrated through her system, and his smile made her stomach go hollow.

She punched him in the arm because…damn it…he was right. "You're a bad man, Tex Avery."

"Damn straight."

God, she loved this man. He was an impossible, cocky ladies' man, but he was also sexy, charming, and caring. She loved the way he took care of his mother and was willing to learn as they went along. Worrying about his mom took so much out of him, but when she was with him, she never felt short-changed or as if he wasn't there with her. She didn't know if he was meaning to or not, but he was selling Patience to her.

Decisions...decisions...decisions.

Chapter Nineteen

Anna's office was exactly the way Liza envisioned it. The wall storage behind the desk was perfect. She was lucky to come across it at an antique shop between Patience and Knight. Em framed pictures of all the people Anna loved and hung them in a collage pattern on the wall. Everything from the cheap metal filing cabinet to a small throw pillow situated on the couch was a reflection of Anna's style.

Liza sensed Tex's presence as soon as he entered the room.

"You did good, sweetheart," he said from the doorway.

She fluffed the pillow one more time. "Was everyone quiet when they left?" To make sure everything got set up, she and Em had recruited the help of Tommy, Bradley, and of course Tex was there to lend a hand.

"Yeah. I even peeked over at the apartment, and there was no light on."

Liza laughed. "Jake probably slipped her a sleeping pill."

"I still can't believe you did all this."

"It was just as much Em as me. It really was a team effort." She felt him approach from behind. As he wrapped his arms around her waist, she melted into him. "Thanks for helping tonight."

He kissed the top of her head. "You don't ever need

to thank me for doing something that's important to you. I should be thanking you for spending the day with my mom. She can't stop talking about the party tomorrow night. Are you sure it's a good idea for her to go?" Concern colored his voice.

She turned to peer into his eyes, eyes filled with such worry. She only wanted to take away his burden for him. Even if it was for just one day. "I do. Please don't worry." He agreed not to, but she knew he would anyway. "She will have us and Edna there."

"I just don't want the whole town to think I knocked you up. It won't look good for you."

She laughed. "Big. Tough. Man, going to defend my honor."

"I'm just warning you what will happen if word gets out," he said. He acted as if she really were pregnant and they were planning a wedding for March.

"It's not true, Tex, so I say who cares what everyone else thinks. The only people at the party are going to be our friends."

"Okay." He seemed to let go.

She massaged his shoulders and watched the tension ease just a bit. He ran himself so hard and deserved a break. He deserved to be the one taken care of. She wanted to do that for him.

"I trust you, Liza."

He did—she felt him starting to trust in her a little more every day. Trust wasn't something he gave freely, and so she cherished it.

"Can we go home?" She didn't even care that she referred to his house as home, as if it were a place they shared together. He did say she made his place seem less cold and more like a home. She appreciated those words more than she was able to express. Building a home, a place always full of love, was something she wanted for her life.

"That sounds like a plan," he said.

****

As soon as they entered the house, Tex dragged her to his bedroom. She didn't mind being controlled when it came to Tex steering the way. Thinking about what he planned for them excited her. The dangerous look in his eyes made her quiver.

She stepped out of her heels as he stripped her of the rest of her clothing. He looked ready to devour her as she stood before him, completely naked, while he was fully clothed. A shiver ran up her spine.

"Lie back on the bed," he said.

She moved her body slowly and seductively, because she wanted him to know she was giving him control, and she could take it back anytime she liked.

"I was going to try to take this slow…but screw it," he growled.

It was just the response she was looking for. She laughed. He lost control himself. Before she could say a-ma-zing, he was nude. He was so hard for her, and that knowledge had her close to orgasm.

He lowered himself. Sighing, she arched her back, her breasts pressed against his chest. She spread her legs, preparing for him to enter, and while she knew she enjoyed the anticipation as much as she did, he was also impatient. He nuzzled her neck before licking toward her ear. Shivers ran up her spine while he nibbled at her earlobe. He then took it farther by suckling it into his mouth.

Slipping his hand between her thighs, he murmured

close to her ear, "You're ready for me."

The pleasure of his words and skillful hands sent a jolt through her system. His fingers stroked and tugged until she was on the verge of losing herself. "No. Not yet." He pulled his hand away from the wonderful things he was doing to her.

"Uh…" she cried.

Their gazes met before he captured her mouth with his. At the same time, he plunged inside her as they both groaned. "Ohhhh…" she murmured.

Like all the times they were together, everything else seemed a million miles away, as if everything against them were in a distant galaxy. The thought of her leaving and him being so wrecked with worry over his mother's illness—it was just him and her in that moment, in the bed they'd made love in so many times before. His bed. His home.

He was so perfect. Her body tingled when he located the sensitive part of her side and let his fingers glide ever so lightly over her. She tried opening her legs wider so she could take him deeper. She needed to feel his hard thrusts vibrate through her very core. "Deeper, Tex, deeper."

He readjusted their positions to go deeper, then slowed the pace. She was about to protest until she realized how much better he felt.

"How does that feel?" He raked his teeth over her neck and down the length of her shoulder.

A sigh left her lips, all words lost. She couldn't express how perfect he felt moving inside her. She was an educated woman, but still no words came to mind.

Could she stay? Did she have the courage to really give her heart to a man? This was something more than what she had experienced with Greg. To the deepest of her core, she knew she could have a never-ending kind of love with Tex.

She could see herself walking down the aisle on her father's arm to meet him. A vision of herself seven months pregnant splayed through her mind. She could even see her and Tex sitting in a porch rocker in thirty years, still very much in love and having crazy, wild sex.

She was so close. "Oh God…"

"Me, too, honey. Me, too," he groaned. With that, he exploded inside her. It took all of her willpower not to lose control and wither below him in such a way she didn't know if she could stop.

"Tex," she sighed as she reeled with tiny aftershocks of pleasure. "Wow."

"I couldn't have said it better." He rolled over, bringing her with him until she nestled in the crook of his arm.

She'd never felt so relaxed and exhausted at the same time. It had been a long, tiring, yet satisfying day. They hadn't started moving things into Anna's office until ten, so she figured it had to be close to two in the morning, if not later.

"Sleep, baby," he whispered, pulling the hefty comforter on top of them.

She kissed his chest and snuggled close, wrapping one hand across his waist. All was right, and nothing was complicated in that moment.

****

"Wow, Anna, you look amazing." Liza stared at her friend, blown away at her sexiness. She knew Anna was a true beauty, but she had never seen her friend look quite so… She didn't even know the word to describe her

357

knockout of a friend.

Anna had added a little more mascara than she probably ever used in her entire life. "I like how you and Em think I'm incompetent when it comes to looking good."

"It's not that we think you're incompetent. It's just…well…"

"You think I'm clueless. You can say it."

Liza looked Anna up and down. "You just don't usually wear these types of clothes."

Anna wore a snug red dress with black, open-toe pumps, and instead of the usual ponytail, she wore her hair down and tousled. She was definitely a sex kitten tonight.

"Just because I don't wear knee-high boots and tight-fitting skirts to go to the post office doesn't mean I don't know how to look nice for a special occasion. I dressed up plenty of times for Em's wedding parties, and I think I looked damn good," Anna added with a smug nod.

Liza surrendered. "Okay. I'll try not to be hurt by your little knee-high-boot comment if you'll forget I said anything about the way you dress." She stood beside Anna, staring into the hotel-size mirror hanging in Anna and Jake's apartment.

"Deal," Anna said with a smile at the corners of her lips.

Liza followed Anna out of the bathroom to the all-in-one bedroom, sitting area, and kitchen. Liza plopped down on the bed. She was so tired. After last night, she could sleep for a full twenty-four hours and still require more, but it had been worth it. Getting Anna's office ready for tonight was a must, and having the help of the others, she and Em were able to pull it off.

Butterflies swarmed in her stomach. She was so excited to show Anna what took so much of her time, and then she couldn't stop thinking about the unbelievable night she'd shared with Tex. He was so gentle and…yet demanding at the same time. She'd felt safe and happy in his arms this morning. If she stayed, she could have that feeling every morning.

"I'm going to stay in Patience," Liza blurted out before thinking better of it.

Anna stopped in her tracks, letting her handbag fall to the floor, blankness on her face as she stared at Liza as if she were a ghost.

"Say something," Liza said.

"I don't know what to say. You've kind of blindsided me here." Anna sat beside Liza on the bed and stared at nothing.

"I know it's a shock, but—"

"A shock?" Anna gaped. "I'm damn speechless, Liza. I know I printed all that stuff so you could see how to open your own practice, but I guess I thought Tex and I were wishful thinking. I honestly never expected you to agree to it."

"I didn't either, but I love him, Anna. I've never felt anything this strong before. Staying here is the only thing that makes sense. If you feel anything with Jake that is close to what I feel for Tex, I can see why you stayed. I don't think I can walk away without trying first."

Anna wiped at her eyes. "You're ruining my mascara." She took Liza's hand into hers. "I'm just so happy. I'm happy that we'll get to see each other every day, but I'm even happier that you've finally found love, and it's even better that it's in Patience," she added with a smile.

"What do you think Tex is going to say?" Liza knew Tex wanted her to stick around, but she wasn't sure what else he wanted.

"He's probably going to have the reaction I did, except he will kiss you senseless."

Liza chewed on her bottom lip.

"I wouldn't worry about Tex."

She sometimes sensed that he felt he didn't deserve her—that he in some way couldn't give her what she needed. That wasn't true. "I hope you're right."

"I am. When are you going to tell him?"

"After your party tonight." It wasn't something Liza thought of doing before now, but the present seemed like the best time to reveal how she felt about him. It was now or never.

"Where are you going to live? Are you thinking of moving in with Tex? What about work? Are you still going to open your own practice? Have you told your parents yet? What did they think?"

She couldn't process everything Anna was saying because every question was running together. She didn't have an answer. All she knew for sure was that she loved Tex to the point she wanted to uproot her life and move. That was the only answer she could give at the moment. "Anna, cool it. I've just said it out loud. I haven't thought past telling Tex. After that, I will work everything else out."

"Sorry, I'm just so excited."

"Me, too." She was also scared, but with Tex, she knew they would figure everything out together.

****

Tex had never cared about the way he looked in the

past. He didn't have to. Women were drawn to the scuffed worked boots, broken-in blue jeans, and sweat-drenched T-shirt look. However, everything about his life was different with Liza. He wanted to be better for her, and that meant dressing in black polished loafers, pressed khaki pants, and a cream-colored sweater his mom had bought him last Christmas.

He stared in the mirror as he slipped his wallet and keys into his back pocket. A knock came at the door, and he wondered why Liza was knocking instead of just making herself at home as usual.

Shrugging, he opened the door. "Leah." This was so not what he needed. "What do you want?" He didn't care that he sounded agitated, because he was. He was expecting, wanting, Liza, but instead, he had to deal with whatever shit Leah brought to his doorstep.

A smile spread across her face as she pulled down her shirt, revealing the top of her bra and swell of her breasts. "Don't you look spiffy."

He couldn't believe this was the type of woman he'd once been attracted to. "Again…what is it you want?"

"I came to remind you how good we are together. I can't stop thinking about you since that night at the bar. Haven't you been getting my texts?" She swayed her body and began touching her breasts. Instead of looking sexy and provocative, she looked silly.

"You must have me confused with Bradley because you and I have never and will never be together." He'd been hitting ignore on her many messages. He was past the point of irritation at whatever game she was playing. He had places to be and a woman he couldn't wait to see.

"Oh, but we could be. You've changed since that slut came to town."

"I think it's time for you to leave," he said between gritted teeth. He was not about to stand there and listen to anyone bad-mouth his woman.

"No. It's time for you to come to your senses and take me to bed. We've been playing this game long enough." She stepped toward him, trying to push her way through the door, but he was able to block her with his body.

He ground his teeth so hard his jaw ached. "The only one playing a game is you." He was never interested in what Leah had to offer. Besides her being way too young, something about her rubbed him the wrong way.

Her fingers started at his chest, but he was able to block her hand from moving any lower. The woman was crazy.

"You're only embarrassing yourself, Leah," he bit out while pushing her hand away. He was proud of himself for not being the slightest bit tempted. It only confirmed he couldn't let Liza go. She was *his woman*.

"You're trying to be strong. I know you can't resist me."

She took one step backward, as if making an attempt to move away from him, but instead tripped over her high heels and fell into him.

"Shit, Leah…go." When she stood, smiling with pouty lips, he added with a lot more force, "Get the fuck off my porch. I'm with Liza. Get used to it."

Her smile faded, and she looked shocked. Probably, not many guys turned her away. She crossed her arms, making her top slide farther down her chest. "You'll regret this."

"Not likely."

She stomped off the porch, having no issues walking

in her heels. He was about to slam the door when she added, "You and I are the same. You'll never be the type of man Liza wants, because you don't do commitment."

He slammed the door behind him. Was there any truth to what Leah said? Was he only kidding himself to think he would ever be the type of man Liza needed?

Tex didn't know if she needed him, but God, he needed her. He needed to feel her body pressed to his, taste her kiss on his lips as the warmth of her mouth swarmed through him. She was staying in Patience whether she liked it or not. He was going to find a way to be the man she deserved.

****

After leaving Anna's, Liza drove straight to Tex's. She was eager to see him. At first, she thought it would be best to wait until after the opening at Nora's to tell him about her life-changing decision, but she couldn't hold it in any longer. This was life-defining for her. It was important she tell him as soon as possible.

As his house came into view, she noticed a sedan parked behind his truck in the driveway. She ran through all the people she knew in town, which was very few, but it was a car she'd never seen. Not wanting to intrude if it was one of his employees, she decided to drive past his house and go around the block. She couldn't help her curiosity, and she slowed as she neared the house.

She sucked in a breath and nearly laid on the horn as she watched Tex holding another woman. Not just any woman…Leah. She wore the same painted-on jeans that were far from flattering and another low-cut blouse she used to attract men.

Gripping the steering wheel tight, Liza felt her hand cramp as she crawled past his house. She stopped at the end of the street, threw the car in park, and tried to calm her breathing. The pain was gut-wrenching. He'd betrayed her. How could he do this to her?

She was ready to give her heart to him, and he didn't care. Had she just been the new girl in town, someone different he could pass the time with? No. She felt the connection. He felt it, too. Didn't he?

Tears pierced her eyes, clouding her vision. She cursed herself for once again picking the wrong man. That was it. She would switch sides before falling into bed with another man who didn't appreciate her.

Right after the thought entered her head, she knew she was lying to herself. She wanted a big, strong man who loved her, who wanted to have sweet babies with her. She'd thought Tex was that man, but she was wrong. Everyone in town knew his reputation, and still she'd given in and not only had sex with him, but worse—fallen in love with him.

She closed her eyes and slowly let out a gush of air. She was through. Through with Tex and through with Patience.

****

Tex had been worried. He waited thirty minutes past the time Liza was supposed to be at his house before he drove to her hotel to see if maybe she stopped there after leaving Anna's. He knew how women could be about getting dressed for a big night. He thought it likely she'd gotten caught up and lost track of time. After pulling into the Town's Inn lot, he found her space empty. His mom had already called before he left home to ask what the holdup was, so he drove straight to her house from the hotel.

As soon as he helped her into his truck, she asked

where Liza was. He only grunted, which made his mom ask, "Did you two have a fight?" When he didn't answer, she shrugged and stared out the window. He wasn't trying to be mean or short with her, but he was confused. It wasn't like Liza to not at least let him know if she was going straight to the party and not pick him up first. And what about his mom? Liza knew how excited Pearl was for the invite, so where in the hell was she?

Nora's shone brightly with outdoor lighting. If he wasn't so upset about Liza, he would have taken pride in being a part of such a night. Tonight was about Anna showing off her *baby*, but in a way, Tex felt as if he were showing off a part of himself. He'd put a little of himself into Nora's and was excited for Patience to see it. He was also excited for his mom to get a glimpse of what he'd been up to.

He pulled around to the back lot because the parking spots in the front were taken. He immediately noticed Liza's metallic SUV and found a spot in the next row over.

He started to guide his mother to the back entrance but wanted her to get the full effect. While entering through the front, he knew he'd made the right decision. His mother's face reflected so much.

"This is lovely," she said in awe. "Did you do this?"

"I helped." His heart swelled twice its size as his mother peered up at him.

Her eyes glistened.

"Don't cry, Mama."

She cupped his face, very much as she had done when he was a small boy. "You did good, honey." She patted a hand over his heart. "So good. I'm so proud of you. I can't believe I didn't know you were working on this."

He took her coat and hung it on the coatrack by the door. "Thank you. That means a lot coming from you." He kissed her cheek.

His mom found Edna in the small crowd of people, and Edna cracked a half smile when she saw Pearl. It was good for them to be together again. Edna was a hard woman to be around, but his mom always seemed to see something else entirely when it came to her.

He needed to find Liza. He searched the sitting area but only found a few of the locals. He nodded to a few people he'd known since birth before making his way to the kitchen.

The soft scent he'd come to recognize as uniquely hers wafted through the air. She stood with the bartender from Ollie's, Minny, along with Jessie and Bradley. She wiped her eyes as they all hysterically laughed at something Minny was saying. He could tell by her body language that she knew he was standing beside her, but she refused to acknowledge him. He went on high alert. Something was wrong.

"What's so funny?" he asked.

"Tex." Jessie knocked him in the side with her hip.

"Minny was just telling us that Slick Jefferson came into the bar this week trying to use the same damn pickup lines he used on Liza with some other woman from over in Knight…" Bradley seemed to enjoy telling the story.

Jessie finished by adding, "…and it actually worked. She left with him. Can you believe that?"

Liza shifted from side to side, as if uncomfortable being near him.

He took the chance and gripped her arm. "Can I talk to you?"

Okay, so touching her right now was not the best idea. She jerked away. "Not now."

The group fell quiet as they witnessed what was going on between him and Liza.

"Please?" he asked. He noticed the set of her shoulders and knew she wasn't backing down.

"I have to see if Anna needs anything." She walked away without even a glance his way.

"What was that about?" Bradley asked.

"The hell if I know," Tex muttered. "Has she said anything to you?" He turned to Jessie.

Jessie and Minny both shook their heads. "She's looked pretty happy to me all night. A little too happy, but I just thought it was the wine," Jessie said.

He knew Liza wouldn't get plastered on a night so important to Anna. She was laughing and acting as if she were having a good time, but she was hot about something, and he was sure it had to do with him.

In a few gulps, he put away his first glass of wine. He stood back, propping himself against the fireplace mantel and watching Liza make her rounds of the room. She never looked in his direction.

She talked with Jason and a few of the firefighters he worked with. Tex knew she wasn't interested in Saunders, but his gut tightened at the sight of her standing near him. Em approached her, and after she excused herself, she followed Em to the table where Em's parents sat. He watched as she made pleasantries with Mr. Bradshaw.

A waiter offered him another glass of wine. He glared over the top of it, itching to go to her and tell her she was being silly and unreasonable. She shouldn't be mad at him for something he didn't even understand. He had a right, damn it, to know why he was on her shit list.

Jessie and Bradley headed up the stairs with Georgia not too far behind.

"Come on, Tex. We're going to show Anna her office," Em whispered as she walked toward him. He followed her and Tommy, not seeing Liza.

Sadness was in Liza's eyes along with pure joy when he found her in Anna's office. She straightened a picture on the wall, then draped a blanket across the chair in the corner. Everything was already perfect because of Liza, but he knew this was important to her. Anna was her best friend, and Liza only wanted to give her what she deserved.

Damn it, he wanted to give Liza what she deserved, too.

****

Everything was perfect. Liza was pleased with what she and Em had created. Everyone in the room had contributed in some way. Anna was so lucky to have such close friendships, and she was lucky to have Jake.

Liza never thought she would think Anna was lucky to have Jake in her life.

But after witnessing Tex and Leah together, feeling such loss, she knew how hard it was to find love and keep it. Anna had that in her life, and she rightfully deserved it. Liza wasn't jealous, but she wanted that for herself.

She hated standing Pearl up since she'd extended the invite, but she couldn't be in close proximity to Tex. She'd made sure she saw Pearl and reassured her that she and Tex were fine. Hell was where she was going for that big fat lie. They were not fine and never would be again.

He'd waltzed into Nora's as if nothing had

happened, but something had, and he knew it. She noticed how he'd stayed in a corner with a sour look on his face. He knew he'd messed up, and he deserved to feel miserable about it.

"Shhh," Em said in what she would consider a whisper. "I think I hear her coming."

They stood around the room as Anna and Jake entered.

Anna's face lit up, much like a small child on Christmas morning. "What's all this?" She looked around a room she expected to be bare. "Who did this?"

"We all did." Em put her arms around Anna's neck while Anna looked shell-shocked.

Anna went straight to the piece of furniture Liza loved and wanted for herself. "Is this an antique?"

"I found it at a shop just before you cross into Knight," Liza answered.

Anna rubbed her fingers across the chipped wood and smiled. Liza and Anna both appreciated the imperfections.

Anna sat in her swivel chair behind her desk, spinning it around a few times. "I love how I can look into the whole room." She crossed her arms over her desk and looked ready to start handing out orders.

"That was my idea," Em said, sounding very satisfied.

"And look at this chair." Anna left her office chair to check out the big, comfy chair situated in a corner. She propped a knee on the arm of the chair and glanced over the pictures Em had hung on the wall. "I think I'm going to cry." She started wiping at her eyes.

Liza knew what picture would choke her up. Em had found an old picture of Anna's mother and framed it.

They'd hung it in the middle of all the other people Anna loved. To Anna, her mom was the center of her heart. It only made sense to put Nora's picture in the middle. Anna rubbed her hand over each picture.

"What do you think, Anna?" Liza asked.

Anna just gaped at them. "I'm speechless. I can't believe all of you did this for me. I don't believe I've ever been given a more special gift in my life. This tops them all. How did y'all do this without me knowing?"

Jake laughed. "I broke the damn door handle on purpose."

"I knew you two," she said, pointing at Jake and Tex, "were giving me the runaround. I would be mad, but after seeing this, I can't be." She went around the room and gave each person two hugs.

Georgia, of course, cried while Jessie made fun of her for being such a girl.

"You haven't seen the best part," Liza said. She went out of her way to make sure the biggest surprise was there on time. And to Liza's amazement, Jake had followed through on his promise.

"I can't think of anything that can top this." Anna had one arm looped through Jake's arm.

"Well…" Liza shut the office door.

"Oh. My. Gosh." Anna threw her hands in the air and literally bounced up and down, which was hard to do since she wore heels for the occasion. "Where did you get this? How?"

Before she and the others got there the night before to set up the office, Jake had already had the picture of Sparks Stadium hung on the wall behind the door. Liza thought it was only going to be a large area photo, but Jake had gotten something better. He'd been able to get a nicely framed picture with all the signatures of the players, coaches, and managers from the previous season.

This time, Anna let the tears fall, and Liza laughed. *Show her pictures of her friends and family, and she gets glassy-eyed. Show her a photo of a baseball field, and she bawls like a baby.*

"Jake did it," Liza admitted with a slight grin.

Anna gasped. "Jake?"

"It was Liza's idea," Jake said.

Anna wiped at her eyes. "Ahhh…look at you two playing nice."

"Don't get used to it," Liza sputtered.

"And don't think I can support your unhealthy obsession with New York," Jake added.

Anna wrapped her arms around Jake and Liza's waists. "I love you guys."

Jake drew away from his future wife and without a bit of humor said, "You should. Because of this damn picture, Liza was forced to ask me for help, and I had to take all kinds of hell from my former agent and some of the guys I used to play with."

Eventually, everyone ventured back downstairs. Liza tried to do the same, but before she was able to slip away, Tex gripped her by the arm and pulled her across the hall to the library. Her cheeks flushed at the memory of the last time they were together in that room.

He was spitting mad. "What in the fuck is going on?" he roared. With his hands on his hips, he was ready to argue.

Good, because she needed to get some things off her chest as well. "I don't know, Tex. Why don't you tell me?"

He paced the room, staring at nothing in particular. "I thought we were done with this bullshit. I thought we had a good thing going, or did I miss something? Why did you stand me up tonight?"

How could he be so stupid to think he wouldn't be caught holding another girl in his arms and she wouldn't have a reaction to it? "Do you think I'm stupid?"

His expression turned serious. "No, I don't think you're stupid. You're one of the smartest people I know."

"I don't mean book smart. Do you think I don't know when a man is being unfaithful to me? I'm beginning to think you men think I'm just blind or clueless."

"Who's unfaithful?"

She crossed her arms and met his gaze evenly. "You."

He jutted out his chin. "Me?" He pointed a finger back at himself. "Don't you dare start comparing me to your ex, Liza. I will not stand here and let you insult me. Not all men are cheating assholes."

Funny he chose those words because that was exactly what he was. "You're right," she admitted. "You're better-looking than Greg, way better in bed, and you sure are good at laying on the southern-boy charm. You are a better man than Greg will ever be, but the one thing—" She held up a finger, narrowing her eyes at him. "—the one thing you two have in common is that you both are cheating assholes. Did you think I wouldn't see you with her?"

"With who?"

If she didn't see it with her own eyes, she would have thought by the look on his face that him kissing

Leah was not true. He did look almost convincing.

"Don't give the innocent-boy crap. You're better than that, Tex. Leah. I saw you with her tonight." The boiling rage she'd felt when she saw them together came flooding back. Her heart rapidly beat in her chest to the point she could hear the pounding in her ears.

His face turned pale.

"Aww, I see I've refreshed your memory," she sneered.

"I can explain what you saw—"

"Shut up," she ground out. His mouth snapped shut. "Did you seek out Leah because you knew I would blow a gasket?"

"No. I would never purposely try to hurt you." He reached out to touch her, but she retreated a step.

Her emotions decided to run rampant. "Huh…so you expect me to believe your hands on Leah were nothing more than you two being friendly? Because I don't." She raked her hands through her hair, turning away from him. "How could you do this to us? You asked me to stay, and I was. I can't go through this with another man." And she wouldn't, especially not with Tex. Thinking of him with anyone other than her hurt too much. "I love you, damn it."

Everything around them fell quiet. "You what?" he asked softly.

She spun around because she refused to be ashamed of how she felt. So she loved him. She owned her feelings. "You heard me."

"You love me? You're staying in Patience?"

Did he really not know the extent of her feelings for him?

"I do love you, Tex. So much that you've actually

broken my heart—" She took a deep breath. "—but I'm not staying."

"But you love me."

Yeah, she loved him, but there had to be more. She told herself she would only stay in Patience if it were good for her. Before a couple of hours ago, she'd thought staying with Tex was the best thing because she cared so deeply for him. Now she didn't know what to do or how to feel.

"That's not enough. I was stupid enough to think I actually found love. That, finally, I found someone who knows me better than I know myself. I could picture myself planning our wedding with your mother, us having a child with your blue-green eyes, and us setting the town on fire with our wild lovemaking when we're in our sixties."

"I want that, too."

"No, you don't," she spat. "I'm sure you want me to stay, but you aren't the marrying kind, Tex. You don't want a family with me. I shouldn't have let myself get this attached when I knew our goals in life were different."

That was why she was mad. He cared for her too much to turn to someone like Leah. She and Tex had something rare and special, and that was why it hurt so much. Finding him in an awkward situation with Leah was not why she was angry. She was mad because she knew she was going to lose him, that in the end she feared he wouldn't want to be the man she knew him to be.

"How do you know? I'll admit that I'm scared of my feelings for you and the thought of passing a terrible disease to our children, but I'm afraid more that if you leave, I'll fall apart."

She quickly glanced away, and he tilted her chin to him.

"I love you, Liza Dyer. I love you so much it consumes me. When Leah came to my house tonight, I told her I only want to be with you. You have to believe me."

His words stole her breath away. When he finally declared his feelings for her, nothing else mattered. "Repeat that."

"Leah came on to me, and I—"

"No," she interrupted. "I don't want to talk about Leah. Say that first part again."

"I love you, Liza. Only you…forever." He leaned in to kiss her.

She circled her arms around his neck, needing to be closer to him. She wanted to feel the extent of his emotions, and the way he kissed her brought home his love for only her. His kiss sent her head spinning. "Mmmm," she said against his lips.

Tex touched his forehead to hers. "If this is going to work between us, you've got to stop thinking the worst of me. I'm bound to mess up over the next thirty years, but I will never cheat on you. I will not ruin the family we're going to have."

She softly laughed. "I'm thinking more along the lines of the next sixty years."

He, too, chuckled and nodded.

A tear slid down her cheek. "But I do trust you."

Gently, he wiped her tears.

"I was going to tell you I not only wanted to stay but that I wanted to have a life with you. I was nervous, but I also knew that with you is where I belong. When I saw you holding her, I thought I'd lost you. I was so angry because one minute I have everything planned, and the next minute everything's shot to hell all over again. I deep down knew the interaction wasn't your idea. I could tell what kind of girl she was when I saw her at Ollie's the night Anna sent her packing. Just seeing her all over you sent my blood pressure spiking."

"I don't ever want to be a disappointment to you. That's my fear. I'm afraid of turning into my father one day and abandoning everybody who loves me."

She wrapped her arms around his waist and laid her head on his chest. "You are not your father, not even close. You are a strong man who doesn't run when things get hard. You've dealt with your mother's Alzheimer's the best you can, and you've never given up. You are a good son. I don't want to ever hear you say you're like your dad, because I don't see any comparison. You are your mother's son."

"What if—"

She put her fingers to his lips before he could ask the question she knew plagued his mind. "We will deal with it *if* it happens." She lifted her fingers.

"I want kids with you, Liza. I really do, but what if I pass this on to them? It pains me to just say the words aloud."

"And there's a good chance they will grow up to be healthy adults. We will not deny ourselves a good life because of fear. You will be an amazing father and just think about your mom. She's already beyond thrilled."

The chatter and laughs from the party drifted from below. They were the people who made Patience the town it was. She was going to raise a family in this town with the man she loved. "You know," she said. "You

376

haven't exactly asked me yet."

He pulled back from their embrace. "Asked you what?"

She frowned. "To marry you, you jackass."

Tex angled his head at her, the corners of his mouth turning up into a grin. "Do you think I honestly would forget to ask you a question like that?"

"Well, you haven't done it yet," she pointed out, pouting.

"I wanted it to be perfect, and I don't have a ring yet. I know how you women and your rocks can be. I was thinking I should wait."

"Don't get me wrong—I want a big fat diamond so I can show all the women like Leah and Carly you're mine, but that is not what's important. You just asking the four little words will do just fine."

"Will you marry me?"

They'd just talked about their future family together, but until he asked the most important question she'd ever been asked, it hadn't felt real. It did now. Everything she experienced in her life before now had prepared her for this moment. She could stand in front of this man and say without a doubt she wanted nothing more than to share a home and family with him.

"Yes."

Tex leaned in to lightly brush his lips across hers. As soon as they met, a gentle touch turned into a kiss until they couldn't stop kissing…kissing…and even more kissing. She slid her hands up the front of his sweater as the tips of his thumbs stroked the naked skin just beneath the hem of her blouse.

When they finally pulled away, breathless, he asked, "Do you think anyone from the party will miss us?"

She was afraid to ask. "Why?"

A mischievous smile formed on his lips. "I was thinking about the last time we were in this room."

"Oh."

"What do you say, baby? Want to make this—"

Before he could finish the rest of his sentence, she was pulling his sweater over his head. "Let's celebrate our life together."

Epilogue

Five Months Later

Liza stood in the back of the church, just behind the double doors. With her father standing to her right and her friends and family waiting just inside the church, she felt blessed.

Pachelbel's *Canon* softly played as the wooden doors opened. "Are you ready, honey?" her father whispered.

She nodded. Waiting the past five months to be Tex's wife had been torture. With Pearl, Anna, and her mother's loving help, she was able to plan and give Pearl the spring wedding she'd envisioned all those months ago.

She and Tex had decided to keep it small, so he'd asked only Bradley and Jake to stand beside him, and she had Anna and her sister. Her sister's husband, Carter, and Tommy were ushers. Brayden, her adorable two-year-old nephew, was the ring bearer, and the young daughter of one of her closest friends from Linden was her flower girl. Everything was better than she'd thought possible.

Her father kissed her cheek and shook Tex's hand before handing her off.

"I love you, Daddy," she whispered for only him to hear.

The most handsome man she'd ever laid eyes on

379

stood before her in his black tux and lavender tie. Their eyes immediately locked. Her best efforts to not ruin her mascara were ruined. A single tear streaked down her cheek. Smiling, Tex wiped it away.

They went with traditional vows because they didn't feel the need to convince an entire church of the extent of the love they had for each other. She and Tex knew they both respected and loved each other. Tex's eyes looked moist when the preacher said, "In sickness and in health." Even though he tried to hide it, she knew him all too well and knew he still worried about the disease he could inherit.

She squeezed his hand and mouthed, "We will get through it."

He nodded, with so much understanding and trust in his eyes. From now on, they were going through the bad and good things life brought their way together.

With the preacher's instruction, Tex dropped a firm yet sweet kiss on her lips. When they turned to face the crowd and were announced as *husband and wife*, Liza smiled at her parents and Pearl, who was seated next to her mother. Both of them wiping at their eyes.

"How did we get so lucky?" she asked him after he pulled her outside.

And lucky they were. After Nora's opened officially, Liza had begun working part time for Anna. She wasn't giving up the idea of opening her own practice in Patience. The timing just didn't seem right. Tex encouraged her, and it took a while for him to realize that she could still help people without an office. Whether it was her helping at story time or listening to Georgia pour out her romantic heart about how she was never going to find the kind of love Liza found with

Tex—Liza felt as if she was helping. She was making new friends and forming bonds in the community where she and Tex were going to raise a family.

After the shock of her engagement and meeting Tex and Pearl, her parents supported her decision. And while her mother was thrilled to plan another one of her girls' weddings, she was also concerned about Liza's job. The sentiment warmed Liza to know her mother did in fact understand her need to work and the satisfaction she felt after helping someone have a better life.

The wedding planning seemed to help Pearl's mood. Tex continued to stay at his mother's house at least twice a week, but now Liza stayed, too. He set up a bed in his old bedroom at Pearl's urging. Liza liked being in his childhood home and room. In some small way she felt connected to that young boy who had to be the man of the house at such a young age. She liked to think just by being there, she helped Tex and Pearl in some small way.

Girls' nights were still every Friday night, she still sparred with Jake for old time's sake and got to see Anna almost every day, and now she was standing with her husband. *Her husband.* It sounded good.

Tex pulled her to his chest. "I don't know, sweetheart. I just don't know how we got this lucky. I love you, and I wouldn't trade this day for anything."

"I love you, too, Tex."

In coming to Patience, Liza had found lasting friendships, never-ending love, and a place she was glad to call home.

A word about the author…

Jennifer has always been an avid reader, but it wasn't until she became a stay-at-home mom that she started to read romance. Her passion of reading romance turned into another passion she had as a child—writing. One late night of writing about sexy heroes and strong-willed heroines turned into two nights, until seven months later she had written her first novel.

She lives in a small, Tennessee town with her supportive husband (whose dream is to be on the cover of one of her books), a beautiful daughter, and two dogs who can't seem to get along. If she's not writing, you can find her reading, hanging out with her family, or cheering on the New York Yankees.

http://www.jennifersimpkins.net

Thank you for purchasing
this publication of The Wild Rose Press, Inc.

For questions or more information
contact us at
info@thewildrosepress.com.

The Wild Rose Press, Inc.